Praise for *Meet me in London*

'A classic romance with the added bonus of a festive feel.
I loved the passion, the romantic tension, and the way the
characters leapt off the page. An ideal Christmas escape.'
Laura Jane Williams, bestselling author of *Our Stop*

'Uplifting, romantic and festive – the perfect book
to curl up with. I couldn't put it down.'
Rosie Nixon, Editor-in-Chief, *HELLO! Magazine*

'Fresh, fun and full of romance! I loved it!'
Heidi Swain, *Sunday Times* bestselling author of *The Secret Seaside Escape*

'A perfect escapist, heart-warming read!
I was hooked from the first line!'
Katie Ginger, author of *Summer Strawberries at Swallowtail Bay*

'Unwrap and enjoy this Christmassy treat of a read.'
Mandy Baggot, bestselling author of *My Greek Island Summer*

'The perfect escape… it's like one big warm hug.'
Kelly McFarland, editor at *CelebMix*

Readers Love *Meet me in London*

'This was an absolute joy to read…It honestly
ticked all of the boxes for me.'
5★ NetGalley Reviewer

'*Meet me in London* is the perfect winter romance. Get
snuggled up and cosy with this joy of a read.'
5★ NetGalley Reviewer

'This has to be one of my favourite reads this year.
From the first page to the last I was hooked.'
5★ NetGalley Reviewer

'*Meet me in London* will without a doubt
warm your heart this winter.'
5★ NetGalley Reviewer

Georgia Toffolo is a broadcaster and British media personality. *Meet me in Hawaii* is the second book of her quartet, and her second fiction novel. She lives in South West London with her dog Monty.

Meet me in Hawaii

Georgia Toffolo
with Rachael Stewart

MILLS & BOON

Mills & Boon
An imprint of HarperCollins*Publishers* Ltd
1 London Bridge Street
London SE1 9GF

www.harpercollins.co.uk

HarperCollins*Publishers*
1st Floor, Watermarque Building, Ringsend Road
Dublin 4, Ireland

This paperback edition 2021

First published in Great Britain by Mills & Boon,
an imprint of HarperCollins*Publishers* Ltd 2021

Copyright © Georgia Toffolo 2021

With thanks to Rachael Stewart

Georgia Toffolo asserts the moral right to be identified as the author of this work. A catalogue record for this book is available from the British Library.

ISBN: 978-0-00-837588-1

MIX
Paper from
responsible sources
FSC™ C007454

This book is produced from independently certified FSC™ paper to ensure responsible forest management.

For more information visit: www.harpercollins.co.uk/green

This book is set in 10.7/15.5 pt. Bembo

Printed and bound in Great Britain by
CPI Group (UK) Ltd, Croydon, CR0 4YY

This book is dedicated to the dreamers, the round pegs in a square hole. Never give up because you have the power to change the world.

**Also by
Georgia Toffolo**

Meet me in London

MEET ME IN HAWAII

CHAPTER ONE

MALIE PUKUI CLOSED HER eyes and raised her head to the setting sun. She took a long, soothing breath and smoothed her corkscrew curls back from her face, holding her hands either side of her head as she bobbed on the surfboard and let the water lap around her knees. This was her favourite time of day. This and dawn. When it felt as though it was just her, her board and the beautiful ocean...

Peace. Calm. Tranquillity.

No expectations, no nothing.

Just me, she thought, *me and Koa, against the world.*

A bark from the deserted shoreline told her that wasn't quite true. She had Nalu, her four-legged friend and the surf school's honorary mascot with her. But he didn't encroach on this time.

She'd chosen this stretch of beach because it was secluded by the natural flora that had overtaken the public access long ago. It meant she was free to surf in peace, free to reconnect with her late brother and take time out from her full-on schedule.

There was no need to put on a front, no need to be anyone but herself.

She lowered her hands to her board and turned to look at Nalu now, playing in the swash, his tail wagging as he pranced back and forth.

'I'll be back soon,' she called out. And she would, really soon.

Just a few more minutes, one more perfect wave and she would paddle back in. She had a function to attend after all. A function that was important if her charity work was to grow and flourish like she hoped.

Still, she didn't feel ready to be that perfect face again. To smile and be polite, to laugh and be merry with those that held the purse strings and likely didn't do anything unless it rewarded them financially to do so. And she knew she had a mouth on her, that keeping it tight-lipped would be a challenge, but she'd do it if it meant she could help more people. People like her friend Zoe.

Now she smiled. The memory of seeing Zoe and her two other besties – Lils and Victoria – back in England last week. Learning of V's engagement, a real bona fide one, and not the pretend shebang it had started out as. It had been lovely and had certainly taken some of the sting out of Christmas with her parents.

One week back in Hawaii and the strain of it was still hanging over her like a cold she couldn't shake. And maybe that was the real reason she was sticking it out with the waves when she should be back at the apartment preening for tonight's cocktail party.

'Urgh!' She thrust forward on the board and paddled, her well-trained eye on the water now as she sought the right swell, duck-diving and paddling until she was forced to accept it was more about avoidance of her life than it was the perfect wave.

England persisted. Her parents. When would they just smile and approve? When would they be able to talk about Koa without filling her with guilt at being the one still here, and the one that didn't deserve to be?

Let it go, Malie.

It was as though her brother was in her head telling her to just chill, to enjoy the surf, the last for the night. And then she felt it, the familiar tug of the ocean beneath her; she could see the swell in the sea ahead, the perfect green wave. *Here it comes.*

She rose up and swivelled her legs beneath the water to turn her board. She lay forward, lifted her chin and paddled. A deep, outstretched motion tight with the board that had her gliding through the water. She checked the wave again, matched her speed and grinned wide. *Wait for it. Wait for it.*

Her board lifted with the sea. *Now.*

Up she popped. 'Thank you, Mother Nature!'

Nalu barked, frolicking into the water at her excited yell. This was why she surfed. This was why she couldn't give it up, not for her parents, not for anything. Harnessing the power of the ocean, the adrenalin rush of being propelled along, of getting it right and flicking the board this way and that... taking control.

She glided with the wave, heading into shore and already she knew, she just needed one more.

It wasn't like she'd spend *that* long getting ready anyway.

She turned and dropped down onto her board. The sun was settling on the horizon, beckoning her out, its orange glow stretching far and wide and mirrored in the sea. She fell forward and started to paddle, her eyes on the sun, her heart not ready to leave.

Nalu barked and her conscience pricked: *You're going to be late.*

She ignored it. It was just one more ride.

She stopped paddling, the lull in the waves giving her time to sit and ponder, to take in the beauty before her.

The geographic gap fell away and she could just as easily be sitting on her board back in Devon, in Hawke's Cove. Sunsets were much the same when you were staring out at the never-ending sea.

A longing came over her, an ache she couldn't quite shift – if only she were back in the Cove. If only things were different.

It would always be home to her. Even if it wasn't the right place for her anymore. She couldn't be trapped by it again, by her parents and their fears, their disapproval of her surfing, their pain over Koa's death. Hawaii gave her the freedom that she needed, and she was so grateful to her godfather for giving her the job at his surf school.

And she loved it, really loved it. She got to surf all day, teaching others about the magic of the ocean, the power of the wave, the freedom.

As though sensing her mood lift, the waves started to swell before her.

Maybe one day her parents would accept her. She swivelled her board around. Maybe one day she could return.

She dropped forward, felt the rush of the ocean beneath her, behind her, as familiar as her own heartbeat. No, she would never give this up. And until her parents could accept it was a part of her, she would just stay away.

Crazy when she considered that it was them who had given her this addiction, the surf school they'd run once-upon-a-time being her home from home as a child. But that had all been before the unimaginable had happened, the—

Her thoughts quit, there was movement in the sea ahead, Nalu was in the water, barking. The sound was sharp, incessant, like the rise of an alarm.

What the—

'H-help… Help…'

The yell sounded male, an accompanying spluttering the unmistakable sound of a person taking on water. The lifeguard in Malie had her scanning the water, the hairs prickling at her nape.

The sea, the shore, was shrouded in darkness and she squinted into it as her eyes adjusted from the sunset. How long had she rocked out here for? How long had she sat—

Oh goodness, no.

She caught a glimpse of someone in the water, their strokes hurried, panicked. She could no longer make out Nalu, but they were definitely in trouble. Either side of them the waves were breaking, the perceived stillness of the water in which they swam telling her the person was caught in a rip current and instinctively fighting for shore.

'Don't fight it,' she yelled. 'Go with it!'

She was already paddling for them, her head raised and eyes trained on their position. They didn't seem to hear her and she cursed, yelled again, 'Hey, over here!'

The waves were picking up, getting bigger, but it worked in her favour, propelling her closer until she was almost parallel to the person.

'Swim to me!' she yelled, one hand waving at him to come her way.

Finally he saw her, his eyes wide as he flicked his hair off his face and continued to strike for shore. He was going nowhere and if anything, he was struggling more, fear making his strokes ineffective and sending him under.

'You can't fight the current.' It was difficult to stay close to him now as each wave urged her into shore, but she couldn't let it. She had to stay with him. 'You need to get out of it, come towards me.'

5

She could see the disbelief on his face, knew the look of fear well. He wasn't coming out. She was going in.

'It won't take you under, I promise.'

He shook his head, his mouth filling with water as he gasped.

'If you can't swim to me, float on your back, go with it and I'll get you.'

It was as though he wasn't listening now, just propelling his arms forward in a jagged front crawl that was too exhausting to watch, let alone deliver.

She cursed under her breath and thought quickly.

She couldn't enter the current where she was, she'd only get swept away from him, but she needed to get him on her board before he lost his ability to stay afloat.

'Please, trust me, stay calm, float, I'm going to come and get you...'

She kept shouting back to him, explaining what she was doing, not knowing whether he could hear or if he was even paying attention. People often didn't when they were in a life-threatening situation. But maintaining that contact was crucial to getting him through this.

She paddled into the current closer to shore and let it take her.

'Grab on,' she ordered as she approached, slipping her own body off the board but keeping one arm over it as she helped him take hold. 'Now grip it.'

She wrapped her arm around his back, which was so broad she had to pull away from the board a little and push her hip into his back to keep him up. 'We're just going to go with it for now.'

She spoke close to his ear, certain he'd hear her, even over his ragged breaths, and she wondered how much water he'd taken on, whether he was even lucid enough to stay with her.

Nalu barked from outside the rip current, swimming to keep pace with them; he wasn't silly enough to join them, like Malie he was waiting for the strength of the current to ease, enough that she could power them both out of it.

If the guy had just done as she'd asked… But then what on earth had he been doing in the first place? Swimming where there was no lifeguard and at this time of day, without the knowledge it took to understand the water.

Foolish, foolish, fool.

And she'd tell him as much just as soon as they had dry land beneath their feet.

She felt the tug of the water start to ease and kicked out, each strike of her legs taking them further into safety.

He was bigger than her, muscular too, and… in a shirt? Who goes swimming in an actual *shirt*?

'Thank you,' he suddenly blurted, his voice rasping as he leaned forward to rake one hand over his face and look to her.

'You want to thank me,' she said, looking to the shoreline, 'you can help swim us back in.'

It was a short, snappy retort, but then, he'd been an absolute idiot and he wasn't dead, so he could pull his weight.

It worked to get them in quicker and as their feet hit the sand, she slid the board away so that he could crawl up the beach. She walked up behind him, the board hooked under her arm. He turned onto his back, his eyes closed as he laid one hand on his chest, the other by his side. He dragged in a shaky breath, then another.

She dropped her board down and stood over him, aware that she was staring but unable to look away. She was relieved he was OK, angry that he'd been a fool, but now that he was on dry land

and not spluttering up half the ocean, she was struck by just how good-looking he was.

Considering that she dealt with ripped surfer dudes day in, day out, some novice in the sea shouldn't really be touting this much appeal.

'Hey, you OK?' she asked.

His lashes fluttered as he gave a choked hum – they were thick, dark, almost feminine, if not for the fact they fanned cheeks that looked like they'd been chiselled from granite.

'What the hell were you thinking?'

He wet his lips, lips that made her think of kissing. It was an impulsive reaction, it wasn't rational. She'd just rescued him, for God's sake. But they were so full, full yet firm, a flush of colour in his otherwise pale and clean-shaven face.

Was it the ordeal that made him so pale, or was it just the light of the moon? Either way, it gave him a sexy vamp-like edge, a total contrast to the tanned Adonises she was used to. Perhaps that was why she found him uniquely appealing. And then his throat bobbed as he swallowed, the move drawing her eye lower... and oh my, would her stomach just quit its fluttering.

He opened his eyes and the fluttering became a full-on typhoon. It was too dark to determine their colour, but his eyes met her own with an intensity that took her breath away. He swept his hair off his face unveiling an angled brow that gave a surety to his features, a confidence that belied his fear of seconds ago.

'I'm sorry I got you caught up in that.'

His voice rasped and her body positively purred over it. Was that how he always sounded, or was that just the effect of the sea?

He was English too; a Londoner, if she were to guess.

Well, English or not, hot-vamp or not, you should be rollicking him, not standing here drooling like a sex-starved nymph.

Where's your good sense, Malie?

Back out in the sea, it would appear…

★ ★ ★

Could this day get any worse?

When Todd Masters pulled himself up the beach on his hands and knees, thanks to his jelly-like legs that had refused to support his weight, he'd hoped he could feign passing out and she would just leave him to it. Let him regather his wits and his pride alone. If only…

Someone up there was clearly having a laugh at his expense today. First his father had refused to accept his help which had resulted in a phone call from hell, and then he'd tried to save a dog from drowning only to find himself the one in need – *in need?* He was *never* the one in need.

And now his rescuer was mad, real mad, judging by her silhouette that showed her hands were fisted on her hips.

'Never mind sorry,' she erupted – *definitely* mad. 'You could have got yourself killed.'

He let his head loll back, his eyes closed again, like he could somehow magic away the whole situation. He'd been an idiot and he'd likely put her in danger too. It had been foolish, reckless, stupid even, and to his horror, he could feel a foreign surge of heat creeping into his cheeks.

Beside him there was a swoosh as she dropped to her knees, a soft curse falling from her lips as her hand fell to his chest. Her palm was warm despite the clinging wet fabric of his shirt.

He couldn't peep, if he did, he knew the blush – *a blush, for goodness' sake* – would spread. And he was trying to force it back. He didn't blush, he didn't get embarrassed and he sure as hell didn't need help. He was always the one to give help. And yet... the sea water swishing around in his gut, currently threatening to make a reappearance, and the way his knees almost knocked told him he'd definitely needed that help.

'Hey.' Her hand pressed into his chest. 'Hey.'

Still he didn't react.

'Hey!' There was nothing soft about it now, her palm was hard, urgent as it shoved at him. 'Are you OK?'

He took hold of her wrist before she could shake the sea water out of him and gave a laugh. Not that he really felt like laughing. And that made it a nervous laugh and he hadn't produced one of those since... well, for ever.

'I'm OK, save for my ego. That's taken a hit.'

He opened his eyes to look up at her and the whole world seemed to stop. For the briefest moment, all he saw were a pair of piercing eyes only a foot away, close enough to feel her harried breath mingle with his. They were cat-like, so dark as they glittered at him, captivating him, and he had the ridiculous notion that he was drowning all over again... until they narrowed and flashed with another surge of rage.

'Your ego is the last thing you should be worrying about.' She pushed off him, rocking back on her heels. 'What on earth did you think you were doing out there?'

It wasn't just her eyes. It was the angle to her cheekbones, her perfect almond-shaped face and lips that were plump in spite of their tight, grim line.

He swallowed. He really needed to get a handle on this situation. He felt unsteady, rocked to his core, and now he wasn't so sure whether that was from his near-drowning or her.

'Are you going to answer me?' She fisted her hands back on her hips and continued to loom, the angle drawing his eyes to her chest, the narrow slant to her waist, and swell to her hips... and he wasn't overheating with pure shame anymore.

He scrambled up onto his elbows with a cough and she scuttled back, just a little, but the space was good, really good. It gave him the clarity he needed, to drag in air that wasn't tainted by her coconut sea scent.

'I'm really sorry.'

'Wading straight into a rip current and refusing to listen to a single instruction I gave you.'

'Hey, I listened.' He raised a hand to ward off the onslaught of her words. 'I just couldn't understand why you wanted me to do that.'

She shook her head so fiercely droplets of sea water fired at him, her mass of hair already springing up into corkscrew curls as they released her fury on him. 'You *never* try and swim against it, no one can beat it.'

'I just wanted to get back to shore before the riptide pulled me under.'

She laughed. The sound sudden, unexpected and glorious. At least she wasn't livid now. 'For your information, you were caught in a rip current, and no one gets dragged under by it, you get swept out.'

'OK.' He said it slowly. 'That's not what I've seen on the TV.'

'This is real life. So in future, you get caught like that, you do as

I say and you either swim parallel to shore, or you go with it until you feel the pull soften. *Then* you get out of it *before* attempting to swim to shore. Understood?'

Understood? He couldn't remember the last time someone had spoken to him in such a way and he had the ridiculous urge to roll his eyes. 'Yes, Mum.'

'This isn't funny, dude.'

'I didn't say it was.' But she'd just called him *dude* and now he really did want to laugh. How interesting it was to be stripped of his identity and just be one of the masses again, or the dudes, as she put it.

She was studying him intently and he realized too late that his amusement certainly wasn't amusing her. He tried to straighten his face, to look serious. Was there another lecture brewing?

'You could have died out there,' she admonished, but it was softer now.

'Yes, I got that much, thank you.'

'Unless that was your intention?' She frowned and swept an eye over his length: shirt, chino shorts, socks… at least he'd had the foresight to toe off his trainers and drop his mobile in them before running in. 'It's not normal to go swimming dressed for dinner.'

'Look, I was trying to rescue a dog.'

'*A dog?* You ran in the water where there's no lifeguard, the light is almost gone, to rescue a dog?'

She didn't sound like she believed him. Great, did she now think he'd put himself in danger intentionally? His amusement morphed back into embarrassment just as swiftly. This was getting better and better. Where was the dog anyhow? He started to scan the beach and then a thought occurred to him.

'Hang on, *you* were way out in the water when I got here, *you'd* gone in with no lifeguard, limited light... *yada yada yada.*'

She lifted her chin. 'I know what I'm doing, plus I'm a qualified lifeguard.'

'Oh, so you can rescue yourself when in difficulty, yes?' He'd swear she was the one blushing now, and even if she wasn't, it suited him to think she was. 'That's a cracking skill.'

She shook her head and shoved at his chest. 'I wouldn't have swum into the rip current for a start.'

'No, I got that loud and clear.' He looked back to the sea, to where he'd been making an idiot of himself minutes before and frowned. 'Not that I understand how you spot one in the first place.'

She turned to look at the water too. 'You see that channel you were in; you see how the waves are breaking either side, but that strip looks calm, virtually still...?'

He shifted higher onto his elbows and looked to where she motioned with her hand. 'Yes.'

Her eyes came back to him, sharp, direct. '*That* is a rip current.'

'Got it,' he hurried out, which he did, and he would certainly remember it in future. 'But at the time I was more focused on the dog that—'

As if on cue, said dog trotted up and like his rescuer shook off his hair, showering Todd in another layer of sea water. Only this time the effect wasn't quite as appealing.

'It was this one as it happens.' He nodded his head in its direction and noted how the hound looked far too innocent and in no way in need of rescuing at all. The dog gave a sharp bark in agreement, or to rattle him further – he couldn't decide.

'Nalu?' She still didn't sound convinced.

'Na–who?' He stared at the dog like he could blame it for everything that had gone wrong that day.

'Nalu…' She leaned over and ruffled its great big head. 'He belongs to the surf school further down the coast.'

'He does?'

'Yup and that's why he's called Nalu, it's Hawaiian for wave or surf.'

'Very apt.' He knew he sounded disgruntled, but he couldn't help it. If it hadn't been for Nalu, he wouldn't have made such a complete fool of himself. 'I take it he knows all about rip wotsits then?'

She laughed again, the sound even lighter and easy now. 'Yup.'

Nalu gave a little snort and plonked himself down.

It really was time to bring an end to the whole emasculating experience, but the idea of just walking away from her was worse than enduring it.

Instead he found himself asking, 'Well, now that I know Naa-luu is safe and I certainly am, because of you, how about a drink to say thank you?'

Her eyes widened. 'A drink?'

'Yes… you know one of those things people do for fun?'

She nibbled her bottom lip, a move he found strangely contrary to the confidence she projected both in and out of the water.

'I can't, I already have plans.' She glanced at her watch and gave a curse under her breath. 'And I'm going to be late.'

She looked back to him as she shot to her feet. 'Will you be OK getting home?'

Her obvious concern was sweet and frustrating – *no, humiliating* – at the same time. It would probably be better all round if they never saw one another again. His ego certainly thought so.

'I'll be fine, my place isn't far.'

She hesitated, leaning on one foot then the other. 'OK. But if you want to swim, maybe stick to the more common areas next time. This section doesn't get many visitors with it being so overgrown.'

'That's what made it perfect.'

Her eyes narrowed and he knew she was trying to suss out his reasoning.

'Well, next time, maybe just avoid the water and the acts of heroism.'

'You're on, I'll leave those to you.' He laughed as he said it, expecting her to take that as her cue to leave. Instead she went back to chewing her lip as Nalu trotted around to sit at her feet.

'You can stop worrying, you know, I'm not about to go back in.'

'Of course, yeah...' she glanced away and then back to him. 'I'll see you around... come on, Nalu.'

Then she was off, ducking to grab her board on the way and jogging into the foliage that bordered the beach. He was left with his ego in pieces but a strange excitement thrumming through his veins. The comedown of the adrenalin, he supposed, only he had a feeling it wasn't just that...

And he hadn't even caught her name.

He knew where she came to surf, though... if ever he wanted to engineer a future meet-up...

'You need to move,' he suddenly heard from the foliage, not that he could make her out. 'The tide is about to take your designer trainers out.'

He shot up, she was right, the water was already lapping at his toes.

He launched himself at his shoes, his wet and sandy clothes making the entire move awkward and her soft giggle trickled through the air, tailing off as she went further into the greenery.

He found himself smiling down at the footwear now in his hands. *Smiling?!*

He could have died and instead of reeling from it, he was grinning like a fool.

He pulled his phone out of his shoes and checked his home screen, cursing when he saw the time.

No more grinning now, she wasn't the only one about to be late.

CHAPTER TWO

'NO. NO. NO. NO.'

Malie was tugging her fingers through her hair and getting nowhere. It was one thing to think she didn't have to do a lot to get ready. It was another to forget about her painfully belligerent corkscrew curls that wouldn't be tamed even with a vat of oil poured over them.

Why had she even agreed to this? Cocktail parties weren't her thing. Give her a foam party in Ibiza with Zoe, Lils and Victoria and she'd be on it in a flash. Although this time they wouldn't lose Zoe for a whole three hours. Now she giggled. Fun times. Real, fun times.

Before the cancer took Koa.

Before the car accident that took away V's chance of having children and Zoe's ability to walk.

She shivered, the familiar guilt sparking.

Losing Koa had left her bereft and made her invisible to her parents. They'd immediately shut down their surf school, unable to keep it going when their champion surfer, their pride and joy had died. They'd forced her to give it up too, but she couldn't. Instead she'd hidden it from them, and thus had begun the separation: their life and hers.

Her friends had been her lifeline. Zoe hiding Malie's board for her so that she could sneak out on the waves. Sometimes with Zoe. Sometimes alone.

And then the accident had happened, and life had changed for them all.

They'd been buzzing that night a decade ago, on the way to the school's summer ball, not realizing that life was about to change for ever. And then bang... literally.

Malie had come away with nothing more than a few cuts and bruises, Lils' injuries had been similar. And to see their best friends, as close as sisters, suffer as they had... survivor's guilt was a real thing.

First, she'd experienced it with Koa, and then the accident had thrown her in deep again.

Working hard to help others, particularly those considered disadvantaged or vulnerable or disabled – or for whatever reason in need – was the one way she knew how to climb out of it.

By helping them, by opening their eyes to what they were still capable of, to face what life throws at them and keep on trucking, the ocean made all that possible.

Surfing was therapy. It had helped her to cope and now she used it to help others. She'd taken inspiration from Zoe. When her friend could easily have wallowed, closed in on herself, she'd fought, she'd made something of herself.

All Malie had to do now was get Zoe back on a board and she would be happy. Which is exactly what they would do later this month when Zoe came to stay. Finally, her friend would be here, in Malie's world of surf, sea and sand, and nothing would stop them getting out on the boards then.

She gave an excited little *squee*, twirling on the spot and... stopped dead. *Oh dear.*

Her *fabulously airy apartment with sea-facing views* looked more like the *before* scene from one of those domestic goddess SOS TV shows. It would likely send Zoe into a flat-out tailspin and she'd start pulling out mops, cloths, bleach... that's if she didn't refuse outright to stay and check in to the nearest available hotel.

Yup, she would have to find time to clean from somewhere.

But right now, she needed to get her hair sorted.

She picked up her brush and tried again. And again. It wasn't having it.

She turned back to the mirror and let go of the brush handle. It didn't move. It sat on the side of her head like some random accessory – *great. Just, great!*

She stuck her tongue out at her reflection and flung out her hands in surrender.

Look, you are you, she mentally reasoned, *you can do a good job selling the work that you do without perfect hair. You can channel Zoe's can-do attitude and get it done.*

It was the reminder she needed. Tonight's cocktail party wasn't about looking the part, it was about representing the surf school and making sure that the charitable foundation knew that the programme was in safe hands with her. That investing in Surf Therapy was the right way to go for the disabled and disadvantaged children they helped.

And if she could pull it off tonight, and over the course of the next few weeks while representatives from the charity were visiting, then hopefully they would send more groups her way.

She yanked the brush out and tossed it onto her bed to join the mountain of discarded outfits, and scooped up more coconut oil, smoothing it through her hair as best she could. Au natural it was going to be!

She washed her hands and picked up the dress she'd decided on. Victoria had made it for her especially, the baby blue fabric with its delicate white swirl was so light against her skin and perfect for the Hawaiian climate. Its halter style and loose skirt complimented her frame, or as her friends would say *enhanced her fabulous assets* which to her were just a royal pain in the proverbial.

She stepped into it, tied the neck and returned to the mirror. Not bad. Even with the wild hair.

Just a sweep of lippy, mascara and… hmm, maybe just a little blusher wouldn't hurt. It was the most made-up she'd been in… well, months… not even for Christmas Day had she gone this all-out.

Kalani would be pleased. And that's what mattered. He was her godfather, her boss, the owner of the surf school in which she worked and the man who'd said he would back this venture of hers. He believed in her so she would too.

She grabbed her silver sandals and slid them on – they weren't the heels her friends would have told her to wear but hey, she still had a beach to cross. She could take the road and go with heels, but it wouldn't be half as atmospheric or soothing, and she wanted the latter. Nerves weren't really her thing, but so much depended on tonight being a success, of making the right impression, that the belly-butterflies were rife.

She headed out into the night, knowing her route like the back of her hand. Coincidentally, the private residence where the function was being held bordered the stretch of beach she'd surfed at earlier that evening. Tucked away. Usually deserted.

Not today though. She felt the flutters ramp up and pressed her palm against them. *It's just nerves. Not him.*

She was used to ripped, surfer types. Long, shaggy bed head, tanned, god-like bodies, abs to die for. Not pale-skinned, trainer-wearing, hoity-toity rich dudes that looked like they'd been plucked out of Victoria's upmarket wine bar back in Chelsea. Not that he'd sounded rich. In all fairness, his accent had sounded more South London to her. But there'd been an air about him, it hadn't just been his clothing that had spoken of a definite affluence. And when he'd looked at her, when they'd been so close on the beach… even now she felt her body heat up.

It was a good job she'd been too busy to go for that drink he'd offered. She had a feeling that any more time spent in his company she'd be in trouble.

'*Aloha*, Malie.' Her uncle embraced her when he saw her. He'd arranged to meet her at the entrance to the private drive, that way neither of them had to go in alone. They dealt with the rich daily – providing lessons – but this was different. This was on their territory.

'You look… *Nani* – beautiful!'

'And so do you, Uncle.' She grinned as she took in his colourful shirt and trousers. 'I never thought I'd see the day you'd don a pair of chinos.'

He grimaced as he took her arm in his. 'Mention the trousers again, and you can do a double shift tomorrow.'

She giggled and he was saved from any further ribbing by the security guard at the gatehouse. He stepped forward, his smile polite. 'Invitations, please.'

Kalani pulled one out of his pocket. It was the colour of sunrise with the silhouette of several surfboards and their owners, one in a wheelchair, one with a prosthetic leg, one with only one arm, some with no external injuries at all but clearly all united by the beach and their boards. She loved it.

'They really have gone all-out,' she said to him as the security guard opened the gates.

'Wait until you see inside,' he said. 'I've heard some of the locals talking about it this afternoon. It seems Mr Masters, the guy who heads up the Foundation and is staying here, has a lot of passion for this project. I think you'll have a lot in common with him.'

'Really?' Maybe this evening wouldn't be such a chore after all. Maybe she did stand a chance of not only doing some good but also getting to talk that passion through with someone who shared it. 'I'd kind of had a different expectation in my head, it's not often you meet people that aren't in it for their own financial gain, good PR or otherwise.'

'Well, maybe this guy will surprise you.'

She nodded as they followed the perfectly manicured driveway that weaved through the landscaped grounds. She could hear music now, the celestial sound of a steel guitar playing the chilled-out music of the island mingling with the gentle hum of chatter in the distance.

'Do you know much about the people coming tonight?' she asked.

'Anyone who's anyone, Mr Masters has roped them all in. I think he's hoping to raid their pockets before the night is out.'

'Now that's a plan I can get on board with... oh wow!' Where the path forked ahead there was an old surfboard sporting a sketch of cocktails and an arrow pointing to the left, towards the rear of the house and closer to the sea. At its base were various-sized lanterns, lit up and adorned with shells. 'I *love* that.'

Kalani grinned. 'Look, there's more.'

Sure enough as they turned down the path, more shell lanterns ran along its edge, their soft glow accentuating the trail and she felt herself smile. This really wasn't like any other cocktail party she'd been to and her beach dress fitted right in – *thank you, V!*

As the music and voices grew louder the path curved off to the right and just ahead, she could see a beautiful pergola. Fairy lights weaved with creeping vines through the wooden pillars and along the lattice roofline, small tables made of what looked like driftwood and varnished to a warm rich colour were decorated with flickering lanterns, sand and shells. Straight ahead was a wooden stage featuring three propped-up surfboards with the charity name – Fun For All – written across them in wave-like writing. To the left the ocean rolled, its waves crashing peacefully in the distance. To the right, the impressive house ran for as far as the eye could see.

People milled everywhere, some readily recognizable like the mayor, the chief of police, famous local author Idris Magnum, as well as some of the island's hottest surf talent. And they were all fixated on the stage – local DJ, Eddie, had them eating out of the palm of his hand. Everyone was smiling, everyone was happy, and hopefully that meant money for the Foundation and a successful start to their relationship with the surf school.

'They're in the middle of the auction,' a young woman explained, coming up to them and smiling at Kalani. She was dressed impeccably in a black bodycon dress, her dark hair perfectly smooth and make-up flawless. Malie didn't recognize her. 'Mr Masters has had them here for over an hour already and the drinks haven't stopped flowing.'

'Bidding while under the influence, hey? You sure Harry isn't going to complain?' Kalani gestured to the chief of police.

'You know, I think he's actively encouraging it.'

They both laughed and Kalani turned to Malie. 'This is Grace, she's the lady we have to thank for Mr Masters coming to us with this venture.'

'Ah, Malie, it's so lovely to meet you.' Grace turned her smile on Malie and a genuine warmth lit up the woman's eyes. 'I loved the piece you wrote on Surf Therapy and the work you have been doing here.'

'You read it?' Malie didn't know why she was surprised; she wrote it as a feature article on their website with this exact goal, to bring charities like Fun For All her way. Zoe with her travel-writing expertise had even cast her eye over it and said it was great.

'I did. I also liked how you incorporated an awareness of the invisible hurdles young people face and how you carefully craft your lessons to boost self-esteem and tackle social awkwardness too.'

She'd really read it. It wasn't just some PR babble to make her feel special.

'I'm so pleased you liked it.'

'Loved it! It was just what we were looking for when we decided to trial this initiative.'

Malie felt her smile widen and looked to Kalani to see he was just as pleased. 'Well, I'd love to offer my thanks to Mr Masters personally, if he's around to be introduced?'

'Of course.' Grace scanned the crowd, craning her neck and frowning. 'He did have a call to take earlier, I think he might still be on it.'

She turned back to Malie, 'As soon as he returns, I'll bring him to meet you. I know he's keen to discuss the initiative with you directly. In the meantime, I highly recommend the Fun For All cocktail we've had mixed specially, it's going down a storm.'

A waitress appeared as though beckoned with a tray of tall cocktail glasses and a drink that very much resembled a Tequila Sunrise, complete with colourful umbrellas, orange slices, cherries and straws. Malie picked one up and grinned as Kalani did the same.

Her godfather was a tower of a man and broad as a bodybuilder, seeing him with such a drink topped off his alien outfit rather brilliantly.

He sipped at the straw and she felt the giggle bubble up in her belly.

'Say anything…' he said around the straw as Grace walked off into the crowd, 'and that double shift will be a triple.'

She took the straw between her lips, fighting back her smirk, and sucked down the sweet drink. She looked to the stage and tuned in to what Eddie was saying.

'We have a fabulous item up next; you'll all want to get your hands on this one, especially if you missed out on the surf lessons with our very own Kalani that were on offer earlier this evening.' Malie felt her cheeks colour as she realized where this was going. Eddie chose that exact moment to catch her eye above the crowd. 'We have a package of five private sessions, only this time they are being offered by the legend that is, Malie Pukui!'

There was a round of applause and she felt her cheeks heat further.

'We arrived just in time,' Kalani murmured, clearly amused to see the discomfort transferred to his goddaughter.

'Who's going to start us off?' Eddie asked the crowd.

'A thousand!' someone shouted.

'Twelve hundred!'

'Fourteen hundred!'

Figures were flying through the air and the excitement in the room was palpable. She took another sip of her drink and felt her pulse racing with the thrill of it, her embarrassment forgotten. To know that this was something she was able to offer personally and have it raising so much money for the Foundation was wonderful.

'This is fantastic, Malie, fingers crossed they secured something similar for mine earlier.'

She nodded, her eyes fixed on Eddie and wondering when the bidding would end.

'Tell you what, ladies and gentlemen, why don't I bring the lovely Malie up here and you can see for yourself the amazing company you will have for those five lessons – her smile alone is worth it! Hey, Malie!'

He sent her a wink across the room and she shook her head with a laugh.

'Come on...' Eddie waved his hand at her and the crowd started to turn, hunting her out. Kalani nudged her with his elbow.

'You can't leave him hanging.'

'You're only saying that because you managed to escape!'

Kalani shrugged. 'You only have yourself to blame for taking so long to turn up.'

'I was having a hair emergency.'

'Be that as it may, your hair can't save you now.'

She laughed again, 'I'm gonna kill him.'

Kalani chuckled. 'Best save that for after the auction, he's doing an epic job of it.'

Her godfather was right. Eddie was doing a great job and she had to trust him. If her going up there raised even more money, then it would be worth every step.

She walked forward, her drink still in hand, and smiled at the crowd parting before her. Eddie filled the air with her numerous surfing accolades, and she tried to tame her smile; it wouldn't do to look too arrogant about it all but hearing it listed like that made her heart pound harder and her lungs feel fit to burst. She really had achieved a lot and sometimes it was easy to forget in the day-to-day running of the school.

'Hey, Malie.' He grinned down at her, holding out his hand to help her onto the stage; she took it, stepping up and turning to look out over the crowd.

It was hard to make out Kalani – to make out anyone – with the lights now directed onto the stage, onto her.

'Here she is, folks. Say hi, Malie.'

She leaned into his mic and gave a soft 'Hi', her fingers fluttering in a wave.

'Four and a half thousand!' The shout was instant and Eddie laughed.

'Remember, it's just the lessons, folks!'

Oh, God. She wasn't one to blush, that was Lils' trick. But right now, the heat flushing her body had less to do with the hot lights and everything to do with the suggestion in Eddie's statement. The laughter rippled through the crowd, along with a flurry of further bids. She squinted against the lights, trying to make out who was bidding but it was impossible.

'Five thousand!'

'Five and a half!'

'Si—!'

'Twenty thousand.' The male bid stole through the crowd, steady, level, controlled. Nothing like the previous shouts had been.

An amazed hush swept the room, Eddie made a choked sound like he'd swallowed his own mic and then he coughed, his brow hitting the heavens.

'Did I just hear twenty thousand dollars?' he said, leaning towards the crowd with his ear and giving Malie a quick smile, bringing the reality of the sum home for her too.

'Yes, twenty thousand.'

She tried to follow the voice in the crowd – there was something so familiar to it, disturbingly familiar. But it couldn't be. It *couldn't*.

It was just the familiar English twang that made her think of *him*.

'Wow!' Eddie declared, one hand raised in the air. 'Well, in that case, I think we have a winner who definitely deserves to take to the stage too. Come on up here, twenty-thousand-dollar man!'

The crowd applauded, the excitement travelling through the room as the sea of people began to part and the lights on the stage found him in their midst.

Her heart leaped into her throat the second her eyes hit upon his. On *him*. Her smile faltered, her lashes fluttered.

'Why, it's our very own host,' Eddie erupted. 'Todd Masters!'

He – who – what, now?

Mr Masters.

The Todd Masters.

The man she had to thank for his business.

The man she wanted to discuss ideas with.

The man she now had to deliver *five* lessons to… was the man she had decided she was best staying well clear of!

She swallowed, made her smile lift again and watched him approach. There was nothing chaotic or flustered or wet about him now. He was every bit the slick millionaire she expected Todd Masters to be. Not a hair out of place in its flicked-back style, his black shirt falling over the abs she knew existed beneath – she'd felt them, after all, when she'd pressed her hand into his chest and they'd flexed beneath her. Her fingers tingled with the memory and she clenched them at her side, her drink cooling the other palm.

It couldn't be him.

Maybe it was just a trick of the light, she could barely focus straight after having those lights on her seconds before. Maybe her memory was playing tricks on her, it had been dark at the beach, easy to mistake him for someone else.

She kept on staring, wishing herself wrong.

Eddie was still talking, making some joke about whether it was a valid bid if it came from the owner himself, which only had the crowd cheering more, patting Masters on the back as he smiled and ribbed Eddie in return.

She heard it all but it was distant, drowned out by her ears that rang with her racing heartbeat. And then he looked back to her again, his eyes locking with hers as he closed the remaining distance and she couldn't breathe. They were bemused, surprised even, but above all she could read something else in their depths, she could read it because she felt it too. An awareness, an attraction. It pulsed through her, out of her control, impossible to resist.

She wet her lips and realized this was how a mouse caught in a trap must feel, only this was a trap of her very own making.

Five lessons… up, close and personal…

What had she let herself in for?

CHAPTER THREE

IT HAD ALWAYS BEEN his intention to purchase *something* at the auction, of course it had. How could he expect others to cough up if he wasn't willing to do the same?

But *surf lessons*? And *five* at that.

It wasn't like he had the time for it. His foundation may be treating the kids to a holiday of a lifetime, but it was still work for him.

Work with some surfing on the side, it now seemed.

He climbed up onto the stage, careful to place Eddie between him and the infamous Malie – how had he not known it was her? He must have seen pictures, come across something, but he'd scoured his brain and come up blank. He certainly hadn't recognized her on the beach earlier and if they'd crossed paths before, there was no way he would have forgotten. She was unforgettable.

The last few hours had already proven that. Didn't matter he had work to tend to, she'd been there, her smile, her laugh, her presence… and now here they were, paired up by his outrageous bid. He hoped he knew what he was doing…

'So, Mr Masters,' Eddie turned to him, his grin wide.

'Todd, please.' Mr Masters made him think of his father and the phone call that afternoon that had sent him running to the beach for some breathing space.

'Very well, Todd, I think you will agree you're in very talented hands with our Malie here.'

'Gentle hands, I hope.' He looked to her with his tease and was relieved to see the wide-eyed panic he'd caught a glimpse of when she'd recognized him had fallen away.

'If you want gentle, Mr Masters,' she said smoothly, 'you might be best with Kalani.'

The crowd laughed, as did Todd. He'd met Kalani briefly and *gentle* was not a word he would use to describe the giant.

'In that case…' He rolled his shoulders, cocked his head from side to side, giving the impression of a boxer about to hit the ring. 'Give me all you got, I'm sure I can take it.'

She rewarded him with a laugh that rolled with the crowd. 'You're on.'

'Now I hate to kick the boss off the stage…' Eddie gave him a grin before looking back to the audience, 'but the band are itching to set up, so I need to shoo the pair of you off and get the last item sold.'

Todd jumped down and offered up a hand to Malie. For a second, he wondered if she'd refuse, the challenge he'd read in her expression told him as much. It had been similar to the look she'd given him at the beach after ranting at him. But she didn't. She placed her hand in his and the simple touch had his palm alive, his body eager to maintain the connection as it slipped from her hand to her lower back to lead her off to the side, away from the speakers and the general hubbub.

'You should have told me who you were.' She rounded on

him, her hair captivatingly wild as its curls flounced around her shoulders with the sharpness of the move. He could see golden streaks running through the dark mass, something he'd not spied when they'd been wet from the sea.

She crossed her arms, her stance accusatory, as she stared up at him and blew an errant curl out of her eyes. They were green. Green and sparkling, hitting with the blue of her dress and making him think of a blue lagoon with its varying shades and something he could dive into and get lost in. He'd had the same thought at the beach and it had been just as ridiculous then. There would be no getting lost in anything. There would be surf lessons, some harmless fun, then back to business. He had no room in his life for more.

'Are you not going to say anything?'

Caught staring, he wanted to slap himself. After that afternoon's embarrassing encounter, the least he could do was show her the real him. The man who was always in control of himself and the situation.

'You ran off so quickly, I didn't get chance to… and it wasn't like you introduced yourself either.'

'I'm Malie, surf school instructor, ex-champion, it's a little different to, *I'm Mr Masters and I'm the millionaire staying at the private residence beyond the overgrown foliage.*'

'I have to say I prefer your introduction, it's way cooler.'

Her eyes softened with her smile. 'You're a charmer, Mr Masters, I'll give you that.'

'Enough with the Mr, it makes me want to turn around and look for my father.'

'And that's a bad thing?'

'When the guy's partly to blame for my storming onto the beach earlier and making a complete fool of myself in front of you, it is.'

She frowned up at him. 'You didn't make a *complete* fool of yourself.'

'A partial one then.'

She gave a soft laugh and shook her head. 'Now that I think on it properly, it's really quite sweet that you thought Nalu was in trouble and jumped in to help him.'

'You do?'

She gave him a nod. 'And now that you know how to spot a rip current and how to deal with them you can keep yourself safe too, but maybe next time leave it to the lifeguard.'

'Maybe I should just take you with me everywhere, then I wouldn't need to worry.'

What the hell, Todd?

He felt his own eyes widen over his impulsive response, watched hers flash in tune as her cheeks coloured. And then she gave a breathless, 'Maybe,' and his good sense to take it back left him.

The auction was underway behind him, the band hurrying back and forth past them with their instruments and equipment, but he was barely aware of any of it, only her eyes locked on his and the strange connection that seemed determined to pull them together. It had existed on the beach and now here, it was undeniable.

It's not like he'd lived the life of a monk all these years. He'd tried dating, tried relationships of a sort. But they never lasted long. He couldn't share his life with another, couldn't give them what they needed to stick around, and he hadn't mourned their loss when they'd eventually given up and moved on. It was to be expected. It was what *he* expected because he was incapable of loving another. He couldn't risk what his father had suffered after his mother had died giving birth to him.

33

Love had the power to destroy a man.

It was fickle and weak, too. Foster homes had taught him that. Love couldn't be trusted.

Love was a frustration. The only person he truly loved was his father and the guy was driving him nigh on insane with his refusal to accept financial help.

And his mind was wandering down a crazy path that had no place in the here and now. What was wrong with him?

'If the idea makes you frown like that,' she suddenly said, 'are you sure you don't want to retract your bid and run away right now?'

He forced a smile, at least, he forced it to begin with, but looking into her eyes he didn't need to force anything. She made him feel it.

'Believe me, that has nothing to do with the prospect of time with you and everything to do with *Mr* Masters.'

'You want to talk about it?' The question looked like it surprised her as much as it did him. *Did* he want to talk about it? He never spoke to anyone about personal stuff. He'd stopped doing that long ago after one too many case-worker interviews that were getting him nowhere. But did he want to now, with her? It seemed so easy. Too easy to say *yes* and it's that which had him opting for diversion.

'How about a dance?' And he didn't dance. Ever.

She looked past him to the crowd, to the band. 'Won't people talk if you're spied dancing with your surf instructor?'

'I think they'll see it as me taking an active role in the evening.'

'Like your bid?'

'Sure, like my bid.'

She shook her head and took a long sip of her drink, her cherry-red lips smiling around the straw.

'You don't strike me as the kind to worry about a little gossip.'
She didn't. She seemed carefree, easy, unless she was rollicking
someone for their stupidity in the water.

'OK, Todd, a dance it is.' She placed her drink down on the
table nearest to them and sauntered past him, looking back over
her shoulder. 'But no funny business, you hear, or me not being
gentle on a surfboard will be the least of your worries.'

He laughed. Again, with the laughter. What was it about her
that had him behaving, no – feeling, so different?

He didn't know the answer. And for once, he didn't need to know.

He was happy to go with the flow.

★★★

'You need to lighten up.' Malie stifled another giggle, her body
moving effortlessly to the music as she maintained eye contact
with Todd. She didn't dare look any lower, it would only set her
off and she didn't make a habit of laughing at people. But his stiff
corpse-like swing was killing her.

'Lighten up?' he said over the music, leaning in so that she could
hear. It didn't stop him clicking his fingers off beat or doing his
little sidestep that was as rigid as a soldier on sentry duty.

He really didn't dance often, or if he did, no one had been kind
enough to point out his... er, unique style.

When he'd asked her to dance, she'd assumed he was a bit of
a closet clubber, not a jagged puppet. It wouldn't be so bad if he
didn't stand out so much. But his six-foot-plus of presence drew
every eye in the room and it was a crime to have his ripped physique
so tight when the music was so fluid, fun, easy.

'Do you dance much?'

He shook his head, his eyes dancing in the fairy lights. 'Not if I can help it.'

She grinned wide, caught on the amusement she could read in his gaze. She liked that he could laugh at himself too. 'That explains it, then.'

'That bad, hey?'

She nodded, softening her confirmation by placing her hand on his arm as she leaned in. 'You dance like you have a stick up your backside.'

She'd intended to pull back but as he raised his brow to look at her, so close, only a foot separating their faces, but found she couldn't. His cologne filled the air that she breathed, spicy and all masculine, his arm beneath her fingers was taut and warm, his eyes flicked to her lips, their intent as easy to read as her own.

Remember where you are.

Remember who he is.

This is not Ibiza, or some club you can just hook up in.

She flexed her fingers, then became immobilized by the conflicting urges to back away and close the distance.

'A stick, you say?' His voice rasped like it had on the beach, or did she just imagine it? Was she hoping he was as wrapped up in the sudden proximity as she was?

'Yes.'

'Do you always say it how it is?'

'Pretty much.'

But she wasn't about to say anything on their underlying chemistry. She knew attraction, the power of the pull when it was reciprocated and it was there, between them. And never had a guy been more off limits to her than Todd Masters. He was invaluable to her plans for the surf school, she wouldn't muddy the waters for a fling that could only be just that, a fling. She wouldn't.

She broke away, forcing her focus on the music, the rippling beat that had her hips gyrating as she twirled on the spot, all the while she felt his eyes follow her. She wasn't intentionally teasing him, she moved on impulse driven by the music, like she did with the sea and her board. And he needed to get a sense of that too if he was going to stand a chance at surfing.

But he wasn't even trying to dance now as he watched her, his grin and the shake of his head looking more awestruck than anything else. 'I envy you.'

She frowned a little as she kept time with the music. 'You do?'

'Your ability to say what you want, dance how you want, to just let go.'

'Well, I hate to tell you this, but you're going to need to learn to do it too.'

'I am?'

'Unless you want to take a pounding in the waves...' He folded his arms across his chest and she danced around him, using her body for emphasis as she explained, 'You need to loosen up, to flex your body as the sea dictates, to move with it. Just like you should ease your body into the music now.'

'Ease my body into the music...?' He sounded less than convinced.

'Uh-huh.' She had ways to get him to loosen up – if he'd been anyone else, she'd have her hands on him now, teasing him into the rhythm, but each time she touched him, she wanted more.

Words. Words would do. She was an instructor after all. She used words every day.

'Try widening your stance...' He did as she bade. 'A little more... try shoulder-width... better, it gives your hips more freedom to move.'

He laughed but did exactly as she asked.

'Now bend your knees a little, keep them soft as you shift your weight from one foot to the other, letting your hips flow naturally.'

'Like this...' He tried left to right, but completely out of time and it baffled her that he could do it, defy the music. To her it came so naturally, the beat, the move, the beat, the move...

'Kind of... but listen to the music, to the rhythm, let it dictate your tempo... not so harsh, flow with it.'

She was watching him and trying not to laugh again. He was trying, he really was; his look of concentration was what she'd expect from him in a boardroom a million miles from where they were now. It softened her to the core. The millionaire businessman trying to learn to dance, to do what she dictated. But all the while his arms were rigid across his chest –

it didn't matter how much his hips moved, those arms were going nowhere.

'You're doing this on purpose, right?' she said eventually.

'Doing what?'

She shook her head and waved a hand in front of her face to hide her giggle. 'Nothing. Nothing.'

He stopped altogether. 'I don't think my ego can cope with your company much longer.'

'I'm sorry, I don't mean to... it's just...' It's just – what? She hadn't danced with anyone so stiff before? She hadn't danced with anyone she wanted to kiss more before and couldn't? That was hardly his fault. And she was hardly being fair. With anyone else she'd simply take a hold of his hips and move him into the movement.

And the truth was, she was going to have to get her hands on him at some point if they were to have five whole surf lessons together. She'd never taught anyone without physically moving them several times over.

No, the sooner she got used to defying the attraction the better.

'Come here.'

'Come here?' He stilled, his eyes wide and dancing with his own laughter now. 'Are you ordering me about, Ms Pukui?'

The way her name sounded in his London accent shouldn't have sent her belly erupting with tiny flutters, but it did.

'Are you going to disobey me?' she pushed, openly shaking off the sensation and fighting back.

'I wouldn't dare.' He stepped towards her and she held her ground, readying herself for the sensation she knew was coming, every nerve-ending alert to his approach.

'Good,' she said, lowering her eyes to his chest. She couldn't stare up at his eyes this close, not now she knew how blue they were, how they danced with his amusement, or burned with reciprocated awareness or just *looked* at her.

She eased one hand onto his hip, the other onto his chest, over his heart and took a small breath.

'You need to get used to it anyway,' she said, 'there'll be a lot of doing as I say during your ridiculously expensive twenty-thousand-dollar training.'

'You saying I'm going to get more stick per buck?'

She smiled at his chest. 'Precisely.'

He gave a groan that she felt rumble through her fingers and she closed her eyes briefly.

Just dance, Malie, concentrate on the music.

'Enough talk,' she said, and then she bit the bullet further to say, 'Put your hands on my hips and feel how I move.'

She saw his Adam's apple bob before her, his jaw held tight, as he moved to do as she asked. Was he finding this as hard as her? As hard and yet...

His fingers closed around her hips, their warmth seeping through the delicate fabric of her dress and triggering a rush of warmth that far exceeded their gentle pressure. She tried to breathe through it, tried to stay fixed on the pulse beating in his steadfast jaw as she focused on the music, the rhythm urging her to move. She didn't want to dwell on just how perfect, just how thrilling his touch, his proximity was, or the fact she could feel his breath brush over her hair, his scent—

'Now feel how I move and move with me...' her voice rose above her heightened senses, 'like this.'

She eased his hips with her fingers, nudged his stance wider with her foot and felt his eyes upon her head as he concentrated and mimicked her. And he did. He really did.

'Better already – do you feel that?'

His answer was another rumble in his chest, a more confident sweep of his hips. She strummed her fingers over his chest, over his heart.

'Feel the beat,' she whispered, not knowing whether he heard her or not. She was losing herself in the music, the feel of his body moving beneath her touch, moving with her, heady, intoxicating.

She found her hand softening against his hip, less guiding as he did it under his own steam. She could – *should* – let go but even as she thought it, their bodies eased closer together, the music and something far more visceral wrapping around them.

'You're a good teacher,' he said against her hair.

'And you're a good pupil.' Her eyes lifted before she could stop them and collided with the dark intensity of his own. She felt his fingers pulse around her hips, her own breath catching as her breasts brushed against his chest.

Just keep dancing.

Remember: Student. Teacher; Student. Teacher; Successful Businessman. Surf Teacher; Philanthropist,. Big-Hearted Charity Do-er; You. Do. Not. Mix.

'Fancy taking a walk on the beach?'

His question broke through her internal mantra, shocking and effective in equal measure.

No, Malie. You don't fancy going anywhere that private, at this time of night, with him.

She bit into her lip, killing off the impulsive yes, the impulsive no.

She used to know her own mind.

But with Todd, it seemed her mind was lost beneath a multitude of other, far more gratifying sensations.

'I'd love to tell you more about the Foundation and the work we do, the kids you'll be teaching...'

She felt her cheeks flush. Again. Lils would so love this reversal in her composure which had her suffering the same affliction as her beloved friend. Malie really didn't.

Seriously, there she was getting carried away with the idea that the super successful, intelligent and sexy beyond measure hunk with

41

his hands on her hips was as caught up as she was in this magnetic attraction, when really all he wanted to do was talk about her passion. Their passion. Something they shared.

'Of course.' She stepped back abruptly, hating how high-pitched her voice sounded.

She distracted herself by brushing down her dress, keeping her tingling palms busy. It wasn't enough. They were still so warm, so fuzzy, from him. She tried to snap out of it by seeking out her drink and grabbing it up. Using the sweet, cold alcohol to drown her embarrassment and loosen up her dry mouth.

'I'll get you a fresh one.'

She was about to say *there's no need*, but he was off weaving through the crowd to hunt down a member of the serving staff.

At least it gave her time to cool off and get her head straight.

At least she hadn't outright kissed him.

At least she didn't have that to worry about.

To remember.

To dream.

Her fingers went to her lips that thrummed at the thought of it alone and she shook her head.

There'll be no dreaming, no kissing, no anything.

Talking. Walking. Surfing. Working.

A perfect list of -ings to stick to... and she could do that.

Surely, she could?

CHAPTER FOUR

IF HE COULD REWIND time by mere minutes he would. To take back his idea of a walk and not witness the look of alarm that had crossed her features. Not to mention his own panic. What the hell had he been thinking?

Truth was he hadn't been thinking at all. He'd been so caught up in the moment, so convinced that she'd wanted to kiss him as much as he did her, that the only thing separating them had been the crowd and he'd wanted them all gone. He'd wanted it to be just the two of them so he could satisfy this incessant need to stay close to her, and closer still.

But it was foolish, reckless even, and it wasn't like him.

Maybe the beauty of the island and the sea air was going to his head. Maybe his phone call with his father had done more damage than just the suffocating helplessness he had become accustomed to.

He'd quickly tried to rescue the situation by using the charity work as an excuse and escaped so fast under the pretence of getting drinks when really what he wanted was time to acclimatize to her appeal. Time to regain his control so that he could approach their walk on far more solid ground and make it all about the charity and not this irresistible pull he felt towards her.

43

He caught a passing waitress and took up two glasses, then debated putting his glass back – he didn't need alcohol to lower his inhibitions any further, he was already being tested to the limit by Malie's unique charm. But then it didn't seem right only returning with one. So, two it was.

Shaking his head at his own uncertainty, he turned to retrace his steps. All he needed was to be his usual, normal self. He never let his countenance slip. He never let the physical override the mental.

He lifted his gaze, seeking her out, and there she stood waiting for him. Her beauty, her smile… his stomach flipped like he'd gone over a hump in the road. He knew he was in trouble, yet he kept on walking. They had people to help and, together, there was so much good to be done. He wouldn't jeopardize any of that for whatever temporary affliction this was.

'Here.' He proffered a glass and she took it with a smile, her lips surrounding the pineapple-adorned straw as she took a sip.

'You like it, then?' He gestured to the glass. 'The Fun For All cocktail?'

'It looks…' she took another sip, 'and tastes remarkably like a Tequila Sunrise.'

He laughed. 'Close, it's a Tequila Sunrise with a *fun* twist.'

Her smile warmed him through. 'You going to tell me what the twist is?'

'Top secret, I'm afraid, it would be more than my life's worth.'

She laughed, the sound so easy, so perfect. 'For real?'

'For real.' He looked past her to the path which led to the beach from the pergola and through a part of him, the part that was aware of the crowd and kept this side – the *right* side – of professional, he said, 'We can get to the beach this way.'

'Perfect.'

Lights secreted away in the ground lit up the path. Palms swayed in the sea breeze and the noise around them turned from party music and chatter to the waves crashing on the shore and the wildlife.

He hadn't actually done this yet, taken a stroll on the beach at night, enjoying the beauty Hawaii had to offer. By the time he closed his laptop or came off an overseas phone call he was either ready to sleep for the few hours he routinely had, or he'd hit the gym to try and get his mind to quit. It seemed it took the appearance of someone like Malie to make it easy to do just that.

'It is beautiful here,' he murmured, and she turned to him with a smile as stunning as the view, although her response was cut off by a particularly high and piercing *Ko-Kee* cry from the undergrowth.

She looked in its direction, as did he, half expecting to see its source staring back at him.

'They're loud, aren't they?' she said.

'What is it that makes the noise?' He squinted into the darkness but still he could see nothing obvious. 'There must be loads of them, it's quite incessant.'

'They're Coqui frogs, the sound is in the name. They're native to Puerto Rico but people say they were accidentally imported here on shipments back in the late eighties... They're seen as a nuisance, but I kind of like the sound. It beats the quiet any day.'

'I can't imagine Hawaii ever feeling quiet.'

'True.' She took a long breath and let it out slowly. 'It's part of the reason I love it here.'

'Not a fan of silence?'

The beach lay just ahead, the white sandy stretch illuminated by the light of the moon alone and for a second he was stunned still. How had he not done this yet? It was beautiful. No light pollution to ruin the night sky, not like the city skylines he was used to. The moon was bright white, turning the few clouds into wisps of silver, stars littered as far as the eye could see.

'I've always lived by the sea,' she said. 'The sound of the waves breaking is home for me.'

'And where is home? Or where was it?'

She gave him a wistful smile. 'Devon.'

'You miss it?'

'Sometimes.' They reached the path and she dipped to slip off her sandals. 'When I think of my childhood, I miss it. Like Nalu, I was practically born in the ocean. My parents owned a surf school in Hawke's Cove and my brother and I took advantage of that every chance we got. Even when we should have been doing homework, we'd sneak off, grab a board and hit the waves.'

She gave him a cheeky grin and he was transported back in time, imagining a younger Malie doing just that. She stood and walked onto the beach, her faced lifted to the moon and Todd just watched her, his mind on what her childhood must have been like. To have had one where you shared in your parents' joy, had a sibling to conquer the waves with, had a home. A *real* home.

'You coming?' she called over her shoulder.

He started to move after her and she turned to face him as she backed away. 'Take your shoes off, honestly, the sand will feel amazing beneath your feet.'

He shook his head and smiled. It was such a simple thing to take pleasure from. He toed off his shoes, his socks, and stepped into the sand. The cool grains eased between his toes, his feet sinking into the softness.

'See?' she cooed, her fingers holding her straw before her lips, her eyebrow raised.

He nodded. 'OK, I'll admit it's... *different*.'

And nicer than he expected...

She stepped backwards, luring him closer to the shoreline and he followed, wanting to know more. All about the girl, Malie. Adult, Malie. The whole package.

'What brings a woman from Hawke's Cove all the way to Hawaii?'

'It's a long story.'

'I have all night.'

She gave a soft laugh. 'I'll give you the cut-down version. My father and Kalani – he's my godfather – grew up together, and when I was done travelling the world conquering the surfing circuit, he offered me a job here.'

'Conquering the surfing circuit, hey?'

'Total world domination.' Her eyes laughed with her words and he knew she wasn't taking herself seriously. But she didn't need to. The surfing world did that for her and he knew from the research his team had done just how impressive she was on paper. He just couldn't believe he hadn't worked out who she was sooner, like on the beach, in his semi-drowned state...

'But there's only so much competing you can do, and it wasn't enough.' Her eyes stopped dancing, her smile once again turning wistful. 'I wanted to help people find what I do in the sea. I wanted them to realize that no matter what their disability or their background or their rough lot in life they could find some magic in the waves... sounds corny, hey?'

She was suddenly all coy as she looked to him and he realized she was embarrassed, feeling foolish even, her hair fluttering across her flushed cheeks as the sea breeze picked up around them. And he couldn't understand it. She was remarkable, her ability on the waves and her decision to use that skill to share that joy with others was something to be celebrated, to be proud of.

'No,' he said softly, watching her lashes flutter, her eyes dark and glittering in the moonlight as they held his own captive. 'It's not corny at all.'

Before he realized, he'd closed the distance between them, his hand reaching out to tuck the loose strands behind her ear, his fingers soft as they stayed to cup her cheek and he couldn't seem to pull them away.

'To want to help people isn't corny, Malie,' he spoke over his inability to act, taking advantage of her gaze on his as he told her the honest truth. 'It's special, admirable, and the desire to help comes off you in waves... if you'll excuse the pun.'

Her laugh was quiet, caught in her throat as she continued to look at him. Then she took a breath, stepped away, her head shaking, her eyes averted.

'Yes, well, that's me, that's why I'm here. How about you?'

He was slow to move in step with her again, to counteract the desire to bring back the intimacy of seconds before.

'I own the charity,' he said simply.

'Cheers, Captain Obvious, I never knew!' She turned to him with a laugh, punching him gently in the arm, the brief contact stirring up the skin beneath. 'Here I am practically telling you my life story and...' She waved her free hand through the air and he knew she was trying to make light of the connection swelling between them.

'Fair point.'

They reached the water's edge and she dipped her toe in the damp sand, tracing patterns in the grains as she waited for him to divulge a part of himself, a part he never really discussed with anyone. And it wasn't easy. It didn't come naturally to him. His motivations were private, they weren't part of the sales spiel that his PR team produced, even though they insisted it should be. Telling him it would be good for others to read, to see how far he had come from nothing, to see what's possible if you have the drive and the commitment to succeed.

She lifted her gaze to him suddenly, a frown marring her expression.

'You don't have to tell me... not if you don't want to.'

But he wanted to. That was the truth of it. He'd known her just a few hours and the desire to open up, to share that passion and the reason for it with someone who also sought the same, was strong.

'I understand completely if you don't, but you'll find no judgement here, just someone who shares your desire to help people.'

Her earnest words were wise beyond the fun aura she gave off and he felt something resonate. Something that told him there was so much more to the reason she gave for her life in Hawaii now and he wondered if she would share it with him in return.

'You could say my childhood was very different to yours...' His mouth dried up, a physical sign that he *never* did this. He cleared his throat and wished he hadn't brought the drink with him as his hands longed to dive into his pockets. Instead he took a sip through the straw, his nose getting assaulted by the vibrant umbrella as he did. 'Good grief.'

She laughed a little. 'They look pretty until they almost take your eye out, don't they? Here, let's leave them with our shoes.'

She took his glass and whizzed them back up the beach, returning in seconds, surprising him by hooking her arm through his and encouraging him into walking beside her.

'In what way was it different?'

It took him a few seconds to realize she was back on his childhood, he was too busy reeling from her arm being in his and just how comfortable it felt, how natural...

'My mother died when I was born,' he said eventually. 'There were complications... unexpected and sudden. They were lucky to save me.'

He felt rather than saw her eyes looking up at him, the sympathy he knew that would exist in those enchanting green depths.

'My father... well, you can imagine... he returned home with no wife and a new-born baby to take care of...' Even now he could feel the pang of guilt, the idea that his own birth took away his mother, his father's childhood sweetheart. He'd come to terms with it so long ago but still, the idea of it – the idea that he'd ruined his father's life – haunted him.

'That's so sad, I'm so sorry...' She shook her head, her eyes still on him but he couldn't look at her, he was too afraid of the raw emotion painted in his face to let her witness it too. 'Your poor father, and you, not to have known your mother...'

His chest squeezed painfully as her arm dug into his side, pressed there by his own. He loosened his grip, forced an even breath. 'It was what it was. We lived in the poorer suburbs of London and with him struggling… he was drinking heavily…' He swallowed past the tightness persisting in his throat. 'I got put into care. He couldn't look after me properly, but he couldn't bear to give me up for adoption either. So, the authorities moved me back and forth between him and foster homes.'

'Your entire childhood was spent like that?'

'Pretty much.'

'No stability, no family life?'

Exactly.

'On the upside, you don't know what you're missing if you've never had it in the first place.'

She curved into him, her other hand coming up to rest on his upper arm. 'I can't imagine how you must have felt.'

'Scared, lonely, confused, helpless… the list goes on.'

Too much information!

He took a deep breath and let it out slowly, his face angling to look down at her as he forced himself to smile to take the edge off his words. 'It's not all bad, though, it taught me to survive, to work hard and prove my worth. All those school teachers who said I would amount to nothing, I proved them wrong.'

She smiled up at him, her eyes filled with such wonder that they stole his breath.

'You sure did, Todd Masters.' Her voice was soft, the emotion in it so raw… He was used to such praise from people who discovered his background, those people like his PR team that wanted him to use it to push his business, his interests, but with her, it was different, it meant something.

It made him *feel* something.

'So that's why you run the charity, to help kids like you?'

'Precisely.' He tried to dodge where his heart was taking him, to get back on safer footing, on what he understood and knew how to deal with. His motivation, not the alien feeling she was stirring up within. 'I want to help those that can't help themselves. Some of the kids don't have any visible disability, no scars, nothing. It's buried deep inside and they need an outlet, a way of bringing it to the surface so that it doesn't have a chance to fester. They need to learn from it, forget the anger, the pain, and move on.'

'But how did you realize that? You were just a child yourself back then…'

'I don't know.' He shrugged as he considered her question. 'I guess I realized that if I wanted a better life, I needed to take control of it, I needed to work hard, make myself independent of the system, earn my worth, so to speak. With wealth comes the ability to control your own destiny and I wanted that more than anything.'

'It is incredible to have achieved all you have, especially when you think how different things could have been.'

'Don't I know it. It didn't happen overnight, but I got there eventually. Life was hard and full of obstacles, but I faced them head-on and got through it, it made me stronger.'

She took an unsteady breath and he frowned down at her. Had he hit a nerve? He hadn't meant to distress her, only to be honest.

'Sorry, Malie, I didn't mean to go on, to get all—'

'No, no, I'm fine,' she waved him down, 'you just talk a lot of sense.'

'I do.' He grinned. 'Are you giving me a compliment?'

Her own smile was slow to come. 'Don't get big-headed about it.'

'I wouldn't dare.'

She tugged him forward again. 'How are things with your father now?'

'You want the honest answer?'

It was a rhetorical question and the look she sent him told him she knew it.

'Difficult... OK, awkward... fine.'

'That good?' she queried.

He gave a gentle laugh. 'It's complicated.'

'I can imagine, what with everything you've both been through. He must be proud of all you've achieved though?'

He laughed harder this time, cynical, his mind returning to their phone call that afternoon. 'I'm not sure about that, I think I'm a giant pain in his backside at the moment.'

She shook her head. 'I'm sure he doesn't see you that way.'

'If you'd heard him on the phone this afternoon, you wouldn't be saying that. He's the reason I ended up on that stretch of beach. The house was teeming with PR reps, journalists, collaborators. I took his call and knew I needed to get away, clear my head before I went back to it.'

'And instead you almost drowned, that's some head-clearing.'

'Well, it gave me an early introduction to you, and an eventful one at that.'

'True...' She looked to their feet as she pulled him along and he could tell she was building the courage to press him about the call.

'He won't let me help him.'

She looked up at him questioningly.

'Crazy, isn't it? You'd think having a wealthy son would be

a huge advantage, but he won't take anything from me, not a penny. He still lives in the house I was born in.'

'Maybe it's because he feels close to your mum there.'

'Maybe...' He felt the familiar tension building between his shoulder blades, the throb kickstarting at the base of his skull and he rubbed at it with his free hand. 'But it's falling apart, it needs work, and personally I'd rather just buy him somewhere new, get him to start afresh.'

'I can't imagine it's easy for him to accept help from you.'

'From his son?' he snapped, instantly regretting it. 'Sorry, it's a sore point.'

'I get it. But put yourself in his shoes,' she said gently, 'he will feel like he failed you growing up. Even if you never doubted his love for you, he will still feel like he wasn't there for you in all the ways that mattered.'

She was right, wasn't she? Didn't he know this already? Wasn't that exactly how his father felt. Wasn't it how *he* felt?

Hadn't he wanted a normal dad, one that took him to the park to play footie on a Saturday, one that would care when he got into trouble at school, one that was strong enough to resist the bottle and sort himself out, to fight to keep him.

'Maybe there's a way to reach a compromise with him, or maybe you'll just have to accept his wishes and let it go.'

He smiled down at her. 'Now who's the one talking sense?'

★ ★ ★

Malie returned his smile and looked away just as quickly. What was she doing?

She wasn't kidding herself. *She* was the one who had linked arms with him. *She* was the one who had probed into his past and cared about what he had to say. *She* was the one enjoying their stroll along the moonlit beach and likening it to something out of a romantic film.

Soft. Perfect. Dreamy.

And none of it was real.

Tomorrow she would take on the role of surf instructor and he would be the guy that ran the charity from which her students came. Yes, they would have lessons together. But they would be just that: *lessons*. Nothing more.

Although right now, she couldn't seem to care. She only cared about the bond building between them. The warmth enveloping her as they strolled along. The moon, the stars, the surf washing over her feet.

'Do you think you'll go back to Hawke's Cove eventually?'

The question was like an iced spear straight through the comforting warmth, and she faltered mid-stride.

'I assume your parents are still there,' he continued, unaware of the messy terrain he had hit upon. 'And what about your brother?'

She swallowed, her grip over his arm tightening.

'Malie?' She could hear the frown in his voice.

'My parents... my parents live in Hawke's Cove still. My brother...' Another swallow. 'He died a long time ago.'

Todd stopped walking, forcing her to do the same as he pulled her around to face him. 'I'm so sorry.'

She waved a hand between them, but it took her longer to speak.

'He had cancer. The big C.' She said it dramatically, in a feigned *I'm OK* action. 'Such is life, hey?'

He cupped her cheek just as he had before, and again her skin heated beneath his touch, coaxing back the warmth, the comfort, the desire for more.

'I can't imagine what that must have been like for you, for your family…'

She rested her head in his palm, unable to speak as she lost herself in his soft gaze, so filled with compassion that she could feel the tightness in her chest, her throat build. She raised her palm to cover his, took his warmth to find her voice. 'It was a living nightmare, watching him… watching him waste away, so slowly but surely, and not be able to do anything, only watch as the light went from his eyes.'

Oh, God, she was going to cry, she could feel the tears burning behind her eyes, see her own emotion reflected back at her in his gaze. But she'd cried all the tears, she'd lived through the pain, she'd been there and done that. No more.

His lips parted as though to say something, drawing her eyes lower to their soft, alluring appeal. It would be so easy to forget the pain in a kiss, to lose herself in him and this crazy heat he ignited in her.

Don't do it, Malie.

But desire beat pain.

She wet her lips, saw him do the same, lifted her eyes to his and saw the passion building there.

'Malie?'

He was asking her permission; she knew it just as she also knew it was wrong. It was messy. It was too intense. She shook her head and turned away before the madness won out, forcing her legs to walk.

He came up behind her, his hand gentle on her hip as he met her step for step. 'Is that why you left?'

'It was a part of it...' She wouldn't lie, she had no reason to lie, not with him. 'The final decision came when I was eighteen.'

'The age of adulthood?' he teased softly, and she laughed, but even she could hear the sadness in it. 'Keen for your own independence?'

'Kind of... I was in a car accident.'

She felt his fingers pulse on her hip. 'A bad one?'

She nodded, her 'yes' a choked-up hum. 'My friends and I were on our way to the school summer dance, when a car drove into ours.'

Even now goose bumps prickled across her skin, the memory, the terror, the sight of so much blood and crumpled metal. She shuddered and Todd pulled her closer to him, his body warmth soothing hers.

'I came out practically unscathed... Lils and I were cut, bruised, but nothing serious, except for the nightmares that soon followed. But my friends Zo and V...' She swallowed. 'They were trapped by the car, Zoe caught between the rear and the driver's seat, V by the steering column.' She shook her head. 'They had to cut them out... we all survived but...'

'But?' he pressed softly.

'It doesn't feel my place to say... though it's not like you're ever going to meet them, are you?' She gave a shaky laugh, expecting him to agree because in what world would they ever become friends on that scale. She wasn't foolish enough to expect – *no*, to *want* more from this. 'V can't have children of her own, and Zoe... Zoe lost the use of her legs. She's wheelchair-bound now...'

Wheelchair-bound but boy, had she shown the world what she was capable of. She smiled as she thought it, even as Todd pulled her closer, offering her more support. 'You should see her, though, that woman is fearless, there's nothing she can't do if she puts her mind to it.'

'I can imagine,' he murmured. 'It seems I've found the answer to your passion, the reason you do all this...'

He turned her to face him again, his eyes so full of that passion he spoke of.

'Is that so?'

He cupped her face again, held her eye. 'Your brother, your friends, Zoe... they've all inspired you.'

'They did, they still do.'

'You know what I think?'

She searched his gaze, her 'What?' so soft, so tight, as her throat closed over but not with sadness, or grief this time... he was so close now, his mouth hovering just above hers, his scent assailing her senses once again and making her sway into him.

'I think you're an inspiration, Malie Pukui – you and the strength you've found to survive all you've experienced and still be able to give.'

'I'm nothing.' It was so quiet she wasn't even sure she'd said it aloud and then his thumb brushed over her lower lip, his eyes intense as they traced the move.

'Don't ever say that.'

'But...' Her argument trailed away. In truth she had none, she couldn't think straight with him this close, with the desire to kiss him burning away every thought, every action save for one. 'Todd, *please*...'

She was already reaching up on tiptoes when his lips found hers, their gentle softness in no way comparable to the sparks that alighted inside her.

Never had a simple kiss done this to her.

Not one so soft, so gentle, so... *oh, my...*

She was immobile, her whole body alive to the feel of his mouth as it moved over hers, his hands as they slipped into her hair, held her close. She heard a whimper and knew it had come from the very heart of her.

The warnings were there, dizzying up her mind, but she couldn't think past the warm pleasure swirling through her body. He slanted his head, his tongue nudging her lips apart and the whimper escaped again, her hands lifting to his wrists like she would pull him away, but she couldn't. It was too nice, too all-consuming. Instead she brushed her tongue against his, tentative, probing, and shivered as the thrill of it rippled through her. No, she didn't want this feeling to end. She wanted it to grow, she wanted more.

And that's when it hit her. The timely reminder that everything had to end.

Fun, enjoyment, love, life.

And when it ends there's pain, so much pain.

Yes, he could block it out for her for now. But what about tomorrow, and the day after that, and... She pulled at his hands, her head shaking, her eyes squeezed shut. 'I'm sorry, I shouldn't have.'

'You didn't, it was me... it's OK, Malie, we can forget—'

But she was already turning to run.

'I have to go.' She hurried away from the heat of the kiss, her shame burning at her cheeks. 'I have to be up early for the first group, thanks for a great evening, for... for... this.'

And then she turned her back on him and kept on going, collecting her shoes as she went. She didn't stop to get her drink, she didn't even stop to say her goodbyes at the party. She was too busy berating herself for her own stupidity.

What the hell had she been doing?

Having fun. Going with the flow. Getting lost in the appeal that was the millionaire Todd Masters and the man underneath.

She shook her head, the painful stomp of her bare feet against the harsh ground the perfect distraction to the chaos underway within.

She never should have kissed him. Never let him get beneath her skin. Never should have cared. *Really* cared. Her brother's death, the accident, they'd taught her how fragile life was and letting Todd in could only ever complicate things.

Get a grip, Malie. You've only just met the guy and he'll be gone again soon enough. It's not like you've fallen head over heels, the whole love-at-first-sight nonsense is just that – Nonsense!

She pressed her fingers to her tingling lips, felt them mocking her internal lecture and knew the next few weeks would be a challenge like none other.

CHAPTER FIVE

HE WAS LOSING HIS mind, the beauty of Hawaii making him unable to focus on work, and that never happened. Ever.

He lived for his company and his charity work. They filled his days and his nights when needed. He stayed busy. Flying from city to city, making money, investing more. He didn't take holidays, he didn't *need* holidays. They were a waste of good, productive hours.

But here… here he wanted to be at the beach, he wanted to be in the water, he wanted to be near her. And that's what it came down to. It wasn't the location, it was Malie.

He knew it. He just didn't know what to do about it. In any normal situation he would propose some fun while visiting and move on when he was done. But this was different. *She* was different. Not to mention the fact that the Foundation's kids relied on her to make their holiday perfect and he had no right messing with that.

He'd certainly had no right to kiss her last night either. But he'd been so caught up in her pain, the emotion swimming in her gaze, and the chemistry that promised to take it away, even if it was only temporary.

He breathed a heavy sigh. It had been a foolish move, one that he *should* regret. But he wasn't so sure he did.

In fact, if he had his time over, he knew he'd do the exact same thing again.

He'd exposed himself when he'd told her all he had, he hadn't felt like himself… and yet he'd never been more true, more open, more honest, and it had left him in some weird state of limbo where he couldn't settle.

He rubbed a hand over his face like it would somehow clear the brain fog, but it was no use. The kiss, the way it had made him feel… yes, there had been the carnal urge, the desire, but it had been the overriding emotional connection that had made it impossible to resist. And it was that which unnerved him too.

Sexual attraction was something he could deal with, something he could manage and keep within his control. He never mixed business with pleasure, be it charity or otherwise. But with Malie… he dragged in another breath… it had been different.

And there was that word again. *Different.*

He stared at his laptop screen, trying to focus on it, instead of the constant replay underway in his head, but it continued regardless. He'd been reliving it every waking moment since. The beach, the moonlight and her. If he closed his eyes – his lashes lowered – he could still feel her. Her soft, pliable mouth beneath his, the taste of her so sweet, and that little whimper which had quivered through her as she'd leaned into him.

His body reacted instantly and he shot his eyes open. He *had* to get a handle on this.

She'd run. At the end of the day, she'd run. It didn't matter that she'd kissed him back, that for a few seconds it had been perfect, she had ultimately chosen to end it. And whatever her reasons were, he should be grateful to her for seeing sense when he hadn't been able to. He didn't want to jeopardize the success of this trip, especially when it could only ever be a bit of fun, a temporary lift to his otherwise monotonous and controlled existence.

Life was how he liked it, orderly and straightforward, so long as he didn't dwell too much on his frustrations with his father.

All he had to do was keep his relationship with Malie professional and platonic. He had five lessons to get through and a few weeks on the island, nothing in the grand scheme of things for him, but plenty for the kids who'd make memories that would last a lifetime.

Now he smiled, his hand massaging the knot at the base of his skull as he glanced at his watch. It was four o'clock in the afternoon, Malie would be coming to the end of her second group session now. He thought of the kids in that group: Jonny, Louis, Sky and Tara. They were a great bunch, but Tara was the one that really caught his attention. Her visible scarring from a house fire had made her withdraw into herself and he hoped, really hoped, that this trip would bring the ten-year-old girl out of her shell again. Not to mention help her parents, who'd lost sight of their marriage long ago.

Only a handful of kids had their parents come along on the trip and Tara was one of them. He hoped they would use the time Tara was busy to enjoy some holiday time of their own and that they would soon realize that giving her some space was just as important as loving her.

If they only saw their daughter happy and enjoying life again, they would hopefully relax their tight hold over her and learn to relax with one another too. And if anyone could see Tara happy again, he had faith Malie would. Her easy smile that lit up her entire face, her bright green eyes that danced with humour, fun, joy… even though he knew deep down she carried her own scars.

And maybe that's another reason he felt so drawn to her, maybe he wanted to help her too. To understand why, when she missed home like she did, she still chose to live in Hawaii. Her parents had owned a surf school, the perfect place for her to do what she does now, and yet she did so thousands of miles away.

But then he hadn't missed the past tense either, they'd *owned* a surf school, which suggested they didn't anymore. And surely they must miss their daughter. Having lost their son, to have their only child living miles away… he shook his head. He had so many questions, so many scenarios playing out in his mind as he sought to understand her better, even though he knew it wouldn't help him to keep his distance. To keep it professional.

He shoved back from the desk and stood. It was no good sitting here and getting nothing done. If he hurried, he could catch the end of the lesson and see how the kids were getting on.

And if the opportunity arose, he would apologize for overstepping the line last night.

He headed outside feeling the pressure ease between his shoulder blades already. It was only a short stroll along the beach to get to the surf school, the fresh air would do him good too.

Fresh air.

Chat to the kids.

Apologize to Malie.

Safe and simple.

The beach was busy, but he could spot his crew almost immediately. They all wore the same bright pink rash vests, Malie's sporting the word INSTRUCTOR in bold white print. He smiled, the gesture lifting him inside and out. She was in the sea, the water up to her waist as she held onto the board with ten-year-old Louis lying on it. He was small for his age, malnutrition leaving him way behind his peers, but what he lacked in size, he made up for in noise and laughter.

Behind them fifteen-year-old Jonny was already standing, his hands whooping in the air, and fourteen-year-old Sky was paddling as she shouted up to him, their smiles painting a thousand happy words.

But where was Tara?

He frowned and scanned the other boards, those playing in the shallow surf, the shoreline – and then he saw her. She was sitting in the sand, hunched over as she tickled Nalu at her feet, her board lying untouched beside her. He felt the weight of disappointment in the pit of his stomach but shook it off. No one could expect her to make a turnaround in just a couple of hours.

He walked up to the surf school and saw Kalani hosing down a row of surfboards.

'*Aloha*,' he called out.

Kalani looked up and grinned. 'Mr Masters! It's good to see you.'

'It's Todd, please.'

'Sorry, Todd.'

'How long have they been in the sea?' He nodded towards the water just as Louis let out a small whoop and launched himself up on his board. Didn't matter that Malie still had hold of it, the boy was in his element.

'Most of their lesson. It's a bit unorthodox, but she finds it works better that way with kids; they're always so impatient to be in the

65

sea, it helps them concentrate and feel like they're getting there quicker. Even if in reality it will take just as long.'

'Makes sense.'

'Sure does! It gets them confident in the water too, especially if they haven't been in the sea much before.'

Todd watched Malie swing Louis through the air and down into the sea with her. The boy gripped her shoulders: 'I did it, Malie, I did it!'

He heard her laughter across the distance as she wiped her face down, undoubtedly getting a spray of sea water from Louis' lips as he cheered at her. 'You did, dude, you were awesome, give me five.'

He felt his chest warm, he wished he'd come down earlier and witnessed the entire lesson, this morning's too. Maybe he could bring his laptop down here, work from the surf school occasionally.

'Don't worry, she won't put you in the sea immediately, she'll subject you to land work first.' He looked back to Kalani and spied his smirk.

'If the kids can do it, I can do it, too.'

'You surfed before?'

'No.'

Kalani just nodded, but his smirk was still there as he continued hosing down the boards.

'What's so funny?'

The guy looked him up and down. 'I'd say you're fit enough for it, but you're going to need to loosen up before you hit the water.'

Malie's words came back to him, their dance immediately after – his body overheating with the memory – the intimate movement of her body against his, and the kiss...

He swallowed. 'Right... well... I can loosen up.'

Even he could tell he didn't sound convincing and was about to make his excuses before heading down to the shoreline when he saw Malie come out of the water, Louis on her tail. The boy lay his board in the sand and hung back as Malie approached Tara.

Todd froze, not wanting to catch her eye and distract her. Especially when Tara had never looked more isolated than she did right now, still hunched up, her only companion Nalu, while all around her people laughed, cheered, played ball games, enjoyed the water... what would she say to her? What would she do?

And more importantly, would it work?

* * *

Malie was careful as she approached Tara. She wasn't overly tentative, but she wasn't quite as full-on as she'd been with the others.

She knew the girl's history thanks to the detailed case file provided by the charity – her heart ached each time she thought of it. A house fire four years ago had claimed the life of Tara's younger brother and left Tara herself scarred, half of her face suffering burns that no amount of surgery could conceal. And Malie knew well enough that the visible scarring would be nothing compared to what lay beneath.

Her suspicions had only been reaffirmed when Tara and her parents had turned up an hour into the lesson, the parents delivering Tara personally with an anxious apology for their lateness. It had taken some coaxing to get her to come forward and numerous reassurances from Malie to her parents that all was OK enough for them to leave. They'd done so eventually, but the sight of Tara continuing to hold herself back from the group, barely responding to the greetings of her friends as she'd looked the other way and kept herself apart, was hard to witness. It didn't matter that the girl knew everyone in the group from back home, she wasn't ready to trust Malie or the water enough to get involved.

She trusted Nalu, though. That much was obvious. Even now she was crouched down before him, the black hair of her bob swinging forward to hide her face as she rubbed Nalu's belly and murmured too low for Malie to hear what she said.

And that's when the spark of an idea hit...

'Hey, Tara, do you think you'd like to come and try the water now?'

The girl lifted her chin and looked to the swash, her hand still tickling Nalu. 'No thanks.'

She lowered her gaze back to her buddy, not once turning her head and Malie knew it wasn't rudeness that kept her eyes averted, but the desire to hide the right side of her face. The scarred side.

Malie's heart squeezed in her chest, her wish being to hold the girl and tell her it didn't matter, it didn't dictate who she was on the inside, she was more than the scars and the pain they brought. But she knew she couldn't, not yet, she had to earn Tara's trust first.

Instead, she played the hand that she knew would work. 'You know, Nalu can surf.'

And just like that, her head lifted to Malie, her eyes wide, scars temporarily forgotten. 'He can?'

Malie nodded, her smile instant and heartfelt. 'Shall I show you?'

'Really?' The girl's eyes sparkled as she looked back to Nalu who'd shot to his feet at the first mention of his name and now gave a bark.

'See, he's even telling you he can.'

Tara smiled at the dog. 'You want to surf, Nalu?'

He barked again and her smile grew.

'Come on.' Malie reached out her hand and Tara eyed it suspiciously. 'You have to come now, else it would be like telling a dog *walkies* and not taking him out. It would be teasing and mean.'

Tara chewed over her lip, her eyes going back to Nalu.

'We don't want to disappoint him, do we?' Malie softly pressed, her hand still outstretched.

Tara shook her head.

'And he'll have so much more fun knowing you are watching.'

Slowly but surely Tara slid her hand inside Malie's and got to her feet, the rise of her body in tune with the happiness lifting inside Malie.

'We're gonna need my board for this,' she said, subduing her voice so as not to jar Tara and risk unsettling her.

She led them over to where her board lay in the sand. 'How about you paddle by the shore here and that way you'll have the best view of us coming back in?'

Tara gazed up at her. 'You're going to surf *with* him?'

'He needs me to push him out and give him power, but he can surf with me or without me.'

'Wow!' Tara's eyes widened as she went back to watching Nalu prancing in and out of the water.

'You mean he can ride a wave standing up?' It was Louis who asked. In the time it had taken to get into the water, they'd gained a mini audience of the other class members who were all looking on, fascinated.

More importantly, Tara wasn't hiding her face, she wasn't shying away, she'd forgotten it all in her excitement. Exactly as Malie had hoped.

'You bet he can,' Malie said.

'But it's so hard to balance,' Louis said.

'He's had many years of practice, haven't you, Nalu?'

Another bark which had Jonny saying, 'This is so cool.'

They entered the water and Malie set the longboard down on the water, letting go of Tara's hand as she helped Nalu to hop on. Once he was ready, she started pushing him out.

'What do you reckon, Tara, with or without me?' she called back.

'With you,' she blurted, her excitement shining in her face and making Malie smile even wider.

'Good choice! Come on, Nalu, let's show them what we're made of.'

She carried on out, spying where the waves were breaking and picking the best spot, the one that would give them something decent to watch, but at the same time keeping herself close by. She shoved up onto the board and paddled, turning the board at the right spot and letting Nalu find his balance. His tail was wagging, his tongue hanging out as he watched the kids back on the shoreline and lived through the fun with them.

Malie looked over her shoulder, assessed the waves approaching from behind, and waited, waited, and then, 'Here we go, Nalu!'

She lunged forward, her arms propelling them through the water at a speed to match the wave. As the board started to lift, Nalu gave a bark and Malie popped up to standing. It was exhilarating to feel the board take off, but it was more exhilarating to watch the awe in the faces of their all-important audience. The magic of it.

Tara tapped her fists together beneath her chin, her body taut with the thrill of spectating. There was no anxiety, no worry about what people thought, of being an outsider, she was wholly involved in that moment, very much a part of the group.

Malie knew she still had some way to go but it was a start. A start she could work with and as she leaped from the board back at shore and watched Nalu being fussed over by all four kids, she felt elated. The greatest sense of achievement that only this job could provide.

'Hey, that was impressive!'

She started. It was Todd. She knew it without looking and then when she did, she wished she hadn't. Her heart was already high on the kids, the waves, the lesson, now it practically fluttered up and out of her throat.

He was wearing a lightweight shirt, black and unbuttoned at the collar, swanky beige shorts that could have been part of a suit had they been longer, and his hair was swept back, perfectly groomed. He looked more boardroom than surfer, but he'd lost the trainers this time. It had her remembering their moonlit stroll, the whole thing unfolding in fast action replay and setting her body on fire as she reached the pinnacle – their kiss.

'How long have you been here for?' It came out clipped as she forced the memory out, her body to chill, and his eyes narrowed on her, not much but enough to know he caught the edge to her tone. She wanted to kick her tactless self and was grateful the kids were too busy with Nalu to notice. 'Sorry, I just meant, how much did you see?'

His expression softened, a smile lifting the corners of his mouth as he looked from her to the kids. 'Enough to see how amazing you are at your job.'

She felt her cheeks heat, her heart throb in her chest. She heard compliments all the time when it came to her skills on the board: *you ripped it up out there; way to go on the hang ten; wow, check out the air you caught.* She also got positive feedback on the lessons she ran; it was an integral part of being able to meet the needs of the children by having them and their parents offer up such insight after their lessons.

But hearing Todd say it, and in such a way…

'Malie!' It was Tara, her head poking up above that of her classmates. 'Can I have a go?'

'With Nalu?'

She gave her a beaming nod, and it melted Malie's heart to see she didn't avert her face, she looked right at them both. 'Hey, Mr Masters!'

All the kids turned to look then, each shouting their own cheerful greeting before going back to Nalu, save for Jonny who eyed Todd suspiciously. 'You here to check up on us, Boss?'

Todd laughed. 'At ease, Jonny, I trust you guys to do me proud. I'm only here to get a sneak peek at what I've let myself in for.'

'You're here to surf too?' he asked.

'Too right I am.'

Jonny grinned wide. 'Have you surfed before?'

'No. I'm a newbie, just like you.'

Malie watched their little interchange and realized, Todd wasn't just the money and the face of the charity, he *knew* these kids. And they knew him. The easy way they spoke to one another, the mutual respect, even affection, it was written in their faces. She shouldn't be surprised, not anymore, but she was. How could a man like Todd, with his success, his company commitments, his workload, find the time to get to know these kids individually?

Even more surprising was the rush of warmth she felt towards him, pulsing around her heart, far too close to where she didn't want it to be.

'What do you say, Malie?'

They all looked to her expectantly.

'Sorry?' She frowned, missing their question entirely and wishing her cheeks would cool.

'They asked if they can watch me take my lesson now?' Todd filled in for her, his eyes dancing with amusement. Had he guessed at the cause of her distraction? Was she that obvious?

She snapped her eyes away and gave a flustered, 'Are you sure you have the time for it, right now?'

'If you do, then I do.'

She looked to the eager faces of her students and accepted that if she hadn't, she'd still make time. To have him involved when he clearly had such a good relationship with them all made perfect sense.

She swept an unsteady hand through her hair and nodded, 'Of course I can.'

And with the kids as an audience... well, any temptation for a repeat of last night's kiss would be non-existent.

'Just let me take Tara out with Nalu first...' she felt better about it already, 'and then I'm all yours.'

I'm all yours... Really, Malie?

She turned away as his brow quirked up and headed for the kids, her feet stomping through the sand at her own ineptitude. Why did he do this to her? Set her on fire with the merest look, make her come out with ridiculous declarations: *I'm all yours.*

'Hey, Mr Masters, will you watch me?' Tara shouted, the open affection Malie had so easily spied when he'd arrived, shining in the girl's face once more, reminding Malie that this had nothing to do with how she'd successfully lowered the girl's guard through Nalu, but everything to do with the relationship he'd forged with Tara himself prior to this trip of a lifetime.

Malie looked back to see him nod, and then his eyes were on her and she struggled to breathe. He was too perfect, damaged in his own way – and still perfect.

Never mind Tara's guard, Malie needed one, because the more she learned about him, the less he became a passing tourist with a fleeting presence in her life, and a man capable of making tracks on her heart. Something she never wanted to risk. Never mind the fact that he was too important to her plans for the surf school and their charity collaboration.

'You're going to need a rash vest and some board shorts.' She eyed his inappropriate ensemble and wished she hadn't. It just led to more inappropriate thoughts and she really didn't need those right now. She lifted her eyes back to his face. 'Kalani should be able to sort you out.'

'Great, you ladies get set up and I'll be right back.'

She dragged her eyes away from his tight behind as he walked off, though her mind wasn't so easily distracted. She was pondering how it was possible for his rear to look so appealing when he wore swanky shorts that had no place on the beach…

'Ready, Tara?'

Thank goodness the kids were too young to realize the reason her voice had shot up a couple of octaves. It was hard enough that she was aware of just how attracted to him she was, she didn't need it becoming public knowledge with his kids too!

Then she caught Jonny's eye and his smirk.

Too young… you're too obvious, more like.

CHAPTER SIX

KALANI HAD TAKEN ONE brief scan of his body and tossed him some clothing. A pink rash vest similar to the one the kids were wearing, only adult-sized, and some shorts.

He stood in the surf school's changing rooms and toyed with not going out at all. He felt ridiculous, and... exposed. Maybe it was the colour of the top – he couldn't say he wore pink much.

Yeah, it's just the colour that's your problem, and not the fact that its unforgiving style shows off every taut ridge.

He worked out, he looked after himself, but he did it for him, he didn't do it to flaunt it in skin-tight, body-popping, fluorescent colour!

As for the board shorts, they forgave far too much. If he dared think on the kiss they'd shared the previous night, or even looked at Malie in any way other than platonic – which let's face it, when she was wearing nothing more than the same figure-hugging vest and bikini bottoms would be a challenge – he'd likely be done for indecent tent-like exposure. And the risk wasn't funny.

He tried to tug the top lower, but it was no good. He was just going to have to play it cool. *Be* cool. Easy.

'Hey, Boss, you ready yet!' Jonny burst into the room. 'Tara's getting naggy.'

The lad gave an exaggerated eye-roll, but he couldn't fool Todd, the teenager doted on the girl like he would a little sister. It was in his nature. Not that you'd guess it to look at him. Plenty of people had judged Jonny wrongly over the years, very much like they had Todd back when he'd been of a similar age. But then Jonny had given them reason to in the days before the Foundation had found him or rather, he'd found the Foundation.

And those days had left their mark. He still bore a scar that slashed through his right eyebrow, a centimetre gap where hair would never grow again. His favoured buzzcut failed to conceal the intricate star that had been illegally tattooed to the base of his skull by an ex-gang member. And as for his body, it was far more chiselled than any fifteen-year-old should be, but Todd knew better than most what had motivated Jonny to bulk up. Fear. Fear of being weak, fear of being crushed, the need to be the biggest, the strongest, to protect those you care about above all else.

Yes, Todd could forgive anyone for being a little intimidated by the lad – even when he sported the same pink rash vest he now did.

'Don't you dare,' Jonny suddenly said and raised a hand towards him in warning as his scarred brow quirked up.

'What?'

'You say one word about this pink thing and there'll be more than words going down between us, Boss.'

Todd laughed, he couldn't help it. 'Have you seen me?'

He plucked at the offensive number and Jonny cocked his head with a nod and a choked laugh.

'Fair point.' The lad caught sight of himself in the full-length mirror that divided up the wall of lockers and rolled his shoulders back. 'You think next time we can insist on black, though?'

The door shifted open again before Todd could answer and in walked Kalani, 'You still stirring it up over the colour of our gear?'

'Hell, no,' Jonny rushed out, his instant respect for the big guy obvious. 'Just the Boss here, he's having a moment.'

He threw his thumb at Todd and grinned.

Kalani looked to Todd, his expression grave. 'Like I said to the boy—'

'Man, jeez!'

Kalani ignored Jonny's outburst. 'It's to keep you readily identifiable on the beach. If you go under, we'll have a greater chance of spotting you, *maopopo*?'

Todd frowned. 'Mao-what-now?'

'He means, *understood*, Boss.'

Feeling well and truly the student, which was even more disconcerting than being seen in this ensemble, he nodded. 'Got it.'

'Good,' Kalani said, satisfied. 'You ready to get fitted out for a board?'

'Sure am.' Todd tossed his clothes and valuables in the locker Kalani had given him to use and slammed it shut. 'Lead the way.'

They followed Kalani outside and within ten minutes they were heading down to the beach, a surfboard hooked under Todd's arm and what he now knew to be called a leash – like some dog walking gear – in his hand.

'How's she been getting on?' he asked Jonny, trying to ignore the way the rash vest clung to his own body, the sun's rays making it feel even more cloying.

'Tara?'

He nodded and Jonny gave a smile so full of pride it had Todd's own lips lifting. 'She's nailing it, Boss.'

'Glad to hear. It's good seeing her take to Malie so well.'

Jonny sent him a funny look, kind of coy, kind of admirable as he shrugged. 'She's a pretty neat teacher.'

Neat and then some.

Todd switched the conversation up swiftly, throwing the focus on Jonny. 'You speak to your mum this morning?'

'Yup, all's good, your lot even took her a home-cooked casserole with pudding too, she couldn't believe it.'

'She was happy?'

'More than.'

'Good.'

It really was good. He'd promised Jonny daily calls back home just to give him the reassurance that all was fine. And to see the lad actually starting to relax was more than just rewarding, it was an affirmation of why he did this in the first place.

For Jonny, back home meant responsibilities, being the man of the house to his single mum and three younger siblings. The opportunity to get a few weeks away and recharge was a huge deal and it had taken lots of assurances from the Foundation, from Todd directly too, to convince him to leave, to convince him that his mother would be OK with the Foundation stepping in and providing the support she needed.

But it seemed leaving his responsibilities didn't mean Jonny would change, his brotherly instincts were already in play here as he looked out for the younger members of their group like he would his own blood.

Todd studied Jonny's face, his relaxed posture, his eyes that seemed to dance with laughter now. He looked younger, less guarded, even with the signs of his past, and not for the first time he felt an affinity with him, a realization that Todd himself could have very easily ended up in a similar gang at a similar age had he taken a different path.

To know that his charity had been able to help Jonny escape that life, to know how much better things were getting for him, for his family… he breathed in, his chest filling with hard-to-suppress pride.

'Thanks for, you know, looking out for Mum,' Jonny suddenly blurted.

'Hey, it's not me, it's the charity.'

His grin turned lopsided. 'You know what I mean, Boss.'

'I do… and so long as you're having a good time, that's all that matters.'

The lad's eyes widened, 'Good time? You're kidding, right! This the best! When you get out there and rip it up on the waves…' he weaved his hands in front of him, 'it don't get much better than that, you'll see!'

'That's—'

'And seriously, have you *seen* Malie, like, proper seen her?' Jonny looked at him now, an all-knowing look in his eye that Todd really didn't want to recognize and find resonant. 'Like not just on the waves, but in the flesh.'

'Hey, that's not cool, she's here to teach you, not be ogled.'

'I'm only human, Boss, and there ain't a red-blooded male out there that wouldn't be *ogling*… 'S'OK though, I think you're more her type.'

'What makes you—' He killed the question. He shouldn't be engaging in such talk let alone encouraging it. Not only was it inappropriate, it didn't fit with his desire to keep his distance and avoid anything close to what had happened the previous night. 'So, you think the kids are enjoying themselves too?'

Jonny clearly caught his change in topic but thankfully knew well enough not to press, he just grinned instead and nodded. 'Totally, check it out...'

He pointed out to the water where Malie and Tara were in the surf. Tara was lying on the board while Malie held it steady. Nalu stood at the nose end making the younger girl laugh as he nuzzled her cheek, his tail wagging happily.

Sky was also in the water, testing out her freshly learned skills, while Louis was happy on land making what looked to be a moat around his surfboard.

'Mr Masters, Mr Masters!'

It was Tara, her hand waving at him excitedly and he felt himself grin. It had taken him a long time to earn the girl's trust, but it seemed Malie had done it in one lesson. Watching it play out as he had, to see Malie coaxing her into getting involved, using Nalu as a loving accomplice, it had been brilliant, and he'd meant it when he'd said as much to her.

The warmth flooding his chest, just as it had when he'd observed it all play out, returned and he was powerless to stop it. Try as he might, he couldn't dampen his instinctive response to her and the effect she had on those around her – another reason to keep these interactions brief, even as the appeal of working from the beach and hanging around more persisted.

'Come and see what I can do!' Tara beckoned and he realized he'd slowed to a halt, Jonny now several strides ahead.

'I'm coming.' He picked up his pace, the reminder to play it cool on repeat in his head. He lay his surfboard down next to

Louis and ruffled the boy's hair as he examined his moat. 'Looking good, mate.'

Louis grinned up at him. 'You going in?'

'Yup, you coming?' The more kids around him and Malie the better!

'In a bit.' He went back to his task, scooping up sand with his hands and piling it to the side. 'I told Tara I could get down as far as my armpit.'

Todd laughed. 'Good luck with that.'

And then he carried on into the surf, every step closer to them, to Malie, teasing his quickening pulse. That sensation would surely ease at some point, she couldn't hold this power over him for the entire duration of his stay. He would become accustomed to her beauty, her smile, her fun-loving and caring persona, wouldn't he?

He reached the board. Malie looked at him from the other side, her face so vibrant, and he knew she'd been as caught up in Tara's joy as he had been. Her eyes sparkled off the water, her brown honey-streaked hair a mixture of windswept and sea-crisped curls that blew around her flawless bronze skin. He wanted to reach out, take hold of one corkscrew curl and wrap it around his finger, lean in to kiss those lips that he knew would taste of the sea now and be just as sweet as they had been last night... *distance, keep your distance.*

'She's learning to pop like a pro,' Malie said, her eyes dropping to Tara, but not so quick that he missed the way her lashes flickered, a hint of colour streaking across her cheeks. Had her thoughts gone down a similar route or had she simply read it all in his face?

Way to go at playing it cool...

He snapped his attention to Tara.

'Pop like a pro, you say?' He gave a wide-eyed nod, grateful his voice sounded suitably impressed, rather than strained. 'How cool.'

'It's totally rad, Mr Masters.'

'Learning the language too, even better, I'm sure your parents will approve.' He gave her a wink and she giggled.

'They'll be happy when they see what I've learned.'

'I'm sure they will, they'll be along shortly to pick you up.'

She gave him a pout. 'Can't I just go back with the rest of the gang?'

'Not today, kiddo.'

She huffed. 'Fine.'

'Hey, don't be like that, I want to see the fun from seconds ago – don't forget I'm here to see you surf.'

Now she grinned. 'Too right, you are.'

But the girl had a point, the fact her parents insisted on being her transport to and from the hotel was madness. And he knew it stemmed from their over-protectiveness. It was something he would have to work on if he was to help Tara feel normal, just a part of the group this holiday, and have her parents relax, take some decent time out together.

'You OK, Todd?' Malie's voice was soft and he realized she was frowning up at him.

'Yeah, of course.'

She nodded and studied him a second longer before breaking off to scan the sea and bend down to Tara. 'You ready?'

'Yup... ready, Nalu?' Tara nodded to the dog who gave a quick *woof* and wriggled back into position.

Malie moved to the rear of the board. 'You best stand back a little, Todd.'

He did as she asked and braced himself for the wave that was approaching.

'1... 2... 3!' She shoved the board forward with the surge of water and it caught the wave. In the blink of an eye Tara was up on her feet, crouched low and not a wobble in sight.

'That's awesome, Tara!' he called out.

The other kids were all watching her now and yelled out their own much cooler accolades and his entire body lifted with happiness for her, their group and... he turned to look at Malie as she gave an excited whoop and his breath hitched. She was captivating. Her grin electric, her eyes alive and sparkling with... *tears*... tears of joy?

She must have sensed his eyes on her as she flicked him a quick look. 'Sorry... it's just such a rush when your kids catch a wave.'

'No apology necessary.'

It *was* such a rush and he could witness it all in Malie: the colour in her cheeks, the brightness of her eyes, the elation in her voice. He could feel it in himself, too. And the connection that had been building from the moment they'd met tugged at him now. He'd never needed to share his passion with another, never craved the companionship of a friend or anything more, but he couldn't ignore the glimpse of what that connection might be like, if he stopped fighting it and let her in.

And then what?

It ends in whatever way life dictates and you go the way of your father.

No. Just no.

She turned to look at him properly now and he snapped himself out of it. He was being ridiculous and fanciful, and he blamed it entirely on the euphoria of seeing the kids excel. Nothing else.

'I love that you still get a kick out of it, regardless of how long you've been doing it.'

She gave him a smile and started to walk towards the shore. 'I can't imagine ever not. I'm sure it's the same for you, no matter how many children you help.'

He followed close behind her, 'That's true enough.'

'Although I can't understand how you have the time to do it all...' She looked back at him briefly, her frown curious.

'*All*?'

'Yes, your work and your charity. I thought you were just the pretty face of it...' She gave him a teasing wink that made his pulse trip over itself... again, ridiculous. 'But you clearly spend enough time with these kids for them to feel as comfortable around you as they do.'

'I work at the centre when I'm in London, it's how I fill my spare time.'

'I'm surprised you have any.'

He shrugged. 'I enjoy it, and it's not like—'

He broke off, knowing what he was going to say and not feeling comfortable putting words to his feelings.

'It's not like—?' she pressed.

He aimed for another nonchalant shrug, but it was stiff with guilt and something else he didn't really want to examine too closely. 'I don't have family and friends to share my downtime with.'

'No one? You have your father...'

He could hear the continued surprise in her voice.

'I see him occasionally.'

'And that's all? Don't you get... lonely?' The last was said so softly but he could feel her sympathy, her worry in that one word.

He could imagine it softening her green gaze even as she watched Nalu and Tara approach the shore.

'Life's just easier that way.'

She sent him a look and he could see so much, feel so much in that one glance that he tensed and pulled his eyes away, focusing on the surfing duo instead. It was easier, it was less... *hang on...* He squinted at them still standing on the board, saw Nalu flexing and shifting...

'Don't tell me Nalu is helping to balance the board?'

'He is...' she said vaguely, her mind presumably still on their conversation.

He kept his eyes locked on the duo, on the safe subject. 'That's amazing.'

'Yes... he is.' She looked from him to Nalu now and his shoulders eased. 'He's great for helping those that need the extra assistance. Although to be fair, I think Tara has got it.'

The board slid up the beach and both Tara and Nalu jumped off together. They could hear the girl's excited chatter as she rubbed Nalu's head, congratulating themselves on their ride.

'That was sick, Tara,' said Louis, offering his hand up in a high-five which she quickly swiped.

'I'll never understand how *sick* came to mean *cool*,' Todd said to Malie.

She laughed, the easy sound working away the rest of his unease. 'Now you're just showing your age.'

'Hey, I'm hardly ancient.'

She studied him for a second, a little crease forming on her forehead. 'How old are you?'

'I'm thirty-three. You?'

'Twenty-eight.'

'Oh.'

'*Oh?*' She sent him a look, 'What's *oh* supposed to mean?'

'Nothing, I just assumed… you just look younger, I guess.'

'You guess?' She laughed and shook her head.

'I'm sorry, that came out wrong, it's more… you have an aura about you, a fun-loving edge, it made me assume you were younger.'

'Well, you act older than your years.' She turned to him then, her eyes glinting with mischief, her lips quirking up at the edges. 'Are you ready to loosen up a little?'

'Try me.'

'Your turn now, Mr Masters!' Tara called out as soon as they were on dry land. 'It's a real buzz, you'll see.'

He did see. He didn't need to experience it for himself, just viewing it through the eyes of the kids, through Malie's, feeling their positive energy, their vibe, it was contagious.

'She's right, you know.' It was Malie who spoke. 'You ready to catch a wave?'

'Absolutely.' He strode over to his board and was about to pick it up.

'Na-ah. Leave it there, make sure the fins are in the sand, we'll do some land work first.'

He didn't know why but the idea of being the only surfer in their group trying to conquer the board while they all watched on made him feel oddly foolish. But a group session… now that was different.

'How about you kids do it with me? I could do with the moral support.'

The excited gabble around him told him it was a definite yes, only Jonny played it cool.

'I'll show you how it's done, Boss.'

Malie laughed. 'I thought you paid for private lessons, Todd?'

'I'm hoping we can start those when the kids leave for the day.'

He'd meant nothing by it, no innuendo, yet the colour in her cheeks, the heat he could feel rising in his own, suggested that neither of them was thinking of surfing.

'We're ready!' Tara shouted, slicing through the sudden atmosphere and they both turned to see all five boards lined up, Todd's taking centre stage. Just how long had they stood staring at one another for?

He shook out his fingers as he made his way to the line-up and took a deep breath... This was going to be interesting...

★★★

'And *pop!*'

Out came the instruction, complete with laughter. And Malie knew she shouldn't laugh, she knew it, she kept telling herself, but it was impossible not to. And it was all his fault. Never had she seen someone pop and produce windmill arms as swiftly as she could say the word *pop*.

And the result... Todd face-planting each and every time.

Even better, the kids were absolutely loving it. Great big belly laughs filled the air as a sand-covered Todd brushed himself off and lay himself forward on the board once more.

Louis piped up, 'Like this, Mr Masters.' Both he and Tara had taken it upon themselves to manhandle Todd and demonstrate the entire movement again and again, their patience never-ending. Meanwhile, Sky and Jonny had given up after fifteen minutes to go and enjoy the last few waves before their minibus arrived to take them back to base.

The thing that got her the most was the change in Tara, from when she'd first arrived to now. She wasn't self-conscious, she wasn't anxious, she was wholly wrapped up in teaching Todd to surf.

'I think I may have been wrong about you,' she spoke up as Todd popped to Louis' instruction and Tara stood beside him braced for his failure, her arms outstretched to offer a counter-force should he fall her way.

'You don't say,' he said, wobbling this way and that but managing to stay on his feet this time.

'Yup…' she folded her arms as she eyed him, 'you're far *too* loose.'

'Yeah, you're like a jelly,' blurted Tara, shaking her head, her eyes tearing up with her laughter.

'And I can't believe you're all laughing at me.'

'Hey, it's not just us!' piped up Louis as he acted out a perfect pop on his board. 'Sky and Jonny were laughing when they ran off.'

'They were?' He dropped onto his board and gave Louis a deep-seated scowl. 'Just wait until I speak to chef about the dinner menu tonight, none of you will be laughing then. Can you get sprouts in Hawaii, Malie?'

'Eugh.' Both Tara and Louis grimaced.

She played along, loving the interplay between the three of them. 'I'm sure something suitable can be sourced.'

'Hey, did someone mention sprouts?'

It was Jonny coming back in from the sea, his board hooked

under his arm and Sky not far behind, their faces flushed from exertion and the unmistakable joy of catching waves.

'Mr Masters reckons he's gonna poison us at dinner for laughing at his board skills.'

'What skills?' Jonny said it so seriously and everyone cracked up, even Todd who shot to his feet, notably solid, not a wobble in sight. *How interesting…*

'Someone's in need of a dunking,' Todd lunged forward and Jonny dropped his board, legging it to the water, Todd hot on his tail, their laughter pealing after them. Water flew through the air as they each tried to outdo the other. Todd's hair took a thrashing, its perfect, swept-back curve falling forward over his face, his grin wide and flashing dimples in his cheeks that Malie hadn't noticed before.

'I'm not sure who's the biggest kid,' Sky said, smiling at their antics.

Malie pulled her attention off them to look at the fourteen-year-old girl. She was mature for her age, quiet and sensible, a good companion to her single mother Malie was sure. She had no siblings. It was just the two of them, and it was obvious she was close to Jonny. Malie couldn't help wondering whether there was something more developing between the pair. Sky was certainly pretty, in a porcelain doll kind of a way, in fact she reminded her a lot of Zoe. Especially with her pale blonde hair, long and fine, her pale skin, even paler with the sunblock Malie had insisted she layer up with.

'It's nice seeing Jonny like this.'

Malie wondered at the quiet sincerity in Sky's remark. 'Like what?'

'Relaxed, happy, laughing even.' Sky looked to her and gave a shrug. 'You know he's the eldest of four, right?'

Malie nodded, it had all been in his file.

'What with his dad running out when he was a baby, and his mum having so many children, Jonny sees himself as the provider.'

'It's a big responsibility for someone so young.'

Sky gave a shrug. 'It's not that uncommon where we live. I think it's why we get along so well, we get what it's like growing up without a dad, but I don't have all the pressures he does. It's just Mum and me.'

'And your mum is lucky to have a daughter like you.'

Her smile was small. 'I've had my moments, getting into trouble, not coming home, bunking off school...'

Malie thought about her own antics, of lying to her parents and sneaking off to Zoe's to grab her board and hit the waves, of staying out late because she couldn't face the pain at home. 'We all deal with the rough in different ways.'

'I'm not so bad now, the counsellors at Fun For All really help... you know, just having someone to talk to, to help you realize you're not alone, even when you think you are. I mean I had Mum, I've always had Mum, but sometimes it's not enough, is it?'

It was a rhetorical question, Malie knew, but she found herself murmuring her agreement anyway. 'My brother died when I was sixteen,' Sky turned to look at her but Malie's eyes were fixed unseeing on the ocean now, 'I felt invisible to my parents – even though they were around and I knew in my heart they loved me, their presence wasn't enough. If it hadn't been for my friends, I don't know how I would have got through it.'

'I'm sorry about your brother but I'm glad you had friends around you. I met Jonny at Fun For All...'

The rest went unsaid. She didn't need to say it. The affection she felt for Jonny, whether it was platonic or something more was written in her face.

'Oh no...' Sky shook her head as she looked to the guys in the water and started backing up.

'What are—?' Malie didn't bother finishing the question as she registered what had set her off. Todd and Jonny were heading for them with a look in their eye that spelled trouble.

'*Behave*,' Malie warned them, backing up too.

'What?' they both said in wide-eyed innocence, their slow stride unhalting.

'You know what...'

Both Malie and Sky turned to flee, Louis and Tara backed out of the way laughing, but it was no use, Todd's arm snaked around Malie's waist as Jonny's did the same with Sky and they were both being taken back to the water. They squealed, trying to wriggle free.

'Don't you dare, Todd Masters.' Malie pulled at the arm around her but it was locked tight, his strength surrounding her and sending a surprising surge of warmth through her lower belly.

She sucked in a breath but it was filled with his cologne, spice and sea, and it only made the tingling heat spread. This was crazy. She was about to get a dunking; she shouldn't be enjoying the threat.

'Todd!'

The male call came from up the beach and Todd stilled. She looked up to see a couple approaching from the surf school and recognized them immediately: Tara's parents. *Oh God.*

'Anne-Marie, Charles! Great to see you!' Todd quickly

straightened, propping Malie up before she fell and giving her an apologetic look. 'These are Tara's parents.'

'Yes, I met them briefly this afternoon,' she mumbled, brushing her hair out of her face and cursing the burn in her cheeks. She felt flustered, like they'd been caught out doing something they shouldn't even though they were just having fun.

'We've come to collect Tara,' said Charles Davidson.

Both parents paused halfway towards them and coming no further. They looked edgy, her mother's hands wringing together as she looked to her daughter briefly and then gave a tentative smile to Todd.

He brushed his hands down his top and she could have sworn his cheeks flushed too. Granted, it could have been the pink bouncing off his top... yes, definitely the pink, because they hadn't been doing anything bad. Nothing at all.

Though they had been messing around when they should have been teaching... and it had been more than just giggles erupting in her belly...

At least only she knew that, though, not even Jonny's hormonally charged brain could spy it surely. Not that she was going to spare him a glance.

Preoccupied, she almost missed Tara's 'So unfair' muttered under her breath.

She looked across at her and frowned. The girl was already folding in on herself, her arms wrapped tight around her, her head bowed. Malie was transported back in time, over a decade, to Koa's bedroom, his body so slight in the bed that looked so big, their mother fussing, their father standing back, withdrawn, closed in, and her – she'd been in the corner in that exact same position. Hunched in on herself, blending into the background, not wanting to be noticed.

She shook herself out of it, the past was the past, it had no place in the now. They'd both lost a brother, though, both lived through the grief of their parents, and for Tara... she was still locked in that life.

She headed over to her, leaving Todd to speak to her parents.

'What's up?' she asked, bending forward to lift the girl's board for her.

Tara sent her parents a death stare. 'I don't see why they can't leave me to travel back with everyone else.'

'Hey, it's nice that they have come.'

'They treat me like I'm a baby.'

'I don't think—'

'No one else has their parents on this trip.'

'I don't think that's quite true.' Malie could hear Todd chatting to her parents behind them, far enough away that they wouldn't overhear their daughter's outburst. 'I'm sure there are a couple of others here.'

'Not many.'

'I think it shows they care.'

She harrumphed and refused to meet Malie's eye.

'Don't you want to show them what you've learned today?'

Her shoulders lowered just a little, her eyes coming back to Malie briefly. 'Maybe.'

'There should be no *maybe* about it, come on, let's go see if they want to watch.'

Tara chewed her lip, her dubious gaze now on her parents.

'Come on, let's go ask them to watch and if they love it – *which they will* – maybe we can ask them about you travelling on the bus with the others.' Malie offered out her hand and was relieved when Tara finally took it, a small smile lifting the corners of her mouth.

'So long as you make them say yes… *to both!*'

Malie laughed and ducked her head low to speak in Tara's ear. 'I'll do my very best, and if I fail, I owe you a trip to the ice cream parlour, my treat!'

'Just me and you.'

'Just me and you.'

'They'd never let you.'

Malie frowned at the girl's surprisingly sad and fatalistic outlook. 'I think Mr Masters could charm a yes out of them if I fail…'

She looked up at Todd and realized just how true that was. Already she could see Tara's parents relaxing into their conversation with him. Was there anyone he couldn't charm at the drop of a hat?

Well, so long as he doesn't charm his way into your pants, you're all good…

Oh. My. God. Why are you even thinking that?

She squeezed Tara's hand in encouragement. 'We got this, right?'

'Right.'

Pants are off limits!

CHAPTER SEVEN

'DO YOU THINK THEY were happy?'

He could hear the concern in Malie's question as they stood watching the Davidsons climb into their small blue hire car that they'd parked at the edge of the beach. Around them people bustled, kids leaving the beach to grab some dinner, the adults arriving after a day's work looking to chill in the last hour of sun. Tara turned and gave a little wave which they both returned, their smiles momentarily genuine.

'Of course they were, they would never have left her with you in the first place if they weren't.' He turned to face her. 'And the joy in Tara's face when she caught that last wave with Nalu – no parent could fail to feel her happiness too.'

'But they hardly stayed long.' She met his eye, her disappointment dampening his own pleasure.

'They stayed long enough to witness her new-found skills and congratulate her,' he said, 'and let's face it, the minibus came and took the others, so they probably felt they were encroaching.'

'Encroaching on what?'

He almost said *our time*, but he'd learned his lesson there. Instead he grinned. 'My lesson, for starters.'

She didn't smile, though. She was too busy watching their car drive away.

'Don't you think they seemed... I don't know... *deflated* about it all. I mean, she stood up on a wave, twice! And all they did was pat her on the back and say *well done*. There was no excitement, no thrill.'

'Hey, just because everyone's not bursting with the buzz of surfing the way you are, doesn't mean they're not impressed, and it's a big deal for them, seeing their daughter conquer a sport that's far from safe.'

'This is totally safe – you want unsafe then you should see the surfing up strip!'

'But they're risk-averse. Nothing's safe. You've read Tara's file, you know what happened...'

'You mean the fire?' Her words were weighted with sadness.

'Exactly. I only met them a year ago when things had got to a point that they knew they needed help. I can't comment on how they were before the fire, maybe they've always been this protective but...'

'But you don't think it likely?'

'I can't imagine what it's like to lose a son – hell, my father... it crippled him when my mother died, but a *son*... and to almost lose their daughter too.'

Her eyes glistened as she looked to him. 'It was the same for my parents. I was much older than Tara when we lost Koa, but they stifled me, all the more so after the car accident, and I knew they only wanted what was best, what was safe...'

She shuddered and wrapped her arms around her middle. He had to fight the urge to reach for her, to offer her comfort like he had the previous night, knowing the trouble it had led to, the kiss, crossing a line that neither of them wanted to go beyond.

'I just couldn't live that way,' she said quietly.

'Did you tell them how you felt?'

She scoffed gently. 'I tried, but it never came out right, we always ended up arguing instead.'

'And so, you chose to avoid it?'

'Yes… They weren't going to change, and I couldn't live their way, so I left.' She looked back to the car in the distance, her mind clearly switching to Tara now. 'I wish we could help them, though, as a family, not just Tara.'

'I do too.'

She gave him a small smile. 'Why doesn't that surprise me?'

He gave her a hint of a smile in return, but it fell away as he went back to watching the car disappear on the horizon. 'It's hard. It's not just about protecting Tara and keeping her safe for them, it's the fact they suffer under the weight of their own guilt too.'

'Guilt? Over the fire?'

He nodded. 'From what I've gleaned, the fire alarms in the house weren't working, and the fire was caused by a set of hair curlers left plugged in.'

'So, they blame themselves for the fire, for their son's death and their daughter's injuries?'

'Exactly.' He turned back to her. 'Their marriage is under a lot of strain and the fact they focus so much on Tara, suffocating her in the process…' he shook his head, 'it's an impossible situation, but they need to loosen the reins a little and they need to spend some time together as a couple.'

Her brow lifted, her eyes bright with realization. 'And you're hoping this trip is going to help them do that, don't you?'

'If it makes them realize that their daughter needs her space just as much as she needs their love, it'll be a start. And if in the process they can use the time she's busy to actually have some time alone together all the better.'

'Clever.'

He smiled. 'I like to think so.'

She smiled with him, her frown from moments ago easing with it.

'Malie, Todd!'

They turned to see Kalani standing in the entrance to the surf school, waving at them, Nalu at his feet. 'You good to lock up when you're done? Everything is tidy, there's just your boards to hose down and put away.'

'Sure,' Malie said, 'I'll see you tomorrow.'

'Cheers, Kalani!' Todd looked back to her. 'Lesson time?'

'You're on… but no more messing around, no dunking!'

'Hey, that was all Jonny's idea.'

She laughed, shaking her head. 'Whatever.'

She started off towards the shore, to where their surfboards lay side by side in the sand. She scooped hers up and looked over at him, her grin loaded with teasing. 'Although judging by your performance on the sand earlier, I think you're going to experience plenty of dunking.'

'I wouldn't be so sure.' He bent and lifted his own board. 'You know I was doing that for the kids' benefit, right?'

She giggled, and threw her hair over her shoulder. 'We'll see.'

He would have had some cheeky retort if not for the fact that he was momentarily stunned again at the sight of her. Board under her arm, her face looking out to sea, all golden in the sun as her hair fell wild down her back. His stomach felt tightened by a spasm of heat and his mouth turned as dry as the sand beneath his feet.

'You ready to—' She turned to him and her words trailed off. 'What?'

He swallowed. The idea of putting some water between him and her sounded mighty sensible right about now. With any luck it'd be cool enough to come to his aid too.

'Ladies first...'

It had been his intention to get her eyes off him and give him the chance to recover, instead he had her perfect rear to follow into the water, the trace of coconut in the air, the trail of her curls over clinging pink, her slim waist and the perfect swell of her hips... none of it helping.

He ducked to waist level in the water as soon as possible, thankfully, before she turned to him.

'We'll practise paddling first, get you to catch a wave, *then* we'll see how you fare popping up.'

She was enjoying this, he could tell. The twinkle was back in the green of her eyes. What he couldn't work out was whether it was the teacher in her excited about getting him to catch his first wave, or the idea of him losing his cool when he failed to pop?

He'd play along for now, but he was pretty sure his skateboarding days were going to work in his favour...

'Whatever you say, Boss.'

She laughed. 'I love how Jonny calls you that.'

'I tell them to call me Todd, but none of them will have it, the whole *Mr* thing wasn't for him though.'

'No, I can imagine.' She slid up onto her board and he followed suit, grateful their conversation had distracted his body enough to calm him in more ways than one.

He followed her direction, paddling out to sea.

'Slip back a little on the board, your nose is digging water.'

He shuffled back and the nose lifted, his paddle becoming more efficient.

She nodded. 'Better.'

When she turned, he turned with her, her eyes scanning the water behind and coming back to him as the first promising wave approached.

'Now check the wave, the speed... and paddle.'

He threw a look over his shoulder, paddled and assessed, changed his pace to suit.

'That's it...'

He felt his board lift, felt the wave take him and went with it, the urge to pop burning through him. He had this... he drew his hands below his chest and pushed up, only this time he did what felt natural, launching his right foot forward. He adopted the stance he'd used as a kid with his skateboard and the adrenalin rush was instant.

For a second the world fell away; he was a child again, weaving through the streets on errand after errand, forgetting his troubles at home... and he was forgetting everything now, save for the rush in his bloodstream, the power of the ride as he weaved his board this way and that, testing, adapting, controlling...

The wave was running out of steam, the shore fast approaching, and he jumped off into the water, already buzzing with the need to go bigger, faster, longer.

He emerged from the water, flicked his hair out of his eyes and scoured the waves for Malie. She was sitting on her board out where he'd left her, mouth agape, her eyes pinned on him.

'How was that, Boss?!' He waded towards her, the board under his palm as he pushed it with him.

She shook her head, her grin building. 'You could have told me you were goofy!'

Goofy?

There were so many compliments she could have given and instead she was giving him *goofy*. As the water level rose, he hopped up onto the board to paddle the remaining distance.

'Goofy, that's the best you got?'

Her eyes danced at him. 'It means you lead with your right foot.'

'And that makes me goofy?'

She shrugged. 'Afraid so… what I want to know is why you were popping with your left foot forward back on the beach?'

'Isn't it obvious?'

She looked at him for so long he thought she wasn't going to answer, not verbally at any rate, but her eyes were ablaze with what he wanted to see, appreciation, respect, want – or was it because he *wanted* to see all that, he thought it was there?

'You were putting on a performance for the kids?'

'And they loved it, didn't they?' Was it his imagination or had her voice softened, was it laced with interest? The kind of interest that had led to their kiss. 'It had to be worth hurting my pride a little for…'

She turned her smile to the sun rather than him. 'You're an intriguing guy, Todd.'

'I'll take intriguing over goofy any day. Now, how about a bigger wave?'

She came back to him, her smile lifting to one side. 'You sure you're ready for one?'

'I was born ready.'

★ ★ ★

'Oh yeah, that was incredible!'

Todd shook the hair out of his face with his exclamation and Malie made herself look away. Every time he did it, his fringe would flick back, his eyes would land on her, so alive and blue against the white of his skin, and she would feel her entire body pulse, the heat swamping her and taking out any rational thought she might try and cling to.

The problem was Todd Masters wasn't just some deliciously hot and charismatic millionaire, he was a total philanthropist, his heart as big as his wallet. And seeing him interact with his kids, hearing him talk about his Foundation, the things that mattered to him, it was getting harder and harder to ignore the way he made her feel, to forget the heat of his kiss, the power of it.

No matter how many times she tried to tell herself that her type was definitely the hunky Adonis kind, her body was all for the hot-vamp do-gooder.

'Having fun?' she asked.

He pulled himself up to sitting on the board. 'Hell, yeah!'

She smiled. 'I can tell, but we should head back, the sun's getting low.'

He looked towards the horizon, his face glowing now as the sun's rays stretched warm and orange across the sky. 'It's beautiful out here.'

She followed his gaze, shared in his appreciation. 'It's my favourite place to be.'

'I can see why.'

'When you're out here, you can forget everything,' she said softly, feeling the view work its unique magic. 'Leave your troubles on the shore, so to speak.'

He hummed his agreement. The low sound strummed through the heart of her and she took a deep breath then swivelled her board around. 'We should get back.'

He'd had his lesson and she needed to put some distance between them again. If they got back now, she could have the boards away and give Zoe a call, get planning her visit – No, scratch that, Zoe was visiting the Caribbean, not at home in Sydney, quick mental arithmetic told her it would be far too late to call her.

She could call Victoria and Lily though. *What and wake them up at the crack of dawn?* No, she couldn't do that. It wasn't their fault she was desperately in need of distraction. She started to paddle even though he hadn't moved.

'Hey, Malie...'

She closed her eyes and knew she wasn't being fair to him, it wasn't his fault either.

She looked to him over her shoulder, all relaxed and happy and far too appealing. 'Yeah?'

'Can we stay a bit, just enjoy the sun going down?'

She hesitated.

'If you haven't got to rush off, that is?'

No, she didn't *have* to rush off. She *needed* to.

But she had no plans. Other than gaining the distance she needed. And it just felt foolish, selfish even. He was enjoying himself and when she imagined how busy his life must be with work as well as his charity efforts, to bring an end to his day just because she couldn't keep a lid on how she felt was just... well, it sucked.

'Sure.' She brought the board back around and lined it up alongside his, pushing her body back up to sitting. 'I guess you don't get to do this much.'

He gave a gentle scoff. 'I can't remember the last time I sat and did nothing.'

'You should find the time for it,' she said, trying to avoid looking at him and failing miserably.

He smiled. 'Do you get to do it often?'

'I always try and see the sun rise or set.'

'Like you were last night... when I rudely interrupted.'

'You didn't rudely interrupt.'

'No?'

'No, your rude interruption came *after* the sun had set.'

He laughed, the sound low and husky and stirring up her insides.

Keep a lid on it, Malie.

Thor is your type.

Not Edward Cullen.

She laughed at her own madness.

'I love your laugh.'

Her eyes snapped to his and his own flared with what looked to be surprise. He hadn't meant to say it. But he had, and... *oh, God.* She swallowed, her tongue suddenly feeling too thick for her mouth.

'Sorry, I didn't mean to...' He raised his hands palm out. 'I just... well, anyway... it was just a fact.'

A fact?

'Well, keep your facts to yourself…' her words were hot with the whole thing, the effect of his praise, his appeal, the way her mind wanted to find out what else he loved, 'especially when they're all personal.'

He dropped his hands and her eyes traced the move as they landed on his scrunched-up board shorts and the exposed length of his thighs that were as toned as the rest of him. Not that she needed to remember the rest of him right now. *Every. Toned. Inch.*

She launched her eyes back to his face and felt her entire body overheat as they locked with his.

'I apologize. Best behaviour from now on in – *scout's honour.*'

'*You* were a scout?'

'Er, no, but I have it on good authority that the saying still stands.'

'Good authority?'

'Jonny… but the rest of the crew agreed.'

She laughed now, good and hearty. 'I bet they did.' She shook her head. 'You're as bad as them, Todd Masters.'

He shrugged his shoulders and looked back to the horizon, to where the sun had now started to dip into the sea. 'I'm going to take that as a compliment, they're all pretty great.'

'You know…' she began thoughtfully, 'for a man who avoids friendships and family bonds because it keeps life easy, you sure care about these kids a great deal.'

He looked to her, his face suddenly sombre with her shift in focus. 'That's different. If I do my job right, if the charity does what it's supposed to, they will all move on eventually. I'll just be part of their past.'

'You give them the tools, the social skills, the ability to move on?'

'Of course, otherwise I've failed them and I'm not a man to take failure lightly.'

'I'm not suggesting you are – but what about your family, friends, those that do stay around?'

'There isn't anyone, save for my father.'

'And you're happy living like that?' She couldn't imagine not having Victoria, Zoe and Lils. To have no friends at all. She knew she was pushing the same conversation from earlier but now she had him to herself, she couldn't let it go. A man with a heart such as his, he shouldn't live in a closed-off way, be so shut down.

'Love and loss, Malie.' His voice had turned husky, rough. 'I think we both understand why it pays to avoid it.'

She hadn't expected his brutal honesty, or the way it cut so deep. She'd never agreed more and felt so sad and regretful all the same.

'But you must be close to your father now, even after...?'

'It's difficult, especially when every time I visit him, I'm reminded of all the ways he won't let me help.'

His gaze dropped, his mouth forming a tight line as he seemed to withdraw from her and into his thoughts.

'It's really getting to you, isn't it?'

His eyes came back to her. 'When you have the power to help people and your own father won't let you... It's driving me more than a little crazy.'

'How often do you see him?'

'A few times a year, when I'm back in London and have the time to call in. I try to avoid the house as it only makes things awkward. When I have its condition thrust in my face like that, I can't help but bring it up. And that always ends badly.'

'Do you talk on the phone much?'

He went quiet, his face going back to the sun.

'We've never had that close a relationship,' he admitted eventually. 'He was too interested in the bottle when I was younger, and now... now, I'm not really sure how to have a relationship with him.'

She could feel the hollowness of his words, knew he was hurting beneath it all. She thought of her relationship with her own parents, the distance between them, the Christmas she had just spent with them – the emphasis on time for families making it all the more pronounced – and her skin prickled. 'What about Christmas? Did you spend it together?'

He let go of a drawn-out breath. 'I put an event on at the Foundation, some of the kids are a little old for Santa but most turn up, a lot of effort goes into choosing gifts and putting on a festive spread. My father came along and chipped in.'

'That sounds nice, really merry.'

He smiled a little. 'It is the season for giving, after all. I guess you could see that as spending Christmas together, doing something we both care about.'

'Sounds like you have more of a relationship than you think.'

'Perhaps... He's been sober for a long time now and he uses his personal experience to help with the counselling side of things; you'd be surprised how many kids start to find sanctuary in a bottle.'

'I can imagine.' She gave an involuntary shudder. 'Is your father a volunteer?'

'Yes. I tried to pay him, but he saw it as charity... Can you believe it?' He threw her a look. 'I pay everyone else involved but him, he won't take a penny.'

'He might see it as a way to make up for the past.'

He looked at her long and hard, his voice quiet as he said, 'I never thought of it like that.'

She gave him a small smile. 'If it makes you feel better, I think you're doing better than me, I don't have much contact with my parents at all.'

'I must admit I was surprised when you hinted as much earlier. I know you obviously work thousands of miles away, but I got the impression you'd grown up close, that you got your love of the ocean from them – surely with what you do now, you would still share that bond.'

You'd think so, wouldn't you? The chill set in. The ache of loss and longing. 'They quit surfing when my brother became too ill to surf himself.'

It was her turn to stare out at the setting sun now, unable to look at him for fear of what he'd see in her, of how weak and vulnerable she would be in that moment and how easily he could become a distraction from it all again.

'They shut down the surf school and locked up our boards – if he couldn't surf none of us could.'

'They forbade you?'

'Yes,' she said it so quietly, 'to the point that I had to hide my surfboard at Zoe's and sneak out with her.'

Her throat closed over with the memories – of being devious when she didn't want to be, of hurting and not being able to escape it in the water because it was shrouded in guilt. 'I'd never needed that time on the water more and...'

She shook her head, her eyes lost in the beauty of the sunset, her heart lost to the memories.

'And so, it created distance between you?'

Slowly she turned to look at him. 'Pretty much… and when Koa died…'

Tears pricked at the backs of her eyes, just as they had the previous night, tears she hadn't let fall in so long. She swallowed and took a breath, but the compassion in his gaze kept them coming, forcing her to look away.

'It was worse. I carried on sneaking about and they carried on ignoring me, and then we were in that car accident and suddenly they were all over me. I knew they were scared they could lose me, too, but that made them ever more watchful, ever more controlling, and I couldn't stand it any longer.'

'So, you left and pursued your dream to surf?'

'Yes.'

'It was brave of you.'

'Selfish, I think they called it.'

'But surely they must be proud of you now, to see what you have achieved, to see how you are helping people, sharing your skills, teaching people to find solace in the ocean.'

She laughed but it was harsh, angry. 'They don't see it that way – they think I'm an adrenalin junkie destined to live a short life. Hell, maybe they're right.'

'They're not right, you do what you love, and you share that love with others. There's nothing wrong with that.'

'No?' She turned to face him, the depth of feeling in his face tugging at her, making her want the other kind of intimacy back, the lustful distraction she knew he could provide, regardless of the consequences.

'Absolutely not.'

'You've not seen my real passion yet, though.'

He grinned. 'Which is?'

'How about I show you?'

Malie, what are you doing?

She ignored her freaked-out self and raised her chin, uncaring.

His eyes narrowed. 'Now?'

'No,' she laughed, 'not here, tomorrow morning. If you're free?'

'I can make myself free.'

'You heard of the Banzai Pipeline?'

'Is that a place?'

'It's just off the North Shore, Ehukai Beach. If you can get there tomorrow morning just after sunrise, you can witness my passion for itself... then tell me you don't agree with my parents.'

He looked at her quiet for a moment and she didn't look away. She was too caught in the emotions flickering across his face and trying to decipher their meaning.

'I can't work out whether you're trying to push me away by inviting me to witness whatever this crazy act is, or if you're letting me in on the real you.'

He had a good point. She didn't know either but the idea of him being there watching her rip it up on the waves filled her with more excitement than just the prospect of surfing Pipe. 'Does it matter which?'

'I guess not.'

CHAPTER EIGHT

IT WAS AN HOUR'S drive to the North Shore and when he saw the state of the parking, he was glad he'd set off early. Cars lined the roadside and the designated car park was already full.

It took ten minutes to find a gap big enough take his hire car and he wished he'd opted for a smaller vehicle. He wasn't sure what possessed him to get the convertible Mustang... OK, that wasn't quite true. He'd got it because it suited Malie's personality best. Vibrant red, it was fun, sexy and impossible to ignore. Not that she'd given any indication she would go anywhere with him after, and he knew he shouldn't even be hoping for it. But he was.

Didn't matter that there was no future, no crossing of lines, nothing, he wanted to spend as much of the day with her as possible.

He parked up and followed a group of surfers, listening to their pumped-up talk of *double overheads* and the *ultimate tube riding*. He had a fair idea of what they meant and even though he could hear the roar of the waves, it still didn't prepare him for the scene that greeted him beyond the trees that lined the beach.

The sky was clear blue, the golden sand dotted with people, but beyond that the waves were insane. It was the only way he could describe it. If *double overhead* meant twice as tall as a man, someone had forecasted wrong because they were at least twenty feet and they were swallowing up surfers left, right and centre.

And Malie was somewhere *here*?

Was she out there already? His heart was in his mouth as he thought it. Surely not. He knew she liked to live a little crazy – she'd hinted as much the night before – but this?

And he felt foolish now, with all the people here; how was he supposed to know where to look for her? Why hadn't he thought to ask her?

Stupid question. He knew why well enough. He was too busy being caught up in her and her invitation to think straight.

So here he now was, surrounded by sun-drenched men and women all looking perfectly at home laughing, cheering on their mates, groaning at what they called wipe-outs, and there was he, a city boy, dressed in his usual shirt, shorts and trainers. He toed off the latter, stuck his socks inside and pushed his aviators up his nose – at least they helped hide his sudden confusion.

'Hey dude, you lost?'

Some shaggy-haired guy, lanky but muscular and wearing just a pair of low-slung board shorts, paused before him and raked his hair out of his eyes as he squinted at him. He sounded Australian, hardly a local himself.

'I'm that obvious?'

''Fraid so,' he said, taking in his ensemble. 'You here to watch?'

He nodded. 'You don't happen to know Malie Pukui, do you?'

What a stupid question. The place was teeming with people, he might as well have just walked into the centre of London and asked a tourist if he knew his father.

The guy's eyes lit up. 'You're kidding, right?'

Todd frowned. 'No…'

'Everyone knows Malie, she's a beaut! Not many that can handle a wave like her, male or female.'

Now he felt extra foolish; of course a surfer would know who she was. 'She told me to come watch her surf. Is she around?'

'Is she around?' He gave a laugh. 'She's out there, dude.'

The guy turned to face the sea, his hand over his eyes as he scanned the surfing dots. How he could identify anyone from here, Todd had no idea.

'See that cluster of surfers off to the left, in the line-up?' He gestured with his hand and Todd felt his heart lurch again as he watched the waves swell and curve.

'Yes.' His voice sounded distant as he strained to make her out, not daring to believe she was being lifted by waves as tall as these.

'She's in the pink and white, matching the colour of her board… and it looks like you're in luck, this wave's hers.'

'How can you—' He was about to ask how could he tell but then she was moving, taking off on the lip of the wave, its face colossal and curving as she ripped down it so fast he couldn't breathe. And then she was turning back into it, taking it horizontally, as it curved over the top of her, dwarfing her. She looked tiny, vulnerable, and surely she was going way too fast?

The spray kicked up in the air, one minute she was visible, the next she was gone. *Gone.* His stomach lurched.

'Wait for it. Wait for it…' It was the Aussie who spoke – Todd couldn't have found his voice if he tried – and then suddenly she erupted from the closed end of the wave, her arms outstretched. He could imagine her *whoop* from here but any sound was drowned out by the thundering crash of the wave, the cheers from the shore.

'Pretty special, ain't she?' The Aussie fist-bumped his upper arm, waking Todd from his trance.

He swallowed. 'Yeah.'

'You can come sit with us if you like; knowing Malie, she won't be in for another half an hour.'

It beat sitting like an outsider. 'Cheers.'

He couldn't tear his eyes off her as she navigated the waves, taking on another and swinging the board up through the air.

'Yeah, go, Malie!' the Aussie bellowed, his fist pumping the air now. 'You see the air she just caught with that one?'

Yeah, he saw all right; the leap of the board, the image of her as she twisted round to come straight back down the wave, the speed, the power, the control, it was mesmerizing – and he almost walked straight into a red flagpole. He sidestepped it and looked up: WARNING. Rip currents. You could be swept out and drown. IF IN DOUBT DON'T GO OUT.

Alongside it was another: WARNING. NO SWIMMING.

He could see further red flagpoles dotted down the beach.

'No swimming doesn't apply to surfers then?' he asked.

The Aussie laughed, 'You're funny.'

He wasn't intending to be.

'Whoa, not cool.'

Todd looked to him, but his eyes were on the water. 'What's not?'

'She just got dropped in on.'

'Dropped in on?'

He tried to see her but the bright pink and white had vanished. Then he saw the board fly up through the air, no Malie. His chest convulsed. 'Where is she?'

'She wiped out; someone took her out. Not cool, not cool.' He shook his head and carried on walking.

'Hey, shouldn't we get the lifeguard?' He stared at the spot where he could make out glimpses of her board in the white froth. Surely, she'd been under too long. 'Hey... hey...' he chased after him, 'what if—'

Before he could finish, she appeared, tossed out by the wave, her body launching from the water and relief swamped him, his skin awash with goose bumps.

'See, she's got this, and she's seen worse, believe me,' the Aussie said, clearly unperturbed.

It wasn't even 9 a.m. and Todd suddenly needed a drink.

'Hey, don't look so spooked! It's all good.'

He nodded, knowing his voice wouldn't work.

'She'd be Queen of the Pipe if only she'd put her name down, it's crazy that she doesn't.'

'Queen of the Pipe?'

'Yeah, it's the big wave-surfing competition that hits this spot in a few weeks' time. It's all over the TV and everything. She'd take the crown easy, it's not like we haven't gone on at her about it either, but she reckons she's too busy at the surf school.'

Todd thought about it and wondered if that truly was the case. 'Do you think—'

He was cut off by a shout, 'Hey, who's your friend, EJ?'

It came from a group of four surfers lounging off to the right, all in a similar state of dress as the Aussie.

'A friend of Malie's, I said he could hang with us until she quits.'

'You mean Todd?' The guy who spoke looked like Kalani, only a younger model. He'd put money on them being related.

'Oh yeah,' the Aussie he now knew was called EJ drawled out, giving a nod as he looked at Todd with fresh eyes. 'Malie told us to look out for you.'

'She did?'

'Yeah, I just forgot.'

'Too many reef hits to the head, dude,' the Kalani lookalike said, walking forward. 'I'm Akela, this idiot is EJ, and this is Kai and Sammy.'

They all gave him a nod in greeting and though they were all various shades of bronze which made him stand out further alongside them, he felt welcome enough.

'I'm going to grab some juice,' Akela said, 'you want one, Todd?'

'Sure.' He dipped into his pocket for his wallet and Akela waved him down.

'I got this.'

'Cheers.'

He went off and Todd dropped his trainers to the sand, turning to scan the waves for Malie again.

'She's right there, dude.' EJ shook his hair from his eyes and grinned as he pointed her out. He felt his shoulders ease as he saw her back on her board paddling out again, diving into an extreme wave and reappearing, all steady and controlled. It was quite something to watch. Something else to experience, he was sure.

He thought of her parents and their aversion to the way she lived her life, to this, and he'd never sympathized with an opinion so much, and disagreed with it all at the same time. It was a crazy contradiction but as he lost himself in watching her – the way she handled the immense swells, the adrenalin rush she was sure to be experiencing – he couldn't imagine her ever not doing it.

How could there be so much beauty in something so terrifying?

Or was he just getting lost in Malie all over again?

Would he feel this way if it was EJ he was watching? Would he be this mesmerized, this hooked, this in awe?

He had a fairly good idea of the answer... there were dozens out there harnessing the power of the waves, but he only had eyes for one.

And he shouldn't... he *really* shouldn't.

★★★

What a rush!

She'd had good days, epic days, and out-of-this-world days. This was one of the latter. She was buzzing head to toe as she emerged from the water with her surfing buddies, all laughing and jostling as their feet sunk in the sand. They were on an absolute high. And then she saw him. Todd.

He was standing with the rest of their crew, his pale English skin, his deep blue shirt, and dark swanky shorts all a striking contrast to the rest of them and her heart skipped a beat. She stopped thinking altogether and launched herself up the beach.

'You made it!' She threw her board down and without thinking wrapped her arms around him, pressing a kiss to his cheek.

She felt his entire body tense in her hold and she fell back just as quickly. She'd been so wrapped up in the euphoric surf then the cherry of seeing him waiting up the beach, she hadn't thought twice, she'd just thrown herself at him.

Smart move, Malie.

You idiot.

She smothered her panic in a grin. 'Sorry, I'm just buzzing, it was a rush out there!'

To her relief he grinned back. 'If that's how you're going to greet me, you want to go back out there, load up some more and come back. I'd love to know what I get next.'

She laughed and punched his shoulder. *There*, more mate-like. Only, the urge to actually jump him was shockingly strong. Maybe the adrenalin rush of surfing pipe and seeing Todd on top was a step too far. Her inhibitions seemed to be drowning beneath a sea of excitement.

She looked to the guys. 'Thanks for taking care of him.'

'No worries,' Akela said, his grin as he eyed both her and Todd revealing that her little display of affection hadn't gone unnoticed. 'Your turn to watch the stuff, we're going in.'

She high-fived him and watched them head towards the sea, reaching around the hem of her rash vest to strip it from her body. She pulled it over her head, shaking out her hair.

'I'm thirsty, you thirsty?' She looked to Todd over her shoulder and his eyes were lost in her lower back, the intensity of his gaze making her breath catch.

She looked down too, popping her hip out as she sought to see what he could, even though she knew what it was. The tattooed butterfly at the base of her spine was an effective, if not teasing, image.

'You like it?'

He swallowed, his eyes coming back to her face. 'It's pretty special.'

'Hey, Malie,' Pika called out from the group now joining them at a far more leisurely pace and setting their boards down far more

119

gently than she had—*oops*. 'We're going to grab some juice, you want some?'

She eyed Todd looking for an answer to the same question she posed to him seconds before and he shook his head. 'Your friends sorted me out earlier.'

'Just one for me.'

They all headed off leaving her and Todd, and the sudden heat hanging in the air between them.

'You sure you're not thirsty? It's pretty hot out here.'

He gave a soft chuckle. 'I'm good.'

Forget the sun, her body felt the burn of *him*. She looked back to the waves, to the people catching the lip and the surfer that took it. She felt the rush in tune with his move and threw her focus into that. It was less... complicated.

'You were incredible out there.' She could hear the appreciation thick in his voice and wondered whether it was more than just her surfing skills that had put it there. 'Don't you ever get scared, though?'

She shrugged. 'It's all part of the thrill.' She looked to him briefly and then back to the waves. 'There's nothing like it. When you're riding inside the tube, surrounded by water, and all you can see is that hole getting narrower and narrower, you can feel the power of it feeding through your fingers as you trail them along... it's immense. I feel immortal, free, empowered...'

'You should write poetry.' He'd come up behind her, she could smell his cologne on the breeze, feel his presence radiate down her bare back.

She laughed and dared to twist her head to look up at him. 'Don't worry, I'm not about to take you out there.'

'Thank heaven for that.'

She laughed more. 'Scared?'

'Hey, I'm as alpha as they come, but I'm not so macho that I can't acknowledge the terror I'd feel at the thought of being taken out by one those barrel-things.'

'It's not so bad… OK, it is, but I wouldn't quit it.'

'No, I get that, but I thought my breakfast was going to make an unwelcome appearance when you were wiped out by that other surfer.'

'You saw that?'

'No, I saw the result of it, your board flying through the air and no you.'

'Yeah, well, not everyone is so hot on obeying the rules of surf etiquette.'

'You guys have an etiquette?'

She ribbed him with her elbow. 'Cheeky.'

'Well, I could have done without witnessing that episode.'

'Worried about me?' She shouldn't have asked that. It was too personal, too suggestive and everything she'd told him off for being the previous night.

He wet his lips, his blue eyes burning into hers. 'Would it be OK to say I was?'

She couldn't speak, her throat had closed on a swell of heat that ran from her pelvis all the way to her chest. She was hot, bothered, and none of it was down to the sun. Definitely time to change the subject.

She looked away, back to the sea. 'You up for doing something else today?'

'What did you have in mind?'

Her eyes flew back to his, a betraying thrill running through her.

Why did she have to read anything inappropriate in that? Because truth was, she flirted, she was a natural flirt, if she fancied a guy there was nothing stopping her, and having to put the reins on it with Todd was proving trickier by the day.

'Do you like pineapple?'

His eyes narrowed, his lips primed to laugh. 'Not the question I was expecting, but yes as it happens.'

'Did you see—'

She was interrupted by his phone ringing. 'Sorry.' He checked his watch as he pulled it out of his pocket. 'I just need to get this.'

He turned and walked away a few steps, his focus on the call, which gave Malie the opportunity to study him unobserved. Although what she should have been doing was calming down.

'Hey, Malie, juice is up!'

Saved by her mates.

She turned and smiled. 'Thanks.'

They dropped down into the sand and she joined them, supping at the sweet, cold liquid and getting rid of the lingering salt from the sea. She looked to Todd to see him heading back over, his fingers tapping away at the screen. His eyes lifted to hers, his smile instant and making her belly flutter.

'Sorry about that.'

'Work?' she asked, then felt awkward that she'd said it. What business was it of hers who he was speaking to?

'Yeah,' he said easily, making her feel better. 'No rest for the wicked.'

He dropped down next to her and she eyed him – he was with her, but he wasn't, and she felt the call hanging over him. 'Do you ever take a day off? From work *and* the charity?'

'Not really, it's the curse of being successful.'

She nodded and sipped at her drink. 'Surely being successful means you employ people you trust enough to take care of things for you.'

'I guess. But I like to keep busy, you know.'

She could take a guess at the reason why and wondered if he'd *known* she'd understand. She hated the quiet because it allowed for too much thinking, too much dwelling on all she'd lost and her broken family. She'd take a guess at him being the same. But at least she took time out to surf, for herself, no one else.

'It's not good for you,' she said gently. 'To be constantly busy all the time.'

He made a non-committal sound in his throat and his phone pinged. He was straight on it.

She eyed the phone in his hand and wondered what it would take to separate it from him. Just for a day.

'You want some POG?' She offered him her drink.

'Some what?'

She grinned, happy to have his attention. 'Passion fruit, orange, and guava juice.'

He pocketed his phone. 'So that's what it was, I admit I didn't ask, it was *just* juice.'

'Well, this *just* juice is a fave here. You should try it again, now you know what's in it.'

His lips lifted to one side, his eyes sparkling. 'If you insist…'

'I do.' She offered it out to him again and watched as he took it. It shouldn't feel intimate, it shouldn't be provocative… but watching his mouth wrap around her straw, the straw that had been in *her* mouth, felt as sensual as a kiss upon her lips.

'So pineapple…' she forced out, finding her voice '…yeah?'

He nodded.

'I'll get the guys to take my stuff back with them, if you're happy to give me a ride.'

He choked on his drink and covered his mouth as he gulped it back. 'Absolutely.'

She didn't want to think over the cause of his splutter, her body had already raced ahead and done so, the swirling warmth in her lower belly knowing exactly what kind of ride they both had in mind.

And it wasn't happening. Ever.

But even her mental pep talk sounded weak. Her ability to resist him was weakening the more time she spent in his company, the more she felt for him – for the boy he was and the man he had become.

Even her reasoning for backing off was starting to get hazy now that they were away from the surf school and the kids and her responsibilities. When she was high on the waves and – she eyed Todd in all his outsider glory – *him*.

CHAPTER NINE

'NICE WHEELS.'

She gestured to the Mustang and the wild glint in her eye told him he'd chosen well.

'Thought you'd appreciate it.'

He distracted himself by pulling open the door and sliding in to get the engine running. He needed to stop looking at her, but it was proving impossible.

She'd left him briefly to chuck on some clothes and grab her bag. But those clothes were barely covering more than her bikini had. Her green vest top hung loose above her midriff, the teasing straps of the multi-coloured bikini she still wore were tied in a bow at the base of her neck, which he could now make out as she'd scraped her hair up into a mass of curls high on her head. As for the shorts... the washed-out denim ended so high the cheeks of her bum peeked through and her legs appeared even longer in all their bronzed glory.

'Are you saying you had this planned all along?' She walked around the front of the car, her eyes finding his through the windscreen, her teasing smile making his heart pound harder.

OK, just get the roof down and drive. Concentrate. Road, not her.

Anything to ease the heated rush that seemed to be a constant companion in her presence.

'I wouldn't say planned,' he said once the roof was down, 'hoped, more like.'

She tossed her canvas bag onto the back seat and climbed in – he had to pull his eyes away from her legs and shook his head with a laugh.

'What?' He could hear the mix of curiosity and confusion in her voice; did she have no idea the effect she was having over him?

He gave her a quick glance, his grin lopsided as he worked out how to phrase it without freaking her out. She wanted them to go about as what? Friends, acquaintances, nothing more. And he did too.

But she wasn't making it easy for him and admitting it wouldn't help, he didn't want to risk ruining whatever this was. A day out. Some fun.

'Absolutely nothing.'

She eyed him, her lips pursed.

'It's *nothing*.' He shook his head, his grin widening. 'Now, are we going to do something with pineapples or are we going to sit here and give each other the eye?'

Now she laughed. 'Pineapples, definitely.'

'Which way?'

'Back the way you came. Did you see the signs for the Dole Plantation?'

Did he? He couldn't recall. He'd been too preoccupied with seeing her. Something else he was struggling to accept, let alone admit. 'Not that I can remember.'

He felt rather than saw her roll her eyes. 'Pay attention, much?'

To you, hell, yeah.

He swung the car around and caught sight of her friends loading up their pick-up trucks. 'You sure you want to bail on your mates?'

'As much as I love them, it can get a bit much being the only female at times. There's only so much eyeing up the babes on the beach that I can handle.'

He laughed. 'I'd noticed they were all male.'

'Did you now?' she said it suspiciously, like she was trying to assess whether he was jealous. It may have crossed his mind once or twice whether they were all purely platonic friends. How could it not when they looked like they did, and she looked like she did, *and* they shared the same talent?

He avoided giving her an answer. 'They seem like a nice group.'

'They're great, always up for a laugh and they love to shred the gnar just as much as me.'

'Shred the *gnar*?'

'You know, tear it up, Go Big or Go Home, that's what we live by.' Her face flushed with excitement as she added, 'We actually had some triple overheads last week, it was epic! The bigger the waves, the fewer surfers in the line-up and that means more fun for us.'

'Greater the risk, the bigger the adrenalin hit?'

She gave him a daredevil grin. 'Too right.'

He almost mentioned her parents, they were the reason she'd invited him along today after all. To show him that risk first-hand and let him decide if having seen it for himself he still disagreed with their stance. But he couldn't do it. He was too afraid of tainting the moment and spoiling her happiness. He took a less contentious angle instead. 'Not many women out there, I guess.'

She shrugged. 'It's just a fact, but I don't see why I should hold myself back based on my gender. If a guy can do it, I sure as hell can.'

He admired her determination and could read the defiance in her tone, knew it had to stem from battling sexism in the sport over the years.

'Sorry, I don't mean to sound bitter; you'd think in the twenty-first century we wouldn't have to face off against sexist jerks who can't stand to have a woman do as well, or heaven forbid, better than they can.'

'Speaking of being better, I'm kind of surprised that you're not taking part in the Queen of the Pipe tournament coming up.'

'How did you…?'

'EJ mentioned it, said you'd be a dead cert to claim the title.'

The mood in the car shifted as though the sun had gone behind a cloud. He glanced across at her but she was looking away, her hands twisting in her lap, making him worry.

'Malie?'

Her lashes fluttered and she looked back at him, her smile not quite reaching the green of her eyes. 'EJ should keep his mouth shut.'

'I think it was meant as a compliment.'

She looked away again. 'Yeah, well, they know I'm not going to do it so they should just drop it.'

He wanted to ask why, wanted to press, but there was something so sad in her demeanour that not even her smile could reassure him enough to go there.

'At least they're not sexist about your skills.'

'No, that's true.'

'I have to say, though, I think you're all slightly insane.' He grinned as he said it, relieved to see her smile turning real.

'Insane?'

'Yes, you guys can keep your triple overheads, in fact, you can keep any kind of overheads, I'm quite happy on the baby waves.'

She laughed. 'I think you'd nail daddy size with a bit of practice, you were pretty awesome yesterday... in fact so awesome, I'm actually beginning to think you were telling me a porky and that you have been on a board before.'

'Oh, I've been on a board, just not the surf variety.'

'Ah, snowboarding?'

'Nope. Skate.' He looked to her and caught her raised brow, her choked laugh. 'What?'

She shook her head, her eyes dancing. 'I figured with your entrepreneurial lifestyle, snowboarding would fit, but skateboard-ing...?' She laughed openly now. 'I just can't see it.'

He laughed too, but only at the idea she conjured up. Of him. Now. On a skateboard. Never. 'Call it a wasted youth, I've not been on one in almost twenty years.'

'It sure came back to you on the water.'

'Some skills you never quite lose, I guess.'

'You must have been good. What was it? Stunt parks at the weekend? Racing down the streets with your mates?'

He scoffed. 'I wish. It was work. Fun too at times, but mostly work.'

'Right, rewind, what kind of work involves the use of a skate-board?'

'Running errands, delivering parcels, being a paperboy... whatever I could get and handle with my board. I was too young to drive.'

'On a *skateboard*? I get the whole bicycle thing but...'

'A skateboard could travel with me, back and forth between foster homes, a bike wasn't so easy to transport, plus they'd only get nicked. At least I could keep the skateboard with me at all times.'

'*Wow* – how old were you?'

'I don't know, eight, maybe a little older. It got me out of the house too, and who could argue if I was bringing money in? I had a nice little enterprise running by the time I could drive and managed to buy my first car. It was a clapped-out banger, but I paid for it outright. There weren't many in our neighbourhood who could claim the same.'

'And the businessman was born.'

She said it jokingly, but he could hear the open admiration in her tone. He didn't have many nice memories from that time but what he *had* gained was a determination to succeed.

'Something like that.'

'I'm impressed. I can't think of many children who would have skateboarded their way around the streets to earn their pocket money. Well, save for one guy, Finn, he'd have been right out there with you.'

'Finn?'

'He worked with Zoe at our local Crab Shack when we were teenagers, a walking advert he was, attracting all the local girls to spend money there, much like you—'

She cut herself off short, her eyes snapping away.

'Much like me...?'

'Na-ah, I wasn't saying anything.'

'You sure? Sounded to me like you were about to pay me a compliment.'

'Maybe.' Her shoulders eased as she looked back to him and he felt his body warm over the admission. 'OK, I was, but not *just* because of your looks, what I was trying to say is that I'm impressed since most kids I knew would have freaked at a paper run on a bike.'

'Well, I can't say it was fun in winter but…' He shrugged. He'd done what he'd had to. He'd craved freedom, control over his own life, and knew to gain it he needed to make himself financially independent. For all she may have joked, he knew his upbringing was the reason he was the man he was now, a man beholden to no one with more money than he knew what to do with. But that's why he was giving back too, trying to help people like he'd once been, to inspire them into wanting more and taking control of their dreams.

He felt her eyes still on him and he looked to her. 'What?'

She shook her head, a smile slow to form.

'What?'

'I wish my friends could meet you, they'd never believe me.'

'Haven't I already met your friends?'

'No, I mean my friends from Hawke's Cove.'

'What wouldn't they believe?'

'That a man that looks like you, talks like you—'

'Don't be going all *Jungle Book* on me.'

She laughed. 'You had time to read when you were younger with all that running around?'

'I watched movies occasionally, it wasn't all work.'

She was quiet for a moment and he could practically feel the cogs turning in her brain.

'Well, if you have some time next week, my friend Zoe is visiting. She's stopping off on her way to another resort somewhere, not that I can remember where, she travels so much with work.'

'What does she do?'

'She's a travel writer, she gets to stay in loads of fancy-schmancy places reviewing them for accessibility.'

'Has she visited you before?'

'No, none of my friends from the Cove have, but Zoe coming out...' her voice had turned soft, wistful, 'it'll be amazing.'

He wondered at the look in her eye, the tone to her voice. 'What do you have planned?'

She took a long breath, 'We're going to surf... it'll be her first time back on a board since... well, you know.' She turned to face the window; her eyes unseeing on the passing world. 'Zoe was my surfer pal, after Koa, she helped fill that void, she was my sanity, my partner on the waves, and after the accident... well, it wasn't possible anymore.'

He could hear the weight of it in her voice. 'You shouldn't feel guilty, you know.'

She gave him a sharp look. 'I didn't say...'

'You didn't have to, it was the way you described the accident to me, how you compared yours and Lils' injuries to those of V and Zoe, how you look when you talk about it.'

Her lips quirked a little. 'Well, I don't need to worry about V anymore, she has her man who loves her regardless, just as he ought to.' She gave a soft sigh. 'They got engaged at Christmas and it was so perfect, so lovely, and they're happy, really happy.'

He couldn't help wondering from her dreamlike tone whether for all she acted like she didn't want that for herself, deep down it was there, a need she couldn't completely quash. He shook off the thought, he had no business probing there, and turned his mind to Zoe's visit instead.

'And Zoe, getting her on a board again, surely that will show you it doesn't matter what has gone before, that it's the future you should be focusing on.'

He could feel her eyes on him, feel his words sinking in.

'It'll be nice to share the waves again with her, for sure.'

'And you can let go of the guilt.'

'I—'

She was cut off by the in-car system ringing. He scanned the screen and cut the call. He didn't want work to interfere with this. He could sense a potential turnaround for her, if he could just keep her talking about it, get her to acknowledge that the guilt should no longer be a burden, then what a difference it would make.

'What were you—'

It started up again, cutting off his question.

'They're persistent,' Malie commented, looking at the caller ID. 'Who's Rachel Mann?'

'She heads up my Asian operations.'

Her eyes widened as she pulled a downturned smile and nodded. He didn't know whether she was secretly laughing or impressed.

He was going to have to take the call, Rachel wouldn't call again unless it was urgent.

'Do you mind if I get it?'

She shook her head and raised her hands. 'Not at all.'

He flicked the call to answer. 'What's up, Rachel?'

'Good lord, where are you, Todd? It sounds like you're in a wind tunnel.'

'I'm driving with the roof down.'

'Really? How nice! Well, in that case, I'll keep it brief...' He nodded, even though she couldn't see him, and sneaked a look at

Malie. She was watching the world go by, her hair blowing back off her face, her skin glowing from the morning's exertions in the sea. Did she ever not have that glow? Would she look the same in London, miles away from the ocean, with grey skies overhead and rain beating down? What would it be like to show her where he lived, to show her his HQ and take her out to dinner? To wine and dine—

'Todd?'

Malie turned to look at him as his name came through the speaker and he realized Rachel was waiting on him to say something. 'Sorry, Rach, say again?'

He put his effort into the call this time, so much so that Malie had to tap his leg to get his attention to take the next left turn. The fleeting contact sent a shock-like current along his thigh, that had him hitting the indicator far more aggressively than it needed and he swallowed before he could nod to her and respond to Rachel.

Smooth, real smooth, Todd.

Malie did the same again minutes later, a light brush of her fingers and a nod to the exit. He started to hope for more turns, but he was out of luck. Ten minutes later, he'd finished with Rachel, called his PA to set some reminders for him to action when he got back to the house, and Malie was telling him to turn into what he could only describe as Hell. On. Earth.

'Here?'

'Yup.'

He eyed her but did as she asked, pulling into a car park as crowded as the Underground in rush hour. Probably not helped by the three buses full of tourists just offloading and meandering around the car park like lost sheep. 'What is it about being a tourist that means you lose all common sense?'

'Hey, easy, tiger, they're just taking in the beauty.'

'The beauty?' He narrowly missed a woman stepping into the road, her phone outstretched before her as she sought the best selfie. 'I can't see anything but people right now. You sure you meant to come here?'

'Believe me, when you get your mouth around a whip, you'll be begging me to come back again.'

He gave a disbelieving chuckle as he swung the car into an empty space. He'd never been so glad to be stationary for fear of running someone over.

He looked across at her as he cut the engine. 'A whip?'

'A Dole Whip to be precise, pineapple ice cream heaven…' She'd gone all dreamy-eyed and licked her lips…

OK, definitely time to get out of the car and get moving. He opened his door, realizing even as he did that if she did that again, with the actual whip, he wasn't so sure he'd fare any better, if he could cope at all. 'We best get moving else there'll be nothing left by the time these lot get served.'

She laughed. 'Do you always do everything at a million miles an hour?'

'I'd say that was more your way of living.' He stepped out of the car, not bothering to put up the roof.

'Only when I'm on the waves… things like this, you just need to chill out and go with the flow.'

'Go with the flow?'

'Something tells me you haven't queued for anything in a while.'

'No.' It was the truth. 'You want me to put your bag in the boot?'

She reached into the back and picked it up, swinging it over her shoulder. 'Nah it's OK, I'll keep it with me, but you probably want to put the roof up else these seats will be toasty warm when we get back.'

She had a point so he ducked back in and set the engine going, the roof next. His phone started to ring through the speakers, and he checked the display before cutting the call.

'You're a man in demand, Todd Masters.'

He shook his head at her teasing tone and locked the roof into place before joining her in the car park.

'Ready to tickle your taste buds?'

He eyed the masses and gave her a wary, 'So long as you know what you're doing...'

'It's a historic landmark visit and a culinary delight in one. What more could you want?'

Fine dining for two on a deserted beach, just him and Malie, that would be perfect... and again, not the answer she would want to hear, or one he should want to give.

'Not a lot, apparently.'

She grinned and surprised him by lacing her fingers through his to pull him along. He eyed their entwined hands as he fell into step behind her and suddenly he was willing to take any amount of queuing, crushing, tourist-trap-hell-ing.

It was a bad, bad sign... only it didn't feel bad.

★ ★ ★

'Right, close your eyes.'

Malie grinned up at him, her pot with its swirling, whirling yellow creaminess poised mid-air in one hand, her spoon in the other.

'Close my eyes…?' Todd looked from the ice cream to her, his hands deep inside his pockets. 'Why?'

'Because it'll taste even better – I promise.'

His eyes flitted over the swarm of tourists surrounding them. 'Are you crazy?'

'No, I just want to make your first time the best.'

Laughter sparkled in his gaze, his closed-mouth grin trapping the sound inside. 'You seriously are crazy.'

She shrugged. 'And you need to trust people more.'

He cocked his head to the side, frowning slightly. Had her choice of words hit a chord? But then his expression lifted, and he was straightening up, rounding his shoulders.

'OK.' He gave a nod. 'Ready.'

He closed his eyes, his lashes fanning his cheeks and Malie was transported back to that first night on the beach when she'd been struck still by his appeal. She felt it even more now, with all that she knew of him and his Good Samaritan act. Only it wasn't an act, it was all him.

Could he be any more perfect for her? Was she a fool to keep putting distance between them? What if it didn't jeopardize her work at the surf school at all? What if she could find happiness without guilt, without fear—

'Err, Malie, I'm starting to feel a little foolish.'

She refocused on his face, his eyes still obediently closed, adorably so, and gave a soft laugh. 'You're too impatient.'

'We just queued half an hour for this thing, I'm practically saint-like.'

She shook her head, her body warming through as she scooped up a generous portion and licked her own lips.

'Open up,' she commanded, her eyes lifting to watch his lips dutifully part and the warmth combusted, an excited ripple swelling into a throbbing ache low in her belly. She wanted to kiss him, so much she had to hold herself rigid, forcing her fingers to lift instead and slip the spoon inside his mouth, watching as he closed his lips around it.

Slowly she pulled it away clean, his low hum filling her ears, the sight of his perfectly kissable mouth moving it around inside, the gentle bob of his clean-shaven throat as he swallowed it down... oh, God, she was in heaven just watching.

'Nice?' It came out high-pitched, her elevated state shining through and she scooped up another healthy spoonful, stuffing it in her own mouth and chilling her body down before he could open his eyes and see it all.

'Delicious.' His lashes lifted, his eyes locked with hers, soft and lazy. 'You're right, that is heaven.'

Her lips parted on a nod, her eyes wide, her brain still screaming: *You can't kiss him. Not after everything you've said, your good intentions. You're friend-zoned for good reason.*

Someone knocked her bag behind her as they brushed past and she turned with them, feeling Todd's arm snake around her middle to bring her closer. *Oh, God.* She could smell his cologne, the heat of his arm against her bare midriff, his breath caressing her hair.

'What do you say we find somewhere to sit with this before we get run over?'

'I have a better idea...' No way could she sit still without doing something stupid. 'Fancy getting lost with me?'

'Lost?'

'Yup,' she blurted, eager to enact her plan. 'The world's biggest maze is here, or at least it used to be the biggest, it's probably not anymore, but still...'

He was about to answer when his phone piped up. He gave a grimace and released her to reach in his pocket and take it out. She eyed the device and did a mental recap of the number of calls he'd taken already and the likelihood of it continuing. He cut the call and looked back to her. 'Let's do it.'

'On one condition...'

He chuckled. 'OK.'

'Take this off me a sec...' She gave him the ice cream to hold and then before she could chicken out, she held his eye and slid her hand inside his pocket. She didn't miss how his entire body tensed and the way his eyes flared, his breath caught, but nothing would deter her from this. She located the offending device and pulled it out. 'This, goes off...'

His brow creased but she held her ground, her finger hovering over the off button.

'You are the boss, right?'

He nodded.

'Well, you need to trust your employees to survive without you. The world won't end if you turn this off and relax, just for a few hours.'

His lip quirked to one side. 'A few hours, that's how long you're planning on getting us lost for?'

'Maybe...'

He laughed. 'OK, deal, turn it off.'

She felt her entire body lift, happiness at his agreement making her almost dizzy. She turned the phone off and looked back up at him. 'A few hours won't cut it, though, Todd, you need to learn to take holidays. Actual, real chill-the-hell-out time.'

'Like you do?'

She could read the scepticism in his tone. 'What do you mean?'

'I saw the schedule at the surf school, by my reckoning you work almost seven days a week.'

'That's different.'

'Is it?'

'Yes, I love my job, I get to spend it in the sea, doing what I adore and passing that love on to others.'

'I love what I do too.'

'In an office, four walls, indoors?' She shook her head and slid the phone back into his pocket, his arm eased around her again and this time she was convinced it had nothing to do with being run over and everything to do with bringing them close again.

She took the ice cream back off him and scooped some up. 'I just can't imagine it.'

'It's not all bad, believe me. Take now, for example, I'm in Hawaii with my charity work and—'

'And your phone hasn't stopped?' She stared up at him, offering him the spoonful. 'No, you won't convince me.'

'Right this second...' He bowed to slip his mouth around the scoop, cleaning it off with a satisfied swallow that had her entire being thrumming afresh, the desire to kiss him almost painful. 'This is definitely not work.'

His voice was thick, laced with the same need. Nerves flared inside her as her brain raced with all the reasons she'd said they couldn't go down this road but struggling to hang on to a single one.

She looked down at the pot in her hand, the creamy yellow sweetness and breathed in his heady scent. 'So I've taken you captive for a few hours?'

He swallowed again, only this time there was no ice cream, only the tension building exponentially between them. 'I suppose you have.'

She dared a quick look up and his arm flexed around her. 'Malie?'

It was breathless, it was asking, demanding... and she wanted to say yes, to hell with all sensibility... but then what?

'Come on, let's go get lost.' She moved away from him before she could reconsider. 'We have a maze to conquer and judging by your workload, not long to do it.'

'I have a counter condition.'

She turned to look at him. 'You do?'

He nodded, his eyes probing hers in such a way that her breath hitched.

'You forget work too, for the next few hours, the day even, the school doesn't exist and we're just two people having fun together.'

'Two people?'

He nodded again and reached out, pulling her traitorous body back towards him. 'There's no working relationship between us, nothing to jeopardize with whatever happens today; we're just going to go with the flow, just like you said.'

'I did, didn't I?' And the flow was determined to pull them closer together, her words coming out like a whisper as she met his eye and the people milling around them fell away, the pot in her hand forgotten as she let her chest brush against him.

His eyes fell to her lips. 'Do we have a deal?'

'Yes,' she breathed, her lashes fluttering closed, ready, waiting, anticipating… and *nothing*, just a rush of air as he suddenly released her. *What?*

'Lead the way.'

She opened her eyes and he was smiling at her, his eyes ablaze with the heat she'd read in every word he'd spoken, every flex of his arm around her. He must have read the question in her eyes, her prolonged silence, and he dipped his head to say, 'We have an audience.'

He dropped his gaze low and to the left and she followed his direction to see two kids, probably no older than five, staring up at them, wide-eyed, their tongues frozen mid-lick to their ice creams. Her cheeks flushed and she tried to smile. It took a good second for them to realize they'd been caught gawping and they looked at one another, burst out laughing, and legged it after a woman paying at the ice cream stand.

'Oh, God, do you think we could be fined for indecent behaviour in a public place?'

'I don't know, that depends, just how far are you willing to go?'

She punched him gently in the chest. 'Don't push it, dude, deal or no deal?'

He laughed hard. 'I still find it hilarious that you call me *dude*, I've never been called that in my life.'

'Well, that's another first for you to log. Let's see how many others we can squeeze into our day.'

'Oh, so it's a day now?'

'You suggested it first.'

'So I did…'

She shook her head laughing and again her hand found its way back into his, just like it had in the car park. She reminded herself that they had an agreement; today they were going with the flow, there was nothing serious to worry about, nothing to jeopardize.

So why the persistent niggle at the back of her mind? The weird sense of... fear... guilt.

Because she was starting to have real fun, she was starting to care.

She closed her eyes briefly, the acknowledgement there even as she tried to bury it. It was all wrapped up in the same pain, the same worry. She couldn't compete in big wave competitions, because she couldn't bring herself to follow in her brother's footsteps. She couldn't find true happiness, the kind that comes from having another to share your life with, to love and be loved, without feeling the guilt of it weighing down on her. Of experiencing what Koa never got to. She couldn't allow herself to get caught up in another person only to have life take it all away.

But for a day, to only let go for a day, you could?

No promises, no future, just a day... a mere twelve hours... no risk, no guilt...

She looked back at Todd and forced away the inner monologue. Yes, for a day, she would just *be...*

CHAPTER TEN

'GOTCHA,' MALIE DECLARED AS one of the secret stations within the maze came into view, her step picking up as she raced towards it and then she turned to him, her green eyes bright as she bobbed excitedly on her heels. 'Your turn!'

He laughed. 'You're a big kid.'

'And?' She pouted up at him, offering out the pencil and the hunt sheet. Did she know how much he wanted to draw that bottom lip into his mouth? Seeing it all glossy and so close, he could almost taste it.

'Down, boy. Stencil!'

Yes, she knew, and she was teasing him every inch of the way. From the second they'd made their deal, it felt like a weight had lifted, a feeling of freedom, a freedom to feel and to act on it. Because it was temporary. A short reprieve from the rules they lived by, the rules that safeguarded their emotions and kept them from being torn apart. He just needed to keep in mind it was temporary and do as he promised, go with the flow.

He shook his head and took the items from her, bending to slot the sheet under the stencil and dutifully coloured it in.

He offered them out to her. 'Happy?'

'Much!' She took them from him and off she went again, giving him a teasing view of her rear as her hips sashayed through the greenery.

'You coming?' she called back without looking.

He shook his head, trying to dispel the hold she had over him but it was no use, every second they were together it ramped up another notch.

She turned and eyed him over her shoulder. 'Come on, slow-coach, else we really will be stuck in here for ever.'

For ever sounded perfect right about now and the realization snapped some sense into him. He started after her. 'I blame the pineapple whip, the taste sensation has gone to my head.'

She paused to rake her eyes over him. 'You know, it really has,' her gaze reached the tip of his head, 'your hair has gone all floppy.'

'My...' He frowned and raised a hand to his hair, felt the usual groomed affair soften beneath his fingers.

She reached out and brushed his hand away. 'For the record, I like it this way – it's more laidback, softer...'

'*Softer*? I'm not sure I like the sound of that.'

'You should...' She wet her lips and raised herself up on tiptoes, her arms hooking around his neck as her eyes searched his. 'It's quite irresistible.'

Irresistible. He couldn't respond, couldn't move, he was too scared of breaking the connection and hooked on what she might do next. They were so close, almost nose to nose, her coconut scent wafting up to him and he wanted to close his eyes, breathe her in, and didn't dare do either.

'It's sexy,' her lips brushed tantalizingly against his, 'I like it... a lot.'

And then she kissed him, actually kissed him, gentle, coaxing and breaking his restraint in two. He tucked his thumbs into the belt loops on her shorts and pulled her up against him, hard. The need, so painfully acute, driving him to taste her, to feel her top to toe, her pliable warmth as she leaned into him, her lips as they moved with his. It was about all he could do not to press her back into the hedge, to hell with any unsuspecting audience, underage or not.

She dropped back, her teeth pulling at his bottom lip, her arms still around his neck as she looked up at him.

'Definitely sexy,' she said softly.

'I'll take it.' His voice was tight, his body too. 'Especially if it earns me a kiss like that.'

She smiled, slow and sultry. 'We should get this maze over with, I'm hungry.'

He wanted to ask what kind of hungry, was it the same kind that had fire burning through his veins now? But he was scared of spooking her, hell, he was scared of spooking himself too.

'How many stations to go?'

She raised one arm to eye the sheet over his shoulder. 'Two.'

The sound of a family approaching, the giggle of a child and the crunch of a pushchair over the soil reached them and he released her.

'Best make it quick, then.'

She smiled and pressed a kiss to his cheek before spinning around and marching on. This time he was hot on her tail, very, very attentive and helpful. Less delay meant less risk of them rethinking the unspoken promise to pick that kiss up again.

He could already foresee his phone staying off for the rest of the day and he couldn't deny how liberating it was not to feel weighed down by it; ruled by it, even. Although perhaps a quick message to his PA to field everything wouldn't go amiss.

'Wait up a sec, Malie.'

She paused, her frown so utterly kissable. 'Thought we were in a rush?'

'We are, I'm just making my day off official.'

'You are?' Her eyes were alive with surprise as she walked back to him and he pulled out his phone, turning it on.

'I am.'

She made an awkward sound in her throat. 'Now probably isn't the time to tell you I have two hours of lessons later this afternoon.'

His fingers stilled on the screen, his eyes lifting to hers. 'You do? But it's Sunday.'

'You ought to tell yourself that sometimes.'

'Well, I'm telling us both now.'

She gave him an awkward smile. 'And as you so rightly pointed out, I don't really have days off.'

'But you didn't say anything?'

'Well, I didn't think you were serious about a whole day… I figured you were getting carried away in the moment.'

'I don't do *getting carried away*.'

'No?' She grinned up at him.

'No.'

'Not even with me?'

The flirtatious comment struck through the very heart of him and he knew the answer as sure as he could identify the disappointment sinking heavily in his gut at the imminent end to their day.

'You're trouble, Malie Pukui.'

'Now you sound like my friends back home.'

'They sound very wise, you should listen to them.'

'*Oi.*'

She pushed him gently in the chest, and the fleeting contact made him want to pull her back against him; he opted to pull a rogue branch from her hair instead. It had adorned her curls for the last hour and provided a focal point when he'd needed the diversion from her invigorating gaze, her wide smile, her incredible body and the sneak peek he kept getting of her bikini top or her bum cheeks as she leaned forward to shade in a stencil.

'How about I make it up to you?' she purred, the flirtatious lilt to her voice spurring his impulsive response to ask exactly what she had in mind and provide a few satisfying suggestions himself. Dangerous territory.

He opted for the safer, 'I'm listening.'

'We finish the maze, grab a quick lunch – they do the most amazing barbecued corn here...'

'And?'

'*And* after work, this eve...' she cocked her head to the side as she considered him, her fingers curling into the top button of his shirt and making his body throb in its heightened state, 'we could have dinner together.'

Before he could answer her, her eyes flared and she blurted, 'But not out-out.'

'Not out-out?' he repeated, confused by her startled clarification.

'Well, in case you haven't worked it out already,' she said, 'everyone knows everyone in Nani Kumu and I don't want people seeing us together and getting the wrong idea.'

'Because this is a twelve-hour thing?'

'Yes, precisely.'

'It didn't bother you when we danced together.'

'Like you said, people would see it as you taking an active role in the evening, us dining out together won't be so easily explained away.'

'Fair point. So, my place or yours?'

She seemed to consider the question and then did a double-take. 'Yours, definitely yours!'

He laughed. 'Quite adamant about that?'

'You haven't tasted my cooking…'

'Well, in that case my place it is.'

'I assume your… people, at the house…'

'You mean the staff?'

'Yes, although that just sounds weird… I assume they're quite discreet.'

'Of course, although if anyone asks, we can just say you're there to discuss plans for the kids.'

She nodded slowly. 'For the work we're pretending to know nothing about for today only.'

'Yes.'

She suppressed what looked like an excited grin. 'This is getting quite elaborate, don't you think?'

'Our secret, no-work, twelve-hour bubble?'

She hummed her agreement.

'All the best things in life require intricate planning.'

'The best things?' she practically cooed. 'Now for that, Todd Masters, you've earned another kiss.'

His lips were on hers before she could even finish, and it was everything and not enough at once. He wished away the people around them, their work, their lives, their reality.

All he wanted in that moment was her. And he'd never wanted anything as much as he wanted this. It should have scared him, but he was too wrapped up in the taste of her, the feel of her, of what they shared to care…

Twelve hours, a few weeks, in that moment he would take whatever she was willing to give to feel like this for longer.

★★★

Watching someone cook was quite fascinating, especially when they were as skilled as Todd. Malie was most definitely her mother when it came to culinary skill. Useless. So it made it particularly captivating to watch him work, she just had to keep reminding herself not to drool…

'Aside from struggling to find stuff, you're quite the talented chef,' she remarked as she sat on a bar stool at the marble-topped centre island, her chin resting in her hand.

He looked up briefly from the chopping board, all the vegetables neatly arranged to one side of it, the bowls with the sliced stuff arranged in front. 'I haven't cooked anything yet.'

She smiled and gestured to the bowls. 'You've sliced those veggies so thinly, I'd have lost a nail at the very least.'

He laughed as he continued. 'There are definitely no surprise nails in this.'

She lifted her wine glass and sipped at the cooling white liquid, her eyes hooked on him. Who'd have thought watching someone cook could be sexy? Well, not just anyone, of course, she'd watched Lils cook plenty of times and never been as captivated as this. *Sorry, Lils.*

He wore a plain black T-shirt and beige trousers tonight, the fabric doing the most amazing things to his behind as he navigated around the kitchen, bending into cupboards, lifting to bring things down. His hair was soft, no sign of his usual slicked-back look and he'd obviously showered – she had smelled his fresh cologne as she'd passed him at the front door, could still catch hints of it now. Her belly fluttered up with a mixture of nerves, want, and hunger, definitely hunger. And not for food… just as it hadn't been when they'd eaten their corn at the plantation. Especially when he'd licked his fingers and lips clean every few minutes. *Heaven.*

She took another swig of wine. 'So, where did you learn to cook?'

He looked to her briefly, a small smile playing about his lips. 'Would you believe I did quite well in Home Economics at school? That and Maths. Figured they were decent life skills – the rest…' he shrugged, 'I didn't have time for it.'

'Too busy working?'

'Pretty much. You gotta eat, right? And any shrewd business-man, teen or otherwise, needs to get their figures right.'

'You cooked a lot for yourself as a kid then?'

He didn't look up, but she could see the frown lines that bracketed his mouth, saw his Adam's apple bob.

'When I was back with Dad, I did… he was either too drunk or too despondent to care. I cooked the basics, then tried to jazz it up – Chinese, Indian, Italian, you name it, I tried it.'

He brushed off his hands and turned his attention to the hob. Pulling out a wok, he drizzled in some oil and lit the gas beneath it.

'He just didn't want to know.' He still didn't look back at her and she wondered what she would see if he did. Was he trying to hide it from her? Or was he reliving it?

'Then a friend of his from the local pub was diagnosed with cancer. I was twenty-five by then, my business was thriving and taking up most of my time. But Dad was there for his friend until the end – I think it was the sharp shock he needed to wake up to the waste he was making of his own life. His friend had a family – a wife, two kids – and then he was gone.'

'It must have been hard for your dad to witness.'

'It was.' He didn't stop cooking as he spoke and she was happy to listen, even though her heart ached for him. 'He called me the day after the funeral, begging my forgiveness, told me he was getting help, that he was sorting himself out and that he wanted to be a better father.'

'It's sad that it took his friend passing away for him to come to you like that.'

'It was hard to accept at the time, but then I wasn't sure I believed him either. It took months to convince me he wasn't just saying it all, that it wasn't some brief remorse born out of grief for his friend and that he'd fall off the wagon again soon enough.'

'But he did it, he got through it?'

'Yes.' He filled the kettle with water and tapped it on, his eyes finding hers. 'I guess I'm more relieved than angry now. Relieved that I don't have to fear him going back to those days.'

She wanted to cross the kitchen, wrap her arms around him, it didn't matter that he wasn't that boy anymore. He was still inside him somewhere, his haunted blue gaze told her as much...

She gave him a small smile instead, and loaded it up with the emotion she could feel swirling inside of her. She wondered what he'd been like back then, had he worn his hair long or short, had his eyes been as blue, his brow as arched, as defined? She'd bet he'd had the same soul-winning grin, the same flash of confidence that would win over the old as much as the young. And as for how he'd spent his days... her heart ached for him as she appreciated how it had made him the man he was today.

'You were a pretty amazing kid.'

He gave a soft laugh. 'Not sure the authorities would have agreed with you. I had my moments.'

'Understandably.'

He moved the bowls across to the cooker and slowly started adding things to the pan.

'My father was a great cook,' she said, wanting to share too. 'And my brother...'

She surprised herself by adding the last, the gruffness to her voice betraying the depth of feeling the memory evoked. She rarely talked about Koa, the pain was always too much to bear, but it felt different with Todd. She felt like she needed to share, just as he had done with her.

'They used to spend Sundays in the kitchen together while Mum and I surfed.'

'Your mum didn't cook?' he asked, looking to her over his shoulder.

She laughed. 'Not unless you count beans on toast as cooking.'

She could feel his grin, even though she couldn't see his face now. His shoulders had eased, his movements smooth and skilled once more.

'And I'm ashamed to say I don't fare much better in the kitchen. There's something about pans and me that don't mix. I mean, have you ever tasted, let alone cleaned, burned scrambled eggs from the base of a saucepan?' She shuddered over the memory that was as recent as last week. 'It's vile and virtually impossible to get off.'

He laughed. 'I can imagine.'

They fell into an easy silence and she lost herself in watching him again, the muscles of his back rippling beneath his shirt as he tossed ingredients into the pan. The oil sizzled and popped and her mouth turned dry, her legs crossing tight over one another. Definitely not hungry for food... no matter how delicious the scent.

She tugged her dress lower. She'd opted for a simple vest style, brightly coloured and comfortable. Not overtly sexy. Yet every time he looked at her, she felt like she was in her finest lingerie, the blaze of his eyes marrying with the pulsing heat in her core. His power over her was like nothing she'd ever experienced before.

Perhaps it was just the whole forbidden thing, the fact she'd told herself she couldn't have him...

But then hadn't she agreed to forget about that for today, for tonight even?

She didn't know whether to be more scared or relieved. Could she really see herself going there with him and coming away with no regrets? Did she really think she'd be able to walk away from him and let everything return to normal, like it never even happened?

No. That was the truth of it. She couldn't. And where did that leave them now? This evening?

Stop overthinking everything, Malie.

She threw back the rest of her wine and wished away her sensibilities, her rising panic.

'Can I help at all?' She slid off the stool and walked around the island towards him; she couldn't think when he was near and she wanted her thoughts gone.

He sent her a brief look, his grin teasing. 'After what you just confessed to?'

She laughed, 'OK, but there must be something I can't burn?'

The kettle clicked off and he gestured to it. 'You can pour the boiled water over the noodles.'

She swept around him, her fingers brushing his lower back as she reached for the kettle and poured. 'Enough?'

'Perfect.'

She slotted the kettle back on its base, her fingers still resting on his back and didn't move away, his nearness having the desired effect of emptying out her mind.

She looked into the pan, smelled the aroma tangled up in the scent of him. 'Mmm, smells great.'

He turned his head towards her and their eyes locked, she parted her lips, looked at the proximity of his and knew what she wanted. 'Todd?'

He spun, pulling her up tight against him, his lips claiming hers in a kiss as demanding, as desperate as she felt inside. It was everything she'd craved from the second she'd spied him on the beach that day and there was no putting the brakes on now. No audience to interrupt or be wary of, he'd already told her everyone had been dismissed.

He walked her back into the island, the air filled with the smell of food, the sizzle of it cooking, but they were in their own world. He forked his hands through her hair, encouraged her head back as he sought to explore deeper, and she couldn't breathe. She pulled away to try and drag in air and he dipped to her neck, to the sensitive pulse point behind her ear. It was getting out of control and fast and there would be no turning back, there couldn't be…

'Malie…' it was a groan, 'what are you doing to me?'

He pinned his forehead to hers, his hands cupping her jaw as he stared down into her eyes. There was so much passion, so much emotion in his darkened gaze.

'I could ask you the same.' *And this is why you can't go there; you'd never be able to come back from it… you wouldn't…*

She caught the smell of burning in the air, the rational thought her sudden saviour. 'But I think you're about to experience my scrambled egg problem.'

He tensed, cursing under his breath as he flew to the hob and lifted the smoking pan off the heat. She was grateful for the diversion, grateful for the sudden slap of clarity. She couldn't sleep with him. Kissing him was one thing, taking the next step… *no, just no.*

She pressed her fingers to her buzzing lips and wrapped her other arm around her middle, fighting back the ache. She'd never turned down a guy she wanted before. Never had she needed to.

But Todd wasn't just a guy she wanted. He was a guy she wanted so much more from and could never have. They were practically on different stratospheres, not to mention the other reasons she never went down the relationship route. Never settled. Never got comfortable. Because that's when life would bite you on the backside. Cripple you when you least expected it… *no, just no.*

So much for a day's bravado, of being able to let go.

'All saved.' He tossed the pan and sent her a relieved grin. 'Do you want to grab the prawns from the fridge?'

'Sure.' She practically leaped at the fridge, opening the door and contemplating whether she could fit herself in there, just to chill down. She opted for taking a prolonged look through the shelves instead, moving away when she decided her nipples were suffering from the cold and not the prolonged effects of their kiss.

'I thought you were about to climb in there for a second.'

She closed the door and gave a nervous laugh. 'As if...'

As if indeed...

She gave him the prawns and turned to get the wine bottle. 'Can I top you up?'

He gestured to his glass, 'Please...' and threw the prawns into the wok, tossing the contents with the skill of a trained chef.

She poured wine into both glasses. 'Can I lay the table?'

She needed to keep busy, anything to prevent a repeat of seconds ago, or worse, a panicked escape that would make her look like she was crazy.

'It's all ready. I thought we'd eat outside if that's OK?'

'Of course.'

Fresh air would do her good. She took up her wine and savoured the chill of it running down her throat, acknowledging even as she did that maybe more wine wasn't such a great idea. Distance would be better.

She walked across the room, her gold leather sandals slapping against the marble floor and ringing too loud for her strung-out nerves. She slid open the large glass doors that led out onto the elevated stone veranda and stepped out, taking in the beauty of the view and using it to soothe her.

'It's incredible up here,' she called back.

'The view sold it to Grace, my PA.'

His PA, of course. He wouldn't have the time to hunt down places to stay for his business travels. And she already knew he never took a holiday.

She walked to the edge to take in its full glory. In the distance, either side, lofty green mountains punctuated the water, creating the stunning cove within which the house rested. Ahead the moon rippled through the water, illuminating the white sand of the beach that you could catch glimpses of through the swaying palms and the flora.

Down to her left was the pergola under which the cocktail party had been held, to her right was a long wooden table which he'd laid out for two, arranging it so that they could sit beside one another. He'd even adorned it with several lanterns that looked similar to those from the cocktail party, their flickering glow augmenting the accented lighting cleverly recessed in the ground and on the walls of the house.

Beyond the table there were sweeping stone steps that led down to a sprawling manicured garden with luxury cabanas and a curved infinity pool which glowed turquoise, the lava-rock waterfall feeding it filling the air with the sound of water and making her wish she could dive straight in.

It was a house that oozed luxury and an insight into another world, a world that the likes of Zoe would be accustomed to, but not Malie, a surfer chick on the wrong side of the tracks – or cove, as the case may be for her.

It emphasized the gulf between her and Todd, making it bigger, ever more insurmountable.

'I hope you're hungry.'

She practically jumped as she turned at the sound of his voice to see him placing two steaming plates down on the table.

'I'll just go get the bottle, take a seat.'

She took a breath, tried to calm her nerves that seemed to be fraying at the edges.

She didn't want to hurt him by putting distance between them. Not today.

But how did she tell him she couldn't keep up the pretence she'd promised?

That even a day, it turned out, was too much.

CHAPTER ELEVEN

'MMM, THIS IS DELICIOUS.' She covered her mouth with her hand as she said it and her eyes sparkled with appreciation as she looked to him.

'I'm glad you like it. It's good to know I haven't lost the knack.'

He couldn't remember the last time he'd cooked a proper meal, let alone cooked a meal for someone else, and not just anyone…

He wanted to impress her, show her he was more than just the business owner, the charity owner, and her client effectively. Not that he understood why it was important to him. It just was.

It didn't change the fact that tomorrow they would go back to how things were, the line firmly drawn in the sand. Unless… could they extend it? Mid-kiss he'd thought about it. Been convinced even that they could do just that – the next few weeks flashed through his mind, such blissful imagery with a sprinkling of work and charity commitments that he wouldn't dare drop.

But now… he didn't know. Something was wrong.

She hadn't said as much, but he could sense a definite shift in the atmosphere and couldn't work out why.

Gone was the Malie who had readily stroked his back as she'd helped out in the kitchen, the Malie who had talked about her family and joked about her lack of culinary skill, and the Malie who had returned his kisses the way she had.

It had gone from zero to one hundred in a flash. He'd forgotten all about the food cooking and his good intentions to take the evening slowly, he'd been so caught up in her and the fact that she'd reciprocated. Every urgent movement of her mouth against his, her fingers over his shirt, in his hair, neither coming up for air, proved as much.

But when he'd turned away and rescued dinner, the woman he'd looked back to hadn't been the same. A shutter had come down and it was still in place now.

Plus, she was jumpy, on edge, the slightest brush of their fingers and she was snapping her hand away, her eye contact brief, making him want to keep talking just to bring her attention back to him.

'What food did your father like to cook?'

'All sorts,' she said, looking at her plate and twirling the noodles around her fork. 'He was from here so lots of traditional Hawaiian dishes, poke and rice was a fave, but then he's just as great at a Sunday roast – his lamb is to die for.'

Her smile was bittersweet, and he could catch the sudden thickness to her voice. He didn't want to make her sad, but he did want her to open up to him. To understand her better.

'It's been a long time since I've had a Sunday roast. How are his Yorkshires?'

She pinched her thumb and index fingers together. 'The best.'

'It's a shame he didn't pass his skills on to you, then.'

She gave a soft laugh and scooped the food into her mouth, her eyes still distant but more relaxed now. She shook her head as she chewed and swallowed it down. 'That was definitely Koa's territory, he had the patience for it, whereas I just wanted to tear it up and throw it together. I'd drive Dad crazy and the kitchen would become a war zone, hence why Mum started taking me out of the house, leaving the men to enjoy it in peace.'

'Were you not envious of your brother for having that time with him?'

'Nah, it was best for everyone's sanity. And we always ended Sunday with a family surf so long as the weather wasn't too horrendous – in fact, we'd start and end most days in the sea when we could.' That bittersweet smile was back and then she gave a little laugh at whatever memory she was reliving. 'We used to have competitions too.'

She looked across at him and his throat closed over. Her eyes glistened with emotion; her beauty magnified all the more by her sorrow.

'Competitions?'

'Yeah, we'd race down to the water, all four of us, grab our little notepads and pretend to have our own surf comp, we'd do the whole panel thing, scoring each other up, announcing an overall winner.'

He smiled. 'What was the prize?'

She gave a little shrug. 'Anything from the last helping of pudding to getting out of washing up for the week.'

He held her gaze, trapped in the swirling pools of green. 'You miss them?'

'The competitions?' she teased and then her eyes were serious again. 'More than I want to admit.'

She looked back to her bowl, but he could tell she wasn't really seeing it. 'I miss how it was before... I miss the people they were, the people we all were, the times we had before Koa left us.' She lifted her gaze to the ocean. 'I'm not sure we'll ever be able to have anything close to what we had before we lost him.'

He wanted to reach for her. Pull her into him. Ease her pain. But he wasn't sure she'd welcome it, not after the change in her. He took up his wine instead, keeping his fingers busy to resist the urge.

'You should talk to them. I know you said you've tried, but having seen you out there, on the waves, it's a part of you. Asking you to give it up would be like telling you not to breathe.'

She gave him a sad smile. 'You say that even though it's dangerous?'

He laughed softly. 'I can see why they'd prefer you took up knitting, or something else equally safe.'

'I'm not sure about that – you haven't seen me with a knitting needle.'

He laughed with her now, happy that she was still able to joke.

'They loved to surf once too, maybe you just need to remind them of that?'

She shook her head, her smile disappearing. 'It was as much a part of them and they still gave it up. When Koa found out that they'd quit, he was so upset and he told them as much, but he was tired, and they just wouldn't listen.'

'Maybe it's time you tried again? Remind them that Koa would want them to surf too?'

She gave a gentle scoff. 'My gran tried a few years back and it totally ruined Christmas.'

'Your gran?'

'My mum's mum. But it just became a slanging match, them declaring me selfish, inconsiderate, insensitive – you name it, that was me – and I just shouted back, but I couldn't find the courage to say what I really thought, that they were cowards, living in fear and insisting I do the same. That... that Koa dying didn't mean we all had to stop living. I just couldn't bring myself to say it.' She shook her head, her fingers trembling as she raised them to her lips. 'Suffice it to say it didn't end well... I try to see Gran on her own when I go back, but she's still torn between interfering for my parents' sake and trying not to push me away.' She shrugged. 'It's hard.'

'That's families all over.'

She took up her wine glass and saluted him with it. 'I'll drink to that.'

He sipped at it his own, his eyes shifting to the view as he considered all that she had told him and trying to think of a way to help, some advice to give, but then what did he know about fixing family relationships; he couldn't even repair his own with his father.

He was so lost in his thoughts he was surprised to feel her hand close over his own where it rested on the table between them.

'I think you could make things better, you know,' she said it so earnestly and he was momentarily confused. 'With your father, I mean.'

He almost choked on his wine, her ability to hit on the heart of his thoughts unnerving him.

'I just mean, if you backed off a little, stopped putting the pressure on him to accept your financial help... a bit like my Gran tries to take a back seat in my relationship with my parents now.'

He shook his head. 'I'm not sure...'

'Have you thought about offering to do some DIY on the house, the two of you working together, spending time together doing it?'

His eyes widened. 'DIY?'

'Yeah, you're obviously good with your hands…' A blush crept into her cheeks as she snapped her hand away and he knew her brain had pivoted sharply into the X-rated, just as his had. 'Behave, Todd.'

'You were the one that said it.'

She wriggled in her seat and took up her glass, but in spite of her admonishment, her lips curved around the rim, her smile alive with teasing. That was better, that was more like the Malie from before.

'What I mean is, your biggest issue with the house, besides the fact that you could afford to buy him something better, seems to be the state of it. If your father is happy living there, then you should focus on making it homely again. Help do it up, get hands-on together. *And* you'd get to spend more time together, rebuild your relationship.'

He stared at her, silent as his brain processed what she was saying. Why hadn't he thought of doing that? The idea hadn't occurred to him once, but now it had been suggested, he could see so many possibilities.

'It won't happen overnight,' she said, 'but it would be a start.'

She was right. And he was long overdue a holiday, taking some time out… it wouldn't be easy, but then, wasn't it worth trying at least? Before it was too late, and the chance was gone. He frowned. The idea of Dad passing away, their relationship as it was, leaving him cold.

'I'm sorry, I don't mean to interfere…' She wet her lips, clearly nervous and misreading his reaction. 'It's just…'

'No,' he said, unable to stop his hand reaching for hers now and softly squeezing it to reassure her. 'It's a great idea.'

She looked to where his hand held hers and he felt the connection burning a path all the way inside him. He turned towards her, his knee brushing against her thigh and sending a frenzied ripple of awareness through him. He released her fingers to stroke the hair away from her face and she raised her lashes, her eyes intense as they met with his own.

He didn't ask permission, he moved slowly, his intention clear and she didn't pull back. He breathed in her scent, felt her warmth, her softness beneath his palm and felt her tremble as his lips gently moved over hers. He cradled her bottom lip, teased at it, his tongue soft and probing.

She was so still, her hands caught in her lap, but her mouth… her mouth moved with every encouraging sip that he took, her tongue soft, exploring as he slanted his head to push deeper.

He heard a whimper catch in her throat, a reciprocal groan eclipsing his own and it was like a match dropped in petrol. She came alive, her hands forking through his hair, her body turning into him. He leaned back into his seat and brought her with him, let her straddle him and take everything she wanted. She raked her nails through his hair, her legs hooked around him, her body pressing against his hardness and making him drag in a breath.

'Malie…'

'Yes, Todd,' she said between kisses, her thumbs brushing over his jaw, his cheeks, as his hands dropped to her thighs. It was intense, crazy, out of control. But not here, not like this. He wanted to take his time, he wanted their first time to be special – *the first?*

There'll be no other time.

He shot the thought down and stood, keeping her wrapped around him and headed to the doors, crossing the open-plan area, he just needed to get to the—

A shrilling ring broke through the air. He didn't recognize it but Malie did. Her head came up on a soft curse, her body rigid around him.

'It's my phone.'

'Ignore it?'

She looked down into his eyes and he could see the fight in her, and he could see when he'd lost the battle, felt her body weaken around him as she lowered her legs to the floor.

'I should get it. It could be important.'

'Won't they leave a message?'

But she was already pulling away, walking across the kitchen to the centre island and her bag that she'd left there. She pulled out her phone and checked the screen. 'It's my friend, Zoe.'

She flashed him a look, her eyes still blazing but there was a hesitancy in them now, that same hesitancy she'd had through dinner. Didn't matter that her skin was still flushed from their kiss, her lips swollen, her hair thoroughly mussed-up by his attentions. She was slipping away.

He nodded and headed to the coffee machine. He didn't normally drink caffeine so late, but he needed one now.

'Hey, Zo! What's up?'

He could feel her watching him as he stuck the pod in the machine, but he couldn't bring himself to look at her. He needed to set his body to chill and looking at her all flushed and dishevelled... his body pulsed... no, he couldn't.

'Not at all, it's fine, it's late for you, though, or early depending on which way you look at it...' She gave a strained laugh. 'No, I'm totally here for you, lay it on me...' she cursed softly, 'that's awful, just give me twenty mins and I can get myself home, we can talk properly... speak soon.'

Slowly, he turned to face her and folded his arms across his chest, leaning back on the counter. 'Friend emergency?'

Did he imagine it or did her cheeks just get redder as she nodded?

She nibbled over her lip, her eyes not quite meeting his. 'Look, I'm sorry to bail, after... after...' She fluttered a hand around her. 'I had a lovely time tonight, I had a lovely day even...'

'But?' He didn't like the tightness in his own voice, but he couldn't relax it.

'Well... our pact...'

'Is over.' He finished for her and her eyes struck with his.

'Yes...' She dragged in a breath and swept a hand over her hair. 'I have to go.'

'I know.'

She leaned from one foot to the other just as she had on the beach that first night. 'I'm sorry.'

'You have nothing to be sorry for, Malie, we agreed a day and now you have a friend emergency to tend to. I'm not going to stand in your way.' He forced a smile this time. If Zoe needed her then she had to go, that wasn't her fault, but it was the disappointment that came with the understanding that this – whatever this was – was over before it had ever really begun. 'Do you need me to get you a car?'

'No,' she gave an awkward laugh, 'I can manage the short walk.'

'OK.' He pushed away from the counter and started for the door, hearing her sandals against the tiles as she followed behind him.

He pulled open the door and stood back, far enough away that she didn't need to come too close.

'Thanks, Todd.' She paused before him, raked her teeth over her lip again and before he could second-guess her, she planted a kiss on his cheek. 'It's been fun.'

And then she was gone, leaving him in a cloud of tantalizing coconut and his head a mess of what-ifs.

★★★

'What the hell was all that about?'

Malie winced at her friend's outburst, watching as Zoe peered into the screen like she was about to climb through it and call her out on her shameful behaviour in person.

'Sorry, Zo.'

'I'm totally here for you… lay it on me… that's awful…' Zoe mimicked the deceitful flurry of words that Malie had come out with in order to escape Todd's place and she felt her cheeks burn up with guilt. 'I hadn't said anything of the sort.'

'I know, love, I just needed an out.'

Zoe frowned as she smoothed her hair behind her ear. 'Why? What's happened? Where were you?'

She shook her head, struggling to even put words to the mess that was her head, her heart, her entire life, right now.

Zoe leaned ever closer to the screen. 'Are you OK?'

'Yes… no… not really…' She dropped her head into her hands, mumbling, 'I don't know.'

'You're really starting to freak me out, Malie, so either you put words to it that I can understand, or I'm bringing an end to my Caribbean jaunt early and—'

'No!' Her head shot up, her hand palm out. 'There's no need, I'm just being silly, and you can't sack off an article just because your mate's in a tizz over a guy.'

'Oh!' A small smile teased at Zoe's lips and she leaned back, giving Malie a glimpse of the luxurious bed in which she lay, the plush-looking headboard making her friend's petite body look all the more so. 'A guy...?'

'It's not funny,' Malie said.

'I didn't say it was.'

'You're smiling.'

'I'm just curious, that's all.' Her friend cocked her head to the side, her perfectly smooth hair falling over her shoulder and glowing white in the light of her laptop screen, 'I've never seen you in a tizz over a guy, we were starting to think you were impervious to the male of the species.'

'We?'

Zoe shrugged, her smile definite now. 'Lils, V, me.'

'I'm not heartless, Zo. I do care, you know.'

'I know you do, I just mean, you never showed an inclination to get serious about one.'

'And I'm not getting serious now,' she rushed out.

'OK-OK,' Zoe raised her hands in defence, 'get all het up by one, then! They're either your mates or a bit of fun. So, where does he fit?'

She raked a hand over her face. 'I wish I knew.'

'Then come on, spill?' Zoe stifled a yawn and reached across her bed, coming back into view with a glass of water and settling in to listen.

Malie felt a pang of guilt and checked the time. Her friend really ought to be sleeping, not playing therapist to her momentary madness.

'Look, I'm sorry, Zo, you should get some sleep. What is it, one, two in the morning where you are?'

'Three, but who's counting, I'm still on UK time. I swear jet lag gets harder to shift the older you get.'

Malie laughed gently, 'You're twenty-eight, hardly old.'

'The same still applies, and anyway, you're stalling, who's the lucky guy that's managed to turn you?'

'*Zoe.*'

There was no avoiding it, they were talking this through. And who knew, maybe it would help her make sense of it all, because she sure as heck couldn't.

'It's funny you mention being turned,' she said eventually, 'he is kind of vamp-like...'

She remembered that first night on the beach, his pale skin in the moonlight, his intense, dark gaze... the fluttering was instant, her insides coming alive like a whipped-up smoothie.

'Earth to Malie...' She focused on the screen as Zoe waved a hand in front of it. 'So this vamp, does he have a name?'

'Todd... Todd Masters.'

Zoe frowned. 'Wasn't that the name of the guy coming out to...' her eyes widened with realization, 'ooh, I see, so it's slightly more complicated than some random guy you hooked up with on the beach?'

'I don't hook up with—'

Zoe's grin shut her up. 'It's a moot point. What matters is this guy has come to Hawaii with his charity venture, bringing you kids you wish to help, aiding you in your quest to give people a better life and now you have the hots for him?'

Malie fiddled with her laptop keys. 'Pretty much, but I'm also a realist, Zo. Me and him don't mix.'

'What's that supposed to mean?'

'It means…' she looked pointedly at the screen, 'I'm just some surfer chick with a screwed-up fam that has no desire to fall into the' – she did air quotes with her fingers – 'Happily Ever After trap.'

'The Happily Ever After trap?'

'You and me both know that life likes to throw a curveball every once in a while…' She thought of Koa, she thought of the car crash – moments in her life that she would give anything to change and couldn't. '…And the hardest to recover from are those that hit where it hurts most… Where you love most.'

Zoe was quiet and Malie knew she was thinking the same.

'You can't say you don't agree with me?'

Zoe surprised Malie with a soft smile instead. 'Look at V, though, look at the happiness she's found.'

'That's V, she was always destined for love, she has a heart of gold and Oliver is so smitten, it's obvious. Who *could* question that relationship?'

Her friend shook her head with a laugh. 'Have you looked in the mirror lately, Devil?'

Malie smiled in spite of herself, Zoe's use of her age-old nickname giving her a much-needed boost.

'You spend your days trying to help people, not just passing on your love of surfing but trying to help people face up to those curveballs, to not let them define you. It seems you need to give yourself a lesson.'

She ran her teeth over her lip, chewing it at the corner. Was Zoe right? Is that what she was doing? Should she be throwing caution to the wind and letting it take her wherever it may… but seriously, Todd and her…

She shook her head. 'Doesn't change the fact that we could never work.'

'Why not?'

Zoe just wasn't getting it, confusion still wrinkled up her brow, her pale skin looking even paler in the light of her laptop screen, and then she yawned again, smothering it with the back of her hand.

'Zo, you need to get some sleep...'

'I'll get some sleep when you start talking sense.'

'He's a millionaire, Zo!' She felt exasperated, why couldn't Zoe just get it? 'He's like way up here...' she flung her hand above her head, 'and I'm like, way down here.' She dropped her hand lower than the screen to emphasize her point.

'What's that got to do with it?' she returned calmly.

Malie's shoulders slumped, her voice quiet. '*Everything.* I'm a run-of-the-mill surfer chick who's still scraping by on her past surf winnings and he's a guy who's made something huge of himself. He came from nothing and now he walks with the rich and famous.'

If Zoe had looked confused before she looked positively baffled now. 'Who cares if he's best friends with Bill Gates and dines with the Queen, what's his wealth got to do with anything?'

'You're only saying that because you've always had money.' It was out before Malie could stop it and she felt instantly bad. 'Sorry, love, I didn't mean...'

'It's fine.' Zoe shook it off, ever the strong one. 'But I think you're lying to yourself, there's more to this than a simple socio-economic divide.'

More?

Well, there was, wasn't there, but how could she confess as much to Zoe when part of the reason her guilt existed *was* Zoe.

173

She loved her friend dearly, and the fact that she'd walked away from that accident quite literally, while Zoe, while Victoria... She felt tears prick at her eyes and she leaned back from the screen, not wanting Zoe to see.

'Look, I'm just being daft,' she said with renewed strength. 'He's just a guy who will be gone again in a few weeks, and I'll forget about him in less.'

'It doesn't sound—'

'Zo, please, I feel bad that I've kept you awake as long as I have.'

'I'm fine, Malie, it's more important that we talk this through.'

'And we can, when you come out here next week.'

She could see the hesitation written in Zoe's persistent frown but eventually she relented, her shoulders easing with a smile. 'That's what I was calling about, actually, when you went all crazy on me... how does Friday sound?'

Malie grinned, the gesture very real now as excitement bubbled up. There was so much she wanted to do together. She wanted to show her where her father had grown up, take her to the best cocktail bars, eat the exquisite pineapple whip, and surf, most definitely, surf! Todd's words came back to her: *you shouldn't feel guilty; it's the future you should be focusing on; let go of the guilt.* Was he right? Would getting Zoe back on a board help her to come to terms with it all?

'Friday's perfect, Zo.'

Her friend's smile morphed into another yawn.

'And you need to go to bed, now, no more talk.'

Zoe stared at the screen harder, stopping her eyelids from drooping Malie was sure.

'Yes, Mum... but Malie?'

'Yeah?'

'Sort that pig-sty out, or I'm checking into the nearest hotel.'

She swept a look behind her and cringed – *busted*.

She looked back at the screen. 'You weren't meant to see that.'

Zoe gave a soft laugh, 'Consider yourself warned, Devil... Night-night.'

'Sweet dreams.'

Malie closed the lid of her laptop and stared at her hand resting over it. *He's just a guy who will be gone again in a few weeks... you'll forget about him in less.*

If only she could truly feel that away.

She looked across to her bed, knowing she should climb in and get some sleep. She'd be up early tomorrow as per the norm if she was to get her morning workout in pre-surf. But the idea of rest – of being able to sleep – was laughable. Not when their kiss, his touch, his need, still had her heart racing, her body aching.

Maybe she should have stuck to their pact and dived right in, tried the old burn-him-out-of-the-system trick... *because one night would have been enough – yeah, right.*

No, she would just have to distract herself instead and what better way than to sort out her pig-sty, as Zo so accurately called it.

She groaned. The idea of lying in bed tossing and turning over Todd suddenly had its advantages.

CHAPTER TWELVE

'BACK AGAIN?'

Kalani came up alongside Todd, his grin all-knowing as Nalu trotted up behind him, giving a little *woof* of his own. Were they both teasing him?

Yes, it was Thursday, and yes, he knew he'd become a bit of a fixture since Tuesday afternoon when he'd started setting up camp at the beachside café next door to the surf school. But from here, he could work on his laptop, the thatched-palm umbrellas providing ample shade and the staff being kind enough to rig him up an extension lead when his power was running low. And he could take in the amazing progress the kids were making under Malie's expert tuition.

'It's good to see them coming along so well.' He looked back to the water and the group having such obvious fun in the waves.

It was more than good, it was fantastic, thrilling even, but it wasn't the real reason he was there. Truth was he couldn't stay away. He'd tried to and managed one whole distracted-to-the-brink-of-insanity day. That had been Monday and his intentions had been good. He'd wanted to give Malie space after what had happened, not knowing where they now stood in spite of the pact and the agreement to put the day behind them.

But he'd spent the entire time apart stuck on her, he couldn't forget it. Not the kiss and not the life history they'd shared. His heart ached for her even now. The woman who'd lost her brother and effectively lost her place with her parents too. It was one thing to never know family, to have never experienced what it's like to be part of a loving whole, he'd been there. But to have lived and breathed that life, only to have it taken away, to mourn it...

'You don't look too happy about it.'

Todd pulled his eyes from the water again to see Kalani frowning down at him and realized he too was frowning. He forced his face to relax into a smile. 'I'm more than happy.'

'Worrying that the kids are better than you, hey?' he teased and Todd laughed.

'They have age on their side.'

'So true...'

They both looked to the sea as Malie high-fived an exuberant Tara. The young girl was hardly recognizable now. He'd never seen her looking so alive, so happy and carefree. Malie had worked wonders on her and he really was happy, but he missed the way things had been between them.

That one day had given him a glimpse of another life, one filled with fun and laughter, of someone to share it all with, and no matter how much he tried he couldn't shake it off.

It didn't matter that they'd agreed it was best all round, that neither of them wanted to pursue a relationship or anything more – he couldn't stop wanting it.

And he could see the fight in her too. The look in her eye, part fear, part panic, part want, and no amount of trying to act normal around each other eased it.

'So, when are you going to come for your next lesson? Malie tells me you've not booked it in yet.'

He hadn't. He'd been avoiding that too. He didn't want to make her uncomfortable, himself too, especially when she was doing such a great job with the kids. The fact that he'd kept his presence in line with their lessons meant there'd been no need for them to be alone again. But his private lessons called for exactly that and he knew her schedule was such that she was tied up at peak times when the beach and the school was at its busiest, leaving only the quieter, more intimate times of the day available.

'I've been busy.'

'Busy watching from here, yeah, I can see that.' Kalani shook his head. 'I'm starting to worry she's scared you off.'

'Not at all…' He knew the guy was still teasing him, but he could also read the genuine curiosity in his eye and could understand why. A man like Todd had a work schedule to keep, he should be looking to have the times nailed down to be sure he could make it and get them all in before he left. His time here was finite, after all.

'I assume you still want them?'

'Absolutely,' he reassured Kalani, feeling guilty that the guy would even think otherwise.

'Then how about when she's done with this session? It's the last of the day and I can lock your stuff up safe here.'

'Sure.'

His voice sounded odd but Kalani didn't appear to notice, instead he just beamed down at him and looked quite pleased with himself.

'Excellent, I'm just heading down to speak to her, I'll let her know.'

'Great.' Todd swallowed. 'Thanks.'

He watched Kalani make his way across the beach and felt his heart pick up pace as he waited on her reaction. It wasn't like the lessons hadn't been paid for, or agreed to, but...

Kalani waded into the water, Nalu heading in with him. Try as he might, Todd couldn't see her face clearly from here, but he could imagine the flutter of panic, the over-bright smile she'd put on to conceal it and the *of course, no problem* she would deliver. He could see her nod her head, her hand sweeping her hair out of her eyes as she continued to listen to what he had to say. Then Kalani was heading back and he knew that was that. There was no avoiding it now. They'd be having a one-to-one very soon and he needed to get a lid on the chaos inside.

'She's up for the lesson,' Kalani said as he neared, 'but you have a slight detour first.'

'A detour?'

'She promised Tara ice cream and asked if you would call the parents to see if it's OK for her to drop Tara back at the hotel later. She said it might help Tara's parents to say yes if you joined them too.'

He looked back to the water, where Nalu was now riding the surfboard with a laughing Tara and Malie's face all lit up as she watched them.

'No problem, I'll call them now.'

He had an idea forming already. A way to spend more time with Malie, without either of them feeling on edge, and to also make Tara's day, as well as that of her parents. He just hoped Malie would appreciate it too.

If worst came to worst, he could always come up with an out. But hopefully he wouldn't need it.

'Excellent, they should be wrapping up in thirty mins.'

He nodded and pulled out his mobile, found the contact details for Tara's parents and dialled. He listened to it ring, hardly aware that the fingers of his other hand were now crossed beneath the table, a move he hadn't done since his skateboard days when he desperately needed the job he'd applied for.

'Hi, Anne-Marie…'

★★★

Malie watched the kids trooping back to the surf school, surfboards under arm, and listened to their pumped-up chatter. Another great day, another happy group of kids. But she was dragging her feet, nerves getting the better of her. She wasn't the only one, though, Tara was also hanging back, her shoulders slumped.

'Tara? What's up?'

Not that Malie hadn't already guessed. But she was hopeful that Todd had managed to use his charm on the girl's parents by now. She wouldn't say anything though, not until she knew which way the conversation had gone.

Tara paused, turning to look at her. 'I wish we could surf for longer.'

Malie laughed and ruffled her hair. 'You and me both, but we're already looking like prunes.' She waved her fingers in the girl's face and grinned.

'Beats having to go back with Mum and Dad.'

'Hey, I know, love, but it's only cos they care.'

She looked up to see Todd approaching and her heart skipped inside her chest. Strands of his fringe fell over his forehead and she felt a giddy flutter as she wondered if it was down to her. Had he opted for the laidback look because she'd said she liked it? His shirt was also a casual colourful number, paired with beige shorts and no trainers. Definitely laidback and definitely all the hotter for it.

'It's not just that.'

Tara's comment pulled her up short and she dragged her eyes from his approach to look down at the girl. Her face was downcast, her black hair falling forward as the fingers of her free hand twisted in the fabric of her rash vest.

You're supposed to be focusing on Tara, came the guilt-ridden admonishment and she dropped down to the girl's height. 'What else is it, sweetheart?'

Tara lifted her head, but didn't look at Malie, her swirling blue eyes were back on the waves instead. 'When I'm out there I don't think about it...'

Malie frowned, sensing her need to talk and she looked up as Todd paused a few strides away. He gave her a nod and a thumbs-up, code for getting the OK from the Davidsons. She smiled back at him, knowing just how much this would mean to Tara.

'Tell you what,' she said, looking back to her, 'you head in and get changed, and I might have a little surprise for you when you're done.'

Tara's eyes met her own now, curiosity sparking in her gaze as her lips threatened to smile. 'Really? Like what?'

'If I told you, it wouldn't be a surprise, would it? Now, off you go.'

Tara spun on her heel and raced off after the others.

'Hey, Mr Masters,' she said as she passed him by. 'Malie has a surprise for me!'

They both watched her go with a smile, relief making Malie forget her nerves from seconds before. She was just happy to see the girl's spirit back.

'There's a lot going on inside her head.' Todd turned to her as he said it and Malie nodded, not quite ready to look back at him, instead she started towards the surf school.

'What did her parents say?'

'They agreed we could drop her home later… after dinner…'

Her eyes snapped to his. 'Dinner? I said ice cream.'

He shrugged. 'Based on your confession the other night that you're a bad cook I thought you'd appreciate a meal out, and I already knew Tara would appreciate the upgrade.'

'But… I might have had plans.'

'Do you?'

'No, but—'

'Malie…' He reached out, his hand coming to rest on her arm and making her jump at the frisson of excitement the simple gesture triggered. He frowned and pulled his hand back, pocketing them both as he looked away and explained, 'I thought it would be nice to take you both out and give Tara's parents time to enjoy a dinner, just the two of them. I don't think they've had a dinner date in a very long time.'

Guilt coursed through her and she gave him an apologetic smile. 'Of course, that sounds like a lovely idea.'

'Fingers crossed it helps. Kalani recommended a restaurant up strip…'

'Hang on, did you *treat* them to dinner?'

He gave her a smile that was so bashful and handsome in one that her heart squeezed inside her chest, her lungs robbed of air.

'I may have.'

She shook her head, unable to stop her smile from widening as she stroked a hand over her crazy sea-crisped hair. 'But what about your surf lesson?'

He shrugged. 'We can do it after dinner.'

'It'll be dark then.'

'Tomorrow then.'

'My friend Zoe arrives tomorrow and I'm taking a few days off.'

'So you *do* take time off?'

She gave a soft laugh. 'Yes, I guess I do.'

'What about a morning lesson? I can get here for the crack of dawn if that works?'

She hesitated. It would be quieter, romantic even, with the sun lifting on the horizon...

'Don't tell me you have plans for then too?'

'No, just my board and the sunrise.'

'Excellent, so dinner now, surf first thing – perfect.'

His words were enthusiastic, but his tone restrained, like he too was contending with the same inner battle: head saying it's a bad idea, body being abuzz with it. And were they crazy to risk dinner together again, especially after last—

'If you're worrying about what happened last Sunday, consider that off the cards.'

She felt her cheeks colour, more at the fact he could read her mind, rather than the actual memory of last Sunday. No, that had another effect over her body, just as hot and just as tingly.

'Tara will be our chaperone.' He winked and flashed his perfect teeth with a grin, the weight seeming to lift from his voice now.

'Funny.' She rolled her eyes, but his grin was infectious and working its magic, whisking away her worries so easily. And he was right, what's the worst that could happen? With Tara around, her libido would be forced to take a back seat. Tomorrow morning, though…

One step at a time, Malie.

'Just give me time to shower and change, I can use the amenities here.'

'Great.'

She felt his eyes warming her back all the way through the doors of the surf school and long after she'd hit the shower.

This was crazy.

This was bad.

This is for Tara and you will do it even if you end up going home a hot mess tonight.

★ ★ ★

If Todd had been offered a choice with no future risk – Malie all to herself, or Malie plus Tara – he may have jumped at the first option, but now, sitting in what he could only describe as a bamboo-and-leaf hut, adorned with wooden masks, shells and rainbow-coloured floral strands, he would actually be torn.

He'd let Malie choose where to eat, her knowledge of the local eateries far surpassing his. It didn't matter that he could afford to take them to the finest Hawaii had to offer, this was the real deal. Tara's flushed cheeks and sparkling eyes told him Malie had chosen right.

'*Aloha!* One mocktail for this lady,' said the cheery waiter, lifting a tall glass off the loaded tray with a tinsel palm tree and straw, placing it down in front of a beaming Tara who sat opposite him, Malie next to her.

'One cocktail for the other...'

Malie's drink looked practically the same as Tara's, he just hoped they'd got them the right way around.

'And a water for you, sir.' He placed it down in front of him.

'Thank you.'

Tara grimaced at his glass. 'You should have had one of these.' She dipped and took a long sip. 'It's delicious.'

'I bet it is... and I can just imagine the sugar content.'

'You need to live a little, Todd.' He looked to Malie as she said it and saw the teasing glint in her eye, it was impossible to take offence. Truth was, when he was with her, he felt very much alive and very much like he was living. More than he could ever remember doing before.

'We need to come up with a plan!'

Malie and Todd both looked to Tara, surprised. 'A plan?' they said in unison.

'We have two weeks left and I kind of figure that Mum and Dad letting me come out tonight shows they're willing to ease up, especially when you speak to them, Mr Masters... so how about you talk to them about me going with the other kids on the bus? Maybe if they start letting me do it here, they'll let the same thing happen at home.'

She sounded so certain, so determined. The quiet, reserved girl that he'd brought out here just over a week ago was almost unrecognizable in the bright, confident girl before him.

'Does it bother you that much?' he asked. To him, having a parent who cared enough to take him from point A to point B as a child would have been a blessing.

'It would bother you too,' she said adamantly, twirling the straw as she spoke. 'It's bad enough to look like I do—'

'Don't say that,' Malie said her hand reaching out to rest on Tara's shoulder as she leaned in to get her attention.

'I'm just stating a fact,' said Tara, holding her eye, suddenly wiser and more confident than her ten years. 'I *look* different, I can't change that, but I can change the way people see me. *You* taught me that.'

He watched their little interchange, saw Malie's gaze waver over Tara's face as she smiled. 'In what way?'

'You made me realize that by hiding away from the group I only made myself different, made myself stand out, I made them uncomfortable around me… as soon as I started getting involved, doing what they do…' she shrugged, a smile lifting her face, 'then I realized I could blend in, I could have fun, I could be just another kid.'

'Because you are,' Malie said softly, she reached around Tara's back and pulled her in for a hug, 'and I'm so proud of you.'

'Hey, gerroff, don't be getting all soppy on me.'

Malie backed away, laughing, but Todd could see the tears glistening in her eyes, her happiness fit to burst from her and reaching inside him too. She was the reason Tara was like this now. She was the reason the girl had grown in confidence. She was the reason he was starting to see more to life than just work.

'You too, Mr Masters.'

He refocused and saw Tara gesture towards Malie. Lord knew what she'd read in his face – another thing he seemed to be losing on this trip, his trusty poker face.

He grinned and raised his glass – 'Deal!' – and threw back a chug. The girl was right, he should have gone for the sugar high.

'So, it's agreed then?' Tara said, looking between them both now. 'You'll talk to them about the bus?'

Malie looked to him hesitantly and then back to Tara. 'We did try before, and they weren't keen.'

'Yes, but now's different. I don't think they would have said yes to this if they were still in the same head space.'

'Head space?' Todd said.

'Yeah.' Tara did a circular motion with her finger alongside her temple. 'And they're starting to argue less.' She said it so matter-of-factly, her approval written in the nod of her head. 'It's been a week but already things feel different. I was worried about them before... you know... they just seemed to argue, or talk about what's best for me. They never seemed to talk like I was there, or pay attention to me and what I thought – it sucked – but now...' She took a long drag on her straw and gulped it down, like she didn't want to pause too long now she had the floor. It made him smile to know she was in such a good place she felt able to speak openly. 'Now, I don't know, they ask about my surfing, they ask where I'd like to go to dinner, who my friends are, and they talk, to each other like, you know, properly.'

Todd looked to Malie and she gazed back at him. Had they really helped this family long term, did the Davidsons stand a better chance at happiness now because of their intervention?

Malie's lips curved up, her admiration shining in her gaze. 'We will talk to them about the bus, won't we, Todd?'

'Of course we can try.'

'Thank you.'

The waiter returned with a loaded-up tray and Tara's eyes bulged out of her head. 'I don't think I can eat all this, Mr Masters.'

'We'll help.'

She shook her head, 'I told you I was rubbish at deciding, you should have chosen for me, Malie.'

Malie laughed, 'No way, if Mr Masters is paying, I say we go for it.'

Tara laughed and started to tuck in. For a moment both Malie and Todd just watched her, and then with a shake of their heads and a smile as warm as Tara's, they tucked right in as well.

CHAPTER THIRTEEN

'YOU OK?'

They were standing outside the hotel, having left Tara inside with her parents, and through the glass doors they could see her chattering away excitedly as they stood either side of her, bending down to listen, their faces full of wonder and such obvious devotion. Malie could feel her chest tighten, as a strange wedge formed in her throat. She tried to swallow it back.

'You OK?' Todd tried again, turning her to face him, his worried gaze searching her own.

She tried for a smile. 'Of course.'

He lifted his hand to her cheek, brushed his thumb over her cheekbone and she felt the wetness spread, a tear she hadn't known had fallen caught in his wake. 'Malie, what is it?'

She took a shaky breath and turned away from him, starting to walk. 'I should get home.'

'I'll walk you back.' He fell into step beside her, struggling to keep up.

She shook her head, she needed to be alone before she cracked completely. 'I can find my own way home.'

'Malie, what's happened? What's upset you? Is it me?'

She didn't break pace, she couldn't even look at him, if she did, she knew she'd crumble, and she didn't want anyone to witness that. She hardly knew what was wrong herself. Seeing Tara like that with her family. Hearing her troubles and how much better her life seemed to be getting and how it compared and contrasted with her own life. It was too late for Malie's family though – ten, twelve years too late. Too much time had passed with her being an outsider, her parents not knowing how to talk to her and vice versa.

'Malie, please? I'm worried about you.' She stopped and he rounded in front of her, his hands gentle on her arms. 'Malie, look at me.'

Her lashes lifted, her eyes meeting with the blazing concern in his. He shook his head a little. 'We had a good night; Tara, her parents, everyone had a good night – didn't you?'

'Of course, I did.'

'Then what is it?'

She gazed into his sparkling blue eyes and for a second wondered what it would be like to offload, to tell him everything that haunted her still – the guilt, the sadness, the regret, the pain of missing what she'd once had and how it controlled her even now.

And then she realized, she'd already told him so much, told him more than she'd even told her best friends. She'd known him a week and spilled her all. And why would she do that, unless... unless...

Her lips parted, her chest painfully still. It was so obvious, so startlingly real. She was *falling* for him.

She'd tried to keep her guard up, keep her distance, keep herself safe and... *oh, my, God.*

You silly, silly fool, Malie.

'I have to go.'

She stepped around him and picked up her pace. How could she have been so stupid? So blind to it?

Trying to shake off the panic, her arms wrapped tight around her roiling stomach, her ears strained for footsteps behind her. Only this time he didn't follow. This time he stayed where he stood and again, she felt his eyes on her back, and it filled her with cold. Because she couldn't accept the comfort he offered, not without wanting so much more.

'Tomorrow morning, then?' he called after her.

'Yeah.' The word caught in her throat as she carried on moving. She'd be home soon, then she could let it all out and tomorrow morning she would be up to focusing on the surf. Teaching him like she would anyone else.

She was saved from the mocking laughter inside by her phone pinging in her pocket. She pulled it out and glanced at the screen, half expecting it to be Todd asking her to turn back. But it wasn't, it was a message from Victoria asking for a Lost Hours call.

She smiled in spite of her mood. Lost Hours was code for 'need to talk stat' and it could be anything from the good, the bad or the downright ugly. And this was definitely one of the 'good' variety.

Lost Hours! Lost Hours! I have exciting news and I'm going to burst if I don't pass it on to at least one of you – who's awake? I'm too excited to do the time conversion for M and Z! Xx

Her smile grew. How could she be anything but happy when her newly engaged friend was as excited as this? It was also a timely reminder of how Victoria had faced her fears by opening up to Oliver, she'd taken her curveball and batted it right out of the park, gaining her perfect man in the process. But as Malie had said to Zo, that was V, it wasn't her, V deserved that happiness and more.

She typed a reply:

Hey, gorgeous! Zoe's mid-air on her way to visit me but I'm one hundred per cent here for this! Give me five to get home! Can't wait to hear! Mxx PS Do I need to have bubbles at the ready?

She sent it and continued on, her mind now racing with what the news could be and providing the distraction she so desperately needed. Anything to take her mind off Todd, off what-ifs, off her parents and how different things could be.

She was unlocking the door to her apartment when Victoria's reply came in:

Bubbles?! I haven't stopped, lol! And this celebration is all Blake Hawkesbury's fault, eek! Xx

All Blake's... *what could he have to do with this?*

Blake owned the sprawling Hawkesbury Estate back in Hawke's Cove. As kids they'd spent their summers *borrowing* boats from old Mr Michaels at the harbour and rowing around to the estate's private beach, catching mackerel and cooking it up on the sand, swimming and generally having a whale of a time. If Blake knew of their antics, he never called them out on it. He was kind and caring to them all... particularly after the car accident.

Her smile dropped a little. It hadn't just been them affected by the tragedy. Blake's only child, Henry, had been a passenger in the car that had ploughed into Victoria's. Henry's girlfriend, Claudia, had been driving and she'd died on impact, Henry escaping with cuts and bruises and what Malie could only see as a shedload of guilt. He'd hit such a downward spiral shortly after that and there were rumours that his father had cut him off financially, their relationship ending with it. Henry hadn't been seen in the Cove since.

Was it any wonder Blake now doted on Lily, and by proxy them, too, filling the hole left by Henry?

And for Lily, having lost her father at such a young age, having someone as talented and successful as Blake sharing his wisdom with her, teaching her all he could about the hospitality industry, about the estate and its winemaking, he'd ultimately filled a hole for her too. Now Lily ran her own restaurant that stocked wine from the Hawkesbury Estate and used the skills he'd taught her daily.

But his generosity didn't end there, he'd even helped Malie all those years ago when she'd mentally broken down after the crash. She'd been desperate to leave the country, to get away from the trappings of her life with her parents but she hadn't had the means or the know-how. He'd given her the financial aid and the confidence to just do it and she'd been so grateful. She'd paid him back, every last penny, as soon as she'd been able. He hadn't wanted her to, but she'd insisted, she wouldn't be a charity case and she wouldn't take payment for any weird sense of guilt he may have felt about his son's involvement in the crash. It had been an accident, plain and simple. They all knew that.

Malie, where are you?! I'm getting desperate here!!!!

Victoria's message lit up on her screen and she shook herself out of the past and into the present. The crash was ancient history and they were all slowly putting it behind them. Weren't they?

Well, V certainly was… and Zoe would be surfing again very, very soon. Todd had opened Malie's eyes to what that would mean for her, to see it, to live it again with her friend.

Calling now!

She tossed her phone onto the bed and pulled out her laptop from beneath it, plonking herself down.

Oops, bubbles!

She shot back up, setting the laptop to ring out and placing it on the bed as she raced into the kitchen and pulled open the fridge.

'Finally... *Malie?*' Victoria's voice filled the room, going from relieved to confused. 'Malie, where are you?'

'I'm just coming!' She yelled over the fridge door. She pulled out a bottle, kicked the door back in place and grabbed a glass from the side, shimmying her way back to the bed and flopping down in front of the laptop.

'Hey!' Malie raised the glass and bottle to the screen, grinning as Victoria's flushed face beamed back at her. 'You look so happy!'

'I am!' Her long dark hair fell in waves around her face, notably dishevelled as though she'd just crawled out of bed and still she looked amazing, amazing and in love.

'Have you just woken up?'

'Pretty much!' There was the sound of a male in the background and Victoria wriggled, her hand pushing someone away.

'Still in bed though, yeah...' Malie teased as she sat the glass between her legs and started to unwrap the foil on the bottle. 'Hey, Oliver,' she cooed.

'Hey, Malie,' came his muffled reply. Victoria pulled the laptop closer and wrapped her fluffy white robe around her tighter before reaching off to the side and bringing a full glass of bubbles into view.

'I was woken up by the delivery man...' Victoria dropped her gaze for a second. 'Where's Lils, come on, Lils, pick up!'

'What time is it there? Eight in the morning?' Malie asked, uncoiling the wire from the cork. 'She'll likely be out foraging for ingredients, you know how she likes to keep it fresh and all that jazz in the restaurant.'

'Never mind foraging, I need her here before I burst.'

'Am I not good enough?' Malie whined, feigning hurt.

'Shut up, you know full well I'd spill all to you, I just hoped to have Lily here because I think she's had a hand in it, and I want to thank her.'

'Now I really am lost, a hand in what?'

'That'd be telling! Shall I ring her on the mobile too, do you think?'

Malie laughed. 'That'll only have the same result, the apps are the same whether they're on the phone or the computer.'

Victoria looked genuinely deflated, her pout emphasizing the luscious curve to her lips. *Damn*, she could be pretty and sophisticated whatever face she pulled. It was a quality Malie had never been able to master.

'Of course,' Victoria murmured, taking a sullen sip from her glass. 'Not sure what I was thinking.'

Malie laughed again, eager to lift her friend's mood. 'Hey, if getting married means you lose your mind, I'm quite pleased I'm set to avoid it for life.'

There was a male grumble in the background as Oliver muttered something to Victoria and her friend batted him away. 'She's just joking.'

'I am…' Malie gripped the cork and twisted the bottle, the pop sounding the same time as her adamant, 'not!'

'Whatever, Malie…' Victoria's soft brown eyes pinned her through the screen, 'one day a guy is going to walk into your surf school and sweep you right off that board of yours.'

She laughed at the analogy and ignored the little voice that said, *he already has, you just left him back at Tara's,* steadily pouring herself a glassful instead. 'Are you getting all fanciful as well as losing your marbles?'

'I'm not being—'

Malie was saved the rest of Victoria's rebuttal by Lils' face filling a new square on the screen. 'Lils!'

'Yes!' Victoria said, crossing her legs and setting the laptop before her so she could peer down into it. 'Where've you been?'

'Hey, sorry, Mum, but some of us have to work this time in the morning.' Lily brushed her hair out of her face with one gardening-gloved hand and managed to smudge dirt across her cheek with it. Malie was about to point it out when Lils frowned into the screen and blurted, 'Geez, are you seriously drinking bubbly at this time in the morning, V? I know you're getting married and you work in a bar, but...'

She raised a disapproving brow and both Malie and Victoria just laughed.

'I am, and not just any...' Victoria raised the bottle to the screen so that they could see the label, 'I believe this is the finest the Hawkesbury Estate has to offer.'

'How did you...?'

'As if you don't know,' Victoria said, her smile bright as she took a sip and hummed with exaggerated bliss. It would no doubt be much nicer than the cheap knock-off Malie had in her hand.

She took a sip minus the hum. 'You're gonna have to give us a clue.'

Victoria closed in on the screen, her face so alive, 'Blake Hawkesbury only went and had a whole case delivered! It arrived thirty minutes ago, woke us right up.'

'Oh wow, how sweet!' blurted Malie, that was Blake all over. 'No wonder you're enjoying breakfast bubbles.'

Lily smiled, clearly not surprised. 'He said he might send one.'

'Did he now?' Victoria grinned. 'Did he also happen to mention the card that might accompany the case?'

Lils couldn't keep a straight face; her eyes were wide with forced innocence as she shook her head.

Victoria laughed, 'You're such a crap liar, Lils.'

'OK,' Lils burst out. 'He might have mentioned an idea and asked if I thought it was a good one.'

'And you said yes.'

'Well, of course I did, what's not to love about it?'

'Nothing at all.'

'And have you replied?'

'No, not—'

'Hey, hey, hey, guys!' Malie felt like she was watching a tennis match, her eyes pinging back and forth the two screens and not having a clue what was going on. 'Can someone tell me what you're talking about before I lose *my* mind?'

'On that note, I'm hitting the shower.' Oliver leaned into the screen, offering a glimpse of naked torso as he kissed Victoria full on the mouth. 'Be good, ladies, not too many bubbles, darling, we're seeing Mum later and she'll likely be opening more!'

'Bye, Oliver,' Lils and Malie chorused and he rewarded them with a grin and a shake of the head before leaving the picture.

Victoria's attention shifted off the call for a long, drawn-out moment and both Lils and Malie coughed loudly.

V's eyes snapped back to the screen, her cheeks flushing pink. 'Sorry.'

'We know he has a fine behind,' teased Malie, 'but seeing you ogling it when we don't get the view, it's just plain unfair.'

'Hey, that's my behind to ogle, not yours.'

They all burst out laughing and Lils dropped back from the screen, unveiling leaf-adorned hair and the picture-perfect backdrop of the Hawkesbury estate. Malie felt a pang of longing and quickly quashed it with a swig of cheap plonk, focusing on the funny smile Lils now wore instead.

'Oh no, are you going all wistful on us, Lils?'

'No, it's just… I'm so happy that V's found someone so perfect for her.'

Malie felt the truth behind her words, the sadness that Lils had thought she'd had that once too, only to find she'd been so very wrong. She wanted to distract her. 'Finding the pickings a little slim in the Cove, love?'

'Slim to none.' Now Lils pouted and just as Victoria had – she looked perfectly beautiful with it, mud-streaked cheek and leaf-adorned hair and all.

'That's not true,' said Victoria. 'What about Ben down the chippy? I heard he'd come back to take over from his dad and is quite the looker now.'

'You are joking, right?'

Malie stifled another giggle.

'I wouldn't date anyone in the Cove if you paid me, not with Mrs Whittaker and her busybody antics. You know, I'm still convinced she knew about Al's intentions to do a runner before I did.'

Even through the screen Malie could see Lils' cheeks colour and knew that the bluster was all front, that she was still messed-up over her relationship with her ex, who'd been far too charming and slick and an overall nasty piece of work. He hadn't fooled the squad – V, Zoe and herself – but he'd had poor Lils fooled.

Victoria shuddered. 'I can't even bear hearing his name without my skin prickling.'

'Prickling?' Malie flipped. 'I wanna punch him, right smack on that pointy nose of his, then knee him in the balls to get him down to my level so that I can face off his arrogant, over-charming, sleaze—'

'Yeah, yeah, we get it, Malie!' It was Victoria staring into the screen at her, her hand doing the whole slicing-of-the-throat action.

Oops. 'Too much?'

Victoria nodded. 'Just a—'

'Nah,' Lils said, her voice resigned. 'In all honesty, I think I would have paid to see it.'

Lils gave a brave smile and Malie felt even more guilt. 'Sorry, love.'

'Are you guys kidding, he was a waste of space, I only wish I'd realized it *before* he'd raided our wedding fund and ran off with it.'

'Well, I just hope he freezes to death up in Scotland, alone and penniless with icicles hanging from his nutsack...' Malie grimaced, she'd been quite satisfied with the imagery until she'd got to his shrivelled meat and two veg. 'Scratch that last bit!'

'No... no,' Lils said between fits of giggles, 'I like it.'

'Yup,' Victoria agreed, raising her glass to the screen. 'I say *amen* to that!'

'Cheers!' Malie said, pleased she'd got them all laughing again.

'Truth be told, I've had enough of men to last me a lifetime. And anyway, I have my hands full helping with your wedding, V.'

'Good job too since I'm going to need your knowledge to get it right.'

'Have you suddenly added wedding planning to your repertoire, Lils?' Malie asked, confused. Lily was a great organizer, knew her food and drink, but wedding planning?

'No, but no one other than Blake knows the Hawkesbury Estate as well as her.'

'The Hawkesbury Estate?' Malie frowned.

'That's what I'm dying to tell you!' Victoria practically squealed. 'Blake has asked if he can host the wedding! We're going back to our summer home, ladies, for my wedding!'

Malie felt her elation through the screen, her own heart dancing with it. 'That's amazing, V, I'm so happy for you.'

'Thank you, and I just know you had something to do with it, Lils!'

Lily smiled, her own eyes glistening. 'I may have mentioned in passing how special the place was to us as kids and how beautiful a wedding venue it made... all off the back of telling him you were engaged.'

They all laughed.

'Well played, Lils!' Malie toasted her drink to her but then her eyes fell on V and the way her smile dropped slightly.

'It is the perfect venue,' V said, but her voice was softer, more reflective and then she looked away from the screen.

'What is it, V?' Malie asked, her heart lurching a little. Why the sudden shift in mood?

'V?' Lils prompted too, leaning into the screen, her eyes narrowed.

Victoria looked back to them and gave a little grimace. 'I have one teeny, tiny problem – Stella.'

Lily's frown became even more pronounced. 'You mean, Oliver's mum?'

'Yes.' She looked away and then whispered loud enough for them to hear. 'She wants the wedding to take place in their home village back in Norwich.'

'And what about Ollie?' asked Lils. 'What does he want to do?'

'He wants to do what makes me happy…' Victoria shrugged and gave a guilty smile, 'which is of course, Hawkesbury.'

'Well, there you go, then,' Malie said. 'Simple. Let him tell her.'

'I don't want to upset her, especially with his father being so sick…' Victoria started to fumble with the sleeve of her dressing gown, her happiness from seconds before dissipating.

'How's his father doing?' Lils asked. They'd all known Oliver's father, Eric, was ill, the whole country did. He was a bit of a British legend, an uber successful entrepreneur, and as such his illness was public knowledge, as was the experimental treatment he'd received recently.

V's expression lifted. 'Really well, against all the odds, even the specialists can't believe how well he is doing.'

'She'll be so happy he's doing so well, a simple decision over the wedding venue isn't going to ruin her mood,' Malie said jovially.

'And it's your wedding day, after all,' Lils said, ever the romantic in spite of her own bitter experience. 'They will want you both to be happy above all else.'

'You think?' Victoria said, hopeful.

'Defo,' Malie said.

Lily nodded. 'Best you break the news sooner rather than later, though, else knowing you it will worry you sick and you won't be able to enjoy anything until it is done.'

'Well, we're going for dinner today and it's bound to come up.'

'It's as good a time as any,' Lils said.

'Regardless of what Oliver said, Dutch courage gets my vote.' Malie threw back her drink to emphasize her point.

'I agree.' Lily grabbed up a water bottle and chugged back the contents. 'I'm pretending it's gin!'

They all laughed and Victoria's attention was once again off-screen, her laugh morphing into a wicked grin. 'Erm, I have to go, guys...'

Malie leaned into the laptop, trying even though she couldn't to see around the screen. 'Oh aye, what's caught your eye?'

Lils laughed, her cheeks flushing pink. 'I don't think we want to know.'

Victoria snuck a look back at the screen, 'Speak soon, yeah?' and her eyes lifted over the laptop edge as she leaned back and the lid was closed for her.

'I think you're right, Lils,' Malie said. 'Only now my head is taunting me with the fact that V is getting some and we're not.'

'Speak for yourself. Like I said, I'm done with the male sex.'

'Very wise, that makes the two of us!' Malie poured more bubbles and took a considered sip.

'Pardon me?' Malie frowned at her friend's disbelieving gaze. 'Did you just say you're done with the male sex?'

'It's overrated.'

'Malie Pukui, since when have you gone off sex?'

'I didn't say I was off sex.'

'Off males then...' her eyes widened, 'are you...?'

'No... although there was this rather feisty ladies' surf champion that paid us a visit a couple of months ago. I definitely considered it.'

'Malie!'

'OK, OK, I just meant...' Hell, what did she mean? She wasn't off sex, she wasn't off men, she was just distracted, exposed, vulnerable, turned on, falling for and quite frankly out of her comfort zone with one in particular. 'I have no idea what I mean, this cheap plonk has clearly gone to my head.'

'Well, on that note, I'm going to have to love you and leave you, honey. I have to get this lot back to the restaurant and get marinating.'

'Sure. Speak soon, babe. Happy marinating!' She blew Lily a kiss and closed the lid of her laptop, placing her glass and the bottle on her bedside table.

The distraction of her friends and getting wrapped up in V's excitement had sure gone well—*Not!*

She'd only managed to turn the conversation right back to her own mess by the end of it. And still, she was no closer to sorting any of it out.

Well done, Malie, well done... She flopped back on her bed, staring up at her smooth white ceiling and watching the fan at its centre go round and round and round.

In less than twenty-four hours Zoe would be here and then she could really avoid sweating the serious stuff. And speaking of Zoe, she raised herself up on her elbows and scanned the open-plan room. She could give it one more once-over. A dust, a hoover, perhaps... yeah, her neighbours in the block would really appreciate that at this time of night. But there was plenty she could get done quietly. She could reorganize the crockery for starters and add some fancy hotel touches to Zoe's room: toiletries, towels on the bed, maybe move a plant in there...

God, what was she doing? She may have teased Victoria about losing her mind but Malie was well ahead of her. Thank heaven for Zoe's visit, her no-nonsense attitude would have Malie thinking straight again... once Malie had convinced her friend that there definitely was no hope, not even a smidgen of a future for her and Todd – *Ah, Todd*... even now her body warmed, the tiny little flutters starting up, well-fuelled by the bubbles she'd consumed. She turned onto her side and pressed her face into the pillow, breathed in her own familiar scent and tried to block him out.

That was how she found herself when her alarm went off at 5.30 a.m., the creases of her pillow ingrained in her face, her body as tight as a coiled spring and Todd's name on her lips. Oh yeah, she'd only gone and dreamed of him, too.

She just prayed her morning workout would burn him out of her system... *before* they started his lesson at dawn. She could always ask Kalani to take her place if not.

No, Malie, it was your charity donation. Not Kalani's.

Perhaps a swap then? She hadn't seen who'd won Kalani's lessons, perhaps it would be some overweight, balding dude with a BO problem. She shuddered. *Better the devil you know than...*

She sprang out of bed, refusing to listen to the rambling of her head, or her heart any longer.

She would get through the morning and then she would be safe in Zoe's company having the time of their lives! Perfect!

FOCUS. ON. THAT.

CHAPTER FOURTEEN

HE'D TOLD HER DAWN but Todd arrived at the surf school long before that. It was still dark, the moon and stars still bright, the breeze rustling in the palm trees and the sound of the waves rushing over the sand the only real noise.

It was serene, soothing to his hyped-up body that had spent the last few hours in bed, wishing sleep would claim him and dreading the ping of his phone telling him she wouldn't be coming to the lesson. Even now he half expected one, and if not that, then Kalani appearing to tell him that he's standing in. And not just for this session but the whole damn lot.

He couldn't blame her either. He'd really overstepped the line last Sunday and in pushing her for more last night, more of her, more of her past, more of what was going on beneath the surface, he'd pushed her away.

He of all people understood not wanting to talk about the personal. He'd kept a close lid on it his entire life. Social workers couldn't even drag the truth out of him. But Malie... she'd managed to crack his life-long hard exterior and she'd done it in less than a week. Maybe that was the reason he couldn't let it go – let *her* go – he couldn't believe that a connection as powerful as this could be one-sided. She had to feel it too. And if she did and was still fighting to hide it from him, heaven knew how vulnerable she was beneath the captivating front.

He'd felt so close to breaking down her walls last night, so close to understanding and getting to know the real her. But then she'd run as fast as she could. Hiding, blocking him out, again.

The swing from sheer joy at Tara's progress, through the sight of Tara being so lovingly embraced by her parents when they'd returned her to them, through their continued chatter through the glass… Malie had watched it all and slowly her expression had changed and it had killed him to witness the tears, to see her cry and not have her confide in him, not to trust him with it.

He leaned against the trunk of a palm tree and stared out at the sea, breathing in deeply and letting it out slowly. It truly was beautiful here, such a contrast to the cities he was used to and the twenty-four-hour hive of activity. To be able to walk and find peace in the sound of the ocean, the quiet of the hour, had its appeal. No wonder Malie loved it.

In the distance the odd boat bobbed at sea, along the coastal road a few early workers prepped their shops and bar fronts for a day of trade, and on the beach there was the odd walker, the odd runner, some with dogs, some… *Malie?*

His eyes narrowed, his heart raced. She was a good distance away but even so, he knew it was her. Nalu too, trying to catch the sand that kicked up on her heels. Her hair was scraped up high on her head, flying out behind her in a mass of curls as she stuck to a pace that was punishing even by his standards and yet she made it look easy, the line of her body lithe, athletic, captivating.

He pushed away from the tree and started to walk towards

her, the movement impulsive, but then his stride faltered. This was her time. Not his. She wasn't here for his lesson – that was at least thirty minutes away – she was here to train and to interrupt her, even without last night hanging over them, would be wrong.

He hung back, gluing himself to the palm tree and hoping it would make him less obtrusive. He wondered if she was interval training and waited for her to slow down, walk, even, before picking up again, but no, she ran and ran, going past the surf school and continuing on. He couldn't tear his eyes away, even when she was no more than a dot he watched, amazed, impressed, and ever more hooked.

He smiled, the image of himself running beside her, of passing up his treadmill for a run outdoors, along a beach, beside a lake, anywhere with her by his side – he shook his head. Why was he even thinking it? The closest he got to a running partner was a personal trainer and he hadn't even used one of those in years, preferring to work out alone, and that made his whimsical imaginings just plain odd. Unsettling, even.

She turned back, her face to the sea as it had been when she'd run past him and still she didn't pause, not until she hit a set of bars positioned at varying heights between the road and the beach. Without pausing for breath, she launched herself in the air, grabbing hold of the high bar and bending her legs, crossing them at the ankles. She lifted herself up. One chin-up, two, three… no way… He'd known she was fit, she had to be to master what she could on the waves, but seeing her training was something else.

He watched her, for how long he wasn't sure, but when an insect took advantage of landing in his gaping mouth, he woke up to his voyeuristic behaviour and snapped his jaw shut. He either made her aware that he was here, or he found himself somewhere else to wait out the sunrise. Question was, which?

Now he'd seen her, now he knew she was only several metres away at most, did he really want to walk away? No.

He looked back to the horizon, to the sun just starting to peek over the deep blue of the sea and decided: that was the sun, it was close enough to dawn in his mind.

He started to walk towards her, watched as she dropped down from the bars and wiped her sweat-banded wrists across her brow. Sweat trickled down her chest, into the valley of her vest top, the Lycra clinging to her body, her shorts just as tight. Every glorious curve was accentuated by the fabric as she stared out at the orange glow starting to build over the sea. Her skin shone gold, even her eyes took on a similar hue, their green absorbing the amber from the steadily rising sun.

She fisted her hands on her hips, dragged in one deep breath followed by another and another, her eyes lost in the view – just as he was lost in her. What was she thinking? Was it about him? Had she suffered all night just as he had done? Was he the reason she was up before the crack of dawn?

It was Nalu who spotted him first, the dog's excited bark breaking the quiet, his tail wagging so fiercely it slapped against her legs.

She turned to look down at him, 'What is—?' and then she saw him, her eyes lifting, her lips parting in a surprised 'O'.

'Morning.' He smiled and Nalu ran towards him, eager for his attention, which worked in Todd's favour since it meant tearing his eyes away from her appeal and keeping his hands busy as he dropped to his haunches and stroked the dog's head, then his tummy as he rolled onto his back.

'I wasn't expecting you quite so early.' She walked towards him, her trainer-clad feet and bare, toned calves inching closer and closer.

'I couldn't sleep.' That was a bit honest. A bit *too* honest. He blamed it on her legs getting too close, her bare thighs, her curvaceous hips and slender waist, her ample... he swallowed and his eyes leaped to hers. His easy grin, forced. 'How about you?'

Her eyes narrowed, her arms crossing over her front. So defensive and the day had only just begun. 'How about I – what?'

'Couldn't sleep?' he said, getting to his feet so that she had to look up at him to maintain eye contact.

'I slept just fine, thank you.'

He didn't believe her, he almost said as much but stopped himself. He'd already scared her off enough, he didn't want to risk losing her completely.

She looked away to the sea. 'For your information, I always work out at this time of day, before the world wakes.'

He followed her gaze. 'I can see why.'

And he really could. The rays of the dawning sun stretched along the horizon, gradients of pink, orange, blue. He felt himself inhale and let go, a sense of calm befalling him until he noticed the watchful, curious look upon her face.

'What?' he said, not knowing whether to smile or not.

'Nothing.'

He smiled now. 'Nothing?' He raised his brow. 'That glint in your eye means nothing.'

'I don't have a glint—' She shook her head, her curls bobbing with the move and sending coconut his way as she laughed it off. 'If you must know, I was appreciating it through your eyes. I guess you don't see this much.'

'I see the sunrise often, it's just that it's normally through the gaps in the skyscrapers beyond the glass.'

'You should get outside more. Don't you go out into the countryside, the seaside even?'

'I've never had the desire to.' His eyes were very much fixed on hers, her upturned mouth so close that if he dipped, he could kiss her.

He could feel the tension mounting in the air, a very different kind of tension to that of seconds before and as her eyes flicked to his lips, he said, 'I didn't know what I was missing out on before.'

Only he knew in that second it wasn't the sunrise he'd been missing, but her... Malie... the thought burned through him, fighting with his survival instincts to back away.

'And now?' she whispered. 'Do you see it now?'

He lifted a hand to cup her jaw, his thumb soft as it caressed her cheek. He did see it. He wanted her, and he wanted her to see it too, the possibility of what they could have if they took the risk.

'Yes,' he said, looking down into her beautiful green eyes fired with amber and wishing her to see the truth in him, in herself. 'Yes, I see it.'

He lowered his head and saw the precise second the shutter fell, the spell broken in the widening of her gaze.

She dragged air into her lungs and stepped back, almost stumbling over a resting Nalu at her feet. 'We'd best make a start.'

She turned in the direction of the surf school and without looking back called out, 'I just need to freshen up and change.'

He watched her go, his body running from hot to cold and back again.

What are you doing, Todd?

He didn't know. He just knew that he couldn't let her go – that in two weeks he may be leaving but life wouldn't be the same. In fact, now that he'd met her, he was struggling to imagine life without her in it.

And that meant one thing, that in spite of his long-held belief that he would never go down the same road as his dad – that he would never let himself love another like his father had loved his mother – he was falling for her... falling fast and he was helpless to stop it.

★ ★ ★

'Did you want a coffee while you wait?' she asked without looking.

She knew he'd eventually follow after her, attuned as she was to every movement he made. She'd swear her heart was pounding loud enough for him to hear, her body thrumming a persistent beat in his presence that only ever became more incessant the more she denied it. Denied him.

'That'd be great, thanks.'

She pulled the shop key from the zipped pouched just above her bum and tried to push it into the lock, but it wasn't just her heart that was unsteady, her fingers were too, and she fumbled over it.

'Here, allow me...' He was right behind her, the deep resonance of his voice running down her spine, the heat of his fingers as they closed around hers taking her breath away.

She said nothing. She couldn't. She was so tightly wound nothing would come out; instead she stepped aside and let him unlock the door, her eyes raking hungrily over him and again remembering her own sweaty state.

She cocked a shoulder, did a discreet sniff, realizing she must smell. She'd really gone for it this morning, trying to burn out his power over her, and one glimpse of the fire in his intense blue eyes, his fringe flopped forward, his grin cocky and sure and yet so full of meaning – *gah*, she'd turned into a hot, sweaty mess for an entirely different reason. All the more so as the sun's rays had lifted on the horizon, dazzling them both in its warm, romantic glow. It had been a perfect moment, it would have been the perfect kiss, with any other couple, just not them.

He looked to her as he pushed the door open and stepped back to allow her entry first. 'After you, madam.'

A giggle worked its way up from nowhere and she knew it had come from nerves. Nerves that were totally shot where Todd was concerned.

'Thanks.'

She took a wide berth around him, but still his fresh masculine scent assailed her senses, his presence making her body hum with awareness. It was ridiculous. She wasn't a nun and he wasn't some forbidden fruit that she couldn't taste. Only she knew a taste wouldn't be enough. No, she'd want the whole damn lot and would go in for seconds, thirds and then some.

She strode to the kitchen and flicked on the light switch, opening the cupboards with more gusto than was required, sending one door bouncing back on itself. She tried again, slower this time, feeling Todd's curious gaze on her.

'Caffeinated?' she blurted.

He folded his arms and leaned into the doorframe. So relaxed, so at ease, why couldn't she be that smooth? She was known for being blasé, unfazed, cool… she was none of that with him.

'What would be the point otherwise?'

'True.' It came out a high-pitched squeak and she grimaced into the coffee machine as she loaded it up. At least all she could smell was ground coffee now and not his heady scent. She breathed it in and tried to reset her heart rate. She was such an idiot. *Do you see it now, Todd?* Really, what kind of question was that?

She took the jug from the machine and loaded it up with water, all the while trying and failing cataclysmically to keep her eyes off him, and each time he caught her peeking his smile grew.

'Tell me, Todd, do most women fall at your feet?'

Where the hell had that come from?

From her frustrations. Her inability to think straight. The need to put a wall up between them and keep it there.

He laughed, but she could sense he was surprised by her directness. 'I hope not, it would make for tricky terrain to walk.'

She ignored his attempt at humour, shaking her head as she clicked the coffee machine on and turned to look at him. 'I think they do… I think you look at me and you can't understand why I'm so keen to do the opposite.'

He ran his teeth over his bottom lip and damn it, if her belly didn't contract with a rush of illicit heat.

'What exactly does the opposite mean?'

'It means I'm not going there with you. We had our… day, and it was fun, we agreed from here on in we're…' She struggled to define them. What exactly were they? Not friends, not business associates or colleagues, not…

'We're?' he prompted softly.

She walked towards him, needing to get past him to head for

a quick shower but he didn't budge and she was forced to stop, to look up at him.

'What are we, Malie?'

She wet her lips. 'You're Todd Masters, my... my pupil this second, which makes me your teacher, and you're going to need to move if I am to get out of this gear and get kitted out for our lesson.'

His eyes raked hungrily over her and she felt every stretch of exposed skin, his gaze burning a path that struck with the throbbing force right at the heart of her. She needed to get laid, like yesterday. Desperately, insanely, and the man that made her want it so bad was the one man she wouldn't let herself have.

He stepped forward, his thought-obliterating scent assailing her senses, the heat of his body engulfing her, his eyes searing down into hers. 'Aren't you tired of fighting this, Malie? I know I am...'

She tried to shake her head but it wouldn't seem to move. She tried to speak but nothing came. She swallowed, her throat bobbing with thickening desire: *just once, just let go once, then hit rewind.*

Maybe it'll be awful. Maybe those fingers that look so strong and capable will suck when they're roaming over her, hungry, desperate.

And then what?

'We have a responsibility to the kids...' she tried.

'We do, but that has nothing to do with this.'

'It will complicate things.'

'The only complication I can see right now is that I can't concentrate anymore, I can't sleep, I can't work, all I can think about is you.'

Oh my God...

'Don't say that.'

'What, the truth?'

'Any of it.' Her voice shook with her body as she held herself rigid, refusing to lean into him as her limbs, her torso tried to do just that.

'Tell me you don't feel it too?'

'I...' The denial stuck in her throat. She was a crap liar, just like Lily. She wet her lips, tried again. 'It doesn't matter—'

'Hey, Malie, you here?'

Her eyes flared and Todd pushed up off the frame. It was Kalani – *crap!*

'Saved by your godfather,' he teased quietly, though she could see the seriousness in his gaze, the continued probing, the need to understand.

She gave him a weak smile and walked past him to find Kalani wedging the front door open.

'Morning!' she said, her voice unnaturally high which made her wince. She tried to lower it as she added, 'You're opening up early?'

'Thought I'd get started on the paint job outside. Been putting it off for ages.' He looked past her as he straightened, his eyes widening in surprise. 'Morning, Todd, I didn't expect to see you here.'

'Morning.'

'Todd's here for his lesson,' she rushed out, hating how her cheeks warmed. She had nothing to feel guilty for. *Nothing.* It wasn't like he'd caught them at it. He could have done, though, they'd been that close... 'I'm just gonna hit the shower, coffee is on, help yourselves.'

She legged it into the changing room, not waiting to read the look on Kalani's face or the corresponding one on Todd's. She didn't doubt the speculation that would exist in her godfather's mind – he knew her too well – and she could do without his judgement, she had enough of her own to contend with.

She checked her watch. Six hours and Zoe would be here. Six hours and she'd have her joyful distraction.

'Sorry, Zo,' she muttered, feeling a new sense of guilt at using her friend in such a way. Zoe wouldn't mind being her saviour though, not when she understood how very real her problem was.

★ ★ ★

Fifteen minutes later, she'd showered, scraped her hair back and donned her surf kit. She was ready. Or as ready as she was ever going to be when it came to Todd.

She pushed open the door into the main room, it was empty; she tried the kitchen, empty. She headed out front and there they were, seated at the table and chairs they used for briefings. Kalani was laughing at something Todd had said, the pair of them relaxed, legs outstretched, coffees in hand. Her belly fluttered at the easiness of the scene. She could almost forget that Todd didn't belong here, that he was a fleeting presence that would soon be gone. She could almost believe he and Kalani had been long-time friends with the way they were chatting.

Todd looked to her and their eyes met, it was a second before she could breathe, another before she could speak. 'You ready?'

She caught the slight pinched look on Kalani's face and knew it was due to the strange tone to her voice. She ignored him.

'Sure,' Todd said, getting to his feet and knocking back the rest of his drink. 'I poured you a coffee, why don't you have it while I change?'

'Thanks.' She stepped free of the entrance to let him pass. She didn't breathe in again until he and his addictive scent were on the other side of the door, leaving her in the far safer company of Kalani. She headed to the table to take up her coffee and felt Kalani's inquisitive gaze on her. Scratch *safer*...

'Don't say it,' she said, lifting the mug for a sip and looking out to sea.

'I wasn't going to say anything.'

'Hmm,' she said disbelievingly.

'He's a great guy, don't you think?'

'*Kalani*.'

'What?' His innocence was so forced that she shot daggers at him, her look doing all the talking for her.

'What I don't understand, *Mea aloha*, is why you look so scared?'

'I'm not scared.'

'What are you then?' he said softly, leaning his elbows into his knees as he looked up at her. 'Because you're not yourself...'

'You won't understand.'

'Try me, I might surprise you.'

She looked to her godfather and though she loved him dearly, she couldn't put this on him. She didn't really want to put words to it herself. She smiled instead. 'In a couple of weeks, I'll be back to my old self.'

'A couple of weeks?' He raised his brow. 'You mean, when he's gone?'

Her throat closed over. *When he's gone*... that was precisely it. She raised her coffee to her lips, forced it down. 'Yes.'

It was all she needed to say and thankfully Kalani didn't press.

'Are you free tomorrow afternoon?' she said once she could trust her voice again.

'I've freed it up to get on with this,' he waved a hand over the shop front, 'she's in need of some TLC.'

Malie scanned the building and agreed, but… 'If I put some time aside to help you next weekend, would you help me instead?'

'Help? With what?'

Now Malie smiled, happier thoughts taking over. 'My friend Zoe is coming to stay and I want to get her out there on the board.'

Kalani smiled. 'For that, I'll definitely pass up the painting.'

'Thank you, I'm so looking forward to getting her on the water again.'

'Right.' Todd appeared in the doorway, his surfboard underarm and the surf school's pink T-shirt pulled taut over his upper body, his grin full of excited anticipation and sending fire licking up her insides. *Oh, God.* 'I'm all set.'

Oh, good.

'Great.' She forced a smile and placed her half-finished coffee back on the table. 'Let's go.'

'Come on, Zoe, I need you…' she muttered under her breath, pulling her board out and setting off down the beach, Todd racing on her heels.

'What was that you said?'

She kept her focus straight ahead. 'Nothing.'

'You know, I'm starting to think that you don't like me very much after all.'

If only…

She looked back at him long enough to spy the laughter in his eyes and realize he knew the truth well enough: the problem wasn't that she didn't like him, it was the fact that she liked him far too much.

And it wasn't funny.

★★★

'That lesson was brutal.'

Kalani grinned at Todd. 'She didn't take it easy on you, huh?'

'I wiped out more times than I can remember.'

'Sounds like playground antics to me.'

Todd shook his hair and raked it back, Nalu trotted up behind him and mimicked his move, showering Kalani and his freshly painted woodwork. *Playground antics*, what was that supposed to mean?

'*Nalu*,' Kalani grumbled, shooing the dog away and looking past him. Todd knew Malie was approaching, he could feel it in the awareness prickling all over his body.

'You going to be OK without me today?' she said, actively ignoring Todd. Pretty much as she had done on the waves, aside from issuing instruction after instruction.

'Of course, my lessons start at ten, if you could pull the gear out for me before you go that would be a huge help – no worries if you can't.'

'I'll help,' Todd offered.

'It's OK, I can do it.' She sent him a quick look, one that he couldn't decipher and then she headed off inside the surf school, leaving Todd standing there.

'She's a big softie really,' Kalani said, snagging Todd's attention. 'I think you've just got under her skin, that's all.'

'Under her skin? You saying I annoy her that much?'

Kalani laughed, his bulky body rumbling with it as he dipped his brush in the vibrant blue paint. 'Annoy wasn't the word I would use.'

'What word—'

'Is it the kids from the resort?' Malie appeared in the doorway preventing him finishing his question.

'That's the one, five altogether.'

She nodded, 'Got it,' and headed back inside, quick as a flash.

'Just don't take it personally,' Kalani said, sweeping the paint over the wooden pillar that held up the palm-fronded roof to the shelter that fronted the surf school.

It was pretty hard not to take it personally, but he could hardly get into it now with Malie coming back and forth and likely listening in right now.

'So, how far is this little refurb going?' he asked instead, gesturing to the school front and realizing that the whole thing probably needed a touch-up. It was a big job and he couldn't spy anyone else that would be helping out.

'All of it. No point doing it piecemeal, it only makes the old look more tired otherwise.'

'You need a hand?'

Kalani looked to him, his eyebrow hitting the palm fronds above. 'You serious?'

'Absolutely.'

Kalani lowered his brush to look at him properly. 'Don't you have more important things to be getting on with?'

'It's time I took a holiday.'

His brow lifted even further. 'Painting is hardly a holiday.'

Todd grinned. 'It'll make a nice change.'

If he was going to consider Malie's suggestion of doing DIY with his father, he might as well start here and help the surf school. They were doing such a great job with his charity's kids after all.

And it gave him a reason to be around Malie more…

'I'll head back home, shower and change. I can be back before you take your first lesson out and you can put me to work.'

'You're really serious?'

'Totally.'

Now Kalani grinned, his eyes warming with his appreciation. 'In that case, thank you.'

'Although, would you mind running inside and getting me my stuff? I'll return this lot later, I think Malie is wanting her space.'

And he probably needed it too. Was he crazy to want to be around her more? To pursue this further? To pursue what exactly? He shook off the crazy riddle and watched as Kalani dropped his brush in the pot and gave him a nod.

'Sure thing.' He headed off inside, coming back seconds later with Todd's bagged-up items.

'Cheers.'

He left before Malie could get wind of his plan and change both their minds. He left before he could change his own too. His instincts told him this was worth taking a risk on and they'd never let him down before.

He was pensive, so distracted by his thoughts that it took him a while to realize his phone was ringing in his pocket. He pulled it out and checked the ID. It was Grace, his PA.

He swiped the call to answer. 'Hi, Grace.'

'Todd, I've had a call from Tara's mum, Anne-Marie. She's asked if you could give her a call back, I explained you might be tied up but—'

'Of course, I'm just heading for the house, I'll call her on the way.'

He hung up, hoping whatever it was, it was nothing bad. Tara was doing so well and as far as he could tell, her parents were benefitting too. Everything seemed to be heading in the right direction.

He located their number and dialled, Tara's mother answered after a few rings. 'Todd, thank you so much for calling back!'

He could hear the smile in her voice and took it as a good sign.

'No problem, how can I help?'

'I… err, we – Charles and I – wanted to ask a small favour, if at all possible, it's fine if you can't, or if it doesn't work for you, or you know, you have plans…'

She was rambling with obvious nerves and he chuckled. 'Hey, Anne-Marie, it's fine, just ask…'

CHAPTER FIFTEEN

THEY WERE ON THEIR second bottle of wine and the giggles were rife. God, how she'd missed this!

'So come on, Zo, spill, there must have been at least one total hottie in the Caribbean that you had your wicked way with?' She topped up Zoe's wine glass before seeing to her own and plonked the bottle back on the table between them.

They were lounging on the cushioned sun-beds Malie had borrowed from her neighbour for the duration of Zoe's visit, having realized the upside-down crate she often used wouldn't cut it and she didn't want her friend feeling like she had to stay in her wheelchair all of the time.

'Please,' Malie groaned out slowly, 'I need to know one of us, other than loved-up V, is getting some these days!'

'You have such a way with words, Devil.' But Zoe's laugh totally belied her criticism as she lifted her glass and sipped at it. 'Since when have you struggled anyway?'

Since a certain someone appeared on the scene, or the beach more like...

'Ah, hang on,' Zoe said, all enlightened. 'It's because of him, isn't it?'

Malie feigned innocence. 'Who?'

'The sexy millionaire who heads up the charity and has you craving more than just a quickie.'

'*Zoe!*'

Her friend laughed harder. 'Don't you go acting all hurt and offended, Devil, you forget I *know* you.'

'And I know you and you're changing the subject.'

Zoe shook her head. 'I'm not, there really is nothing worth telling.'

Malie snorted into her glass. 'Well, that's disappointing.'

'It's worse than disappointing, the fact is there have been men, walking-sex-god type men, but every time we get to the bedroom they morph into airy-fairy nurse types. *Tell me if I hurt you, is this OK, do you want me to move you here, here or here?*' She flapped her hand around her dramatically. 'It's like they suddenly think I've lost the use of *every* limb and that I'll break if they so much as touch me, let alone lose control. And don't get me started on the panic in their faces when I so much as moan.'

'*Moan?*' Malie looked to Zoe and tried to keep the rising giggle in.

'Yes, you know...' Colour crept into Zoe's creamy white skin and her eyes flashed. 'An *oh-yes, God-yes, When-Harry-Met-Sally* moan, they practically leap off me in fear. It's good enough to kill the moment dead.'

'You know what you need?' Malie said, acting the expert and waving her glass at her friend.

'What?'

'You need a *real* bad boy, someone who's been around the block a few times and could really show you a good time. A bit of rough.'

Zoe laughed into her wine glass, humming as she swallowed it down. 'You probably have a point there.'

'It's such a shame you and Finn never… you know…' Malie made a bed-squeaking sound, lifting her mouth at the corner as she gestured.

Zoe shot her a look, choking on her wine. '*Finn?*'

'Yeah, come on, don't give me that look of surprise. You forget, I *know* you too well.'

'You don't know me as well as I think you do, if you believe there was anything going on between me and Finn.'

'*The lady doth protest too much, methinks.*'

'Really, you're going to use Shakespeare against me now? You didn't even read the book.'

'I did so,' Malie protested or rather lied, her lips pursed around the laughter dying to get out.

'Right, which play is it in?'

Malie erupted with a giggle. 'OK you got me, but seriously, the line still holds… he was a bit of rough with a reputation to boot, he would have sorted you out "down there" no problem.'

'*Down there*, Jesus, Devil, what kind of phrase is that?'

'You know what I'm getting at though, don't you?' Malie laughed and Zoe joined her, throwing back a gulp of her wine.

'Yeah, well, that was never going to happen.'

'But why not? And don't tell me it was because of the accident.'

Zoe shook her head. 'No, not that. At least…'

'At least?'

Zoe looked to her and Malie caught a glimpse of vulnerability in her fragile features, a weakness her friend rarely let slip through. 'That summer at the Crab Shack, Finn always treated me like you girls did.'

'Well, not quite,' Malie laughed softly. 'I wasn't eyeing you up like I could strip you naked and have my wicked way with you.'

She was trying to lighten Zo's mood and was pleased to see her friend's lips quirk with a hint of laughter.

'I swear you just see what you want to see.'

'You ask V or Lils and they'll tell you the same, it was virtually impossible to get served promptly at the Crab Shack when you were both on shift, you were too busy getting lost in each other's eyes.'

'I was not.'

'Then more fool you, because he certainly was – he was well and truly lost looking at you.'

Zoe shook her head, clearly refusing to believe her. 'He was never lost. He knew exactly where he was, what he was doing and where he was going, and it wasn't ever about me, except as a friend. And that… that was exactly what I needed, that was *all* I needed. He… he felt the same. I'm sure he did. Friends, nothing more.'

It sounded to Malie like her friend was trying to convince herself as much as her.

'And anyway, I wouldn't have ruined our friendship by blurring those lines, even if I'd had the opportunity, which I did *not*,' she added quickly. 'I liked that he treated me like I was normal, I liked the person I was when I was with him, I liked the person he made me *believe* I was. Why would I have messed with that?'

'Er, because Finn was on every girl's radar – he was the bad boy every female wanted to be ruined by. If you're telling me you were the only girl in the Cove who was immune, sorry, but I'm not buying it.'

Zoe's cheeks sported a hint of colour again. 'He was good-looking, of course he was, I wasn't blind…'

'But?'

'But I was sixteen. And his mother was sick. And, of course, my parents... Let's just say they weren't impressed, even that we were friends – anything more than that would have seen me confined to a convent, I swear.'

Malie laughed at the very idea and Zoe's eyes snapped to her. 'I'm not kidding... and anyway, soon after that summer, I started going out with Brad—'

'Urgh! Brad!'

'He was OK!'

'He was hardly the man of the moment after the accident, that's for sure.'

'No, but then, neither was Finn, you know.'

'No, I don't know, Zo. And the question is, *what* don't I know? I know he came to see you though and after that... *pouf*, nothing.'

Zoe rubbed her hands up and down her legs that were straight out in front of her, her slender lengths made all the more so by her inability to use them. 'It's not a good memory... I don't like to think about it, let alone talk about it. But yeah, he came to see me at the hospital, and all those things that made him so good to be with...? They disappeared, and I saw that he was just like everyone else, wanting to wrap me in cotton wool and tuck me away and... and *save me*. Let's just say there was a full-on scene with my parents,' she shuddered. 'It wasn't pretty.'

'No, I can imagine.' Malie felt for her, really felt for her, she knew how suffocated Zoe had felt at the hands of her parents and then to have it all play out like that with Finn too... She shook her head. 'I'm sorry.'

Zoe waved a hand. 'It's ancient history, the last I heard he'd left for Australia.'

'Australia, really?' Malie's voice went up in pitch.

'Yes – *Australia.*'

'Okaaaay,' Malie drawled, nodding, 'and he just happens to follow you to the same country?'

Zoe shook her head, a small laugh erupting.

'Quit overthinking it, Devil, and carry me into bed. These beds are comfy and the view exquisite, but I don't fancy being eaten alive when my insect repellent wears off.'

Malie laughed too, loving that her fiercely independent friend knew she had nothing to prove in front of her and had asked to be carried in. It made their bond feel all the more special.

Zoe's eyes narrowed. 'What's that funny smile about?'

'I was feeling pretty special.'

'You looked pretty special.'

'Oi, cheeky!' Malie got to her feet. 'I meant *special* in that you still let me carry you around.'

'Yeah, well, you and you alone.'

'See, *special.*'

They both laughed and Malie walked around the table, scooting down to lift Zoe into her arms.

'This is the most action I've had in weeks, you know.'

Zoe giggled, wrapping her arms around Malie's neck. 'Is it all you think about?'

'I'm talking about weightlifting, I'm not sure what you were thinking.'

Zoe was still laughing as they headed inside.

'You know what they say,' Malie sing-songed, 'it's not the mouth it comes out of but the mind—'

'But the mind it goes into, yeah, yeah,' her friend joined in, patting her chest with a grin. 'It was *Hamlet*, by the way.'

'What was?'

'The play – by Shakespeare. Queen Gertrude says it after watching some character's insincere overacting in a play that Hamlet's written.'

'Oh yes.' Malie kicked open Zoe's bedroom door. 'Wasn't that the depressing one with all the death and corrupt family shizzle?'

'You paid some attention, then?'

'I read the Oxford notes,' Malie said, laying her down on the bed and plonking herself down next to her. 'I couldn't even cheat and watch the film, it was so utterly depressing and seriously, what child needs that in their lives when life is tough enough already?'

They shared a quiet look – they knew better than most – and then Malie slapped her knees to cut the sudden chill. 'Right, what can I get you for bed?'

'Just my chair,' Zoe said, raising herself onto her elbows. 'I can sort the rest.'

'No problem.' She got to her feet. 'And you can help yourself to toiletries, I've even laid out the fancy towels for you.'

Zoe smiled up at her. 'Thank you.'

She headed for the door.

'And Malie?'

She paused and looked back at her friend.

'Thank you for schmoozing my parents, you have no idea how nice it is to be free of my shadow for a week.'

'Is Gabriela actually that bad?'

'Not really, she's great, and I like her, I really do. She's also a skilled physio-cum-nurse, but it's suffocating having someone follow you around twenty-four-seven and trying to tell my parents

I can survive a week without her just fell on deaf ears. They listened to you, though.'

'I obviously have the magic touch, if only I could have the same skill with my own parents, hey?'

'I think we're as bad as each other where our own parents are concerned.'

'Lucky us!' They shared another look, both knowing the other hurt and neither knowing how to fix it. 'I'm just glad you could come and stay, Zo. I feel like I have a whole life here but it's not the same without having you guys to share it with.'

Zoe's smile was small. 'I know what you mean.'

'Oh, speaking of which, I haven't asked you: how long have you decided you can stop for?'

'A week, I need to be heading on to New Zealand then.'

'New Zealand – how awesome! Another long-haul flight, though? I don't know how you do it.'

'Hey, no rest for the wicked, right?'

Malie's heart pulsed in her chest as she heard her mind replay someone else quoting that exact phrase to her just a few days ago. Todd, on their day out. She remembered the fun, the easiness with which they'd spent that day and her belly flipped over, her heart starting to dance. *Quit it.*

'None at all,' she said softly, heading out and reminding herself that she had Zoe to help her quit it, quit him. And for a whole week too. That left only another week in which to avoid him and the chaos he'd kicked up inside her.

She could cope for a further week, there was plenty she could throw herself into to keep out of his way.

And she could start by asking Kalani to take over his one-to-one lessons, no matter how much he griped. After that morning's brutal session, Todd may have even taken it upon himself to ask Kalani. Now wouldn't that be a bonus.

She ignored the dead weight forming in her gut at the prospect of not seeing him alone again and focused on seeing to Zoe. Her friend was her first concern, Todd shouldn't even be on her radar. Outside of her work with the charity, that is.

CHAPTER SIXTEEN

'NO ONE TOLD ME we'd have to work today, Mr Masters,' Tara grumbled, bending to dip her brush in the paint pot and blowing her fringe out of her face with a huff. 'This is like slave labour or summat!'

Todd laughed. 'You're getting paid in ice cream, surely that's fair?'

Tara threw him a look but then grinned. 'It is nice ice cream.'

'Plus, you get to spend the day with me here, while your parents get their *boring* sightseeing done.' He was quoting Tara on that.

'True. Not sure why they'd wanna go see that pearl thing anyway. Didn't they get enough history in school?'

Todd shook his head but didn't argue with her. He was just glad he'd been able to help out and the fact that it meant her parents truly were enjoying their chance at a holiday and spending time together was a good sign.

'Right, I think Kalani wants us—'

'Todd?'

His heart pulsed – *Malie.*

He turned to see her staring at him wide-eyed, mouth parted, her colourful rash vest clinging to her upper body, her black swim shorts a mere belt. He smiled, trying to hide his body's instinctive overheating and looked to the petite blonde woman in a wheelchair beside her. She was similarly dressed but wearing fashionably oversized sunglasses and a far warmer expression, although her smile suggested she was amused by something, like she'd just been told a joke that only she was privy to.

'Morning, or is it afternoon now?' He dropped his brush into the paint tray and glanced at his watch – it was almost one.

'If it is, you owe me lunch.' Tara beamed at him before looking at their new arrivals. 'Hey, Malie! Is this your friend Zoe?'

'Hi, kiddo,' Malie frowned, 'How did you—?'

'I might have mentioned you have a friend staying,' Todd jumped in, wiping a hand on his trousers and offering it out to Zoe. 'Nice to meet you, I've heard a lot about you.'

Her smile grew as she shook his hand. 'And I you.'

Todd glanced at Malie as he straightened and combed his fingers through his hair, brushing back the strands that had fallen forward. 'Sounds ominous...'

'Doesn't it just.' He could hear the teasing in Zoe's voice and felt her eyes watching him closely.

'What are you doing here?' Malie's voice was tinged with silent accusation, the flush to her skin making her eyes appear brighter, ever more piercing as they speared him.

'What does it look like?' he said, his tone light and easy in such contrast to hers. 'I helped Kalani out yesterday after you left and when he mentioned he was helping you ladies today, I said I'd carry on with it. Figured it would keep Tara out of trouble too.'

'Hey, I'm not trouble,' the girl blurted out, waving her paint-brush at him and sending droplets flying through the air. Thank heaven he'd thought to put a dust sheet down, as for him, he had to jump back to evade being splattered. 'Say it again and I'll come over there and paint you.'

He chuckled at her threat. 'I would be careful who you're threatening if I were you.'

Tara laughed as she returned to her task, 'Whatever you say, Boss.'

'Cheeky! You've been hanging around Jonny too long.' He looked back to their new arrivals, Zoe was all smiles whilst Malie continued to frown at him.

'But…' she flustered. 'Don't you have work you should be doing?'

'It's Saturday,' he shrugged. 'And wasn't it you who told me I should take some time off and try my hand at DIY?'

'That's not what… that was…'

She opened her mouth and closed it again, Tara coming to her aid. 'If I had time off, I'd spend it doing something fun, not painting.'

'Would you rather be walking around a war museum?' Todd said to her.

She laughed. 'Nope.'

Malie looked ever more baffled. 'So why is Tara here?'

'I'm helping out her parents,' he explained. 'They're having a day out together, checking out Pearl Harbor among other places, and asked if she could spend the day with me.'

'Wow,' Zoe exclaimed. 'DIY and babysitting—'

'Hey, I'm no baby!' Tara's head snapped around so quickly her black hair flared out. 'And I don't need looking after.'

Zoe laughed. 'I can see that!' Then she smiled up at Todd. 'That's really nice of you… *Isn't it*, Malie?'

He'd swear she would have given Malie a shove if she'd been close enough and he couldn't help grinning back. Malie wasn't so pleased, though, her teeth looked gritted, her eyes flashing above her friend's head.

'Yes… yes, it is,' she bit out eventually and letting go of a gust of breath she scanned the area. 'Where is Kalani, anyhow?'

Todd gestured down the beach. 'He's prepping the equipment for you and keeping Nalu out of the paint. I think he's already had to clean blue pawprints off the floor inside.'

'Right, sounds like Nalu.'

'He also mentioned that he'd left the rolling beach chair out for you, it's just inside the door. Here, I'll go get it for—'

'No need, I'll do it… *thanks*.' The last was added as more of an afterthought, her tight smile, too, he was sure. 'Give me your sunglasses, Zo, I'll tuck them inside with our bags.'

Zoe slipped them off and passed them to Malie. 'Thanks.'

Malie took them and fled the scene like she had a crocodile snapping at her heels. He watched her go, not knowing whether to be insulted, hurt or happy that his presence clearly affected her as much as hers did him.

'Don't mind Malie,' Zoe said, looking up at him with another smile, her eyes striking with their crystal-like quality now that the glasses were gone. They were green like Malie's, but lighter, almost ethereal.

She was beautiful, just as Malie was, but couldn't be more different. To Malie's golden bronzed skin, Zoe was creamy white. To Malie's wild curls, Zoe was all smooth blonde waves that ran free down her back. And where Malie was all curves and strength, Zoe was petite and porcelain-like, fragile even.

Though he knew from Malie that she was far from that under-neath. He could fully believe the strength of will that existed behind that smile and her astute green gaze that was now consider-ing him with far too much interest.

He cleared his throat. 'It's OK, she's just surprised to find me here, I get that.'

'I think it has more to do with the fact that we polished off two bottles of wine last night and are now suffering the consequences.'

'*Two*,' he said, and gave an impressed nod. 'Not bad going.'

'Why do you think I was wearing the glasses before?'

He chuckled. It was true it was overcast today, warm but in no way bright enough to warrant the accessory.

'That brutal, hey?'

'Pretty much, Malie's a bad influence.'

'She is that.' Only Zoe wouldn't realize just how much he meant it as he laughed with her. Malie had certainly corrupted his whole life plan. 'It was a good night, then?'

'The best. She's always fun to have around.'

'Very much so.'

Zoe squinted up at him and he knew he'd overstepped, again; she was far too astute not to miss the way his voice caught, the mess of emotions that he hadn't had the time to get a handle on yet coming through.

'You must miss her?' he said, throwing the focus back on her.

Zoe's eyes softened, her genuine love for her friend shining through in her face, just as it had in Malie's when she'd spoken of her friends. 'I miss them all.'

'You're lucky to have that kind of friendship. I think it's rare these days.'

'I think you're probably right.' Her eyes narrowed once more and he could feel the question coming: *Do you have friends like that?*

'So, last week…' he got in before she could, his eyes going back to the surf school, to Tara happily painting in spite of her complaints, 'did you manage to sort out your problem?'

She gave him a confused frown and he immediately regretted his choice of topic.

'*My* – oh!' Her brow lifted, her eyes widening. 'You mean, last Sunday?'

He nodded, wondering whether he would have been better keeping quiet since he now felt like a prize fool. Had Malie played him when she'd run out of his place claiming Zoe needed her?

'No, yeah, everything was OK, just having some… er… guy trouble.' She looked less pale and more lobster-coloured all of a sudden, her eyes now evading his own. 'I was really sorry to interrupt… *things*.'

'Things?' His own brow lifted, just how much did she know and how far was he willing to push her to find out?

'Yes,' she said, her voice rising. 'Dinner, wasn't it?'

Dinner and so much more… His grin couldn't be doused now, played or not. 'That's right.'

'What's right?' Malie reappeared, pushing the all-terrain beach chair in front of her, its fat grey tyres big enough to work over the sand.

'I was just saying to Zoe that she didn't need to apologize for interrupting our dinner last Sunday.'

He saw Malie's cheeks colour, her eyes flitting from him to Zoe and then to the beach. 'Oh yeah, sure, that was fine.'

'Maybe I could make up for it by treating you both to dinner this evening?' Zoe said, and both Malie and Todd looked to her like she was crazy. Not that Todd didn't want to say yes, but Malie…

'We have plans!'

'Do we?' Zoe asked all innocent, 'I wasn't aware of—'

'Right, come on, Kalani's waiting.' She shoved the chair up alongside Zoe.

'Can I help?' he asked.

The words were barely out of his mouth when Zoe said, 'That's very kind,' and Malie gave a sharp, 'No! I've got it.'

She positioned herself between him and Zoe and lifted her friend into her arms as if she weighed no more than a feather. He shouldn't be surprised, really, not when he considered how hard Malie trained and how very slight Zoe's frame was, but still he admired her. Especially when he was gifted the most glorious view of her behind as she bent forward. He dragged his eyes upwards to find Zoe giving him an apologetic smile over Malie's shoulder.

'Maybe we could all meet for a drink later instead?' Zoe suggested as she was lowered into the beach chair. 'I'm sure you guys will be thirsty after all this manual labour.'

He could just imagine the glare Malie would be directing at her friend.

'Sure… if Malie's up for it.'

'I am!' piped up Tara, sloshing her brush about.

'We'll see,' Malie mumbled, with a fleeting look in his direction before starting off down the beach.

He watched them go, unable to stop smiling. So Malie had talked to Zoe about him… Not only that, Zoe was matchmaking, it was as obvious as Malie's own interest in him. She wouldn't be half as flustered if he meant nothing to her.

And you really shouldn't be so happy about that fact.

But he was. There was no point denying it any longer, he wanted to mean something to her...

'Masters and Malie sitting in a tree...' His eyes snapped to Tara who was singing into her brush. 'K-I-S-S-I-N-G!'

'Tara!'

She pursed her lips into a smile and went back to work.

'You need to keep the paint on the brush and the wood, not everywhere else, Tara.'

'Oops,' she looked to the fresh splodge at her feet and scrubbed at it with her shoe. 'Sorry, I got distracted by the love hearts floating around your head.'

He shook said head and walked Zoe's wheelchair inside the school, safe from Tara's splash radius.

The girl wasn't wrong though, was she?

His smile that couldn't be doused was answer enough.

★ ★ ★

'Stop it, Zo.'

Malie adopted the same warning tone she used with mischievous kids who were putting their safety at risk in surfing lessons, only this time, the only thing at risk was Malie's blood pressure.

'What?'

'You're grinning like a fool.'

'You can't even see me back there.'

Malie sensed Zoe risk a glance her way but she was busy avoiding her eye and staring determinedly at Kalani and a bouncing Nalu straight ahead.

'I don't need to see you to know you're grinning so you might as well get it off your chest now before I take it out on you with the waves.'

'You wouldn't dare.'

'Try me.'

'Aw, come on, Malie,' Zoe's plea was full of teasing, 'you must see how funny this is.'

'What's funny?'

'Is that *seriously* him? The millionaire businessman who's up here...' she waved her hand above her head, her body lurching as Malie hit a rocky patch but it didn't stop Zoe's demonstration as she swung her hand down towards the ground, 'and you're here.'

'Exactly.'

She laughed. 'Yeah, he totally looked it in his jeans, painting the school and looking after that girl. Totally untouchable and unattainable by the likes of you.'

'Don't, Zo.'

'Don't what? I'm merely pointing out that every argument you've given me about why you can't go there with him is utterly flawed.'

'It is not.'

'It is so.' Zoe turned to look up at her. 'And you need to see that before this chance passes you by.'

Malie looked down at her friend – she wasn't laughing now, she was serious, her clear green eyes intense in their insistence. 'He likes you, Malie, it's obvious... and you like him too, that's why you're so unsettled about this.'

She went to deny it and couldn't. She couldn't lie to Zo, she'd done enough lying to herself.

She shook her head. 'It's just not that simple.'

'It could be.'

Malie took a deep breath and glanced back to the surf school, to where Todd and Tara were laughing about something, clearly thick as thieves.

'Stop trying to fight it, Devil. You never know what's around the corner.'

'I do, he has a flight out of here in two weeks.'

'So?'

'So, he will leave, and life will go back to how it was before.'

'All I'm hearing are excuses.'

She sighed. Yes, they were excuses, but they kept her this side of safe, this side of a life she knew and understood. She wasn't ready to take that plunge.

'You can't be scared, you're the daring one, you're the one who takes the risks and dreams big.'

No, she wasn't. And how did she tell Zoe that? She'd given up on her big wave-surfing dreams for fear of walking in her brother's footsteps, of replacing him, of failing him too. She'd fled Hawke's Cove rather than fight her parents for what she wanted, to surf, to be heard, to be visible again. And now she was running from Todd for fear of the unknown, of being happy and having it ripped away by a mean twist of fate, of feeling the guilt she was sure she'd feel to have it all where Koa would never be able to.

She shook her entire body out of the funk. Now wasn't the time for it. Now was about getting Zoe back on a board. A dream that she could follow and one that had existed for a decade already. It was long overdue…

'You're just trying to delay this,' Malie said, locking her eyes on Zoe's and pleading with her to drop it.

'No, I'm—'

'Come on, Zo, we've waited ten years to get you on a board again, leave it... for now, at least.'

Her friend looked up at her, her eyes wavering.

'Or are you just chicken?'

Zoe's eyes flashed just as she'd known they would. 'You know I'm not chicken.'

Malie shrugged with a laugh as she leaned forward and pushed the chair forward again. 'In that case, prove it!'

Zoe looked back to the sea. 'I will... but this conversation isn't over, Devil.'

'No, I didn't think it would be,' Malie said under her breath, forcing her head to clear and to focus on the here and now: getting Zoe on a board.

'*Aloha*, ladies, it's about time!' Kalani beamed at them as they neared.

'Zoe, meet Kalani, my epic godfather.' Malie stopped pushing the chair and walked around it to give Kalani a kiss to the cheek.

'Epic?' Kalani's chest puffed. 'I like the sound of that! It's great to meet you, Zoe.'

He held out his hand to Zoe just as Todd had done and she shook it. 'Great to meet you too. I have a sneaking suspicion Malie gets her wild streak from you.'

'Nah, I'm as tame as they come.'

'Yeah, right,' Malie laughed along with Zoe. 'Did I also mention he's a compulsive liar?'

'Ooh, harsh,' He pressed his palm to his bare chest, feigning hurt. 'We best begin before you dish out any more compliments. You ready to get started, Zoe?'

Her friend rubbed her hands up and down her thighs and took a deep breath. 'Yup.'

Malie smiled softly. She could see the need to be brave, the need to conquer her fears, the need to do this written in every line of her friend's face and her tight nod.

'We've got this, Zo.' She offered out her palm for a high-five, a move they'd done as children before they'd tackled any joint project and Zoe's smile became a grin.

'Hell, yeah,' she said, smacking her hand against Malie's.

'You heard the lady, let's do this,' Malie said to Kalani and they got moving, each one focused on the end game. Getting Zoe to surf again.

★ ★ ★

Within an hour, Zoe's confidence outshone Malie's. They were out in the water, Zoe life-jacketed up and lying prone on the surfboard, Malie standing on one side of her, Kalani on the other.

'Are you sure you're ready for this?' Malie asked.

'Definitely.' Zoe gave her a vibrant smile; she looked so small on the board, the life jacket size a large kid's, making her more vulnerable to look at. She gripped the special straps positioned so that she could hold herself in place, but as her confidence had grown over the course of the lesson, she was using them less and less.

Malie looked to Kalani and he smiled encouragingly.

'If you eat it, we'll be there in seconds to get you – OK?' she said.

'I just want to catch a wave already.'

'You've caught plenty.'

'*Alone*, Devil.'

A wave ran through them making the board bob and showering spray over them all. Malie looked out to the sea, judging the waves. It should be OK. It should be safe. She knew she was being overly cautious and shouldn't be. This is what it was about. Freedom. The power to be in control. The power to move unaided. It was exactly what Zoe wanted, what she needed.

'OK, I'm coming with.'

She left Kalani with Zoe and raced out of the water as quick as she could, taking up her board. It was far better for her to surf alongside Zoe than to try and keep up without the board. Her pulse raced in her chest, the thrill of knowing what was to come and the hope that the ocean would behave and deliver her friend the perfect wave.

'Let's do this!' She ran into the surf and leaped onto her board, powering herself out to them with a grin as wide as the sea itself.

'I'll keep watch,' Kalani said when she neared and he stepped back to free Zoe to paddle out with Malie.

'This is gonna be so epic,' she said to her friend. 'Come on, race you!'

'You have a head start,' Zoe complained, but she was already paddling hard and fast, keeping up with Malie stroke for stroke. Which wasn't really a surprise since Zoe's arms served as her legs too, wheeling her day in, day out. They grinned at one another and for a second, time fell away, they were kids again, doing what they loved. Leaving their problems at the shore and living for the wave.

'I can't believe we're doing this,' Malie said just before executing a perfect duck-dive, Zoe too.

As soon as she surfaced, she checked on Zoe – sure enough she was still there, her ponytail slick down her back, her eyes bright and smile big.

'I know. I think my parents would have a fit.'

'Yours and mine. But hey, we're adults now, we do what we want, when we want.'

They paddled out a little further, just beyond the breaking waves. The line-up was relatively quiet and anyone present knew her well enough to stay back and give them space.

They turned their boards and looked back to the shore, then each other.

'OK?' Malie asked.

'Never better.'

Adrenalin pumped through Malie's veins as she eyed the swells coming from behind. 'When I say go, we go?'

'How about when I say go, we go?'

Malie laughed, loving Zoe's spirit and marvelling at it all the same. 'You're on.'

They bobbed on the water, Zoe watching, Malie waiting on her. Happy, so happy. And then her friend nudged her head forward. 'Now.'

They were off, a little giggle erupting as they raced each other as well as the wave, and as it lifted, they took off. Malie popped up, pivoting away to keep a safe distance between them, her eyes flitting between her own path and Zoe as her friend rode the wave to shore, the spray kicking up in her face, her mouth closed against it but her smile obvious.

'Go, Zo!' she shouted and Kalani whooped from where he was positioned between them and the shoreline. It was spectacular to watch, and she knew it would feel even more so for Zoe, to feel the exhilarating power of the move and to do it alone.

As they neared the shoreline, Kalani was there alongside Zoe, helping her to stay on and bringing the board back around as Malie dived off her own.

She was buzzing from head to toe as she waded through the water towards them, her board under her palm.

'How was it?' she called out, already knowing the answer.

'You have to ask?' Zoe laughed, the sound coming in pants with her rapid breath. 'The best! The absolute best!'

'Ready to go again?'

Her friend wiped a hand over her face, across her dainty mouth. 'Definitely.'

Malie launched herself onto her board. 'Race ya!'

'Is everything a race with you, Malie?' It was Kalani who asked as they took off.

'I'm sorry, have you not met me before?' she called back, sending Zoe a wink and realizing her friend was already pulling away.

'You paddle faster than you used to,' she said, coming up behind her.

Zoe laughed back. 'Got to be some perks to being in a wheelchair – and before you say it, no, you're not claiming unfair advantage and getting a head start.'

'I wouldn't dare ask for one.'

'Yes, you would.'

And then they were off again, laughing, duck-diving, paddling, living in the moment. Malie felt the weight lifting from her shoulders. They'd done it... no, Zo had done it. She was surfing again. Just like old times, they were together facing off the waves, relishing them – and the accident, it was the past. It had changed things for them all, but they'd fought back, and it was time to let it go. No more guilt.

'I love you, Zo!' she called out, bursting with the freedom of it, the happiness.

Her friend laughed, the sound filled with her joy. 'I love you too, Devil.'

They were so wrapped up in their own world, the surf, their boards, the fun of it, neither of them felt the time passing or noticed the mini audience that had appeared half an hour later.

As they joined Kalani in the water, he gestured to his watch. 'We should call it a day. You don't want to push it too much on your first real outing.'

Zoe arched her back a little and nodded. 'I think you're right.'

'You feeling OK?' Malie asked, trying to keep the concern out of her voice. It would be tough on her friend's upper body, lying prone like that, not to mention all the paddling and the core strength required to navigate the wave and keep her legs in place, even with the board's special rails and straps.

'I feel amazing,' Zoe looked at her, her face vibrant and alive and boosting Malie as much as a fresh wave would.

'Good.'

'You were epic, Zoe!' It was Tara shouting from the shore, her hands cupped around her mouth. Next to her was Todd, his grin and admiration palpable across the distance. She caught his eye, felt her heart pulse and heard his words as though he was speaking them now: *let go of the guilt*.

She nodded to him, her smile telling him everything she felt inside. Gratitude, relief, love. So much love – and not just for Zoe…

She swallowed, feeling her cheeks flush, the realization swimming in her head, her heart.

'Seems you have a little fanbase, Zoe,' said Kalani, and her friend giggled.

'I think they were Malie's fans first.'

'Well, now they're both of yours,' Kalani said, helping Zoe up and into his arms. 'It's time we grabbed a bite to eat. I told Tara and Todd we should head down to the Tiki Burger Hut, you going to join us?'

Zoe looked to Malie, half pleading, half commanding her to say yes. 'Well?'

Malie shook herself out of her stupor. Today had been huge, monumental for Zoe, for them, and nothing could spoil it. Not even her messed-up feelings that were no one else's fault but her own. 'OK, OK, we'll come.'

'*Yes*,' Zoe said, grinning up at Kalani.

'Don't get too excited,' he said, wading through the water back to shore. 'It's not that special a place.'

Zoe looked back at Malie; it wasn't the place that she was excited about, it was seeing Malie spend some time with Todd. She didn't need to spell it out to Malie for her to know the truth.

Just wait until I get you alone later, she silently warned her friend.

Hell, who was she kidding? She needed Zoe, more now than ever.

CHAPTER SEVENTEEN

TARA LOVED THE BURGER hut, and under normal circumstances he would too. A nice greasy burger, fully loaded with fries on the side, what could be better?

Malie.

Having Malie take the plunge with him. To hell with their pasts and the pain, to look to the future together. He thought on all he'd said to her about Zoe, about her guilt and how she needed to put the past to bed. And he'd seen it all in her face as she'd come out of the water. The small nod of her head, her smile filled with so much emotion. For a second, he'd believed it wasn't just her elation over Zoe, of breaking free of the decade-old guilt, but something more, something akin to how he felt inside…

She wasn't giving him that vibe anymore, though. She'd barely spared him a glance since they'd arrived and if not for their companions, the conversation would have been non-existent.

'Are you not finishing those?' Tara asked, eyeing up his fries.

He pushed the plate closer to her. 'Help yourself.'

She grabbed a handful and put them all in her mouth at once. 'It's like you've never eaten before.'

'I've worked up an appetite,' she mumbled over her mouthful, raising her hand to cover her lips as she said a quick, 'Excuse me.'

'It really is nice of you to give up your time and help out at the surf school, Todd.' Zoe's smile was warm and encouraging. 'Malie tells me you've been having lessons too?'

'Yes, she's quite the teacher.' He smiled at Malie and she immediately lowered her eyes to her food. Not a good sign. He looked back to Zoe. 'She doesn't go easy on you, does she?'

Zoe's laugh was soft. 'She's always been that way – the stuff we got up to as kids, she was always the instigator. I don't think my childhood would have been half as exciting without her.'

Malie said nothing, her continued quietness bothering him more than he could stand. To go from that moment at the beach, that connection, that smile, to this… his hope crushed. He couldn't stand it. He had to leave. Now.

'I'm going to head to the bar for some drinks.' Kalani got to his feet. 'Anyone for another?'

'Not for me,' Todd said before Malie could use it as an excuse to leave. She belonged here, whereas he clearly didn't. 'I promised Tara I'd take her for ice cream.'

'But I haven't finished your fries…' Tara pouted.

He forced a grin. 'If you eat all those you won't have space for the ice cream.'

Kalani looked at her plate. 'The man's got a point… Ladies, same again?'

Both Malie and Zoe nodded.

'I'll see you guys back at the school for your lessons soon,' he said to Tara and Todd as they stood up too. 'And thanks again for all your help today.'

'You're welcome,' Todd said.

'Next time,' Tara blurted, 'can you warn me I'll be working?'

They laughed and Kalani ruffled her hair. 'Sure thing, kiddo, but I'm really grateful, you did the work of ten men up there today.'

Tara immediately puffed up. 'I did, didn't I?'

'Yup.' He gave her a gentle fist bump and left them to it.

Todd turned to look down at Malie and Zoe, almost wishing she'd stop him, ask him to stay, anything but this...

'Hopefully I'll see you again before you leave, Zoe.'

'You too.' She gave him a smile that smacked of an apology. Not that she had anything to be sorry for.

He looked to Malie, 'Let me know when you're next free for my lesson, or if it suits better, with Zoe staying, perhaps I could ask Kalani to take my lessons?'

He said it with his heart in his throat, hoping she would rebuke the suggestion.

'Sure... that would probably be best all round.'

He felt the pang of disappointment deep in his chest, immobilizing him, the silence awkward and heavy; he'd swear even Tara picked up on it as she took hold of his hand. 'Can we try the coconut today?'

He was slow to smile down at her. 'You can try whatever you like.'

Her grin lifted his spirits enough to leave but he couldn't stop himself from taking one backward glance to find Malie looking right back at him. Their eyes met, the world stopped, and for the briefest second, the world fell away again, and the future was full of possibility.

And then she blinked and the wall was back, her eyes turning to Zoe beside her and his heart squeezed tight in his chest.

'Come on, Mr Masters, I bet that queue is going to be huge.'

★★★

Malie averted her gaze. There was too much in his, too much she couldn't acknowledge or accept. No matter how much she wanted to. She looked at Zoe to find her friend too busy watching Todd leave.

She elbowed her. 'Hey.'

'Hey yourself,' Zoe murmured, nudging Malie back but not taking her eyes off him.

'*Hey.*'

Zoe dragged her eyes away and looked at Malie hard. 'Well, if you're not going to appreciate his… assets, why can't I?'

Malie stared at her, hardly able to believe what her friend was saying. Yes, Malie had been clear that there was nothing between them, that there would never be, but she'd also been clear about why. Did Zoe really—

'See!' Her friend suddenly blurted. 'You care!'

It took another second to realize that Zoe had played her. 'Not funny, Zo.'

'I'm just trying to make you see sense.'

'Yeah, well you ogling the first guy I've ever wanted to get serious with really isn't going to help.'

'It just did.'

'What do you mean, it just did?'

'That's the most honest you've been about him to date, admitting that you want a relationship with him.'

'I'm not admitting—'

Zoe's hardened stare cut her off.

'OK, I am admitting that, but it still doesn't change things.'

'Change what? The whole, he's a millionaire and has no place hanging around the little people like—'

'I didn't say little people.'

'It's what you meant though, Devil. And quite frankly it sucks that you would ever think it. And if you bring up my family's wealth again, the rest of my drink's going over your head. There aren't thousands of miles and a WiFi connection between us to protect you now.'

Malie felt her cheeks burn. 'I'm sorry, I didn't mean to upset you with that, it just slipped out, I was desperate.'

'Desperately trying to avoid the feelings you have for him, yeah, I get that. But if you want my opinion, guys like that are in short supply. The way he is with Tara, helping out Kalani, he obviously has the brains to have reached the grand heights he has career-wise and still he puts time and money into his charity ventures, into people that need it...'

Malie picked at the chips on her plate but didn't eat one. She couldn't stomach any more food now. Not with Zoe pointing out the obvious. But how great he was wasn't the issue.

'To have all that going for him *and* to look like he does, I think it's practically criminal that you've turned him down.'

Malie pushed her plate away and said nothing. What could she say other than to repeat herself?

'The thing is, I thought V was lucky,' Zoe continued, on a roll, 'finding Oliver and the happiness she has, but you put him and Oliver side by side, I'd struggle to choose between them. And that happiness she's found, it could be yours too.'

Malie shook her head, 'Don't, Zo.'

'Don't what?'

'Tease.' *Don't tease me with the picture-perfect future that deep down I crave but don't think I can have.*

'I'm not teasing you, Devil, I'm telling you to get out there and take what he is offering. It exists, it's not a figment of my imagination how he looks at you and quite frankly, if I was you and I had him looking at me like that, I'd be wheeling myself out of here and high-tailing it after him right this minute.'

There was a startled cough from behind them and they both turned to find a flustered Kalani staring at a point between their heads. 'I'll just put these down here and make myself scarce.'

'You don't need to—' Malie started to say.

'No, no, it's fine, this has *girl talk* written all over it. I'll be back at the bar... with the men.'

He fled and they watched him go, torn between guilt and giggles.

'Oh dear,' Zoe covered her mouth, 'do you think he'll be able to look me in the eye tomorrow?'

They both laughed, the atmosphere easing.

'Look, Malie, you are one of my best friends,' Zoe said softly. 'I love you like a sister. I wouldn't be a very good friend if I didn't try and make you see what you could be giving up. Why not just give it a go, see where it takes you? Where *he* takes you?'

Malie looked at her friend. 'I can't. You know me, I've never over-thought getting it on with a guy before – they're either hot or not, and if they're hot, I'm straight in there! But with him, it's different, it's insane, Zo. It's like every bit of me goes into overdrive, I want to kiss him so much that I don't dare.'

'You know this sounds ridiculous.'

'It's not ridiculous, because I don't think I could ever get enough of him, that's the problem. I know that if I start down that path I won't ever want to hop off.'

'Who says you have to hop off?'

'Life does, it's never all roses.'

'No, it's not, but having someone like that to share it with, to face it all with…' Zoe sounded wistful now. 'It's worth the risk.'

'I'm not worth the risk.'

'Why?'

'Because I'm not destined to fall head over heels, to survive a whirlwind romance and get a Happy Ever After.'

'Why?'

'Because I don't deserve it.'

'Why?'

'Zoe! Are you trying to sound like a toddler?' She could feel the emotion welling up inside, could feel it bursting to get out. The pain of loss, the guilty ache, the reasons she denied herself love and was denied it.

'No, you just need to make some sense.'

'I can't be in love, he can't be in love with me, because I can't have that kind of happiness.'

'And still I have to ask why?'

'Because it terrifies me. Because Koa never got any of it. Because who's to know what's around the corner. Aren't they reasons enough?' There, it was out, and the wedge in her throat swelled, choking at her, the pain of losing her brother, the pain of life after.

'But Malie, you spend your days helping others live life to the full, doing everything you can to make up for the rubbish hand they've been dealt – me included – don't you think you should allow yourself the same?'

She shook her head and pressed the back of her hand to her mouth. Tried to breathe.

'Come on, Devil, don't you think *you* should be living your life to the full and going after what your heart wants.'

She couldn't answer.

'I won't tell you what to do, I can't, but right now you're treating him badly and he doesn't deserve that.'

Malie's eyes shot to hers.

'Don't look at me like that, you are,' Zoe insisted, though her eyes were soft with sympathy. 'That's not the Malie we all know and love. You swing between ignoring him, being standoffish and downright rude.'

'I am n—'

'You know you are,' Zoe challenged. 'You almost floored him rushing off to get the beach chair, treating him like he had some nasty disease and unable to get yourself away from him quick enough. It's just not nice… and it's not you.'

'It's impossible to act normal around him when my heart feels like it's going to explode in my chest, and I have a million different thoughts racing through my brain.'

'As well as the aching lady bits, hey?'

Malie choked on a strained laugh. 'That phrase sounds so wrong coming from you.'

'Be that as it may, my point still holds.'

'I know and yes, yes to it all!'

'You should just follow your gut.'

'If I followed my gut, you wouldn't have surfed today, and I'd have had him naked by now.'

'Not with Kalani, Tara and me as spectators, I hope.'

Another laugh.

'OK, so all joking aside,' Zoe said after a while, 'if you're not going to see where this connection between you goes, tell him the truth, tell him why you can't, at least let him understand it has nothing to do with him and everything to do with you.

'You mean the whole, *it's not you, it's me*,' Malie laughed into her drink, chucking back a gulp. 'A bit clichéd, wouldn't you say.'

'Frankly, you are being all cliché.'

'Cheers... Anyway, it doesn't matter, I've already told him.'

'What?' Zoe's eyes widened in surprise. 'You've told him about Koa, you've told him about your ridiculous sense of guilt, your avoidance of anything that might cause you future pain. The *whole* shebang?'

'Practically yes, and he agreed, Zo.'

She stared at her incredulous. 'He *agreed*?'

'Yes! He doesn't want to take a chance on love either, his mother died when he was born and left his father crushed. He's seen what happens when you love someone and you lose them, and he has no interest in going there.'

'Absolute... absolute... gah! Something I'm not going to say out loud but let's go with *nonsense*. You're still making excuses.'

Malie shook her head. 'It's not nonsense to want to protect yourself from future pain.'

'That wasn't what I meant. I get why you both feel that way, what's nonsense is the fact you think he doesn't want to take that risk, the way he was looking at you...' her friend smiled over the memory and took a long swig of her drink, 'that man had a love emoji smack bang on his forehead.'

Malie laughed in spite of herself, Zoe's imagery working some magic.

'I'm serious, though, Devil, you need to stop living constrained by the past. Younger Malie would have taken this chance – to hell with the consequences.'

'Yeah, well, younger Malie learned her lesson the hard way.'

'I think it's time for a new lesson… before you lose this chance at happiness, real happiness.'

'I am happy,' Malie insisted, far too strongly.

'Really?'

She was happy. *Wasn't she?*

She thought about the surf school, the kids she'd helped over the years, Kalani, Nalu, her home here, and smiled. Then she thought of home-home, of the Cove, her parents, of the part of her life she longed to have back and avoided at all costs now.

She felt Zoe's hand cover her own on the table. 'Hey, I'm sorry, I just think… I think you should talk to him. At least be honest about how you feel towards him and that way you can come away knowing you were straight with him. I think he deserves that, don't you?'

'I'll think about it.'

★★★

She was still thinking about it a week later. And though it hung over them at times, especially when Todd made an appearance at the surf school when both she and Zoe were there, her friend hadn't pressed her again and she was grateful for it. She wanted to make the most of Zoe's stay, not dwell on the poor state of her love life or lack thereof.

The week had gone too quickly as it was. Days were being split between lessons at the surf school and sightseeing with Zo. They'd devoured pineapple whip, surfed until Zoe was too tired to surf any more, laughed and talked until their voices were raw. Just like old times. They'd even called Lils and Victoria and had a virtual birthday party for Lils. Drinking bubbles and getting giddy over the internet. But now the week was up, and it was time for Zoe to leave.

The car waiting to take her to the airport sat with its engine running outside Malie's apartment. They'd agreed: no airport goodbyes. Too much crying and making fools of themselves in public. So instead they were doing it alone on the threshold of Malie's apartment, with just the cab driver to witness it.

'I'm going to miss you,' Malie said, a tear running down her cheek as she looked down at her friend and wished she could stay.

'Hey, we said no tears,' Zoe admonished, her own cheeks damp.

'No, we agreed no airport goodbye.' Malie leaned down and pulled her friend into a bear hug.

'Jesus, Devil, you're going to crush me.'

Malie just laughed and held her tighter, hearing Zoe sniff and give a choked laugh back.

'Thank goodness we have V's wedding to look forward to,' Malie said, pulling back and pressing a kiss to Zoe's cheek.

'It almost makes a trip back to the Cove worth it.'

'You say that, but I don't think you mean it really.'

Zoe manoeuvred her chair around and gave her a look. 'You can think that if it makes you feel better.'

Malie just wrapped her arms around her middle, feeling suddenly alone. 'Safe travels, Zo, message me when you get there.'

'I will.' She waved her hand in the air and then joined the driver who helped her in. She rolled the window down, her fingers curling over the door as she leaned out. 'And talk to Todd, Malie, please.'

'I said I'd think about it.' She blew her a kiss. 'Love you!'

'Love you too!'

Malie didn't move again until the car became a dot on the horizon, the sun setting around it. She looked back inside her apartment, its orderly state a stamp of Zoe's presence, and realized it was the last place she wanted to be. With Zoe gone, after seven days together, it felt emptier than ever.

She walked through the room, donned her surf wear and grabbed her board off the wall. There was only one place she wanted to be right now, and that was with Koa.

CHAPTER EIGHTEEN

TODD WAS TRYING TO concentrate on work, but it was late, and the later it got, the easier it was for Malie to take over his thoughts. As though he lacked the energy to push them away. Be it a smile, a tease, a lesson instruction, his brain just replayed her over and over and he had no idea what to do about it.

He pushed the papers he'd been reading away and swivelled in his chair to look out at the view. From here he could see the pergola under which they'd danced just two weeks ago and beyond it the beach where she'd saved him from the riptide – *no,* current. And in just one more week he'd be gone, flying to New York on business and in all likelihood, he'd never see her again.

Because why would he?

Now that he'd visited the school – witnessed what it was capable of – there would be no need for him to attend future visits, unless he could fabricate a reason, which was a ridiculous thought to even have. He didn't have the luxury of time to chase a woman who'd made her feelings perfectly clear… only she hadn't.

She was a walking contradiction and the idea of leaving without gaining at least an understanding of what stood between them bothered him more than he'd care to admit. He fisted his hands as his gut rolled with it. No, he did admit it, all right. He didn't want to leave things like this.

But he could hardly *make* her talk to him.

He pushed up out of his chair and didn't really think about where he was heading. He left the study, left the house, walked under the pergola. Didn't think on anything until he'd removed his shoes and sunk his bare feet into the cooling sand, and then she was there, telling him to do just that. Like she had done that night, after their dance.

He could almost see her before him, cocktail glass in hand, her eyes dancing, her laugh soft and alluring. But it wasn't a laugh that filled his ears now, it was the crashing of the waves and a… strange, snuffling sound. The kind an overexcited dog makes, a dog like…

He squinted into the dark – *Nalu?*

And then he appeared out of a ditch in the sand, one he'd likely created, and launched himself across the beach towards him. Todd scanned the rest of the area. Nalu wouldn't be here alone and that meant Malie was here somewhere. But the beach was deserted, the only movement that of the palms and the flora swaying in the breeze.

He looked out to the sea, to the low glow on the horizon as it swallowed the last of the sun, and then he saw her. A solitary dark shape in the water, so still he would have missed her had he not been looking.

'Zoe's gone home, hey, Nalu?' He ruffled the dog's head, but his concerned gaze was on her. Kalani mentioned in passing that Zoe was staying for a week, and that week would be up today. 'Is she OK, do you think?'

The dog made a low whining sound that married with his own inner turmoil.

Could it really all be over in a week? And why did it bother him so much? He'd never sought more from a woman, why did he want it so much from her?

It was a stupid question, he knew why, he just couldn't quite believe it. Despite all his better judgement, his own messed-up childhood and family dynamics, he had fallen for her. He was head over heels in love with Malie.

Nalu started to trot back to the shoreline and Todd followed. If Zoe had left today, maybe she'd be grateful of the company, even if it was him offering it.

He watched her bobbing out at sea. She looked so sad, lost even, and he knew with certainty that he couldn't just leave her. Not until he knew she was OK. He sat down instead and waited, his arms resting on his bent knees, his eyes on her. Nalu gave him a sniff and then sat down beside him, mimicking his gaze.

'You like her a lot too, hey?'

And now he was talking to a dog. But at least Nalu didn't object to his company. Not like the woman who was now turning her board for shore, although she didn't surf the waves like he expected, she seemed to let them plough over her, through her, like she was… like she was broken.

Something caught in his throat, a swell of emotion so forceful he couldn't breathe past it. The urge to call out her name, to startle her into being *her*: fierce, vibrant, full of energy, even if that energy smacked of *go away*, it would be preferable to this. But he was scared she'd run, paddle as fast as she could away.

Instead he sat stock-still and waited.

She spied him the second she slipped off the board and stood.

'*Todd?*' His name escaped her lips in a startled gasp that had him shooting to his feet.

'I'm sorry, Malie, I didn't mean to scare you, I just... I came for a walk, I hadn't expected anyone to be here.'

She waded out of the water and brushed her wet hair out of her face, her eyes glistening in the moonlight and he knew it wasn't just the sea beading on her lashes.

'You don't have to apologize...' she took a breath that seemed to shudder through her, 'you have as much right to be here as me.'

He frowned, pain working its way through him as he witnessed her suffering up close. 'Have you been crying?'

She blinked rapidly and looked away, swallowing hard. 'I've... I'm...'

He closed the distance between them, unable to bear it any longer, and he rested his hands on her arms, bowing his head to try and get her to look at him. 'What's wrong, Malie?'

She wiped a shaky hand over her face, her other still clutching her board. 'It's nothing, I'm just being silly.'

'Crying isn't silly.'

Her eyes looked to him but her face was still averted. 'Zoe left today.'

Her lashes fluttered, her voice cracked, and she looked back to the darkened horizon. 'It was harder to say goodbye than I expected.'

'Oh, Malie, that's not silly, that just shows you care.'

She lifted her chin, visibly drawing strength from somewhere to speak. 'Having Zoe here, it just reminded me of how much I miss home, how much I miss my friends, even my family.'

He took the board from her and laid it down on the sand, reaching for her next, his instincts now driving him and overriding any worry that she would reject him. She needed him this second and he could be there for her, he could at least do that.

He pulled her into his arms and hugged her head to his chest, her hair damp in the palm of his hand.

'I'm sorry,' she whispered, her body trembling against his.

He pressed his lips to her hair, breathed in her scent, all sea and coconut. 'You don't need to apologize for crying, not to me, not ever.'

She sniffed. 'I don't mean for crying, I mean... I mean...'

She tensed against him and pressed up off his chest, her eyes finding his. 'I'm sorry for how I've treated you.'

He lifted his hands to her face, stroked her cheeks as he stared down into her eyes which today looked as black as the sky above and twinkling with both the moon and fresh tears. 'I just wish I could understand why you're still running from me at every opportunity, why you won't give us a chance to see where this will take us?'

'We talked about this, we said we couldn't, we agreed.'

She was shaking her head at him.

'I know, but that was before... before this... before I started to understand how I feel... I don't know, I just know I don't want to say goodbye, that it's too much to ignore... I want to take a chance, I believe we're worth a chance, don't you?'

But her head was still shaking, her eyes staring up into his awash with fresh tears.

'What is it? Tell me?'

He sounded as desperate as he felt inside. Desperate, frustrated, almost out of hope.

'I'm scared.'

He frowned, his fingers pulsing around the delicate skin of her neck as he caressed her. 'What are you scared of?'

'I'm scared of falling in love...' She wet her lips, her choice of words making his heart flutter painfully in his chest. 'I'm scared of the happiness I might find...' she dragged in a breath, the next few words a mere whisper, 'only to have it ripped away.'

'I know, I know, but we can't know what the future holds, I just know that I can't turn my back on this.'

'But your father, my brother.'

A tear ran over one lid, its trail killing him as he smoothed it away with the pad of his thumb.

Hope flickered to life, she wasn't running, she was listening. It was a start. 'Would you rather live a half-life in fear of what may be?'

She couldn't answer him and he could see the fight dying in her eyes.

'I'm scared of the guilt too.'

'The guilt?' His frown deepened, what could she mean by that? She'd faced her guilt head-on when she'd helped Zoe surf again, she'd let go of it.

'The guilt of finding the kind of happiness that will forever be denied my brother.'

He shook his head. 'Malie, you have to stop with this guilt thing – do you honestly think that Koa would *want* you to feel that way?'

She closed her eyes, shutting him out, and it all slid into place for him: It wasn't just her love life this guilt affected, it was everything else too. He remembered their conversation in the car when he'd asked why she wouldn't compete in the Queen of the Pipe, the way she'd closed herself off, just like she was doing now, how her smile never quite reached her eyes.

'It's why you don't compete in Big Wave competitions, isn't it?' he said softly. 'It's your passion but you don't do it... because of him.'

Slowly, she opened her eyes, her surprise that he'd put it together clear. 'I can't bear it... walking in his footsteps, overtaking them or even failing in them, like he doesn't matter, like none of it matters, when it does...' She squeezed her eyes shut, opening them again to blaze up at him. 'It hurts, really hurts.'

'But you wouldn't be, don't you see that? You'd be living your life for the both of you, doing everything you dreamed of doing together.'

A tremor ran through her body, he could feel it through his fingers, see her head shake as her brow creased into a frown.

'Do you really think your brother would want you to forgo doing what you love, what you were born to do? Do you think he'd want to see you like this, torn up with guilt, putting off your own happiness? You saw how sad he was when your parents quit, you lived through it with him.'

She was so quiet but he knew she was listening, he only hoped his words were getting through.

'If your brother was still alive, would you be competing?'

A wet smile lifted her lips. 'If Koa was still here, everything would be different. Mum and Dad would still have their surf school, their boards, their lives, real living, not just going through the motions day in, day out.'

'But can't you see that that's what you're doing too, just going through the motions?'

She shook her head fiercely now. 'No, I've been OK, I got out of there, I refused to quit surfing because they demanded it,

I surfed and surfed and surfed, and then I used that skill to make others happy, to help them. I've made a life for myself away from all that pain and heartache.'

'A life that's still constrained by it.'

'It's not.'

He brushed his thumb over her lip, felt it tremble beneath his touch and fought the urge to kiss her, to make her realize what really living feels like.

'You'd be crowned Queen of the Pipe several times over already if you were living your life to the full – and you wouldn't be pushing me away, you'd be in my arms, my bed, my...' He almost said heart but he knew she was already there and so he gave in and kissed her, softly, heard her breath catch, felt her lips part.

'The truth is your brother would want you to go after your dreams,' he said, his mouth brushing over hers as he spoke, his own body thrumming with awareness of hers, so close and yet so far away. 'If you were honest with yourself, you'd know it's true.'

A whimper worked its way up her throat – was it denial, acceptance, something more? But then her hands were in his hair, her mouth moving beneath his and he couldn't think past the rush of warmth that flooded his body, the tightness, the need...

'Let me take care of you, Malie, please, just let me be there for you...'

★ ★ ★

Let me take care of you...

Malie broke away startled, her eyes wide, her mouth agape.

Let me take care of you...

She stared up into his eyes as black as the night, at the sympathy, the pain, the worry and the pity. Oh my God, he pitied her, he pitied her life and the pain she was in. That wasn't love, it wasn't close.

But for a second, she'd thought it, she'd felt it. She'd taken Zoe's words and used them to reassure herself that this was real. *No.* Don't blame Zoe for this.

You believed it, because you wanted to believe it, because you love him more than you ever thought possible, and now you are paying the price.

She'd got so wrapped up in it, in the moment, in the fantasy, that she'd missed all the signs. How could she have been so stupid? She knew Todd was a white knight. His philanthropic nature, his inherent need to help those that need it, and now he wanted to make her his charity case, confusing it with so much more.

Her stomach twisted tight, goose bumps prickling over her wet skin. 'I have to go, it's getting cold, I need to get dry.'

She was rambling but she needed to get away from him before she broke again, before she convinced herself that this was more than it was. Because now she knew how much she wanted it to be more, how much she had fallen hard and fast, exposing herself to all the pain she had worked so hard to avoid.

'Malie?' He frowned down at her. 'What's wrong?'

She ducked away from him to grab up her board, startling a snoozing Nalu at their feet, 'Don't you see, Todd?' she threw at him. 'I'm your charity case, you're trying to help me like you do all those kids, you care for me only in so far as you want to fix me.'

'That's not true, I want to help you *because* I care about you.'

'No, no, you don't! You're like some bloody white knight so eager to save me!' She shook her head furiously – *don't listen to him, it won't end well, it can't.* 'And I don't deserve it, I don't deserve your pity, your help or whatever this is between us.'

'*Malie…*' He stepped towards her and she backed away. 'Don't presume to tell me how I feel, I know how I feel and I'm telling you now, this is something special and worth fighting for.'

'Like you fought to fix your relationship with your father.'

He stilled, his expression turning stone cold. 'Why would you say that?'

'Doesn't feel so good when the shoe's on the other foot, does it?' She gave a harsh laugh, but it was nervous, driven by guilt at her lash-out. It had worked, though, it had made him stop.

'I know I've made some mistakes with my father, that I've hardly been the model son and vice versa.'

'And yet you think you can stand there and tell me how I should deal with my loss of Koa; I bet you're going to tell me to give my parents another chance to make it right too, aren't you?'

He stared at her, both anger and shock written in every taut line of his face, his only movement the pulse ticking his jaw as he clamped his mouth shut. She floundered in the face of it, her heart fluttering wildly, guilt swelling painfully in her chest. Guilt and a far more powerful emotion that pushed to be acknowledged. The depths of her feelings for him. *Oh, God.*

'Why don't you just do us both a favour, Todd? Go and fix your own family issues before daring to tackle mine, hey?'

His eyes flickered with the direct hit and she felt her palms itch to reach for him, to stroke away the pain of her words, to take them back. She raised her chin to challenge him, to challenge the rising tide of emotion inside that insisted she cave.

'I don't need your help,' she bit out, using her surfboard as a shield now. 'And I don't need you!'

'No... you've made that perfectly clear.' His voice was so low she barely recognized it as his. She wanted to walk around him, to disappear into the undergrowth and not look back but her legs had gone to jelly. She couldn't trust them to take her weight if she so much as moved.

'I'm sorry, I don't want to hurt you.'

He gave a harsh laugh, the sound sending an ice-like trickle running down her spine.

'Lucky for you, I grew up on rejection, Malie,' he rasped, any trace of affection he'd held for her gone. Obliterated by the pain she'd inflicted. 'You're just another to add to a very long list so don't lose sleep over it. I won't.'

Her entire body shivered, her mind screaming at her to say something that would make it all better, that would bring the Todd she knew back. But she'd gone too far. She'd ruined everything.

'I—'

'Save it, Malie, you can have your waves and your board; they seem to do a far better job than me.'

And then he turned, and he was gone. He didn't even look back when she dropped to her knees, her board falling to the sand. He didn't seem to hear her racked sob, or Nalu's whimper.

She'd done it now. It was over. Really over.

'Oh, God, Nalu.' She hugged her little friend to her chest. 'What have I done?'

CHAPTER NINETEEN

TODD STRAIGHTENED HIS BOW tie and wanted to rip the damn thing away.

It was the last day of the programme, the last day for him in Hawaii, and it was meant to be a celebration. A gala ball to celebrate the work of the charity and the surf school, and more specifically, Malie. Pain caught at his chest, took away his ability to breathe, his ability to move. The echo of the words she'd thrown at him that night a week ago punished him even now. She'd been running scared. He knew that, but it in no way softened their blow. Or her rejection.

But tonight, he would have to see her again.

He'd avoided the surf school, the beach too, doing all he could to stay out of her way and not have to suffer it all over again. But he couldn't avoid tonight. He was the host and she a guest of honour.

He yanked at the bow tie ends and turned sharply away from his reflection that judged him such a fool. She hadn't asked for him to care for her, to fall for her, he'd done that all off his own bat.

His heels clipped against the polished surface of his floor as he made his way into the hallway and saw his PA standing there.

'Are we all set, Grace?'

'Against all the odds, yes.' They'd intended to hold the gala in the grounds of the house, just as they had the cocktail party, but it had rained most of the day and was set to continue into the evening. The weather very much like his mood. 'With the doors open between the living and dining area, the room is impressive enough and the dance space ample, it's ideal.'

'Good.'

The doorbell sounded and she stood to attention, hooking the tablet she carried safely into the crook of her arm. 'I will greet the guests while you get yourself a drink.' She frowned and did a quick scan of his overall appearance before patting his bow tie in place and stepping back. 'You look like you could use it. Is everything OK?'

'Of course.'

She hesitated a second longer but, ever the professional, let it go, her smile that of the perfect hostess. 'Let's get this party started.'

She twirled away in a cloud of green silk, her black hair smooth down her back. This was her thing, throwing parties; he knew she'd get a kick out of it and balance his anti-party stance quite perfectly.

He headed through the double doors that led into the space that had been created for tonight's gala ball and paused to take it in. Grace had outdone herself. Where the cocktail party had been beach-themed, tonight's party was all glitz and glamour, and intimate with it. Candles adorned the tables, glassware sparkled, bottles of champagne chilled in ice buckets and an acoustic duo played the perfect background music.

Tonight was about thanking everyone for their hard work. The Foundation hadn't paid for it. He had. It was another way he could contribute and give back. Like the white knight Malie accused him of being.

Was that really all she saw in him? Did she truly think that's why he cared about her?

And why are you even pondering it anyway? She wants nothing from you.

He strode across the room, his intent to pick up a bottle and neck a glassful before anyone came in but he was intercepted halfway across the floor by a waiter. 'Sir?'

He offered up a tray of prepared glasses like he'd spied his intent – of course, he would have, he was paid to be on hand and Todd should have known there would be some ready.

He took it and nodded his thanks, but couldn't trust his voice yet. He threw back a gulp and turned to watch the doors. He prepared his face, his smile. He just needed to get through the next few hours and then he'd be free. Tomorrow morning he'd be on a plane to New York and he could start putting this blip behind him.

Because that's all this was, a blip…

He took another swig and concentrated on it, rather than the internal laughter mocking his resolve.

★★★

'Malie, if you don't get yourself out here now,' Kalani called through her open doorway, 'I swear to God I'm going to come in there and—'

She came around the corner and he cut his rant dead, his mouth hanging open, his eyes wide as he stood holding a bright red umbrella above his head.

'What's wrong?' She smoothed down her front, her hands

patting nervously at the soft silk as her heart went into full-on panic mode. 'Oh, God, is it too much? I knew this was a bad idea, what the hell was I thinking…'

She started to turn away, to race back to her bedroom and find something else when Kalani reached out.

'Don't even think about it.'

'Look, I know we're running late but I can't turn up looking like this, not when it's left you gawping all fish-like!'

'Hey, it's not cos you look bad.' He shook his head, his hand falling back to his side. 'I was just stunned speechless.'

'Kalani, you're never speechless.'

'And I've never seen you dressed in a gown with lethal heels before.'

Her heart did a little flutter, her shoulders easing. 'You mean, I look OK?'

'More than OK, and now I think on it properly, as your godfather I should probably send you back to get changed after all.'

She laughed at that, her nerves almost forgotten. 'In that case, I'll just grab my bag.'

She teetered back into the dining room. It really was alien wearing heels again but it helped her confidence which was already in tatters thanks to her nerves. They'd taken a thorough bashing in the run-up to this evening, knowing it would be the first time she'd see Todd since their… since their argument… if you could call it that.

He hadn't even come to watch over the kids' sessions, not even the last few where there had been tears from her students, even herself. She'd never had the same group for so long and it had been impossible not to become attached.

She'd even promised Jonny that she would investigate surf centres back home and send the details on to the Foundation in the hope that the kids could keep up their surfing. And for the briefest of moments, she'd even thought of her family's surf school, standing empty – such a waste – and the idea of talking to her parents – of opening their eyes to what was possible if she could get them on board with the idea, of the great work they could do. But there were so many what-ifs, so much doubt, so many past arguments to overcome...

And then there was Todd. He hadn't even finished his lessons that he'd paid through the nose for and she knew he hadn't taken them with anyone else. Guilt chewed her up inside and this time it had nothing to do with her past and everything to do with how she'd treated him. She knew she had to apologize, even if she had to drag him away to do it, she had to make him believe how truly sorry she was.

It was the reason she hadn't bailed on the night altogether, that and the fact the people from the Foundation would be there, Tara's parents among them.

Tonight was about celebrating the success of the work they had done with the surf school and hopefully it meant there would be lots more programmes like this one. Programmes that made her happy to be a part of, that got her out of bed of a morning and sent her to bed smiling at night. Only in the last week she hadn't been smiling, she'd been pining. Missing Todd more than she could ever have thought possible. She'd tried telling herself it was because it was straight off the back of Zoe leaving, but she knew she was only lying to herself.

She wasn't the same person she'd been before Todd's visit.

She wasn't the same Malie who was happy in her own company, or messing about with the lads on the waves, or teaching at the school. She wasn't the same Malie, content with sitting on her board patiently awaiting a wave. She wanted more.

But she also knew she wasn't ready to take that plunge. Especially with someone as special as Todd. She'd hurt him enough already.

She just had to make it right. She needed to apologize and hope he could forgive her, then maybe she would be able to move on without this feeling of emptiness swelling inside.

'Don't tell me you can't find it!' Kalani called from the doorway, shaking her out of her thoughts. 'If you don't hurry all the good food will be gone.'

'Sorry,' she said, scooping her bag over her shoulder. 'All ready.'

'Thank heaven for that.' He lifted the umbrella between them as she locked up the apartment. 'Your feet will be pleased to hear that I've brought the car.'

'You're a lifesaver.' She gave him a small smile in thanks and turned to hook her arm through his. 'Right, let's do this.'

He laughed. 'You sound like you're about to head into battle.'

She gave him another smile – *that's because it feels like I am.*

★ ★ ★

Todd checked his watch again. It was getting late and he really wanted to deliver his speech before too much champagne had been consumed. But how could he deliver the speech when she wasn't even here, and neither was Kalani?

'I think you're just going to have to start,' Grace said as she approached him, her trusty tablet still under her arm. 'We've already delayed things by half an hour and the kitchen is wanting to bring the food out.'

'Still no sign of them?'

She shook her head. 'I'm afraid not, I've asked the men on the gate to message as soon as they arrive.'

'OK.'

She looked to him with concern. 'Are you sure you're OK?'

He sipped his champagne and avoided her eye. 'Yes, or I would be if our guests were all here.'

'You were like this before, though, in fact, you've been like it all week. Is there something I can help you with?'

'Not unless you can miraculously make our guests appear.' He eyed the room, hoping for the umpteenth time he'd just missed them in the crowd, but he knew deep down he hadn't. He'd know with every fibre of his being if Malie was in the room.

Was she going to bail on the evening? Were they both going to? Had she said something to Kalani to make him pull out?

Surely not. Not when the surf school's work with the charity was so important. But then, why else would they not be here? Perhaps he should ring her, or ring Kalani at least. He pulled his phone out of his pocket, was about to look up his number when a ping came from Grace's tablet.

She glanced at her screen, her smile instant. 'Kalani's car has just pulled up.'

He felt the tension ease from his body. 'Thank goodness.'

She sent him a funny look and he knew she'd likely spied more than just the professional in his relief, but she didn't comment on it, instead she suggested, 'Why don't you get started on the welcome speech and I'll hurry them through?'

He nodded, calmer this time.

'I'll get the musicians to introduce you.'

He nodded again, took another sip of champagne but he didn't taste it, didn't even feel it go down, he was already preparing himself for seeing her. He had to get this speech right, he had to thank her for her work, he had to make her see that as far as their shared passion went, they'd achieved something to be proud of and to set aside the personal.

He barely heard the introduction; in fact, he was barely aware of the words coming out of his own mouth as he spoke about the Foundation, something that he could do in his sleep. Anything from elevator pitches to the full-on nitty gritty, he knew it all, because Fun For All was his baby and the past three weeks had been a huge milestone in its progress.

Not so much for his heart.

He scanned the crowd as he spoke, resting on certain individuals who had played a role, be it in the organization, the funding, the support workers, the parents – Tara's parents. He paused, they looked so happy, so different to that first day on the island and he took a breath. It's not all bad. So why did he feel so lost, so unfulfilled?

The main doors pushed open and his heart skipped a beat, his eyes landing on the arrivals, only to have it sink in his chest. Kalani and Grace. No Malie.

He was about to look away, to get back on track when Kalani and Grace stepped away from the door and a flash of red pulled him back. *Malie?*

Words failed him, the world tuning out as all he could see was her.

She looked hesitant, her eyes flitting about the room as she entered. Her hair had been tamed into a fountain of curls that spilled from up high, framing her face, teasing over her bare shoulders. Red silk wrapped around her upper body, enhancing her curves, her small waist, and from there the view disappeared behind the crowd.

She was breathtakingly beautiful and now everyone was looking at her, curious as to what had caught his eye and silenced him.

She gave a nervous smile to the room as the doors closed behind her.

'Sorry we're late,' she said, lifting her shoulders in a self-conscious gesture and giving a little wave of her fingers. He could see the colour creeping into her cheeks, feel her embarrassment across the room.

'Not at all, you're right on time,' he assured her. 'I was just about to tell the room all about you, come up here, Malie.'

The crowd murmured as they parted for her, the men virtually drooling, the women beaming. There was no jealousy from the latter and normally it would surprise him. But not with Malie. All these guests knew of her already and his speech was just going to reiterate all that they loved about her. *Loved* – no one loved her like he did, however.

He cut the thought dead and forced his smile to be warm, trying to ease the weariness he could spy in her gaze as she joined him. It wasn't nerves, it wasn't embarrassment, not anymore. She was trying to read him, to understand where they stood.

He broke away and gestured for a nearby waitress to bring her a glass.

Malie took it from the tray, with a small, 'Thank you.'

'No one said I'd be made to stand up front,' she said between her teeth, smiling at the room.

She smoothed her dress down with her free hand and he traced the move, seeing that the red silk fell to the floor with a split that ran all the way up to her thigh – he snapped his eyes to her face as his body warmed and swallowed. Her eyes were almost level with his, which meant her heels were high – he'd never seen her in heels. He couldn't stop himself looking down past the gentle curve of her behind to the delicate point of one heel just visible beneath the hem of her dress and he swallowed again.

'Please tell me you're not waiting for me to speak,' she murmured, 'I haven't prepared anything.'

He pulled his eyes back to her face, to her flushed cheeks and bright green eyes that twinkled in the soft lighting of the room and laughed, the sound low and husky with the need he couldn't shake.

'You're safe, I just want you up here while I thank you.'

She glanced at him, her eyes piercing and full of so much... so much what? He couldn't tell. He couldn't read her – and how it frustrated him.

He gave up and scanned the waiting crowd, shutting that side of him down to do what he was good at. He was Todd Masters, the guy who headed up a charity foundation and a billion-pound firm, he could talk about the woman who had changed the lives of these kids for the better in just three weeks. He could do her justice.

'So, ladies and gentlemen, some of you have already met this incredibly talented woman and for those of you who haven't, this is Malie Pukui.' He smiled at her vibrant beauty and tried to make his heart immune. 'She's the person we have to thank for the progress each and every child on the programme has made over the course of the last three weeks.'

He raised his glass to her as he continued on, 'I'm sure many of you have heard a tale or two about her by now, even if you haven't had the pleasure of meeting her in person. She's someone who has the greatest belief in our cause, giving young lives hope for the future regardless of the path on which they tread. Her passion, her determination, rubs off on those around her, making them realize they are capable of so much, if they just try and don't give in. She gives them courage in the face of adversity. She makes them smile when they feel glum. She makes them feel alive and capable of living. *Real* living. In a world that isn't as inclusive as we'd like, but one in which we can work together to make it so.'

He met her eye and could feel the heart behind his speech pour into that one look. 'To Malie Pukui, and the surf school for their fantastic efforts to make not just this venture a success but many, many more to come!'

He lifted his glass in toast and the room cheered. 'To Malie Pukui.'

Yes, *to Malie Pukui*, the woman who had stolen his heart and yet he couldn't win hers.

She turned to him, her eyes glistening. 'Thank you, Todd…' Her voice quivered with emotion and then she dragged in a shaky breath and smiled to the room, visibly composing herself. 'Thank you all, too. I couldn't do it without the awesome pool of kids coming to my sessions and the support of the surf school itself. In particular, the school's owner, my godfather, Kalani… Don't try and hide now, Kalani.'

Sure enough, the big guy was trying to duck behind tall, slim

Grace and failing miserably. The room all toasted him with their glasses and a mixture of laughter and cheers.

'I think you've made him blush,' Todd murmured close to her ear.

She shivered a little, and he watched the tiny tremor in the curls that brushed over the nape of her neck, his fingers itching to brush them aside, to wrap one around his finger, to whisper closer to her ear all the things he felt, all the things he wanted...

'Yup.' She swallowed and glanced to him, her voice tight. 'He's gonna kill me later.'

He pulled himself up sharp. He was losing himself again. The personal taking over the professional. And she'd made it so painfully clear she didn't want the former. He needed to get away from her, reset his mind and his body. He needed to prep himself for goodbye too, because this was it. His chest, his throat squeezed tight and he coughed, fighting against it, forcing it back as he focused on their audience.

'Now, please enjoy your evening, everyone, let's celebrate.' He lifted his glass one final time. 'To us all!'

Everyone toasted and immediately the buzz of conversation filled the room, their focus on one another freeing Todd and Malie to step away.

'Excuse me,' he said.

'Todd,' she said at the same time, turning to face him and blocking him in, 'I—'

He looked past her and spied Tara's parents, his escape. 'Tara's parents have been asking after you, they'd like to speak to you.'

He saw the briefest flash of disappointment, so brief he wondered if he'd imagined it, and then her perfect smile slid into place, 'Of course.'

On impulse he rested his palm in the small of her back to lead her to them and instantly regretted it. She looked to him, her lips parting over a rush of air, the look in her eyes searing him to the core and then she looked away, and he followed her lead. But he couldn't pull his hand away, it triggered such warmth, such dizzying contentment, none of which he had a right to feel. None of which was healthy to feel. In less than twenty-four hours there would be thousands of miles between them and this would be over before it had ever begun.

And still he didn't pull his hand away.

'Charles, Anne-Marie,' he said as they neared the glowing couple. 'You remember Malie...'

***

Malie smiled at Tara's parents, trying to ignore the continued thrum of her skin from where he'd touched her seconds before, to ignore the echo of his speech replaying in her mind. It had felt like he'd been speaking directly to her at times, rather than about her. To have the courage to face up to life, to live, really live...

'Of course, Malie, we're so glad we get to see you again and thank you in person.' Tara's mum grabbed hold of her free hand, squeezed it between her fingers as she gave Malie a watery smile. 'Although it doesn't feel enough to simply say thank you. Tara's like a different child now, she laughs again, she calls us out when we are too protective, when we argue, when we...'

'Go easy, love, Malie won't have any blood left in her fingers if you squeeze her hand any tighter.' Charles softened his words with a loving smile and a comforting arm around his wife's waist.

'I'm so sorry, I'm just...' She looked up to her husband and leaned into his hold, releasing Malie's hand to place it on his chest. 'We're just so much happier.'

'It's true.' Her husband grinned and looked to Malie. 'We weren't in a good place before this trip, we haven't been for years.'

'Ever since the accident,' his wife said quietly.

'Aye,' he agreed. 'Guilt is a nasty thing, we blamed ourselves, each convinced that the other blamed us too.'

'I never blamed you,' Tara's mum said vehemently. 'They were my hair tongs.'

'And I should've changed the batteries in the fire alarm.'

They both went quiet, reflective, and Todd and Malie looked to one another, their expressions soft with understanding.

'We argued so much,' Tara's mother said after a while, 'about the small things as much as the big, and Tara, she just started to hang back, hide in the corner from it all, making herself invisible to us, but we didn't see it, we couldn't.'

Her husband squeezed her waist as her voice broke off on a tremor.

'It took Tara, would you believe, to make us realize it,' he added. 'She stood up to us, like she was the adult who knew better.'

'And she did, she was right.' Tara's mum nodded. 'Thanks to you she had the confidence to do that, Malie. You brought her out of her shell, brought back our little girl. Thank you... really truly.'

Malie was stunned still, her head spinning. *Making herself invisible to us.* The words kept replaying over and over. Wasn't that exactly what she'd done with her parents after Koa's death?

Hadn't she just hung back, hidden herself from them in the end? Taken herself away?

Was she in some way to blame for their estrangement? With each other and with her?

'Malie, are you feeling OK?'

It was Todd, his voice reassuringly soft in her ear, his hand returning to her lower back, his touch warm and gentle and contending with her sudden chill.

No, she wasn't OK. How ironic that Malie had helped Tara to find the confidence she needed to deal with her parents and the issues they shared when Malie herself couldn't even do the same.

'I just need to get some air.' She looked back to Tara's parents and felt her eyes prick with tears; she was so happy for them, so happy for Tara too, and she wanted them to know it. She didn't want them to think her sudden shift in mood was down to them. 'You don't need to thank me. Tara is a wonderful girl and to know that I have helped you all is enough. She really is special, and you are lucky to have her, just as she is lucky to have you.'

She looked to Tara's mum, to the tears that still welled in her eyes and pulled her into a hug. 'Ask Tara to stay in touch, won't you?'

Tara's mum embraced her and then Malie turned to Tara's father who looked like he didn't know whether to embrace her too or shake her hand. She decided for him, pulling him into a hug and releasing him with a warm smile that matched his own.

She looked back to Todd. 'I'll be back shortly.'

'I'll come with you.'

'No, it's…' She broke off at the look in his eye, she couldn't reject him now, she didn't have the strength for it. She needed him, she realized, more than anything in that moment… *she* needed *him*.

'OK,' she nodded.

His face visibly relaxed as he looked back to Tara's parents. 'Enjoy the evening – food will be out shortly, and I have it on good authority – that is, Tara's – that the dessert is to die for.'

Charles chuckled. 'Yes, she mentioned she'd helped you menu plan.'

'Helped?' Todd managed a laugh too. 'I think she practically took over the kitchen.'

Tara's parents beamed with pride. 'Thank you too, Todd,' Charles said. 'Without the Foundation, heaven knows where we would be now.'

Todd cleared his throat and Malie could see the emotion trying to break free of his stoic expression. 'You're welcome.'

One last smile and Tara's parents walked away, freeing them to do the same, Todd's hand still resting in the small of her back as they weaved through the crowd and headed outside. The rain was still beating down and so they kept close to the house, to the shelter provided by the upstairs balcony and providing privacy to them, too.

'Do you want me to bring you out some food?' Todd asked gently.

She shook her head. 'I'm not hungry…' She gave him a quick look. 'Sorry.'

'What for?'

She'd meant for turning down his offer of food when she knew how much effort had gone into it all. But now she'd said it, it wasn't about the food at all.

'For everything,' she murmured, wrapping her arms tight around herself as she looked out at the rolling waves in the distance, to the sheets of rain breaking the surface of the pool, and feeling the same unsettled force inside her chest.

'You don't need to apologize to me.'

Malie turned into him, her eyes on the crisp white collar of his shirt, his perfect bow tie, his cologne soothing her as she breathed it in and gathered the confidence she needed to be honest with him.

'I never should have said what I did about your father. I didn't… I wasn't… I was upset, and I lashed out.'

He wrapped his arm around her back pulling her up against him gently. 'I know you were.'

He tucked her head beneath his chin and held her, the strength and warmth of his body forming a protective shield that she wanted so much to lose herself in.

'You're not mad with me?' she whispered, her lips brushing against his shirt.

'I was.' His voice was low, husky with his own pain as it rumbled through his chest beneath her ear. 'But I know you're hurting too.'

'Truth is, I didn't realize just how much…' She took a shaky breath. 'It still doesn't excuse what I said, it still doesn't excuse the fact that I did it purposefully… to hurt you.'

She felt him tense beneath her and squeezed her eyes shut, hating her own honesty even though she knew it was the right thing to do.

'Why would you?'

'Because you scare me.' She opened her eyes and made herself look up at him, to hold his gaze. 'I needed to push you away before you… before you hurt me.'

She felt her eyes prick, the burn of tears so quick to return as she looked up into the eyes of the man who had come to mean so much to her and still, she couldn't let herself have.

'I would never hurt you,' he said thickly, 'surely you know that by now.'

'I know you wouldn't intentionally.' She wet her lips, blinked back the tears so that she could see him clearly. 'But I don't feel strong enough to take that risk.'

He pressed his forehead to hers. 'But don't you see, Malie, together we'd be stronger?'

She closed her eyes again. 'I don't see, I'm too messed-up to see. In there, with Tara's parents, I realized just how much I am to blame for what's happened with my parents.' She shook her head still feeling his own pressed reassuringly against her. 'And I know you are right, that there are things I need to do, changes I need to make, to stop holding myself back from living my life.'

She felt the tears escape her lids, felt Todd's fingers gently caress her chin as he raised his head and lifted hers to look at him again. 'There's time for all that, Malie, you can change things for the better, still live your life to the full.'

'To big wave surf?' She gave him a weak smile.

'Precisely.'

'And what about you?'

'I'm going back to England after New York. I'm going to suggest to my father that we get our hands dirty together.'

'DIY?'

He nodded, his eyes raking over her face, his hand on her back taking up a dizzying caress over her skin. 'I think you're right, it's time we spent real time together, it's time I gave up trying to change him and accept him for who he is.'

A bittersweet warmth ran through her as she lifted her hands to his face, her thumbs caressing his cheeks as she held his gaze; a thousand wants, a thousand words, so much trying to get out and not being able to voice a single one. Instead she kissed him – light, uncertain, testing his response – needing him to want her like she did him.

But he didn't respond, he didn't reject her, but he didn't kiss her back either and she dropped back, her eyes searching.

'And what of us, Malie,' he said so softly she had to strain to hear. 'Where do we stand?'

The one question she couldn't answer, fear and love combining to keep her tongue-tied. She tried to kiss him again, telling him with her silence because she wasn't ready to give that answer.

His body stilled, his head lifted further away. 'Malie?'

'I don't know.' She shook her head, her eyes pleading with him to understand. 'I'm not ready for this. I just know I don't want you to go, I don't want to be apart.'

'You could come with me, you wouldn't need to worry about money, I could recruit someone to cover for you here, I could...'

She was shaking her head all the more now, resisting the urge to cover her ears and block out his words, to be tempted by them.

'It's not the money, the school, that worries me, it's... it's me, it's this—' She pulled his hand from behind her back and rested it over her heart. 'Losing Koa...' her voice cracked, 'to almost lose my friends, too, I don't think I could love you and survive if... if...'

'Oh, God, Malie.' He crushed her to him, his mouth feverish as he claimed her almost painfully, but she craved it, every nip of teeth, of the invasion of his tongue as he duelled with her own, the press of his fingers as he clung her to him. So desperate, so pained. She was drowning in him, in the sea of emotion, of everything she felt for him and more.

He broke away, his voice ragged. 'Can't you see I feel the same for you, that the idea of losing you would kill me, but to walk away

and never see you again, to leave tomorrow and for that to be it...'
He shook his head, his eyes clamped shut and when he opened
them again, she could see the torment firing in his glittering black
gaze, feel his pain like her own. 'That would be worse. To give
up on us by *choice*...'

He couldn't finish, instead he was kissing her again, hard, urgent
and her hands were in his hair, holding on to him like she could
never let him go.

She knew he was right, that somewhere in all he said was the
truth. She wanted to be alone with him, she wanted to go to bed
with him, she wanted them to have tonight regardless of what
tomorrow would bring. She kissed him back with the all the love
she felt inside, kissed him until the urgency was burning out of
control, his hardness pressed between them as he turned her into
the wall.

He tore his mouth away, his eyes blazing down into hers.
'Malie... we need to stop... if you don't want this, we need to
stop now, or God help me...'

She shook her head, her eyes intent in his. 'I don't want to stop.'

'I don't think you know what you are saying.'

'I do.'

Still, he hesitated. 'And tomorrow?'

She wrapped her fingers around his neck and pulled him down
to her. 'Let us have tonight, tomorrow can wait...'

'You said that before.'

'But this is different.'

She tried to kiss him again, but he pulled back. 'Come dance
with me.'

She frowned at him. 'Dance?'

'I'm giving you time to change your mind.'

'I don't need time.'

He took hold of her hand and looked to the doors. 'You're upset, and I can't take advantage of that.'

She closed the distance between them and palmed his cheek, turning him to look at her. 'I may be upset, but I know I want this.'

He gave her a small smile but there was a sadness to it, an edge that took hold of her heart and squeezed so tight she couldn't breathe. 'Then you will still want it when the evening is over, and the guests have gone.'

'But—'

He pulled her to him. 'If I am to make love to you, Malie,' he pressed a kiss to her lips, 'it won't be a hurried affair up against the wall here.' He probed her lips with his tongue, a sweet invasion that had her thighs tightening against the thrilling ache. 'It'll be in my bed after everyone has gone.' His mouth brushed against hers as he spoke. 'So I can take my time exploring every last inch of you, imprinting each one in my mind.'

He trailed hot, barely-there kisses along her jawline, coming to rest at her earlobe which he caught in his teeth, his hot breath teasing at her ear canal. 'If I'm only ever to make love to you once, I want it to be something you remember for a lifetime.'

She whimpered, her heightened senses colliding with the meaning behind his words and she clung to his shoulders, scared her knees would fail her.

'OK,' she managed softly. 'OK.'

'So, you'll dance with me?'

She looked up into his eyes as she nodded, knowing that it was so much more than a dance she was agreeing to.

Nerves fluttered up in her belly as she laced her fingers through his and let him lead her back inside, onto the dance floor. Around them people ate, laughed, danced, but they were hardly aware of a soul. Every look, every touch, every move they made was loaded with the promise of what was to come, and she forgot the pain, the sadness, the revelations. They were tomorrow's concern.

Tonight, was about them, and them alone.

CHAPTER TWENTY

TODD CLOSED THE FRONT door on the very last guest and stared at the wood, his palm pressed hard against it, his eyes closed. He half expected Malie to race up behind him, to tell him she'd changed her mind, that she had to leave too. But the hallway was silent save for his pulse racing in his ears.

Are you sure you want to do this?

He didn't know. To make love to Malie, to know her, and to still have to leave...

Was he really strong enough for that?

His father hadn't been strong enough to move on. When his mother had died, it had crushed him, destroyed the person he was. Not that he'd known his father before, but he'd heard stories, seen pictures, witnessed their happiness through the immortal images.

But after...

'Todd?'

He opened his eyes to her soft-spoken call and turned. She stood at the bottom of the stairs, one hand resting on the balustrade, the other reaching out for him.

He raised his eyes to hers, to the unspoken question swimming in her depths. He may not be strong enough to move on tomorrow, but he knew he wasn't strong enough to end this now. That he would take whatever Malie was willing to give and then…

That was tomorrow's problem.

He closed the distance between them, entwining his fingers with hers and pressing a kiss to her lips. 'Are you sure?'

She nodded. 'More sure than I've been about anything in a long time.'

It was all the reassurance he needed to lead her upstairs, their footfall on the surface a delicate clip that sounded with the beat of his heart. He pushed open the double doors to the master room, the bed positioned to take centre stage and make the most of the floor-to-ceiling windows displaying the vista. He turned the lights on low to keep the rolling sea as the atmospheric backdrop to what was about to happen and turned to her.

'It's beautiful,' she murmured as she looked past him to the view.

'Not as beautiful as you.' He half expected her to laugh off the smoothness of his compliment, instead colour crept into her cheeks, her green eyes sparkling in the low light as she considered him with a slow smile.

Silently she stepped up to him, her fingers light on his bow tie as she worked it undone.

'Are you really sure?' he asked again.

She pressed a finger to his lips. 'It may surprise you to know that you're the first man I've ever wanted like this and resisted for so long.'

His brows pulled together as her finger fell away and she continued to undress him. 'That doesn't sound like a good thing.'

'It may also surprise you to learn that I do everything a hundred miles an hour.'

'That I do know.'

She didn't react, instead she watched her fingers as they unbuttoned his shirt. 'You're the first man I've stomped on the brakes for.' She looked up and met his eye, her sincerity making his breath catch. 'That makes you a very good thing.'

She teased her fingers beneath his open shirt and his muscles flexed under the simple touch, the heat spreading like wildfire as it followed her teasing caress.

'That makes you special, Todd,' she whispered, lifting up to press her lips to his, 'very... special.'

She wasn't confessing her love for him but boy, did it feel enough. For now, it had to be, it would be. He turned her so that her back faced him, his fingers brushing her hair to the side so that he could trace the delicate arch to her neck with his lips. 'That makes two of us, Malie.'

She gave a little shiver.

'Are you cold?'

'No, Todd, no... I'm never cold with you near.'

His heart pulsed in his chest, his fingers trembling as he took hold of her zipper and eased it down. Hardly daring to believe that this was happening he imprinted every second to memory. Just as he'd said he would.

He reached the curve of her back, unveiling her butterfly tattoo and seeing it with fresh eyes. He eased the dress from her body, brushed his hands over her hips as he encouraged the delicate fabric to fall, his thumbs meeting at the base of her spine, his fingers fanning out as he caressed the loop of one wing.

She wriggled beneath his touch, her whimper a delight.

'This is beautiful.'

She looked to him over her shoulder, and he could see the question in her eyes.

'The butterfly,' he said in answer. 'It's beautiful, like you.'

Her lashes lowered, her bottom lip caught in her teeth as she rolled into his continued caress.

'What does it mean, Malie?'

Her lashes fluttered open and she turned into him.

'It means I'm free,' she hooked her arms around his neck, 'free to enjoy life as I want, without anyone's judgement or dismissal.'

He could see the meaning in her eyes, knew the answer before he even asked, 'When did you have it done?'

'The week before I left the UK for good. The week before...' She broke off and took a breath.

'The week before you left your parents behind?'

She lifted her lashes, her pained depths pulling him apart inside. 'Yes.'

He kissed her, desperate to ease the pain, the worry, the heartache, both hers and his. 'It's not too late, Malie, you can still be that free and have them back.'

She nodded, her lips finding his. 'I know that now... thanks to you, thanks to Tara and her family.'

She stepped out of her heels, her fingers on her bra as she released the fastening and let it drop to the floor. She gazed up at him, bare but for the strip of her thong and he couldn't speak. She wasn't just beautiful, she was exquisite. The luscious curve to her breasts, their hardened upturned nubs aroused by him, for him, the proud angle to her neck as she let him drink in his fill. And still he wanted, needed, more, his heart feeling fit to burst.

He kissed her with all the passion, all the need, all the love he felt inside. He cupped her beneath the curve of each breast, his hands continuing to tremble, his heart beating out of control. She leaned into his caress, her whimper soft and teasing in his ear. This was happening. It really was.

'Oh, Malie.' He swung her up in his arms, and carried her to the bed, laying her down like she was some fragile possession he didn't dare break.

He stood back and stripped his shirt, his shoes, his socks, not once taking his eyes off her and the emotion in her gaze. It looked like love, it looked exactly how he felt, and if it was, then surely this wasn't goodbye, surely this was just the start.

He lay down next to her and she curved her leg around him, pulling him in against her, his hardness nestled between her thighs as she kissed him. Her hands roamed over his back, his chest, his hair, like she too couldn't get enough and needed to commit every stretch of him to memory. It was impassioned, it was desperate, but when her hands reached into the waistband of his trousers, he pulled back.

He gripped her wrists, forcing her to pause, his eyes searing down into the glazed heat of hers. 'Are you sure?'

'I want you, Todd, more than I've ever wanted anyone in my life… *please?*'

He released his grip to stroke the hair back from her face and press a kiss to her forehead, the bridge of her nose, her lips.

'OK,' he brushed against her mouth, 'no more questions.'

He pulled away to strip himself of the last of his clothing and reached for the protection in his bedside drawer. When he came back to her, he did exactly as he'd promised outside, he took his time, intending to travel the length of her, every dip and curve, every taste to sample, coaxing out every sweet sound she could possibly make as she wriggled beneath him, begging him for more.

'Please, Todd, now.'

He rose up above her, his legs and arms bracketing her body as her own impatience drove her to strip away her thong and then there was nothing, no barrier between them, no holding back.

She took the protection, pushed him to his limits as she stroked and sheathed him and then she lay back, opening herself up to him so that his hips nestled between her thighs.

Never had he felt more at home, more at peace, and as she wrapped her legs around him, her ankles urging him forward, he eased inside her, his eyes locked in the emotional heat of hers. He made love to her. Slow and sure. In body and in mind. Like his whole world wasn't imploding inside, like he hadn't crossed a line he couldn't come back from, like they belonged together, just like this. Always.

Somewhere deep inside he knew she hadn't promised him more. Not yet. But it would come, he had to believe it would come. And she would love him as he did her. He just had to show her how good life could be if she took that leap with him.

She had to see it – *Please, let her see...*

He squeezed his eyes tight against the alternative and let go. His cry, his release, so full of love that, to his ears, it married with her own. And that could only mean one thing...

Malie loved him.

★ ★ ★

She woke to the alien feeling of her limbs being entwined with another's, all naked and hot, and… she froze.

The night flashed before her eyes: the speech, the conversation with Tara's parents, the kiss beneath the balcony, the dance floor, the bedroom, the bed…

The bed in which they were now, the sheets tossed aside, Todd's body spooning hers, his leg hooked over and between her own and brushing just there, her breath caught, her body pulsed. She didn't dare wake him, didn't dare move a muscle. Already she could feel the need stirring within her, the need that should have been well and truly slaked by the night's repeated lovemaking – *lovemaking*.

Not sex, not the basic urge to have fun and be done. No. This was so much more. Just as she'd predicted, just as she'd wanted it to be and shouldn't.

And now what?

His breath caressed her ear, his nose nuzzling in as he shifted and murmured in his sleep, his arm wrapping around her to draw her in tight. Oh, how she wanted to snuggle down too. To close her eyes and let sleep claim her once more. To not let this night be over. But the sun was already creeping in through the glass, the hint of pink and orange on the horizon all warm and comforting and a direct contrast to the messed-up state of her head.

No, not her head, her heart.

Slowly she turned, disentangling herself as she encouraged him onto his back. He was so peaceful in his sleep, younger even. There was no crease to his brow, no lines around his eyes, his full mouth relaxed into something that looked close to a smile, and his hair… she reached out, unable to stop herself and stroked his fringe from his face.

Yes, she wanted to stay, more than anything she wanted this to be her new normality but there was so much she needed to make sense of before she could let herself be with him. She'd spent her entire adult life avoiding anything close to a relationship – to suddenly change that stance now when she had so much else to sort, to address? She couldn't do it.

It was as much about protecting him as it was herself and it was that realization that had her pulling away and climbing out of bed, finding her clothing and slipping it on before picking up her shoes. She felt like a thief stealing away into the night and guilt gnawed at her stomach, tears quick to follow. But if he were to wake up, he'd never let her go without a fight. She knew that, just as she knew she wouldn't be strong enough to fight back, that she'd readily go running straight back into his arms, back into his bed, only to have her feelings for him mess with her head and delay the inevitable.

No, it was better this way.

She owed it to him, to herself, to get her life straightened out first.

And why can't you do that with him by your side?

She reached the threshold of the bedroom – the doors were still open from where he'd led her through them the previous evening, the air filled with the thrum of anticipation – and she looked back to his body laid out and relaxed. Her heart ached, wanting to return, even as she knew she needed to leave. She couldn't think clearly with him by her side, couldn't trust her mind to make the right decisions, couldn't trust anything with her emotions swirling like crazy within.

That's because you love him, you fool.

You shouldn't be leaving; you should be holding on with both hands and never letting him go.

She shook her head and clutched her shoes to her chest. She'd had good reasons to avoid relationships thus far, even if those reasons seemed blurred now.

She turned away and a tear escaped. She brushed it away with the back of her hand and kept moving, her bare feet silent on the floor as she padded across the landing and down the stairs. Her bag rested at the foot of the last step where she had left it the previous night and she stooped to pick it up before letting herself out, the door clicking softly shut behind her.

She dragged in a shaky breath, wishing her head to clear, for sanity to take over and the torrent of emotion to subside but it was no use. She made her way down to the beach to avoid the gate and the road and the people that would be there. She knew she looked a state, doing the walk of shame in her fancy dress, her hair giving away the night's heated antics. Her cheeks warmed even as more tears fell, the cool sea breeze making the strands cling to the wet streaks. She was a mess. Inside and out. Nothing could stop the tears or the sense of emptiness swelling inside.

She took another breath but it just felt worse, nothing could fill the void. She tried to tell herself it was just a hangover from last night's perfection, of the emotional bond they'd shared as much as the physical. But it was no use. She felt open, exposed, raw. As though with every layer of clothing he'd removed, another layer over her heart had fallen away, every time they'd come together, the bond had strengthened until the very idea of being apart seemed impossible.

But it would pass, she just needed time. Time to fix her life, time to see clearly and then she could be objective about the future and whether she could entrust her heart to Todd.

A little late for that, don't you think?

Her body shuddered, its agreement clear, her heart was already long gone, and for the first time in more years than she could count, she wanted her mum. She wanted to talk to her and tell her everything, to have the confidence of Tara to be honest about Koa and how she'd hated living like he didn't exist, like she didn't exist too. She wanted to say she was sorry for running. She wanted to tell her about the surf school and the work they were doing… she wanted to tell her about Todd.

She was already lifting her bag, looking for her phone, her fingers trembling as she dialled Home.

It had barely rung once when her mother's familiar voice came over the line. 'Malie?'

'Hi, Mum.'

'This is early for you – it must be five, six in the morning out there?'

A sob erupted out of her control and she tried to bury it so that her mother wouldn't hear.

'Malie? What is it? What's wrong?'

She could hear the panic in her mother's tone, knew she'd caught her anguish and she couldn't keep it trapped any longer, the time for pretence was over.

'I… I could do with a chat… if you have the time?'

'I always have time for you. You're worrying me, love, what's going on?'

Malie felt her lips curve into a watery smile as her mother's love shone down the line. A small flutter of what felt a lot like hope and belonging once more started up inside.

'It might take a while...'

'Just start at the beginning, love, I'm here.'

It was as good a place as any...

CHAPTER TWENTY-ONE

HE KNEW SHE'D GONE, even before he opened his eyes. He could sense the emptiness of the bed, the room, the house. He was alone. Something that had never bothered him before, but now he felt it like a weighted ache deep inside his chest.

He didn't even strain his ears to listen for footsteps or sounds in the kitchen, didn't try to fool himself into thinking she was making breakfast, or outside enjoying the sunrise, any of those things that would be expected the morning after a night such as theirs. Waking up to a relationship, a real relationship. Not that he'd ever really had one of those. But he'd hoped – no, he'd *convinced* himself things were different now. That she wouldn't run, not this time. Not after all they'd shared, all they'd felt. Because she had felt it too, he was sure of that.

He rolled over and palmed the bed, felt the residual warmth from her body and wondered how far away she was, but even as he thought it, he knew he wouldn't run after her. That he couldn't.

She needed to come to him when she was ready.

If she ever would be...

He closed his eyes against the pang, the doubt, the what-if; he had New York to prepare for, he had work to do, work he could control, Malie he could not.

No matter how much he loved her, he had to let her be free. Free to make her own choices. Free to live her life.

His gut twisted and he got out of bed, crossed to the window and looked out over the sea. The sea that would forever remind him of Malie. The urge to run after her was so strong, like a physical pull that he couldn't ignore. He lowered his gaze and turned away. No, it was good that he was leaving, New York couldn't be more different, and once he was there, he could fill his head with work, far away from this place where the temptation was too much.

He threw his focus into packing before he could decide to do otherwise.

***

A week later, not even the miles between them could stop him reliving that morning and the weeks that had led up to it. No matter how busy his schedule, the back-to-back meetings, the social functions that served to fulfil a business need, she was always on his mind. Like now, as he stared unseeing at the figures projected onto the screen of the conference room.

'What do you think, Todd?'

'Hmm?' He focused through the brain fog to see Nathan, his head of development, looking at him like he'd lost his mind – he couldn't blame him. He'd completely zoned out. Again.

'Sorry, what were you saying?'

Nathan frowned and gestured back to the projection. 'The venture looks quite viable, if you take into consideration—'

A knock on the glass door cut him off and the entire room of ten all looked to it. Grace stood there, gesturing to him. There was only one reason Grace would disturb this meeting, the one reason he had given her all week as a free pass to contact him regardless of the hour.

'Hang on, Nathan.'

He stood up and walked to the door, opening it.

'It's on,' she said in a low voice, her eyes bright. 'You told me to tell you and it's been confirmed, the surf conditions are perfect, the Queen of the Pipe is kicking off today.'

His heart lurched. 'And the line-up? Have they released it?'

Grace nodded, her eyes widening because she knew what this would mean to him. 'She's on the list.'

'What time is it on?'

'Should be airing in the next hour.'

An hour. He had time to conclude the meeting and get back to the hotel.

'Thanks, Grace.'

He strode back into the room, suddenly feeling alive, more alive than he had done in seven days. Ridiculous when he was no closer to having her, but to know she was taking this step, she was going for it.

Go big, Malie. For Koa and for yourself.

'I have half an hour, let's see if we can get this wrapped up.'

He had some place else he had to be.

★ ★ ★

They had it done and dusted in twenty and he was out the door, Grace on his tail updating him with all things urgent. His hotel was two blocks away and she was racing to keep stride with him, taking his instructions and doing her best to keep it brief. When they hit the lobby of his hotel, she left him, heading back to the office with a thumbs-up for luck.

He entered the lift, yanking his tie free and shucking his jacket off. *Don't miss it. Don't miss it.*

The lift took an eternity to get to his penthouse suite but then he was there, his jacket tossed over the back of the sofa, his hand on the remote and keying in the number for the surf channel that he'd memorized this past week.

And there it was. The Banzai Pipeline. The waves immense, the crowd unbelievable. He pulled a beer from the fridge, and dropped onto the sofa edge, his body hunched forward, his elbows on his knees.

The first mention of her name and his heart leaped into his throat, the first glimpse of her smile and his eyes pricked.

She was radiant. Everything about her so familiar, so heart-warming, yet so far away. He cursed the miles, he cursed the screen that sat between them, he wanted to embrace her, to wish her luck, to tell her how proud he was. It didn't matter whether she won, or not. She was about to go out there and do what she'd refused to since she'd lost her brother. And as he thought it the commentator made reference to Koa, the surf legend, and the man she had thought she couldn't replace.

'You're not replacing him, Malie, you're doing him proud.'

He barely blinked as he watched the entire thing unfold and every time she caught a wave, he fisted his hands around the bottle and screwed up his face, his eyes peeking through slits. He knew she had it, knew she knew what she was doing, but the waves were fierce, the wipe-outs he'd already witnessed terrifying and bloody.

Come on, Malie, come on.

It was a constant mantra, his oxygen-starved body going dizzy. He opened another bottle of beer and another and then it was done and my God, she was through to the next round. The commentators were praising her prowess as she walked through the crowd, her grin lighting up her face, her friends running up to her cheering her on.

He shot up and almost showered his room in beer. He stepped closer to the screen, watched every flicker in her face. Kalani came up to her, swung her around and then there was a woman. Todd stilled, his head cocking to the side. She was small, blonde, he didn't recognize her at all but as he looked to the obvious love in her face as she embraced Malie, he knew in his gut who she was. The man behind her wore the same doting expression. Love and pride. Her parents, it had to be.

He raked his hand through his hair, stared at the happy group. *You did it, Malie, you did it all.*

You didn't just conquer the waves, you conquered your fear of your family too.

He couldn't move. Even as the camera panned away and they moved on, he remained standing there, eyes fixed, body still. He missed her. Missed her more than he imagined possible. Did she miss him too? Did she even think of him?

She looked so happy. Could she be that happy and miss him? *Unlikely.*

He raked his fingers through his hair once more and turned away from the screen, the rollercoaster of emotion underway inside too unsettling. Yes, it was great – more than great – to see her doing what she was born to do, but it didn't mean she was ready to move on with him. It didn't change—

'Hey, check it out, folks,' the commentator's voice piped into the room, 'Stevie's managed to tear the awesome Malie Pukui away from her family for a quick catch-up.'

He was already turning back to screen, already eager for more of her, of whatever glimpse he could get.

'So how does it feel, Malie, nailing your first ever Big Wave competition?'

She beamed at the commentator and then the camera. 'Incredible!'

'I bet! Gotta admit, we all wondered why you never took the leap before with skills like yours.'

She shrugged and Todd could tell she was trying to make it seem nonchalant, but he could read the blazing emotion in her eyes, read the truth of it – *Koa*. 'I just never felt I could do it, it… it wasn't for me.'

'So, what changed?' He shoved the mic back under her face and Todd watched her take a breath, saw the way her lashes fluttered before she looked to the commentator, to Kalani and her family behind her, before coming back to the camera.

Her smile was wistful, her eyes sparkled, and her cheeks flushed deeper. 'Let's just say, I met a certain someone who reminded me that life needs to be lived to the full, and this was a big part of that.'

Todd's heart pulsed in his chest. A certain someone. *Him*.

A big of part of it? Was there another part to it too? A part that meant she was ready to commit, ready to take that leap with him?

'A certain someone, hey?' The commentator grinned. 'And are we allowed to know who this special someone is?'

Todd's heart didn't just pulse now, it launched into his throat as he waited on her response, unable to breathe.

'His name's Todd...' The camera zoomed in close to her face and Todd could see it all – her passion, her love, not for the water now, but...

'And he is special; very, very special,' Malie added, as though she was reading his mind and confirming everything he wanted but never thought he'd hear.

The commentator's grin widened; Todd's own grin just as extreme. 'Well, hear that, folks, we have this Todd dude to thank for getting Pukui out there – this guy must be one in a million, hey, Malie?'

She laughed softly. 'Yes... Yes, he is.'

'There we have it, folks, now back over to the judges for their summing up of today's heats.'

Todd shook his head, scarcely believing all he had witnessed, all he had seen in Malie's face, but there was one thing he knew for sure: he couldn't bear the miles between them anymore. Couldn't bear being apart. He understood that it didn't necessarily mean she was ready to give him more, and he wouldn't pressure her to choose. But he had to be there for this competition. This huge moment in her career. Her life.

He *had* to.

★★★

'I can't believe I'm doing this,' Malie said as she looked out at the waves, barely aware of the crowd that had thickened over the course of the week, since day one of the competition. But today was the final, this was it.

'We can,' Kalani said from beside her. 'It's long overdue.'

'Too right, dude.' EJ went in for a high-five which he had to rescue himself from as Kalani left him hanging. He grinned at Malie instead. 'You've got this, you know that.'

'Just be careful,' said her mother, unable to hide her worry as she watched the waves the Banzai Pipeline was famous for crashing in the distance.

Hani, her father, wrapped his arm around her mother and gave Malie a supportive smile. 'As EJ said, you've got this, we know you do.'

She smiled her thanks. She knew how hard this was for them but the fact that they had come out – had been there for a week now and watched her surf every day, even been out on the waves with her – meant the world. Things were already so much better and although her mum was worried, she knew that's all it was. It wasn't the memory of Koa haunting them, it wasn't the kind of suffocating fear she'd endured after his death, it was the natural fear of the unknown and the hope that she would do well.

And boy, did she hate the waiting. She couldn't sit still, bobbing up and down, prepping her board even though it didn't need it, keeping her body physically busy until it was her turn. Trying to keep her mind busy, too, because every time it went quiet Todd was there, and the pain of missing him didn't get any easier. If anything, it only proved how much she wanted him in her life. How much she wished he could be there now to witness the changes she'd made already. How much further she still wanted to go so that she could have him in her life. Because that was the next step.

She wanted to claim this crown and then she wanted to hunt him down and tell him the truth.

That she loved him. That she'd been a fool not to have seen it sooner and recognize it for what it was. To have realized that no amount of separation, no amount of mental talk, no amount of time or fear of the future could change the fact that she loved him. She really loved him.

'You're up, kiddo,' her father nudged her, pulling her thoughts back to the here and now.

She turned to him and grinned. 'Wish me luck.'

'Not that you need it, love,' her mother said.

'Good luck,' her friends and family called, and she raced off, her trusty board under her arm, her heart and focus on the win.

Win the crown.

Win the man.

In that order. She hoped.

It all felt so possible. With the adrenalin racing through her system, the knowledge that her parents were there and that they supported her, the enduring spirit of Koa in the water with her, and in her heart there was Todd, his presence almost tangible, like she could feel his eyes on her now, watching her, cheering her on.

She waded into the water and threw herself onto her board, paddling and duck-diving the waves, feeling Koa's presence, talking to her, encouraging her. From the first wave to the last he was there, and she needed it. It was a tight competition; she wasn't the youngest, she likely wasn't the fittest, but she wanted this. For Koa and herself, she wanted this win.

Time was ticking, it was her final wave and she knew in her gut, this was it. As she rose up on her board and took off down the line of the wave, it wasn't just Koa who was there riding it with her, it was Todd. His faith in her so unbreakable even when she had pushed so hard to keep him away. She felt their power combine with that of the sea and could sense the crowds cheering even as her ears filled with the roar of the ocean curving over her head and forming the perfect barrel. It was immense, epic, the tube ride of her life... if only Todd was there.

The thought stayed with her as she made her way back to shore, the buzz of the crowd drawing out her grin, their hoots and the calls impossible to ignore. There would be time for sadness later. She waded out of the water to their talk of a definite win. A *definite* win. Just as her friends had always told her. And still she couldn't believe it.

Not even when the podium was before her and her name was called, her parents hugging her, her friends high-fiving her, Kalani swinging her a full 360 in the air so fast she almost lost her balance as she climbed the steps, but then she was there looking out, the crown hers, the crowd's cheer like a soundtrack to her dreams.

'Speech,' they called. 'Speech!'

She smiled, felt tears tighten up her throat as she coughed them free, scooped her hair out of her eyes.

She knew what she wanted to say, the words flowing from her with choked-up ease. 'I wouldn't be here if not for the love my parents have for the ocean, which they instilled in me as a child, and for my brother, who pushed me to go bigger, go stronger, live the dream... Losing him was the hardest thing I've ever had to go through, but winning this for him has been the easiest. This is for you, Koa!'

She raised the trophy to the heavens and blew him a kiss, letting the tears fall freely now. As she looked back down, the dummy cheque was passed to her. Her smile grew, her heart pulsed in her chest. This was her ticket to New York or wherever else Todd may be. She'd find him and use the money to secure the flights she needed to win back her man. She clutched it to her, the trophy too, and climbed down the steps, her footing unsteady as the tears continued to swim before her eyes, her body weak in the aftermath.

She'd won, she'd come and achieved what she set out to, but now she needed him, just as much as she needed her next breath. She stumbled up to her parents; Kalani was standing between them, but then he stepped aside and she frowned into the eyes of the person standing directly behind him... no, it couldn't be... she shook her head, expecting it to clear, for it to be a figment of her adrenalin-infused brain.

Surely she'd conjured him up, with all her conviction that he was there watching her while she'd been on the waves, how much she'd wanted him to be there. He stepped forward, ever more real, his eyes glistening, his brow furrowed, his smile so proud, so full of... no... she walked up to him, slowly, unsure, not daring to believe.

'Todd?'

She felt her legs give way beneath her, felt the trophy slip from her grip as his arms wrapped around her, pulling her up against his solid strength and warmth.

She breathed him in deeply, took a moment to find her voice, to feel capable of looking up at him and really believing. 'It really is you.'

His smile was small, but it was there. 'Yes.'

A fresh wave of tears filled her eyes as she tried to blink them back. 'I can't believe it.'

'Is that a good can't believe it, or a bad, because I can leave if you want me—'

She kissed him, every second that she'd missed him pouring

into the gesture. She clung to him, praying it wasn't a dream, that he had really come back for her in spite of all she had done.

'I'm so sorry, so very sorry,' she hurried out as she broke away and stared up at him. 'For pushing you away, for leaving…' she shook her head, 'it was foolish, wrong. I was confused. But I'm not anymore, I'm not.'

He chuckled softly. 'And here I was ready to apologize to you.'

'Apologize?' She frowned. 'Why?'

He squeezed her tighter against him. 'For turning up, for looking like I'm making demands of you, when I'm not, I just didn't want to miss this.'

'Oh, Todd!' She leaped up, kissed him again, deeply, thoroughly, all her love, all her happiness fuelling that one move. She didn't want to stop, didn't want to break away, didn't want this moment to end, and would have carried on if not for the sharp cough directly beside them.

'And this is Todd,' Kalani said, after another good throat-clearing and reminding her that her parents were witnessing this whole crazed reunion without any introduction.

She pulled back on a choked laugh.

'Sorry, Mum, Dad, I just need to get this off my chest first.'

Todd blinked down at her, his eyes glazed by her kiss as they searched for the confirmation he truly needed; she didn't want him to search anymore, didn't want him to question.

'I love you, Todd Masters. I've loved you from the very first second you made a fool of yourself in my surf lesson, I loved you when you almost drowned yourself trying to rescue Nalu, I loved you then, I love you now, and I will always love you. And if you can forgive my stupidity, my ridiculous behaviour that must have driven you crazy—'

She couldn't finish, his lips crushed hers now, his groan one of sheer bliss as he twirled them both on the spot. 'You can drive me crazy for the rest of my life, Malie, if you promise to love me like that.'

She laughed, delirious, heady. 'I will.'

He set her down, grinned down at her, 'I love you, Malie.'

'I know you do.'

Another throat was cleared right next to them, this time Hani's imposing frame took out the sun to their right. 'Er, Todd meet my father. Dad, this is Todd.'

Introductions were made, celebrations were had but all Malie wanted to do was whisk Todd away so that they could be alone. They had two weeks to catch up on, two whole weeks of missing one another and a whole lifetime to look forward to.

Night fell, the celebrations continued back in Nani Kumu and finally she felt able to leave her parents with Kalani and invite Todd back to hers. Anticipation coursed through her – excitement, joy, the realization that they were now together and there was nothing holding them back.

She unlocked her apartment door, turned into him for a long, drawn-out kiss and then flicked on the light and—

'Oh, God, Todd, close your eyes.'

'Malie it's…'

'Please, if you love me… close your eyes.'

He did as she asked and she looked at the flat through Zoe's eyes. Had it really only been a few weeks since her visit? Oh, God. She'd lived on her own far too long. She hurried about the room, pulling stuff into her arms, moving it from surface to surface…

'Malie, look, if you've changed your mind, and you want more time, it'll kill me but I—'

She threw the stuff over her head and ran to him, swinging her arms around him as she kissed him hard. 'I haven't changed my mind,' she said between kisses, 'but *you* might when you come in.'

He laughed, the sound deep and throaty as he kissed her and backed her into the apartment. He broke away, his eyes dancing as he looked at her. 'What are you afraid of, that I'll—' He lifted his gaze to the open-plan space and his eyes widened, his mouth too. 'What the hell happened here?'

'*Me*,' she squeaked, her shoulders up around her ears as she gave him a sheepish smile. 'If you close your eyes, you can't tell.'

He shook his head, amazed and looked back to her. 'You really do need me, you know.'

'You won't hear any argument here.'

He laughed again and swept her into his arms. 'Do you think you can direct me to the bedroom, or am I better off ravishing you on the semi-clear sofa?'

'As much as that sounds perfectly agreeable, I'm all for the bed, that way,' she pointed, laughing and blushing at the same time. She was a slob and still, he loved her.

He kicked open the door and she peeked through squinted eyes. 'Not too bad, is it?'

'In all honesty, Malie, we could be in a pig-sty and even that wouldn't stop me making love to you.'

She wrinkled her nose. 'You're kidding, right?'

'No, I'm definitely not.'

He threw her onto the bed as she let out another ripple of laughter, watching as he dragged his T-shirt over his head, the muscles of his torso flexing with the move and making her mouth water. She climbed up onto her knees, pulled her own shirt over her head and shuffled forward, stripping her bikini top as she went.

'In that case,' she purred, tugging on his waistband, 'get a move on, I'm ravenous over here.'

He looked down into her face and stilled, his eyes softening. He cupped her jaw, his thumb sweeping over her bottom lip. 'This is really happening, you and me?'

She nodded. 'It's really happening.'

'I love you, Malie.'

'I love you too.' And then she yanked his waistband, harder this time, and he fell on top of her, his lips claiming hers. The mess forgotten, the world forgotten, everything but the love they shared, the love and the phone buzzing against Malie's butt cheek. She wriggled and adjusted, pulling it out of her pocket with the intention of tossing it aside.

'Who is it?' he murmured against her neck.

She peeped over his shoulder at the screen, seeing several missed video calls and a text. 'Oh no.'

He lifted up, his hands pressed into the mattress either side of her. 'What's the matter?'

'It's my friends, Lils, V, Zo, they're requesting a Lost Hours call.'

'A what now?'

She frowned at the phone. 'It means it's an emergency.'

'You have to take it?'

She gave him an apologetic smile. 'It's kind of our code.'

'Far be it from me to stand in the way of girl code.' He smiled to soften the blow and rolled onto his back. 'So long as you don't expect me to clear out while you have it because now I finally have you back, I'm making the most of being by your side.'

'You and me both.'

She collapsed down next to him, her head nestled in the crook of his arm and swiped to join the group call.

'About bloody time, Devil!' It was Zoe, her anxious frown filling the screen. 'I've been trying to reach you for the last ten minutes.'

'Hey, Malie,' V and Lils chimed in, looking exhausted in their dressing gowns, their eyes half asleep.

'Sorry, love, it's only just started ringing through now, what's up?' It had to be something huge for her to wake V and Lils up so early.

'I've decided to stage an intervention,' her friend declared, her voice firm and brooking no argument. 'It's time you woke up to…' she broke off, her frown deepening as she loomed into the screen, 'Malie, what's that behind your head?'

'Hmm? My what?'

Zoe flapped a finger at the screen. 'There, behind you? Good God, Malie, are you naked?!'

Malie felt her cheeks colour, looked down at her chest and realized that she was indeed half naked. 'Never mind all that, what's the problem, who needs an intervention?'

'That's an arm,' said Victoria with a yawn. 'Behind her head, it's an arm.'

Lils squinted into the screen. 'It is, you know, a definite *male* arm.'

'Whoa, Malie,' Todd started to wriggle away. 'You didn't tell me it was a video call.'

Malie looked to Todd and back to her friends and gave a guilty shrug. 'I guess now would be a good time to introduce you all…

Todd, meet V and Lils, you already know Zo,' she swung the phone at him and back, 'guys, meet Todd.'

'Todd? Isn't that the guy we're having an intervention over, Zo?' Victoria asked.

'Not being funny,' Lils said, smothering a laugh, 'but Malie doesn't look like she needs an intervention to me. The words *horse* and *bolted* spring to mind.'

Zoe was shaking her head, her smile slow to form. 'So... you and Todd, you're...' she gestured at the phone.

'Well, we were about to,' Malie said, 'but then you called.'

'Malie!' Todd blurted and she looked to him.

'Sorry, we kind of tell each other everything, is that going to be a problem?'

'Don't worry, Todd,' came Oliver's disembodied voice from V's screen, 'you'll get used to it.'

They all laughed, even Zoe, who was slowly coming out of her shock enough to ask, 'So you've seen sense without our help?'

'Not quite,' Malie admitted, 'you helped, Zo, more than you know.'

'Nice to know your friends saw sense before you did,' Todd ribbed her as they all giggled.

'Well, in that case, Devil, we best leave you to it.'

'Please... oh, but before you go...' Malie pulled the phone close, trying to smother it and the microphone.

'I don't need to see your boobs, Malie,' came Lils' voice.

'Just Todd's chest will suffice,' added V with a sharp 'Oi!' from Oliver.

Malie shook her head, grinning as she looked to Todd.

'Would you be free this summer to come to Devon – I kind of have this thing I'm invited to and it has a plus one?'

'You know I can hear you, right?' V piped up.

Malie's grin widened. 'All right, bridezilla, keep your hair on…'
She turned back to Todd. 'Would you be my date to V's wedding?'

'I'd be honoured.'

'Hear that, loves,' she brought the phone back to her face, 'I have
a plus one… *and* an old surf school to check out, it's going to be
a busy summer.'

'A surf school!' Lils blurted. 'What are you saying, Malie? Are
you coming back to the Cove?'

She was already losing her focus on the call, caught up as she
was in the glow of Todd's gaze as he pieced together what she
was saying.

'Malie?' Lils prompted. *'Malie?'*

'I figured since you'll be back helping your dad,' she explained
to Todd softly, 'I could be back working on the family surf school,
looking at recreating what we have here.'

'I love it.' He smiled at her, pulling her in.

'Gotta go, loves, but yes, Lils, I'm coming home.'

She heard Lils excited *squee* as she cut the call, could imagine
the happy faces of both V and Zo too.

'You know they probably got an eyeful when you flashed your
phone back and forth,' Todd murmured.

'They've seen worse.'

He leaned back before she could kiss him. 'Worse?'

'Remind me to tell you all about Ibiza when we have time.'

'Ibiza?'

'Mm-hmm.' She probed his lips with her tongue, teasing him
into kissing her.

'Do I want to know?'

'Maybe save it until after the wedding.'

'Whose wedding? V's or...?'

It was her turn to lean back. 'Are you asking me to marry you?'

'I don't know, were you meaning V's wedding or...?' He widened his eyes, nodded his head.

She grinned, so full of love for him and the promise of a future she never thought she'd have. 'Wouldn't you like to know...'

And then she kissed him, leaving him in no doubt as to whose wedding she'd meant, because she had no doubt whatsoever that one day in the not too distant future, it would be her saying, 'I do.'

Acknowledgements

Writing the acknowledgements for my second book feels slightly surreal, knowing that you are coming on this joyous journey with me is something I appreciate more than words can do justice.

Rachael Stewart - you've made this book incredibly special. I feel so lucky to have embarked on this wonderful writing journey with you.

To my fabulous and incredibly patient editor Becky Slorach, thank you for your guidance and support past, present and future – my WhatsApp warrior! Thank you so much.

Huge thank you to everyone at Mills & Boon as well as HarperCollins, especially to Kirsty Capes, Katie Barnes-Wallis, Sophie Calder and Tom Keane. A second book finished! Pinch me!

Thank you to Lucy Truman and Kate Oakley for such a happy and vivid cover, it suits Malie's warm and adventurous personality to perfection.

To my wonderful managers, your enthusiasm and assurance has been crucial over the past few months of writing this book.

Friends and family who supported me on my journey writing Malie and Todd's story who I am so happy to have in my life. I love you all dearly. My grandfather Bertie who sadly passed away before my first book was released, but whom I consider an endless source of inspiration and strength. Most importantly my darling PH, your support for my career is unparalleled.

I am eternally grateful to all my loyal readers and supporters. Your encouragement has given me the push I needed to finish Malie's road to self-discovery and happiness, I hope her bravery inspires you.

**If you loved *Meet me in Hawaii*,
read on for an extract of Zoe's story
Meet me in Tahiti from Georgia Toffolo
and Mills & Boon**

Coming September 2021

Chapter 1

ZOE TAYLER'S MOBILE PHONE pinged, alerting her to an incoming email.

Her fingers froze on her computer keyboard.

She knew that email would be from mum.dad@taylers.co.uk.

Yep, her parents not only owned a domain name, they also had a dedicated address for corresponding with their only child. That was how serious they were about keeping a not-so-proverbial eye on her.

Whenever Zoe was on an international job her parents' email obsession ratcheted up to frenzy level—particularly on day one, which brought an avalanche. Only gradually did the frequency taper off in the ensuing days, easing fraction-by-fraction with each of Zoe's instantly returned 'I'm-fine-no-need-to-worry' replies.

Today—sigh—was day one, this would be their fourth email of the day, and the just-roll-with-it process of allaying their myriad concerns lay depressingly ahead of her.

It was noon in French Polynesia, which made it 11pm in England. There should only be time for only one more communique before her parents went to bed, so within the hour she should be free.

Unless...

Well, unless she decided not to answer this one. In which case she could be free immediately.

Her fingers twitched on the keyboard as the idea of going off the grid took hold...

And then she laughed.

Futile to hope her parents would shrug their shoulders, assume she was fine and go to bed. The more likely scenario was that they'd call Zoe's mobile, and keep calling, and when Zoe didn't answer (because answering would render her little rebellion redundant) they'd fret over what ills might have befallen her—everything from a fever-inducing cold caught during her plane trip to her lying unconscious on the floor with a cracked skull. Within twenty-four hours they'd be knocking on her bungalow door with an ambulance on standby.

Yeah, hard no to that!

She leaned back in her chair, rubbing her hands up and down her thighs to remind herself why her parents needed to know she was all right, and knew she was going to reply.

'Fight your big battles to the death but don't sweat the scrappy skirmishes if you want to win the long war,' she murmured, and her hands abruptly stopped moving as she realised what she'd said.

Not that those words didn't suit the situation, but it shocked her that she could recite them—verbatim—after...what...twelve years?

Yes, it had been twelve years since Finn Doherty had said those words to her that idyllic summer they'd worked together at the *Crab Shack* in Hawke's Cove.

Her parents hadn't wanted her to take the job at the *Shack*, hadn't seen the need for it given the generous allowance they gave her. But all her friends had summer jobs lined up and she'd pleaded, and her BFFs had pleaded, and even Ewan, the owner of the *Crab Shack*, had pleaded (*such* a softie), and at last she'd been given the okay to be just like every other sixteen-year-old in the village.

Unfortunately, a week into the job she'd had a wisdom tooth out—typical that she'd get her wisdom teeth earlier than any other kid *and* that one of them would be impacted. (Seriously, it was like the universe had it in for her!) Her parents, true to form, had acted like she was about to be measured for her coffin and it had taken two days in bed and an extra day of frantic begging before Zoe was allowed to return to work.

But her parents' capitulation had come at a price: constant phone calls.

After their eighth call on her first day back, Zoe had decided that giving up the job was preferable to having every *Shack* employee lining up to throttle her. She'd hurried out to the storeroom, blinking tears away because she didn't cry, *ever*, phone gripped in one hand, when Finn had…well, materialised.

He'd looked at the phone, at her face, and understood the situation instantly. That was when he'd said those words to her. And then he'd told her that the big battle had been getting her parents to agree to the job but the phone calls? Pfft, they were nothing.

And just like that, the phone calls had ceased to matter. So she'd called her parents, right there in front of Finn, and explained that if she didn't answer a call immediately it didn't mean she was being rushed to hospital, only that she was busy, and in such cases she'd call them back within half an hour, cross-her-heart-hope-not-to-die. Then she'd set the phone to vibrate-only, and whenever it had buzzed in the back pocket of her jeans, she'd smiled at Finn and he'd smiled back, sharing the secret. And over the next few days the calls had tapered off. The way the emails she was currently dealing with always did eventually.

So deal with it, Zoe. The sooner you deal, the sooner you're free.

She switched windows on her computer. For long responses—and she was determined to compose a long one, knocking off every possible issue she could think of as a forestalling tactic—she preferred keyboard typing to tapping on her phone.

She couldn't imagine what there was left for them to warn her about but when she opened the message she saw they'd found something: Cristina, Zoe's regular travel companion.

The email was oh-so-carefully worded; this wasn't a hill her parents were prepared to die on lest Zoe decide no more travel companion *at all*, but nevertheless the dictates were clear: Zoe should remember Cristina was there to help. It was fine for Cristina to enjoy herself, and nobody expected her to hover over Zoe twenty-four hours a day, but Zoe shouldn't see it was an imposition to request Cristina's assistance whenever she needed it. Cristina was stronger than Zoe as well as being a trained nurse, so Zoe shouldn't insist on doing all those transfers to and from her chair herself all the time.

The easy way to head this particular concern off at the pass was to let her parents know that Cristina had become as tedi-ously dedicated to Zoe's wellbeing as they were, to the point where Zoe had to send her on made-up errands to win herself some breathing space. Today, for example, Zoe had asked her to carry out a completely unnecessary accessibility check of the entire Poerava resort. Problem was, though, if she told her parents Cristina had been afflicted with the protect-Zoe-Tayler-at-all-costs disease they'd probably kick off a campaign to get Zoe to hire Cristina as a permanent live-in assistant. Not! Happening!

Zoe wished she knew what she did that made people want to stand guard over her so she could stop doing it! It happened to everyone who came into her life sooner or later, and as for those who'd known her from her cradle…?

Well, gah! Just…*gah*!

Yes, three miscarriages before Zoe was born had conferred 'precious' status on Zoe. Yes, Zoe had suffered all the health issues associated with being premature. Yes, Zoe had been a sickly child, in and out of hospital with bronchiolitis. But—ginormous, important BUT—by the age of eleven she'd been as hardy as any kid in the village. Small, yes, but perfectly formed and perfectly fit! And yet a slight breeze sent half the village running for her coat. A yawn and the other half would urge her to rest. A scratch on her arm and she'd be fending off offers to drive her to Accident and Emergency. As though she were a piece of delicate porcelain teetering on the edge of a cliff and it was everyone's collective responsibility to stop her going over.

Thank God for her best friends, Victoria, Malie and Lily, who treated her like they treated each other: no fuss, no concessions, just love. Without them, Zoe would have spent the span of her life from primary school to coming-of-age peering through the windows of her parents' clifftop mansion—or as the girls called it *Palace de Prison*—at everyone else frolicking on the beach below.

Zoe smiled around a sigh, as she always did when thinking of her friends. She depended on the girls in a way she never let herself depend on anyone else. It didn't feel like a weakness to need them, to lean on them when the going got tough. They had each other's back, always. Knew each other's frailties and strengths. Knew each other's scars. Were always there for each other—whether it was a quick phone call or an all-in session via video conference.

Zoe's visit home last Christmas had come about after one of those video calls. It hadn't been easy, going back to Hawke's Cove. But Victoria had been struggling over a decision that might have torn her from the man she loved (her now-fiancé Oliver Russell) and so Zoe had sucked it up and joined Lily and Malie on a surprise visit to her, because for the big deals you needed to get tactile with your friends. They had a codename for those big deals—the scared-to-death and flying-high ones, the heartbreaks and exaltations, the ones that meant you dropped everything to be there: the Lost Hours.

Zoe was proud of the fact that she'd been the one to inspire that codename. They'd taken a trip to Ibiza to celebrate Victoria's birthday and because V was the last of them to turn eighteen it was all-out-for-freedom that week. *So* all-out Zoe had managed to get lost at a foam party. One moment they'd been dancing as a group, the next the foam had gone right over Zoe's head—she was the shortest, at just over five feet—and pandemonium had apparently ensued as Victoria, Malie and Lily had searched for her for the next three hours. They'd been scared out of their wits and checked her over as thoroughly as a doctor when she'd resurfaced, despite Zoe reassuring them that she hadn't been kidnapped or drugged or conked on the head. Eventually they'd let the matter rest—perhaps reading the gleam of mischief in Zoe's eyes that told them she was thrilled at having had a secret adventure.

It had been two months before the summer ball that would mark the end of school, and with the daring still racing through her blood Zoe had made the decision then and there that the ball would be a turning point, kick-starting a new life.

Careful what you wish for.

That night had certainly kick-started a new life. A new life for all of them. Just not in a way anyone could have anticipated.

Which she was *not* going to think about now.

She was going to think only positive thoughts.

As though by magic, her phone lit up.

Video call.

Lily.

Zoe smiled as she hit the button to accept. 'Hey!' she said. 'It's close to midnight over there! Do you miss me that much?'

Lily opened her mouth…then closed it.

'Lily?' Zoe said, alarmed at the distraught look on her friend's face.

Lily opened her mouth again…and burst into tears.

'Lily!' Zoe clutched the phone so tightly in her hand she was in danger of cracking the case. 'Tell me, *tell* me what it is!'

'Sorry, *sorry!*' Lily wiped furiously at her eyes. 'It's just…Blake.' A little sob escaped her, but Zoe could see her pulling it all together, the way she always, always did. 'H–he's d–dead.'

'Oh Lily! *Lils!* I'm so, so sorry. Do you need me to come? I will, you know I will.'

Lily shook her head furiously. 'You hate Hawke's Cove.'

'This isn't about Hawke's Cove, it's about you.'

'You're on a job.'

'I'm a fill-in, nothing more. It's a *junket*. Like…blerrgh. You know I don't do those.'

A ghost of a smile from Lily. 'And yet there you are.'

335

'Meh!' Zoe tossed in nonchalantly. 'I like the guy who asked me to do it, that's the only reason.'

'As in *like*?'

'As in *no*! Geez! Rolf lives in Germany. It's an online friendship, nothing more. Let's leave the romance to V and Devil, shall we? On the subject of which, this is Lost Hours business. They're joining us, right?'

And just like that, Lily was crying again. 'I was going to dial them in but I…I mean, they're both…you know, with Oliver and Todd. But Mum's not here and I just…I feel kind of lost, and I knew you were in a time-friendly zone and…oh, I don't know what to do!'

Okay, sound the alarm! Lily *lost*? Not knowing what to do? It. Did. Not. Com. Pute. 'Okay, you just stay there, I'll conference in V and Devil and we can all cry together.'

'You never cry. And you wouldn't have to even if you did. You barely knew him.'

'I'll cry for you like a professional mourner. And Malie will cry for real. You know she adored him almost as much as you.' She started tapping at her phone.

'Not V!' Lily said suddenly. 'I mean, the Hawkesbury estate!'

'The estate? I don't see what that has to do with V. Unless it's a will thing? But how could that—? Okay, what am I not getting?'

'Not a will thing, a wedding venue thing. Not that there's going to be a problem, because I won't let anything go wrong, but she might worry.'

'Er…if you think the death of the richest man in Hawke's Cove can be kept a secret for more than an hour you're dreaming.

Or is Mrs Whittaker dead too? Cos I'll bet she's already got the megaphone out.'

'Oh. I just…I'm not thinking.'

'Not thinking? You? You're scaring me with that kind of talk! Anyway, Victoria isn't going to give a damn about her wedding!'

'Victoria certainly is going to give a damn about her wedding,' Victoria said, laughing as she joined the call.

At which point Lily burst into tears again.

'Or…maybe…not…?' Victoria said. 'What's going on?'

'Blake Hawkesbury's dead,' Zoe explained.

'WHAT?' Mali said, announcing herself.

'Today,' Lily said, and kept on crying. 'It happened today.'

'And her mum's out of town,' Zoe said. Imbuing the phrase with as much meaning as she could. Subtext: *someone has to get there fast!*

'Right, I'm coming,' Malie said, and actually jumped to her feet.

'What about Todd?' Lily sniffled.

'We're not joined at the hip you know.'

Lily shook her head, adamant. 'No, you can't come, you've got another surf competition coming up.'

'There'll be other competitions,' Malie said, and then abruptly started crying too. 'But there was only one B-B…' But she choked, and couldn't continue.

She didn't have to. Everyone knew Blake Hawkesbury had loaned Malie the money she'd needed to flee Hawke's Cove after the accident. Maybe he'd done that out of a sense of responsibility— it had been his only son Henry's girlfriend, Claudia, driving the car that night—but Zoe had always thought it was simply that he was kind. The deep down type of kind. To all of them. Especially

Lily, to whom he'd become a mentor, almost like a father, after giving her a job in his hotel kitchen when she was sixteen.

Zoe may not have had much to do with him but the memories she had were good ones. 'Hey,' she said, suddenly overwhelmed by nostalgia, 'remember how he always let us get away with sneaking onto his private beach for our night-time barbecues, pretending he never knew we were doing it?'

'Yes!' Victoria agreed, smiling mistily. 'And how he sent that case of his finest champagne to me and Oliver to celebrate our engagement? He was so happy to be hosting our wedding at the Hawkesbury estate.' And her smile dropped as the tears came to her too. 'And now he won't even be there.'

Silence, except for Lily, Malie and Victoria weeping.

And then Malie blew her nose. 'Right. What do you need?'

Lily heaved in a shuddery breath, then let it out, making a visible effort to get back to her normal self. 'I need *you* to go to that surfing competition and win it for Blake.' Another heaved in breath. 'And Zoe, I need you to stay where you are and write me something poignant to say at the funeral. And Victoria—'

'Save your breath,' Victoria said, cutting her off. 'I'm coming to Hawke's Cove tomorrow and it's not to discuss wedding plans.'

Lily gave a choked sob. 'Of course you're coming. Of course you are, and I need you to come.' Another hitching sob. 'But right now, I'm going to get into bed and cry my eyes out.'

Lily rang off, leaving Malie, Victoria and Zoe staring at each other.

'Will she be okay?' Zoe asked.

Mali blew a corkscrew curl out of her eyes. 'She'll pretend she is, anyway.'

'Maybe I should come over for the funeral...?' Zoe said, tentative.

'Maybe you shouldn't,' Victoria said. 'You think we don't know how much you hated coming back for Christmas?'

'Yes, but—'

'But nothing. I'm not taking the risk that another visit so soon will have you vowing to stay away forever when I need you at my wedding in June.'

'Not to mention *my* wedding when the time comes so don't let the Cove outstay its welcome. Or do I mean you outstay your welcome? Whatever, just don't pretend you don't loathe Hawke's Cove with a passion and would rather swim with the piranha in the Zambezi than come home.'

'I think you mean the Amazon—'

'Details, details!'

'—but okay!' Zoe huffed out a short-lived laugh. 'Hey, do you think Henry might finally turn up?'

Malie rolled her eyes. 'Who knows?'

'Who *cares?*' Victoria said, and then grimaced. 'Sorry, I don't mean that, I take it back. Henry may have been a spoilt brat—'

'Not may have been, he *was* a spoilt brat, and probably still *is* a spoilt brat!' Malie threw in.

'—*but*, if you'll shut up, Malie, for a few seconds, I think he suffered as much as the rest of us. Not physically, obviously, but emotionally. I mean yes it was an accident, but Claudia *died*, right next to him in that car. How do you even start to deal with that?'

'Claudia's parents still blame him,' Zoe said, and then she sighed. 'And so do mine.' Another sigh. 'Talking about my parents, if

I don't email them within the next ten minutes they'll declare a state of emergency. So that's me, signing off.'

'Measurements!' Victoria called out. 'Remember, I need your measurements if I'm going to make your bridesmaid's dress not look like a sack on you!'

'They'll be the same as they were at Christmas—and incidentally I'm wearing that divine pink dress you made me to a cocktail party tonight—but yep, fine. Measurements. As soon as I locate a tape measure.'

Zoe disconnected and returned to the email from her parents, rescanning the words and heaving another sigh.

She was going to have to refer to Blake Hawkesbury's death and she really hoped that didn't have them harking back to the accident. She'd used up a lot of energy over the years putting that night behind her, leaving Hawke's Cove behind.

Lately, though, fate seemed to be conspiring against her.

The Christmas visit.

Victoria's wedding, coming up in a few months.

Now Blake.

And of course, Malie's decision to move back there and reopen her family's surf school in the near future, taking her entrepreneur fiancé with her—not that it was so much taking him with her as it was him being willing to follow her to the ends of the earth.

And on the subject of Malie, *damn* her for bringing up Finn Doherty during that visit to Hawaii in February, because ever since he'd been popping into her head at inopportune times. Damn her for all her talk about how Finn used to look at Zoe like he wanted to strip her naked.

Damn her...but God, how Zoe loved her.

How she loved them all. They were her anchor and her safe harbour.

But they were also the tide, pulling her back to where she didn't want to go.

You hate Hawke's Cove. Lily.

You think we don't know how much you hated coming back for Christmas? Victoria.

Don't pretend you don't loathe Hawke's Cove with a passion. Malie.

She'd tried so hard to escape, she *had* escaped...but because of the precious friendships she'd forged there she was scared she'd never truly leave it behind. In fact she felt a terrible, burning certainty that Hawke's Cove was waiting for her to return, to face a past she wanted to forget—a feeling that had been growing stronger since Christmas.

Maybe it was tiredness getting to her; since December she'd done practically back-to-back trips—Mexico, England, the Caribbean, Hawaii, New Zealand. And yet she'd so easily shelved what she'd thought was a firm plan to chill at home in Sydney for a few months. She should have turned down this job—it was so last minute she hadn't been able to do her usual meticulous research, plus she really, truly hated junkets—but a nagging discontentedness had had her accepting.

And so here she was, batting away memories, replying to yet one more email, drowning in the...the suffocation of her life, the same suffocation she'd fled ten years ago.

'And you think Henry Hawkesbury was a spoilt brat?' she asked herself out loud. 'Get over yourself Zoe Tayler. Blake Hawkesbury just died, Lily is in mourning, Rolf's got pneumonia, and you're complaining? You're alive, you've got a job people dream about, you're in paradise—stop bitching about having to write an email.'

Quickly, she typed:

I just heard Blake Hawkesbury died. Lily's Mum's away at the moment so I hope you'll check on her—you know how close to him she was.

And then she switched to autopilot, and kept typing. She'd been typing versions of the same email for so long she could just about write it in her sleep. Soothe, placate, deflect.

She reread her message, checking for typos, hit send, then returned to her interrupted article.

But stubbornly, the words wouldn't come. As she sat there watching the cursor blink, it struck her that when she'd checked for typos in that email she hadn't absorbed one word of the actual content.

She went back to the email she'd sent, read it again, and knew why the content hadn't pulled her in: it was tepid, it was practised, it was *nothing*. Even the reference to staying in her room all day writing her story on Malie's godfather's surf school was a glib throwaway, nothing but a facile reassurance that they could go—to—bed—please!

Strictly speaking she *would* be working in her room all day. She was going to finish that article, then she was going to write a brief on the surf school for a documentary maker she'd met on a trip last year, then she was going to tackle the research on Poerava she ordinarily would have done a week before flying in. But she had oh-so-carefully 'forgotten' to mention the cocktail party she'd be attending *in the evening*—an omission that suddenly troubled her.

She started to rub her hands up and down her thighs, then stopped herself. She didn't need to remind herself why her parents worried; they never stopped *telling* her they worried. And at almost twenty-eight years old she didn't need to confess every single thing she did or feel guilty about skipping an occasional detail that might cause them unnecessary anxiety.

Especially since she *knew* nothing was going to happen to her at the cocktail party. Nothing interesting, anyway. She'd been to so many of those parties she could describe *exactly* how the evening would unfold. She'd dress up and do her hair and make-up. She'd drink champagne, eat canapes, meet the resort manager if he/she was there, be schmoozed by the public relations executive who'd arranged her travel. She'd talk to as many people as she could, gathering information on the resort and the area's most interesting attractions, and at the end of the evening she'd return to her room with Cristina and go immediately to bed to rest up for the always-busy first day of action.

Boring.

So boring maybe she should just skip it. After her recent travel-fest no one could blame her for preferring a quiet night in. Even when you were being flown Business Class (as she invariably was), air travel was exhausting, especially when you had to navigate airports in a wheelchair. And then, of course, she had jetlag to contend with, which could kick in at any moment, not to mention—

'Oh. My. God! Listen to yourself! Sermonising on the evils of travel! Who even *are* you?'

She sat up straighter. She wasn't going to lie to herself by pretending she was too tired to go to a two-and-a-half-hour party when what she was actually suffering from was a guilty conscience over not telling her parents she was going out. Nor was she going to send a follow-up email mentioning the party. That would be tantamount to asking for permission to attend when she—did—not—need—permission! She also didn't need another email shot back at her listing the dangers that lurked in the unfamiliar dark.

What she *was* going to do was remind herself—visually, since she couldn't trust the tortured inside of her head—that she was living the life she'd always dreamed of.

She pushed away from the desk and wheeled herself onto the large sundeck of her bungalow, gazing at the endlessness of blue.

Blue was her favourite colour, and it didn't get more beautiful than this, laid out in shades shifting seamlessly from crystal to powder to electric to azure to sapphire, all the way out to the horizon where the lagoon collided with a vivid cerulean sky. Her bungalow seemed to be suspended between two worlds—and in a way that was exactly what it was, perched on stilts over water, not earth. There were glass panels in the floor inside that allowed you to see the colourful fish darting freely below, but Zoe preferred this outdoor vantage point. In her soul she was soaring, skimming across the lagoon, rising into the air, flying straight up to the heavens.

This was why she'd fought so hard to not return home to Hawke's Cove with her parents. This beauty, this freedom.

It had been worth every trade-off she'd negotiated—the apartment that had been bought for her off the plan and before construction so modifications could be made for her wheelchair, the physiotherapist who came twice a week, the cleaning service, the detailed itineraries provided to her parents whenever she was travelling, Cristina's assistance, the regular phone calls when she was at home, the barrage of emails when she was working, a hundred other inconsequential intrusions.

It had been a fight for her life…at the cost of her parents' hope for a cure.

'Fight your big battles to the death, but don't sweat the scrappy skirmishes if you want to win the long war,' she said again, looking out across the lagoon.

Once more she heard Finn saying those words. But now she could *see* him, too. His crooked smile with the tiny chip in his front tooth as he'd tucked a hank of her hair behind her ear. She'd looked into his too-blue eyes that day and seen more than a colour. She'd seen, so clearly, that Finn was mysteriously older than his eighteen years. His life had been nothing like her pampered existence—and yet he'd believed, he really had, that she was as strong as he was, capable of fighting for what she wanted, ready to do whatever she set her heart on.

What would he think of all those compromises she'd made to get where she was? Would he see her as a victor or would he say she was…

'Lost,' she said, and closed her eyes, trying to unblock the memory of the very last time she'd seen him.

Impossible.

As usual, only a snippet or two resurfaced, just enough to tell her it had been traumatic; the rest stayed safely buried.

She opened her eyes, stared out at the horizon, and saw again his eyes, the same colour as the French Polynesian sky.

She may not have the full memory of that night but she knew one thing: however Finn Doherty may have looked at her during that *Crab Shack* year, his opinion had gone through a dramatic metamorphosis in the two years that followed.

And it didn't matter. It really, truly didn't.

She hadn't seen him for ten years and she'd never see him again.

Which was just fine with her.

Because she had an article to finish, a party to go to, and a life to live.

Chapter 2

FINN DOHERTY WALKED SLOWLY around the hotel ballroom with Aiata, the resort's PR manager, looking for flaws to be corrected before the guests arrived.

But there were no flaws. Everything was perfect.

No, not perfect.

He hated the word 'perfect'.

'Magnificent' was a better descriptor. He'd go with that.

Yesterday this had been a moderate-sized room running the length of the *fare pote*—the communal house—which was comprised of an airy lobby, Tāma'a restaurant, the Manuia bar, a quiet library room, and a ruthlessly modern but hidden commercial kitchen. Elegant, certainly, with richly-brown teak flooring, fairy lights strung across the ceiling, and full-length glass doors replacing walls on three sides and opening onto a wrap-around deck. The doors offered uninhibited views onto a grass clearing that was ideal for small soirees. The clearing was bordered by stunning gardens landscaped to merge with the island's natural rainforest beyond. Objectively speaking, it wasn't vastly different from any other expertly-designed, well-positioned hotel ballroom.

Now, however, the roof had been retracted, the glass doors

concertinaed all the way back, and teak extensions had been attached to the deck, stretching across the grass clearing so that the gardens became the walls—and the result was enchanting. A secret bower nestled within a rainforest, accessible only via a broad teak ramp that led through a natural opening between two coconut palms and circled back to the communal house.

Nothing was needed to beautify the space except for subtle lighting spiked among the plants. There were no bars set up, no food stations; instead, wait staff would circulate continuously, bringing refreshments through the swinging doors from the kitchen servery. No plinths with flowers anywhere either—just a few high tables scattered with hibiscus petals for those wanting to put down their glass or napkin. And even those hibiscus petals worked some strange magic, looking as though they'd drifted in from the riot of colourfully bold hibiscus plants dotted throughout the gardens—reds and yellows, oranges and pinks, whites and purples.

Finn moved to the edge of the jut of teak, breathing in. Out. In. Out. Warmth. Tang. Green. He'd have sworn he could isolate the creamy lemony scent radiating from the small white blooms of his favourite flower, the Tahitian gardenia—*tiare mā'ohi*—the national flower of French Polynesia, the shape of whose seven-petals had inspired the name of the island. Fanciful to think he could smell that among the crowd of other plants that included equally fragrant frangipanis in the usual white, pink and yellow, as well as several ancient tree varieties bursting with rare red and orange flowers, plus, as a dazzling array, orchids, metre-tall spikes of football-sized red torch ginger blooms, and jasmine—which he preferred to call by its local name, *pitate*, when he was here.

When he was here…which wasn't as often as he would have liked.

He had other resorts to oversee. At the Great Barrier Reef. In Fiji. Bali. Langkawi. The health retreat in the Maldives. This place, though, was special. The first resort he and Gina—his ex-wife and business partner—hadn't bought as a going concern. As satisfying as it was to retrofit and refurbish a property nothing compared to building a success from an idea, which is what they'd done with Poerava. His gem at the very centre of the flower that was Tiare Island.

And okay, it was actually too soon to tell if Poerava could be counted a *success*, but the signs were there. The travel industry buzz, robust forward bookings, media interest. They'd got Poerava into all the key luxury travel brochures he'd personally targeted and anecdotal feedback was that people were clamouring not only for the outrageously popular overwater bungalows but also for the garden suites within the rainforest.

He'd been involved personally in every single part of this development and was proud of it. He'd overseen the design, by his favourite architect; he'd supervised the construction; he'd chosen the décor; he'd even named it, after the exquisite black pearls that Polynesians once-upon-a-time dived for off one of the island's petal-shaped peninsulas. The only thing he hadn't seen through from start to finish was tonight's launch party—not by choice, but because a situation in the Maldives had needed his undivided attention for a full month.

Not that he could have done a better job. In fact, there was only one problem with tonight's launch, and it had nothing to do with Poerava. It was simply that he no longer had any excuse for stonewalling Doherty & Berne's next portfolio acquisition, which Gina, as the Berne half of the partnership, had been working on diligently for six months.

Gina had never made any secret of the fact that her dream was to expand into the UK. She'd joked that one of the reasons she married him was because she had a Brit-obsession! It had been unwavering, that dream of hers, since they'd formed their company seven years ago and he owed her a shot at achieving it.

Problem was, her preferred property was a fortified manor in Devon, which Finn had pinpointed on the map in his head the minute he'd seen the photos. Way too close to Hawke's Cove. Which left property number two: a loch-side castle in the Scottish Highlands. But was it fair to Gina to sway the decision on the basis of his reluctance to go back to a place just because his memories were not fond? At thirty years old it was way past time to put those memories behind him.

'Boss!'

Finn, startled out of his thoughts by the sharpness with which that one word was uttered, saw that the usually strictly-deferential Aiata was regarding him with an expression just shy of exasperation.

'Sorry, what?' he said, wincing because obviously she'd been trying to get his attention for a while.

'The first guests have arrived,' she said.

Which was Aiata speak for *Step it up, get your game face on and get over there to meet-and-greet.*

He glanced round, surprised to note that the wait staff briefing he'd intended to listen to had happened without him, and that one of the staff was offering welcome drinks to a small group of guests. The band hired to provide background music had set up, the singer conferring quietly with the ukulele player.

He checked his wristwatch. Okay, there were five minutes to go before the scheduled start time but how had he not noticed everything happening around him?

In the time it took him to raise his eyes from his watch the number of guests had increased from six to eight...ten...eleven. They were coming in fast *and* early.

At the first strum of the ukulele he examined the guests more carefully. Noted that a VIP—a director of the tourism board—was among the early-arrivers and being charmed by Poerava's manager, the glamorous Nanihi.

'Right,' he said to Aiata. 'I'll join Nanihi and do the VIP schmoozing but I also want to meet all the international travel journos. How many do we have here tonight and how many are staying for the full week?'

'Fifteen tonight, ten are staying,' Aiata said, and the almost-exasperation was back. 'The document I emailed had names, publications, background information on each of them, sample articles, the personalised itineraries I've put together according to their individual preferences, plus—'

'Yes, yes I got it,' Finn said, wincing again at having cut her off. It wasn't her fault he hadn't done his due diligence on the media. He devoutly hoped it would be the last wince-worthy moment of the night. 'Sorry, I didn't get a chance to go through it because of the Maldives issue. Maybe you could give me a rundown now of who they are.' He shot another glance around the space, estimated that around a third of their expected two-hundred-plus guests was already here. It often happened like that. A trickle became a flood and eventually reverted to a trickle. But mid-flood there was no time to talk about which media wanted to do what activities. 'Forget that. Just tell me if there's anyone who needs special attention.'

'There's a last-minute stand-in for Rolf. You know, Rolf Vameer? You asked for him specifically after he did that piece about the Fiji resort but—'

'What? No Rolf?' Finn said, and winced again at having interrupted her. He blamed his impatience on that manor house in Devon. He accepted a glass of champagne from a passing server and took a sip, forcing himself to relax. 'Is he going to be a problem?'

'He?' she asked, frowning.

'Rolf's replacement.'

Her frown cleared. 'She, not he. And no. She's a sweetie. Easy going from what I could tell when she checked in. I was surprised because she normally won't do junkets and she's only doing this one because she's a friend of Rolf's.'

'She doesn't do junkets?'

'No. She thinks junkets put pressure on writers to hide the downsides of a place. Plus she hates seeing everyone come out with the same basic article post-trip.'

'Sounds like trouble.'

'That's not my impression. And I've taken pains with all of them to offer points of difference in their itineraries and plenty of free time, so the issue about everyone writing identical stories shouldn't arise. There are certain things they'll do as a group but each of them has a choice of other activities and I'm talking to them separately to craft individual story angles.'

'Okay, great.' Another sip of champagne. 'Then if there's no one who's a problem I'm happy to wing it and keep things with the media informal tonight. Anyone who needs a corporate perspective will want an in-depth interview which I can't do tonight anyway, so you can set up a time for them to talk to me on the phone once I'm in the UK. For the destination features I'll leave it to Nanihi to give them what they need during the week.'

'You got it boss,' Aiata said.

'And Aiata, thank you. For everything. I can tell it's going to be a great night.'

She smiled at him with her more-usual warmth, murmured something about Nanihi heading his way, and glided quietly away.

★★★

The next forty-five minutes flew by. A blur of faces, chatter, music. Finn gave a brief, well-received speech and introduced his team. The band was perfect. The resort staff managed the flow of people brilliantly so that he met everyone he needed to meet. The flood of arriving guests became a trickle. Everyone seemed happy and relaxed.

Figuring he'd earned some off-the-clock-time, Finn collared Kupe Kahale, owner of the Mama Papa'e restaurant on nearby Heia Island, with whom he'd formed a close bond over the past year. The bombastic Kupe always gave the impression that those to whom he deigned to speak were being granted an audience by royalty—a view with which Finn concurred: Kupe was a legend in these parts and Finn considered he *was* being granted an audience. If Finn hadn't been flying out in the morning he would have sailed across to Mama Papa'e and enticed Kupe and Kupe's wife Chen to share more raconteur-like reminiscences of 'the good old days' in French Polynesia over an excellent meal and a bottle of wine.

It was in the middle of Kupe's story about the invention of his signature cocktail that Finn became aware of a disturbance—actually it was more like a ripple of interest, an impression of people directing their attention to one point in the room. He was curious but not unduly so given there was no crash of glassware, no raised voices, no break in the general hum of conversation. It wasn't until Kupe himself briefly paused as something caught his eye beyond Finn's left shoulder that curiosity got the better of Finn; Kupe was not the type to pause mid-anecdote for anything less than a volcanic eruption.

Sure enough, Kupe picked up the thread of his tale almost immediately, but Finn's concentration was shot: he had to see what was so interesting.

He waited until Kupe had finished the cocktail story and was distracted by a passing tray of canapes, then shot a look backwards, over his shoulder. All he could see was Aiata. No, Aiata wasn't the focal point; that was whoever Aiata was bending down to talk to. Someone in a wheelchair wearing. A lacy, beaded rose pink skirt draped down to the chair's footplate and the sparkly toes of a pair of lilac shoes peeped from beneath the hem of the skirt.

The Rolf replacement.

Aiata's swing of long black hair obscured the woman's face and torso but no way was Finn going to do the stare-and-wait routine. Aside from the fact that it didn't matter what she looked like, it irritated him that the simple fact of being in a wheelchair could get people gawking.

He turned back to Kupe, who'd finished his canape and was

waxing lyrical about a special pork dish offered at the Mama Papa'e restaurant.

Finn tried to locate his enthusiasm but it appeared to be M.I.A. In his head, he was seeing the pink skirt and pretty spangled shoes of the woman Aiata was talking to and remembering that Aiata had described Rolf's replacement as a sweetie. The way she dressed fitted that description. The gauze and sparkle, the choice of those particular shades. He hoped that ripple of disturbance wasn't going to be repeated, that people weren't going to either look or deliberately not look at her all night, because that would get up his nose in a big way.

Oblivious to Finn's waning attention, Kupe reached for another canape and engaged the server in a discussion about the dipping sauce. While Kupe was preoccupied Finn risked another look over his shoulder—not that he had any idea what he'd do if he found his guests ogling the poor woman. He smiled as he imagined himself striding across the floor, shoving people left and right as he raced to rescue the damsel in distress. The counterproductive sort of behaviour that would draw everyone's attention.

He started to turn back to Kupe but just then the crowd shifted enough to give him clear line-of-sight to Aiata straightening and stepping aside.

His smile fell away, the sounds of the party fading until all he could hear was his heart thudding in his ears.

The woman in the wheelchair was Zoe.

MILLS & BOON

THE HEART OF ROMANCE

Keep in touch with...

Georgia Toffolo

Follow:

f ToffTalks

o Georgiatoffolo

y @ToffTalks

For all the latest book news from
Georgia, sign up to the newsletter:
b.link/ToffNews